TREADING THE
TRAITOR'S PATH:

NEITHER THIS, NOR THAT
Book #2

MariaLisa deMora

Edited by Hot Tree Editing

Photography: Wander Aguiar, Photography

Model: James Clippinger

Cover design: Debera Kuntz

First Published 2017

ISBN 13: 978-1-946738-00-4

DEDICATION

Life begins at the end of your comfort zone.
~Neale Donald Walsch

Some stories lie too close to the bone to be easily collected.
To those of you who join me on journeys such as these:
Thank you.

Contents

ACKNOWLEDGMENTS

Po'Boy is quite the character. Near the end of Twisted Pain, he told me a secret that nearly made me drop the idea of writing this book. Something so abhorrent in biker culture, it seemed wrong to write it. Dude's persistent though, and he wore me down, putting people in my path who showed me that the times they are a changing. Once he got me on board, however, it was balls to the wall and full steam ahead as he pushed my comfort levels and boundaries.

I've come to love him. I know I probably say that about every character. Well, nearly every one of them. Some are unrepentant jerks who don't deserve the headspace. But Ralph Lewis, or Motorboat as I affectionately call him, is unique in my head. He owns an interesting dichotomy of characteristics that I've not seen in a single character. He can be a cold-blooded killer, a ride or die brother, a friend like no other, and a caring and sensitive lover.

If nothing else, he's taught me two things:
Lesson One: There will always be someone who feels like you
     don't deserve the things you've worked for and earned.
Lesson Two: Fuck 'em.

The thank you section comes next, y'all hang around and give these folks some love, okay?

Thanks to Wander Aguiar for the image on the cover, it's an excellent capture of a phenomenal model, James Clippinger. James embodies the exact look and attitude I imagined for Po'Boy, and a picture find like this is rare. He's kinda my version of a unicorn. :makes with the jazz hands: It's magic! Thanks to Debera Kuntz for her work on the cover, her artistry was critical in helping set the tone of a series theme.

Hot Tree Editing and Becky Johnson worked their wizardry, making me look so much more intelligent than I am. This is a team I'm proud to have behind me, and I can't thank them enough.

Thanks to my alpha and beta team, Missy, Kori, Megan, MirandaPanda, Jamey, Kristen, Jesse, and (my slow friend) Kay. Your encouragement and insight provide so much more than mere amusement, I promise.

Thanks are also due to you, the reader. You're the one who keeps opening these covers and drinking down the words inside. The ones who inhale the story and breathe out a demand for more. I appreciate every single one of you more than you'll ever know, because while I write these damn things for me, I'd be lying if I didn't say the finished product is (mostly) just for you.

Finally, fuckin' finally, there are thank yous needed for the folks in the life who put up with my Ed and Kay brand of special shit. You haven't killed me yet, and for that I'm grateful. But, you did saddle me with Tinker, so there's that, too.

Love alla y'all. Except Tinker. :P

Wootully yours,
~ML

Chapter One

A groan slipped from the bound man's lips, and Po'Boy reached out, bending over to grip a fistful of hair at the back of the man's scalp, lifting the heavy head as it lolled on a suddenly lax neck. Bloody spittle drooled out of his open mouth, splashing to the floor between their boots. *Jesus*, he thought, *least the guy took a serious lickin' before he went tits up*. He shook the man's head slightly, feeling the pull of weight like a pendulum. "Tick, tock," he muttered, impatient, flexing his other fist. Open, then closed, fingers tightening as the splits at his knuckles painfully complained. "Tick, fuckin' tock. Get off the clock, man."

When the guy's fluttering eyelids opened to slits again, Po'Boy, known to the government as Ralph Lewis, was ready. "There ya are." He gave it another second, waiting until he saw recognition in the man's gaze. "You know who's puttin' the pressure on, my man. I needa know what you got in your head. Gimme somethin', Jones."

"Fuck y—"

Po'Boy yanked back on Jones' hair, stretching his neck near to breaking and stalling midsentence whatever words the guy had been about to spew. The leather straps binding him to the metal chair creaked and strained, the legs of the chair screeching across the cement floor. "Heard enough of them words. Stop postulatin' and fuckin' *talk*!"

Eyes locked on his, Jones found enough slack in Po'Boy's grip to shake his head back and forth the barest measure, indicating a crystal-clear unwillingness to do as Po'Boy demanded.

"No chatter from you? Then, man, you know how this is gonna go." *Fuck.* "You about to pull the trigger on yourself, man, and it ain't gonna go easy. I just need a fuckin' name, man. Gimme a name, and I'll move on, track down the next piece of work to get what I need. It's a fuckin' name. Ain't worth your life."

"I'm no traitor." Hissed words using up the thin amount of air in his lungs, the man again sagged in Po'Boy's grip, wheezing in another scarce measure. "No traitor like you are." Lids closing partway over glazed eyes, his head became a heavy weight in Po'Boy's hand again.

"Jesus. You fucking are." Po'Boy shook his head, releasing the hold he had on the man, a quick flick of his wrist shaking a few strands of blond hair from his fingers. Talking to the unconscious man, he muttered, "If you weren't, you wouldn't have been where I could scoop you right the fuck up."

With hands on his hips, Po'Boy missed the comfort of feeling the bottom edges of his cut skim the inside of his wrists. The supple leather would have been cold to the touch against his heated skin. The man in the chair had on a similar leather vest to the one Po'Boy normally wore, but the back of his carried a different patch. That very difference leading them to where they were now. Po'Boy recognized parts of himself in Jones and knew he wouldn't get anything from him. MLH&R wasn't just a patch on their vest; loyalty, honor, and respect were how they lived their lives. "You ain't gonna give it up, are you?"

A soft groan was his only answer.

"Jesus. What the fuck else am I supposed to do with you?"

Pulling a wide-bladed knife from its sheath on the man's hip, Po'Boy swung it back and forth experimentally, testing the balance and weight of the weapon. The lack of a vest on his back made him feel exposed, naked, off in a way that was hard to define. *I ain't patchless, just anon.* His thoughts were meant to be reassuring, missing the mark by a mile because here he was alone, not surrounded by brothers. *Same as Jones, only he's on that side of the blade, and I'm here.*

On the final side-to-side pass, he extended his arm and executed a tiny arc modification, stepping to one side in a move that felt choreographed. *Done this shit a thousand times.* Over the next ten minutes, he stood, watching and listening, waiting for it to be done. If he could, it was what he did, offering respect to the final moments of whoever had gotten his lasting attention. This man, flaunting a patch from a dead club, using names he shouldn't know to gain entry into a private club in Incoherent territory? He had definitely gotten Po'Boy's attention. Five minutes after that, Po'Boy was back on his idling bike, sending a text to the Incoherent clubhouse.

Chapter Two

Po'Boy came awake with a start, forcing himself to lay flat while struggling to calm his breathing, panting rasps of sound filling the tiny room. It was always like this when he drank. Sober or stoned, his dreams were easy, a way for his brain to sort out whatever he'd been doing recently. Nothing to concern himself with. Sober or stoned, his dreams were good. Always. A drunk dream, however, was an entirely different thing. They always circled the one pain in his life he would never fix. Could never get past.

Sabrina Rotain's voice was loud, taunting him from the other side of the door. When he'd heard her coming, he'd darted into the locker room bathroom that faced the grade school playground, hoping to avoid a confrontation. No such luck. Not today, at least. Ralphie leaned his forehead against the metal door, listening, feeling the burning blaze of mortification in his cheeks.

"Ralphie, you in there alone? Got you a little friend in there with you, Ralphie? Got a little friend?"

Why won't she just go away? Soundlessly he thumped his head against the door. She went through the same taunting routine two more times, finally tiring of her game when he refused to respond. Silence filled the room, and from outside he heard the rhythmic squeaking of the chains on the swings, the solid thud of the teeter-totter hitting the ground. Another ten minutes and the bell would ring, calling everyone back to classes and leaving him a chance to escape, finally.

A quiet knocking on the door, then another girl's voice calling gently, "Ralphie? She's gone." She hesitated, then softer, sounding embarrassed, said, "I gotta go. Can you come out so I can go?"

Swallowing hard, he reached up and drew back the bolt, fingertips easing the metal knob to settle silently against the door. Cautiously pushing against the surface with both hands, he opened it an inch, then two, only seeing the one girl waiting outside. She smiled at him, and then her eyes flashed nervously as she looked beyond the door and he knew. She didn't have to piss. She was the bait to get him out into the open.

No chance of going back now. Shoving the door wide, it thudded against something before it hit the cement brick wall and Ralphie heard a short curse, knowing in that instant he was right. He stepped out and then Sabrina was there, one of her crew of girls slamming the door at his back, cutting off any hope of retreat. He put his head down, trying to push past them, but Sabrina grabbed his hands and, laughing loudly, put them on her tits. Right on her tits, firm globes under his fingers and he gasped, lifting his gaze to stare into her face. Face tight, mouth pinched like she tasted something bad, she asked, "Like what you feel?"

Shocked, with an involuntary shake of his head, he tore his hands free from hers, stepping backwards. The sneer on her lips told him what was coming next, and sure enough, the word that most terrified him blazed through the air.

"Faggot!"

His response was instantaneous, and the sudden movement caught her off guard. Then his palm was stinging, and his eyes were filling with tears as fast as hers, the bloodless mark on her cheek rapidly flooding with red.

5

A heavy hand on his shoulder whipped him around, and Ralphie stared into the angry whiskey brown eyes of the most beautiful boy he'd ever seen, just before that boy's fist connected with the point of his chin.

That had been tonight's dream. The beginning of the most important friendship he would ever have. The beginning of the biggest lie, too. A blast from the past, that action was all back before George Bell became Twisted, one of the scariest motherfuckers to roll twos in Louisiana.

Po'Boy shook his head, levering his legs off the thin mattress and letting his feet dangle to brush against the chilly floor of his apartment. Tapping his bare soles against the grimy tile, he lifted and stretched his shoulders, rolling his neck, chin to his chest. Goose bumps raised along both arms, and he sighed. Memories were the absolute worst, especially in the middle of the night when all his defensive walls were down. Even now, five minutes into being awake, he still remembered the thrilling shock of seeing George for the first time, feeling the rush of adrenaline that accompanied the moment.

George had beaten his ass, knocking Ralphie to his back in the dust of the playground, wooden seats and metal chains of the swings clanging against each other over his head. Then George had done the damnedest thing. *Changed my life.* Stunned, for one long moment he'd laid there, glaring up at the boy who'd bloodied his lip. Ralphie had been busily plotting his next move to get out of the predicament in which he found himself, then a breath later, he could see the fire dampen in George's eyes, and the boy had held out his hand. They weren't friends, weren't even friendly, but it was a clear offer, and not one Ralphie would have ever expected.

In an instant, his mother's words had run through his head, and he repeated them aloud again now, "Nearly always easier to be someone's friend than their enemy." She'd meant them as a warning about his attitude towards her husband, Grover, but they'd been as true at that moment as they had been in this one. He'd hooked his star to George and never looked back. Decades later, the legend of Twisted and Po'Boy walked the bayous, deeds and attitudes granting them a larger-than-life status.

Fuck, kiddie school was a trip. Hard to even remember being Ralphie. Big but soft, he had been the target of every schoolyard bully who felt they had something to prove. Shouldn't have been a shock when not all of those bullies had been male. Bitches were sometimes more brutal than a man ever thought to be.

A different memory of Sabrina Rotain flooded his mouth with bile, of the night he'd struggled to maneuver the weight and heft of the barrel into which they'd folded her lifeless body. It had taken him three tries to get it pushed up and over the lip of the boat, sinking her into the deepest channel in a remote bayou. She'd fucked herself by playing games with Twisted's family. *Pulled her own trigger, like Jones from last night*. A memory of the arcing, pulsing stream of red raced through his head. *Always comes down to the red*. The remembered weight of the modified machete he'd used made his arm ache. It had been Jones' own weapon, an old trademark of the Vicar's Wrath MC.

What a fucked up, longass night. With a sigh, Po'Boy pushed up from the mattress, standing tall and stretching hard, pushing the arch of his back until his muscles trembled from the strain. Experimentally, he clenched and unclenched his fist, feeling only slight swelling in his knuckles remaining. He slid his phone out from under his pillow and thumbed the button to wake it, wincing when he saw it was not yet 3:00 a.m. *Fuck, it's gonna be a longass day*.

Two hours and four cups of coffee later, he sat with his elbows propped on a folding table in the Mandeville clubhouse's main room. He'd gone to the house to use the weights in the back lot, exhausting his body in a satisfying way. Feeling almost like his usual self only lasted until the door opened and he looked up to see the faces of the men walking in. *Jesus, I just want to fucking sit for five minutes*. He tilted his head, acknowledging them, seeing from their expressions they were on the tail end of their night, while he was on the starting end of his day.

"Got more of that?" Wildman pointed to the mug on the table in front of Po'Boy. When he didn't get a response, Wildman shook his head and laughed. "Jesus, you awake, man?"

"Fuck you." Po'Boy lifted one hand and flipped the bird at Wildman who walked towards the coffeemaker on the back cabinet. "Don't ask shit you can figure out for your ownself by just looking across the goddamned room. Useless sack of shit."

"Jesus, what crawled up your asshole and died?" Busk, another member who'd walked in with Wildman, pulled a chair out from the table and flung himself into it beside Po'Boy. "Get me a cup of joe, Wild."

"On it." Wildman's response came immediately, and Po'Boy grinned at the holdover habits from the man's prospect period. "You take two sugars, right?"

"Jesus, gonna ask me if I want my cock sucked, too?" Busk laughed, then leaned forwards over the table, cradling his head on his crossed forearms. "Not that I'd turn down any action these days."

"What's up with that?" For as long as Po'Boy had known him, Busk had an old lady, a pretty little woman called Junebug. "Ole lady holdin' out?"

"She's preggers, man. Had some spotting, so we're holding off. Doc said it's safe to fuck, but I don't wanna take a chance." Wildman placed a full mug of coffee beside Busk's head, and Po'Boy grinned when the man didn't even open his eyes or move. "I'm gonna grab a couple hours of shuteye here, then go home and check on her before work."

"Shit, you shoulda said something. Wild and I could have handled the housekeeping." Po'Boy reached out and traded his empty mug for the full one. "You don't need coffee. You're asleep on your feet. Find a bunk." He realized his gaze was tracing the lines of Busk's shoulders and arms, the arched angle of his neck. *Fuck.* Slurping at the sweetened drink, he grimaced as he said, "Wildman, I'm outtie. I got shit to do for a couple of days. Let Twisted know when he surfaces from his weekend with Yousa." It was past time for him to make a New Orleans run if he was drooling over his brothers, the men who could never, not ever know his secret.

On his bike and headed across the causeway, he automatically adjusted for the constant wind blowing in off the Gulf and let his thoughts fly ahead of the bike to where he was headed. An exclusive club in the Quarter where he kept a suite. They had a price tag to match their promises of private and discreet, and for Po'Boy, ever since he'd been introduced to the place by his mother's husband, it had been his goal to keep a place there. A play place. Now that he could afford it, he did.

It isn't that I'm gay. Po'Boy grimaced at the thought. The fact he'd never been with just a guy was something he kept on his internal tally sheet. Like being bi was somehow less damning in his own eyes. He liked watching other people fuck, liked being part of the act, of what they were doing, liked having another man be part of what he was doing. Loved watching a woman get fucking pounded, and seeing the distracted confusion in her expression when his touch on her breasts or face was soft and sensual, the contrast helping to overwhelm her and open the gates for the best fucking orgasm she'd ever had.

He loved fucking a woman at the same time as another man. Mouth or asshole, didn't make him any difference. Feeling how she would move at the mercy of either man, like a ragdoll at their whim. Doubling up was the best, feeling another dude's cock against his while enveloped in a woman's raging heat—*Fuck.* Po'Boy reached down and adjusted himself.

Be honest, asshole. Po'Boy snorted at his thought. *I don't mind a little dick once in a while, too. Especially in my asshole, rubbing up against my magic fucking button.* Having a guy drill him while he was fucking a chick. *Paradise.* That was an activity restricted to his suite.

Something he'd thought about for the first time when he was fifteen, maybe even obsessed about after watching a series of porn videos one night. Porn had been his outlet for a long time. He snorted again. *Porn, and Twisted.*

His brother didn't mind sharing chicks. In all the time Po'Boy had known him, Twisted was one of the most laidback dudes when it came to fucking. Public or private, it didn't matter to him; he could still get into it and get his nut off even if the entire club had chairs lined up and watching. Sharing with him meant anything goes. Standing with a bitch on a spit between them, taking her mouth while Twisted slammed her from behind, watching Twisted's hands on her ass or hips. Sometimes standing with a bitch on their spits between them, him in her ass while Twisted's cock rubbed and stroked his dick inside her. He reached down again and pinched the head of his cock hard, needing to not pop a painful boner on the bike. A semi wasn't bad, and just the friction from his jeans could keep him half hard for hours.

Then Twisted found his old lady. Penny Dane, or Yousa as Po'Boy liked to call her. No sharing that bitch, and Po'Boy had known this as fact from the very beginning. The idea had never crossed Twisted's mind, not that Po'Boy thought Penny'd be up for it, either. And now he had gotten to know her, Po'Boy would put the brakes on anything, even if Twisted brought it up. *Cain't fuck my little sister*, he thought and realized his dick was rapidly softening in his pants. *Bitch is finally good for somethin'*. Mouth open and laughing behind his bandana, he roared off the causeway and onto the mess of highways leading down into New Orleans.

***

"Jesus," he grunted, pushing himself off the sweaty back of the woman in front of him, keeping his dick lodged firmly in her ass as he shifted backwards on his knees. "Fuckin' tight. Jesus, you're gonna fuckin' kill me, blondie." One hand on her hip, he gripped her waist with his other, pulling her back onto his cock. Angling so he could watch not only his dick moving into her, but also see the dick of the man on the bottom of their pussy sandwich. Wet and gleaming with lube and juices from all of them, the thick cock pulled out and pushed in hard and fast. Po'Boy reached down between them and trailed his fingers along the man's thigh, tugging hard on his sac, grinning as it drew up tight to the man's body.

"Awwww, Lewis, you're gonna make me blow." The complaining voice was laughing, and Po'Boy lifted his gaze to see Greg's face smiling at him over the blonde's shoulder. Po'Boy grinned back and repeated the motion, watched as Greg's eyes rolled up into his head and felt the heat against the head of his dick when the man filled the condom. "Oh, *baaaby.*" Drawn out and breathy, the word jolted in the middle when Po'Boy pounded deep into the woman's ass, moving her on Greg's cock. "Oh, baby. Do that again." With a smile, Po'Boy accommodated the request.

Five minutes later the three of them were reclining, tangled in the huge bed, Greg and the woman on either side of Po'Boy, his arms around their shoulders or waist, his hands stroking their skin. Greg Stanton was a regular hookup for Po'Boy, but didn't know his real name. Once Po'Boy got to the underground parking of the club, he shed the Incoherent vest and became Lewis. This meant Greg only knew him as the man's personal, tatted-up badass. That was how it needed to be. How it had to be.

At the thought of any of the men in the MC knowing him like this, seeing him like this, Po'Boy shivered, and Greg immediately soothed him. "Shhhhh." Fingers moving up and through Po'Boy's hair, Greg gripped and then tugged, tilting Po'Boy's head down. Regular did not mean exclusive, but regular meant Greg knew him really fucking well. He saw something in Po'Boy's expression, and whatever it was Greg didn't like it, a flash of pain showing on his features for a moment. Raising his head slowly, Greg asked permission with the gesture, and Po'Boy granted it when he pressed his lips to Greg's. Soft lips contrasting with hard angles and the prickle of scruff against his skin nearly made him groan, but he bit it back, and Greg settled his head back into place on Po'Boy's shoulder.

Fuck. The guy was getting attached, which meant it was time to move on and find another regular fuck buddy. He lifted an arm and reached across, bringing a bent knuckle under the blonde's chin and lifting so she looked into his face. "You okay?" She nodded, her features relaxed, eyes at half-mast. Satiated. "You sure?" She'd been someone Greg had brought, and Po'Boy hadn't vetted her like he normally did the women he picked up for a threesome. "Not hurting, and not freaked out?" The last thing he needed was some bitch to run to the cops about the encounter. She shook her head and smiled.

"Y'all were good to me." Holding his gaze, she offered him a crooked, one-sided smile. "Not sayin' I'd be up for a round two anytime soon, but it was good. No worries."

He nodded, knowing Greg was offering the same reassurance, his cheek moving against the skin of Po'Boy's chest. "What's your name, doll?"

"Denise." Now her smile lifted both corners of her mouth.

"Leave your number on the dresser if you're interested in a repeat sometime." With a deep sigh, he pushed up on an elbow and looked down at the two people in the bed. "I need a shower." Greg tensed because any version of those words was Po'Boy's code for "and don't fucking be here when I get out." Cupping Denise's cheek in his palm, he bent and pressed a kiss to her lips. Sweet and soft, he intended it as a goodbye. Moving to Greg, he searched the man's eyes for a moment and saw exactly what he had expected to find. Hadn't wanted, but expected. Painful hope that Po'Boy would ask him to stay. *Yeap, time to cut this cord.* "I'm going to be out of town for a while. Don't worry if you don't hear from me." He wasn't, of course. He just wouldn't be calling Greg again. Ever. He kissed Greg softly, letting the other man nibble on his bottom lip, pulling back when Greg tried to deepen the caress.

When he got out of the shower thirty minutes later, the suite was empty. Denise had left her number, and he tucked the slip of paper into the drawer of the tiny desk in the corner. He didn't take anything from this world with him when he left here, keeping his lives strictly separate.

Glancing around the space, he saw the dirty sheets from the bed were piled in the basket across the room. *Fuck.* Greg had remade the bed, even knowing he might not be the next one in it with Po'Boy. That right there was why he didn't have exclusive anything. Hooking up was better, and far easier. Throwing himself into the armchair, he pawed his phone out of his pocket and turned it back on, waiting impatiently through the bootup cycle. Texts started to roll in even before he unlocked it, and he could see names but not messages, a security measure Twisted "strongly" recommended for all Incoherent members. Po'Boy frowned down at his phone, seeing he had more than a dozen contacts. *Fuck.*

Taking a minute to center himself, he closed his eyes and breathed deeply, pulling the club version of Po'Boy back into place like a cloak. Eyes opening a slit, he started working through the demands of being an MC club vice president. National, as Twisted liked to remind him these days, with them starting chapters in Texas and Mississippi, which gave them a presence in three southern states. It took him two hours, but he finally dealt with everything. Outside pressure on their Baytown chapter had caused a threatened outflow of members, but like with nearly everything, he'd found a direct response was the best way to deal. Calling the president of the other club had surfaced info that the motherfucker hadn't known what his officers were doing, and Po'Boy let Twisted and other Incoherent officers know they'd see a quick resolution to the problem. The only other major thing had been three texts from Penny, wanting to know if Po'Boy would help her plan a fucking birthday party for Twisted.

Uh, lemme think. Fuck no.

As he stared at his phone reading a final e-mail, it buzzed in his hand, and he flipped to the text message application.

Why not? :pouting:

USA I'm busy. USA was on the patch he'd gifted her with after the shitstorm which had been her introduction to Incoherent and life with Twisted. Yousa was what he called her, but everyone knew it was an echo of her words, "Upright and sucking air." Pretty much a definition of his life. Not good, not bad, just keeping on and as long as they were all doing the air sucking thing at the end of a day it was a win.

He's your best friend. Help me.

Rolling his eyes, Po'Boy decided to shut this shit down. He missed Twisted too much to want to lose a scrap of time with him, but spending a day with Penny and hearing her talk about Twisted? Torture.

Penny, I just can't.

He flipped back to the e-mail and was tapping out a response when his phone rang, Penny's picture showing above the "Yousa calling …" *Fuck*. He answered the call without trying to hide his irritation, "*What?*"

"What's wrong, Po'Boy?" She sounded worried, and it shocked him, because why would she be worried about him?

"What do you mean, what's wrong?" He tipped his head back and stared at the ceiling. Patterned tin panels decorated the edges, adding a small touch of elegance to the room. "Nothing's wrong, woman."

"Bullshit." He could hear the impatience in her voice. "You never call me Penny unless something's wrong. Now spill, big guy."

"Jesus, you're full of yourself today, little sister." He gave her the title approved by Twisted, something which granted her a station in the club separate from her property patch. As Twisted's old lady, she had been issued a vest she wore whenever the club was around other clubs,

14

at rallies and parties, places where she'd be riding bitch behind Twisted, and flying his PO patch granted her untouchable status. Around the club, and on her bike, she wore a different vest, a set of blacks holding an Incoherent support patch over her heart, and right under that was the nameplate Po'Boy had given her. Calling her little sister allowed her to call him brother, something reserved for only members and select people, like Penny, who even if she weren't Twisted's old lady, would have been issued a PO by the club because of her actions to save him. Saved them all. Po'Boy shook his head. "Ain't nothing wrong. I just don't have time to plan a bullshit party for Twisted. Man wants sammaches and beer, maybe a little bourbon and green on the side. He don't want no fuckin' party."

She was quiet for a minute, and he gave her time, knowing it meant her brain was working overtime. Her response was soft, and he swore under his breath because when she talked like that, it exposed so much of what she felt. Emotions he'd never be able to show anyone. Couldn't even acknowledge. "He loves you, Ralph. Bell misses you. Can't say so. Not my he-man. But, he does. I see it, and I can't figure out how to fix it. I know you love me, and I love you, but I hurt you, too. I thought if we could do this together, he'd see it and...I don't know, it'd be easier for him."

"Penny," he started, but she cut him off.

"Please?" That single word hung between them, and he squeezed his eyes shut tightly. *Fuck.*

"Fine." She made a noise, but he cut her off. "Not today, though. I got shit to finish up in Orleans. I'll call you tomorrow." He didn't even try to fight her, didn't try to turn her down again. That single-word plea had knocked every argument out of his head. "Don't gloat, bitch."

"Wouldn't think of it," she said, and he could hear the smile in her voice. "Talk tomorrow."

He disconnected the call without responding. *Fuck.* If Penny saw this much with as little as he let himself be around the happy couple, then he was doing an absolutely shit job of hiding anything. *I need an uncomplicated hookup.* Just a fuck. Long, hard, and sweaty bodies moving against each other without any feelings involved.

With quick, practiced movements, he downloaded and logged into an app on his phone. A few minutes later, he tugged on a shirt and his boots, closing and locking the door behind him on his way to a quiet bar around the corner. A quiet bar which was his go-to spot here, where his newest hookup would meet him. He deleted the app and locked his phone.

Chapter Three

"So," Po'Boy licked a stripe of frosting off the cupcake in his hand, then glanced up at the redhead seated on the couch on the opposite side of the room, "when are we gonna see some little Twisted-Yousa ankle biters running around?" He licked off another stripe of frosting and then peeled the paper down, taking a big bite of the cake.

"Oh, God. Never, if I have my way," Penny laughed through her answer, holding her cupcake with both hands to keep from dropping it in her amusement. "I'm not mommy material, Po'Boy."

"The fuck you aren't." Frowning, he glared at her. "You got tits and a womb. That's all nature needs." He swallowed, then took another bite. "Actually, I think it's just the womb part. You ken bottle feed the little bastards iffn you needa."

She shook her head at him, tossing a bright smile before she sank her even teeth into her cupcake. Muffled by her mouthful of cake, she said, "I don't have the want to, at least not right now." She swallowed and grinned again. "You got frosting on your chin."

"Fuck," he grumbled, lifting a hand to swipe at his face. "Why are we eating cupcakes again?" He finished peeling the paper back and tossed the rest of the cake in his mouth. He chewed a minute, then stuck his tongue out at her, grinning at her easy laughter. "I mean, don't get me

17

wrong, Yousa, them are tasty treats. Just not sure why we're chowing down today."

"These are the leftovers from the cupcake cake." Looking down, he folded the paper in half, then in half again, only looking up when she called his name. She smiled hugely at him, and he laughed aloud at the green coating her teeth from where she'd smeared frosting on them.

"You made a cake out of cupcakes? Jesus, you're domesticated. I'm telling you, gonna be spawning soon. Look at the place; you've made a great nest. Mama Penny, I'll start calling you that instead." The laughter died in her eyes, and he frowned. "Shit. Sorry. Too far? Did I take it too far? I do shit like that, Yousa. Don't mean anything by it."

"Not too far, asshole," she retorted, then shook her head "I just...I dunno. You know him better than me, better than anyone else could. Do you think he wants kids?"

Pushing up from the chair where he was seated, he walked over and slouched down beside her on the couch. Leaning close, knowing the position would hide his expression, he tipped his head to rest against her shoulder and said, "You know Bell, Penny. If he wanted something, he'd say something. He ain't shy, woman. Do I think he's pining for kids? No." He shook his head, and she made a noise. "Do I think if you wanted kids he'd be okay with it? Hell, yeah. Because it was something you wanted. Man wants to give you the world, and you know it. Don't read anything into my bullshit today. I'm just raggin' on ya."

"I love you, Po'Boy." From his position beside her, he was close enough to hear her rough swallow as she fought for control of her emotions. "Brother."

"Little sister." He gave the respect right back to her and reached down, grabbing her hand and pushing his fingers between hers. She was tiny, so he had to slouch far down to sit like this, but it gave her something she needed, and he knew it because she allowed it as often as he was willing. After a few minutes, he stirred and sat up, and that was when she leaned against him like she always did.

When Twisted first brought Penny home, Po'Boy had been appalled. Her bloodline was enough to warrant caution, since she was princess to the Caddo Hobos. Add to that the fact she'd earned the attention of the Guanyin's Shield, which just happened to be the CoBos rivals. The Shield were also a close support club for the Vicar's, which in turn made them an enemy of Incoherent. Hell, just having the bitch in his house opened Twisted up for all kinds of shit. Po'Boy had avoided meeting her for weeks, avoided talking to Twisted about her as much as he could, still seeing how his brother was hooked, pulled deeper and deeper into something Po'Boy had never seen.

Then the shit hit the fan in a way which meant it got all over every-fuckin'-body, and Twisted was in the wind. It had taken Penny to find him, taken Penny to rescue him, too, and she had more than earned her way into Po'Boy's heart with her determination. "Stubborn as a mule," he muttered, and she giggled. "What's next? We got a food truck comin'. They're gonna handle food. Boys'll handle booze. You made a fuckin' cake out of cupcakes. I ain't hanging a banner for my boy. I think we're done for today." The party was tomorrow here at Twisted and Penny's house, since more than Incoherent would be coming. Given Penny's connections, it wasn't a surprise that when she'd invited her family and friends, the list was mostly bikers and their bitches. "I think we're done."

"We're done," she agreed and sat up, turning to sit sideways on the couch, one leg bent underneath her ass. "You bringing a gal?"

"Fuck, not this again." He let his head tip back, more to hide his expression from her than out of true frustration. "Let it go, Penny. I find my pussy on my own time, and do not need you to hook me up." Last weekend was the best example, not that he could say anything like that to her. The man he'd messaged on the app had shown with a woman, and with the welcome buffer between them, "Lewis" had gotten off just like he needed. "Just leave it the fuck alone."

"Twisted worries." At her tone, Po'Boy rolled his head on the cushion to glare at her out of the corner of his eye. "Seriously, Po'Boy. I heard him asking Busk the other day what was up with you."

He turned to stare at the ceiling again. *Shit.* The exact kind of attention he didn't need. *Where's a fucking MC war when I need a goddamned distraction?* He decided to introduce a level of raunch she probably wouldn't be comfortable with, see if he could pry her off the topic of him getting himself some. "Penny. I'm not wasting away and doing without hot pussy. I'm just not flyin' around my own flagpole for a change. All the bitches who hang around the club are passarounds, and I'm just tired of knowing the hole I stick my dick in has said hello to every other brother's dick, too. Orleans is a good place for anonymous pussy, and that's all I need. Wet and willing to climb my pole. Throw in a little assplay, and I'm a happy bastard."

"Jesus, you're a serious horndog." This voice wasn't Penny, and Po'Boy lifted his head to see Twisted stalking into the room. "Stop talkin' to my ole lady about your fuck habits." Long, dark hair pulled back into a single braid, Twisted's smile would stop traffic, and nearly stopped Po'Boy's breath in his chest. *Never again*, he thought and felt again the wash of loss and regret which had become too familiar lately. *Time to deflect and redirect.*

"Jesus yourself, Prez. She fuckin' asked." Po'Boy grinned as Twisted's scowl turned from him and towards Penny. "You're here, that's my release bell. I'm outtie, brother." Slapping Penny's thigh, he stood from the couch and started walking away. "Thanks for the chat, little sister. I'm going back to Orleans now, see about finding a flag to put on my pole."

TREADING THE TRAITOR'S PATH: OUT BAD

Chapter Four

Crissy

"Oh. My. God." The pauses in between the words were involuntary but distinct, and the pronunciation of God was more like *GAWD*, but Christine Emmerson for once didn't try to check her distinctive Louisiana drawl. "Tell me you didn't just do that."

She looked down at her phone again and narrowed her eyes. "Oh, my." She took a breath, and then wheezed a soft, "God." Stabbing her finger at the button to close the image window on the app, she scrunched up her nose. "You *did* just do that. You sent me a dick pic."

Closing the app entirely, she flipped over to messages.

You would NOT believe that guy. The one from Milwaukee? What a douche! I'm giving up on dating. It's just not worth it.

She waited for a beat, and when there was no response continued.

I'm going target shooting tomorrow. Just in case. Get in a little percussive therapy. He could be a hacker, prolly already knows the address here. Can't be too careful.

She grinned, knowing it was a topic that would definitely provoke a lecture on being safe. After a moment, she typed again.

Dating is overrated IMO. Someday I'll meet my Prince Charming, but it's not going to be trolling endless pages of pictures I'm not even certain is the person who will show up for coffee. I'm done. D. O. N. E. Done.

Without waiting for a response, she locked her phone and tossed it on the table next to her armchair. Curling her feet into the seat next to her, Crissy propped one elbow on a knee and then, chin in hand, she stared out the window at the field behind the house. With a shiver, she watched as a flock of dark birds swooped in and landed around the silo, pecking for any grain spilled on the patches of snow.

Running footsteps sounded overhead, and she looked over her shoulder, smiling as she saw the small body already rounding the top of the stairs. "Auntie Crissy, where *are* you?" The plaintive call sounded as if the little girl had been looking for hours, instead of having just woken up.

"In the sunroom, Missy." With sounds of bare feet slapping the wooden floor growing closer, Crissy opened her arms, preparing, and then gave a soft "oof" when the small body leaped over the arm of the chair, landing in her lap. Snuggling the little girl close, she buried her face into the crook of her niece's neck and told her, "Missy Prissy, you're still supposed to be asleep. Naptime is not over, honey."

"I had a dream." The complaint was clear, and Crissy squeezed Missy a little tighter, knowing it wasn't a good dream chasing the little girl up out of sleep. "Can I stay here with you?"

"Sure thing, butter bean." Crissy slouched a little, drawing the little girl up her chest, smiling when she felt the weight of a head heavy on her shoulder. "I got you, darling girl." With a contented sigh, she leaned her head back against the chair and settled in, resting her cheek on top of Missy's head.

Missy was her sister's only child, three years old, and was quite the handful. Crissy had moved in with her sister's family nearly a year ago to help out and hadn't counted on the tiny girl stealing her heart so quickly or completely. They'd spent hours together each day, coloring and conducting tea parties upstairs in Missy's room. She whispered, lips brushing Missy's hair, "Love you."

Soft and sweet, she got the words back. "Love you, too, Auntie." Then her heart clenched in her chest as Missy continued, "I miss Mommy."

In a voice thick with tears, Crissy choked out a promise. "She loves you, too, Missy Prissy. Always and forever."

The funeral had been two weeks ago, and tomorrow Bob, her brother-in-law, and Missy would be moving to Minnesota to live with his folks for a while. Rhoda had made him promise to go home because she loved her husband and daughter more than anything. Rhoda knew Bob's mother, the mother she'd found as part of the life she'd made with them, would help them heal. Rhoda also loved her baby sister, and knew unless forced out of the nest, Crissy would stay with Bob and Missy, and make their lives better without ever trying to spread her wings.

Crissy had been fourteen when their parents had died, and the twelve years between the two girls meant Rhoda transitioned into a mother's role early. It was a facet of her personality, so much a part of her that even now, after the cancer had taken her away, she was still looking after everyone as much as she could.

An hour later, Crissy watched the birds leap from the ground, flying up to rest on top of the silo when Bob's truck pulled in and parked nearby. He'd been to town to deal with the bank and settling final details of his life with Rhoda here. He climbed out of the vehicle, and Crissy watched as he looked around, hands on his hips, surveying the house and farm. She stirred, gently jostling the little girl still sleeping in her lap. "Hey, little Missy, Daddy's home." A squeeze of the child's arms around her neck let her know Missy was waking up. "Time to rise and shine. Daddy's outside and Auntie needs to get dinner started." This would give him time with his daughter without Crissy underfoot, something he needed even if he didn't know it.

Missy sat up, hands shoving at the honey-blonde hair that had fallen around her face. She twisted to look out the window and with joy in her voice shouted, "Daddy's home!" Limbs still uncoordinated, she tried to slide off Crissy's lap, yelling, "Daddy!" Gripping the little girl under her arms, Crissy set her feet on the floor and let go, smiling as Missy raced towards the door. Outside, Bob's head lifted and even from this distance Crissy could see his smile and knew he'd heard his daughter's greeting.

He was a good man, the best. Fiercely loyal, faithful to her sister through the best and worst life had to throw at them. He didn't hesitate to lay things out, wanting only the best for everyone he loved and hadn't backed away from doing it to Crissy last night when he'd come in from the barn to find her sitting in this same chair, crying again.

"Crissy, honey." She heard Bob's soft voice from the doorway, and she sniffed, lifting her hands to wipe the tears from her cheeks. *"You can't sleep again?"*

"Says the man walking in from outside at 2:00 a.m." Crissy swallowed hard, then whispered, her voice ragged with grief, tearing out of her throat while her chest clutched tight, *"I just miss her."*

"I miss her too, honey." Soft footsteps and she knew it was because he'd left his boots near the door. Rhoda hated stepping in puddles left on the floor by melting slush off footwear and had quietly campaigned to make that not happen in her house. The whole family walked through the house in socks or slippers, and now the idea something so small had made her sister happy caused Crissy to tear up again.

"Things keep coming out of left field." The heat of his palm hit her shoulder, and his fingers dug in tightly, holding on. She whispered, *"I'm going to miss you and Missy."*

"It's the right thing to do, Crissy. Time to start the process, and we both know it." She nodded, and his grip changed as he squatted next to the chair. "We can't make the hurt go away, so we have to find the best way we can to live with it, and push through like she'd want. It's not moving on because this pain's going to be part of us for the rest of our lives. We have to know it's okay to hurt, but it's also okay to laugh. At the end of things, our passing will cause this same pain to someone else, and I want us both to know their pain is worth it. Rhoda lived life as she wanted, and she didn't have any regrets about that. You have this great opportunity, and they've been gracious enough to keep the offer open. It's time, honey."

An ad agency had recruited Crissy even before she'd finished college, having her work as a freelancer on various projects as a trial of her skills and compatibility with their in-house team. Rhoda's diagnosis came just after graduation, and instead of traveling to Slidell and settling into a life of working and relearning her childhood culture, Crissy had come to Wisconsin. Understanding the gravity of the situation, the human resource manager had offered to let Crissy stay on as-needed, doing freelance projects when she could find the time.

When it was clear Rhoda was losing her war against the disease, she'd reached out to the company without telling Crissy, and put things into motion. When Crissy's plane landed tomorrow, she'd be striking out into a brand-new life. Condo, job, leased car—Rhoda had taken care of all the details in between medication infusions and doctor visits, putting precious time and energy into lining out her little sister's world. She'd known Crissy too well.

Phone in her hand, Crissy opened the text app.

Your little girl is so beautiful. She's gonna be a heartbreaker when she grows up. Bob's gonna have his hands full, for sure.

Bob swung Missy high in the air, bringing her body close to his chest before flinging her up again. Crissy heard her laughter through the windowpane.

Thank you for letting me be part of this. Part of your love for your family. Our family. Love you so much.

She turned towards the kitchen to put the already bagged roast into the oven for dinner, thumb moving across the phone's screen.

Maybe dating will be easier in Louisiana. Should I learn French? What if a guy flirts in French, I'd think he was asking where the bathroom was. Eeek. I can't learn a foreign language. Wait, is it foreign if Americans speak it? Hmmm.

She grinned and shoved the phone into her pocket. *Time to fly, little bird*, she imagined Rhoda's voice saying.

Chapter Five
Po'Boy

Po'Boy leaned his ass against the hood of a pickup parked at the edge of the field and lifted a beer to his lips, surveying the crowd over the bottle. *Must be a hundred people here*, he thought and grinned as he swallowed. The party hadn't been a surprise, couldn't be, not with the food truck showing up early and the band needing to get into the field behind Twisted's house to set up their stage. But Twisted had been pleased. Po'Boy had been witness to an intense liplock Twisted had laid on Penny in response, and then gotten a back pounding clinch from his brother when Penny had shared Po'Boy's part in the festivity planning.

He was feeling loose and buzzed, tired and achy in the best of ways from the activities of the previous night. Every time he moved, his asshole clenched and a tiny thrill of pain zipped up his spine. The only near issue last night had been when the other guy wanted to bottom, and Po'Boy had to redirect their activities away from that particular scene. He'd so far drawn the line at plowing another man. "I'm bi" had become his mantra, and for some reason fucking a guy crossed whatever fake-ass line he had in his head. His dick liked to paddle on both sides of the boat, no denying the truth even to himself. He liked to give and receive head, and for penetration it didn't matter if it was takin' pussy or gettin' cock, he'd get off just as spectacularly with either sex. Plus, going down on a woman was a huge turn-on for him. *As is sucking cock*, he thought, smiling again, remembering kneeling on the mattress to bend over the man's lap last night, getting his first taste of the salty musk from the burly bear.

Fuck, I might be drunker than I thought. Po'Boy needed to corral his thoughts, pull back before he got a stiffy from thinking about his hookup. A decent little threesome, which was his preferred way to go, because it gave him plausible deniability in his head. The guy's cock had been short but thick, and he'd taken care easing into Po'Boy's hole while Po'Boy's dick was buried in Denise. "Burns so good," he muttered, an echo from last night, and then jerked sideways, nearly falling when Twisted's voice came from beside him.

"What burns?" The chassis of the truck moved as Twisted hefted himself onto the hood, the muscles in his arms bunching with the movement.

My asshole. Po'Boy checked himself before those words fled his lips, and shook his head. *Fuck*. "My eyes, watching you cuddle up to Yousa." They'd been slow dancing to the fast strains of Zydeco music, and Po'Boy knew Twisted didn't give a shit who saw how he felt about Penny. "Was a boot-stomper, and you were humpin' like a horny hog. Fuck man, get a goddamned room."

"You never used to mind watching me rub up against a woman," Twisted reminded him, and Po'Boy swiveled to stare up at him. "Not sayin' I'm down for putting on a show with my ole lady, and you know I ain't, but it never bothered you before."

"You didn't give a shit about the bitches before." Po'Boy nearly rolled his eyes at himself. *That didn't make any sense, fool*. "It's weird is all, seeing you deep like this."

"I didn't give a shit, you're right." Twisted's gaze stayed on him, unwavering, and Po'Boy was reminded of Penny's words about his concern. "And neither did you. What's changed?"

"Ain't fuckin' no club ho at your fuckin' birthday party. Man, you *are* Twisted. Fuck." Po'Boy forced a smile and shook his head as he turned away, staring across the field to where the prospects were piling brush for a bonfire later. "Plus, didn't invite any passarounds. You havin' an ole lady and all, seemed fucked up."

"Now it's Penny's fault you ain't getting' no 'tang?" Twisted laughed, taking the sting out of his words. "Fuck you."

"Poontang, poontang. I get plenty of pretty, pretty poontang." Po'Boy lifted his beer to find it empty. "Fuck." He stood, staggering slightly as he placed the bottle on the hood next to Twisted. "Gonna shut my eyes a minute." Taking off his vest and shirt, he folded them as he moved to the back of the truck. Opening the tailgate, he sat and then lay back, stuffing the bundle of leather and fabric under his head. The metal of the truck bed bit into his back. "Fuck."

"Here," he heard and looked up to see a wad of material flying at him. Reaching up instinctively, he snagged a blanket out of the air.

"Miracle man."

Laughing, Twisted had already turned away and was walking back towards where Penny stood across the field. Folding the blanket into a messy rectangle, Po'Boy laid it in the truck bed, and then crawled to where he could flop down on top of it. Pulling his vest and shirt closer, he shoved them under his head again with a sigh.

It was full dark when he jerked awake. Fortunately, the dream had only just begun, so he wasn't vocal about it, just shaking and sweating. Tonight it had been the time his mother's husband forced him into a blow job. Po'Boy well remembered how it had fucked with little Ralphie's head for a long time because of just how good it had felt to have the man's cock in his mouth. Voices nearby surprised him, and he recognized them as the probable reason he'd woken when he did. About to thank whoever it was, the tense tones finally registered and he lay still, listening intently to try and pick out the words.

"...seen the way he looked at me." The first voice was gruff, angry.

"You do not want to court that disaster, brother." The second voice was cajoling, level and sensible in tone. "The man would have the ass of anyone who touched his woman."

Who are they talking about? He didn't have to wonder long.

"Penny Dane is bad luck walking on two legs, brother. He's stuffin' his cock into sweet meat and leaving the rest of us to swing, waiting for him to get back to business." The first voice clipped off his words, seeming to grow angrier with every passing moment. "Remove her from the fuckin' equation, and we're back to where we need to fuckin' be." *He's one stupid motherfucker. Fuckin' munt.*

"Not certain that's truth, brother. She's had a mellowing effect on the man, and I suspect when he gets tired of playin' house, and you know he will, he's gonna carry a dose of mellow back into business. We'll be richer men." A laugh, then, "Sweet thing like she is, it might take a while, but when he does get tired of it, and he will, we'll be ready."

Footsteps crunched on the seashell and gravel mix of Twisted's drive, moving away. Po'Boy eased up to one hip, peering over the edge of the truck bed, trying to see who the men were. Didn't mean he could do anything about it right now, but knowing who was riding the discontented train would take him a long way to derailing that motherfucker when it came time. Identical patches gleamed in the moonlight, and Po'Boy sucked in a breath. *That's a fuckin' dead club, at least up here. What in fuck is someone doin' wearin' Vicar's patches at this party?* He watched as they stripped off their vests and bundled them into a bag, shoving it into the backseat of a nearby car before turning to walk to where the bonfire was now blazing brightly.

Po'Boy tried to push to his knees, but a wave of nausea hit him. Too much booze and sweet drinks on an empty stomach. He lay back down, telling himself it was for a moment only. Closing his eyes and sighing, he let what he'd overheard tumble around in his head. *Vicar's Wrath here.* A nonexistent club because all local chapters been disbanded, most of their members rolled into the Incoherent. Those men here, not invited by him or Penny, meant they'd been brought in by someone else. *Who would have—* His reverie was interrupted by a shuffling footstep at the tailgate of the truck and Po'Boy opened his eyes a slit to see a figure looming over him in the darkness. The flaring light from the bonfire was barely enough to let him recognize an ally, Wrench. A CoBo member who had known Penny her entire life. One who had a thing for her once, giving way when Twisted staked his claim. Wrench was looking down at Po'Boy, and he was about to sit up and greet him when the expression on the man's face caught his attention.

It was avid. Hungry.

Wrench's gaze was trailing along Po'Boy's form, pausing at his chest, then moving down to his crotch. His nostrils flared, and the muscles in his jaw tensed, jumping as he ground his teeth together.

Aroused.

Po'Boy's cock twitched, and the movement must have been visible because he watched as Wrench's tongue came out in a languorous swipe across his bottom lip. *What the fuck?*

A sound from by the bonfire pulled Wrench's gaze away, and he took a step backwards, then two, before turning and stalking into the darkness.

What. The. Fuck?

***

Standing near one of the upended fifty-gallon barrels being used for impromptu tables, Po'Boy used deflection techniques to watch Wrench. He knew him, of course. You couldn't be around Penny and not know Wrench. The man held unofficial titles for the CoBos like Po'Boy did

IMC. They were the men who fixed problems, who weren't afraid to do the wet and dirty work needed to find the information that'd keep their brothers safe. A nomad, always on the move, Wrench seemed to have settled down since Penny shacked up with Twisted. Still, his skill set was legend. Never, and Po'Boy was fucking attuned to the idea of gay behavior in the clubs, but never had he heard anything at all muttered or whispered about the man. Straight as they come, at least where people could see. *A lot like me.*

Shaking off the thought, he continued his observation of the group around the bonfire. He hadn't gotten a good look at the men's faces who had worn the Vicar's patches, so he still had those people to find. Plus, trying to figure out exactly what he'd seen on Wrench's face because he didn't trust his memory at this point. The possibility of knowing someone else like him was intoxicating. *Not that I'll do fuck all about it, but Jesus.* Just the idea had his dick perking up to take notice. Just to have someone he didn't have to guard everything that came out of his mouth would be nice for a change.

Voices behind him caught his attention, and he strained to hear. After a few innocuous words, he was certain he recognized the men he'd seen earlier. Twisting at the waist, he made a show of stretching while looking around for the faces matching the voices. Distracted, he was taken off guard when he heard Wrench from beside him.

"Kink in your back?"

Po'Boy whipped around, bringing his raised arms down so fast beer flung out of the mouth of his bottle, splashing on Wrench's chest, bare underneath his cut, just like Po'Boy. He'd slipped his cut in place after leaving the truck bed, but tucked his folded shirt into the waistband of his jeans instead of putting it on. A droplet of the liquid trailed its way down Wrench's torso, dampening the material at his waist. Po'Boy realized he'd been staring and without meaning to, his mouth led the way as he said, "Yeah, I copped some shuteye in the back of a truck a bit ago. Woke up stiff." Total truth, but what had been stiff had been his dick.

A reaction flashed over Wrench's face so fast Po'Boy couldn't register the emotion, then the man smiled. "Lotta bitches here would love to work that cramp out for you."

Lotta bitches aren't you. Strange how his mind knew exactly what he couldn't say first, and then came up with the correct comeback second. "I bet there are." He lifted his beer, taking a drink to keep his mouth closed for a moment, then swallowed and said, "Enjoying the party Penny planned for her ole man?" He knew as soon as he said it the dig was deeper than he intended, because a naked pain danced on Wrench's face for a moment, smoothed away a second later. He noted Wrench's empty hands and offered the man an out, giving him a chance to ignore the previous statement. "You need a beer, man?"

"Yeah." A single gruff word, then Wrench turned to stare at the bonfire. "Naw, you know what? Never mind. I better get in the wind."

"Where you off to? Party is just starting to get good." Po'Boy paused, then surprised himself by leaning in slightly to say, "Walk with me. There're a couple of assholes here I want your take on." *What the fuck am I doing?* "If you wanna talk business, that is. You need to leave, you can go on. I'll catch up with you later."

"I'll walk with you." Wrench inched closer when he muttered the words, and Po'Boy caught a whiff of him. A scent which went straight to his dick, it was filled with wood smoke and expensive cigarettes, a spicy musk underneath it all. *Fucking shit.*

Nothing for it now but to accept his fate. *I'm in hell.* Without looking to see if Wrench followed, he strode across the trampled field towards Twisted's house. Inside, he avoided the groups of people in the kitchen and living room, opening the door and heading into the darkened den instead. Sweeping the room with a glance, he ensured they were alone, then pushed the door shut as soon as Wrench was inside. He opened his mouth, then closed it when he realized he wasn't sure how to begin without revealing he was awake when Wrench had found him in the back of the truck. Po'Boy knew how he'd react if someone knew his secrets, and wanted to avoid having Wrench trying to pound his head into the floor if at all possible.

"At least two men flashin' Vicar's patches are here." Wrench didn't say anything, didn't move, just stared at him. "They were talkin' shit about Penny." Still no reaction, which puzzled him. "I ain't wantin' to start shit tonight, but I want to know who they are and better yet, who invited their fuckin' asses."

"Ragman folded VWMC into IMC." Wrench's tone was flat, unsurprised. "Ain't no VWMC no more."

"Fuck, man, you and I both heard rumors they've reformed, down on the Mississippi coast, where Leswayne had family." He snorted, admitting Wrench's network was likely just as good as his. "I know you have, because I have." Leswayne had been the previous president of Vicar's Wrath, killed by Penny's blade a year ago. His son, Ragman, had only one reaction to his father's death, regret it hadn't been at his hands. "Ragman can't control all the shit his old man stirred through the years. You met Leswayne, knew him as well as the rest of us did. Motherfucker left a world of hurt, and there're those who want to keep that hurt going."

"Heard you ran into one such the other night." They hadn't turned on any lights when they came inside, and the weak moonlight coming through the windows served more to disguise than illuminate Wrench's face. "Heard he had a problem, and you helped him with it."

"A problem? What the fuck are you goin' on about?" Wrench was with the CoBos, and the relationship between the clubs was friendly and supportive, but he and Wrench were not brothers. The idea he could have heard about Jones and the shit that had led Po'Boy the man's way was concerning.

"Heard he had a problem with his circulation, and you fixed it right up." He lifted one hand, palm first. "Not sayin' I wouldn't have provided the same assistance. Just sayin' I know VWMC reborn ain't the old VWMC."

Po'Boy stood still for a moment, then deliberately shoved both hands into the front pockets of his jeans. Rendering himself at a disadvantage was the right move, because the tension which had crept into Wrench's muscles eased, his shoulders lowered as he relaxed. "Deuces is a fucktard." Deuces was the man who had revived the old MC patch, and likely who was behind the pressure IMC had been experiencing, even if Jones hadn't been willing to speak the name. "But Deuces ain't here. These are two munts I ain't never seen before." Wrench lifted an eyebrow in question, and Po'Boy winced because maybe he was laying it on a bit thick. He played up being the hick with a lot of people because when he paired that kind of language with his thick Louisiana accent, they immediately deducted a dozen points from any IQ they assumed he had. "Munt. Male cunt."

That earned him a nod, and then an answer. "Royal and Keister." Wrench said the names with a straight face, but Po'Boy needed clarification.

"Keister? Like...he's called...he calls himself an ass?" He couldn't help it, and a laugh broke free. "Fuck, that's bullshit. Keister."

"Gets better." Wrench smiled, and in his clean-shaven cheek, Po'Boy saw the shallow dip of a dimple. *Fuck me.* "He thinks it means German."

"Kaiser? He..." Shaking his head, Po'boy laughed again and caught Wrench looking at his neck as he did so. Testing the theory, he swallowed and watched as Wrench's jaw tightened, a muscle jumping in his cheek. "He thinks his road name is the same as Kaiser? A German emperor? What a maroon. Definite munt."

"Yeah, he's a piece of work. Royal, he's the smarter of the two. Wish he'd prospected for us, but VWMC offered fucking fast track. Insane. He went from prospect to member in a couple of weeks, then officer in a handful more." Wrench leaned his shoulders against the wall and shoved his own hands into his jeans pockets, but then Po'Boy caught him discreetly adjusting his half-hard cock. Once his attention was snagged by the bulge, he couldn't pull his eyes away, watching as the wrinkles in Wrench's crotch fell away, fabric pulled taut by his dick. "Uh," Wrench grunted and coughed, bending away for a moment.

Po'Boy tore his gaze free, suddenly aware his own cock had woken up. *Fuck*. Turning to the side, he took a couple of steps towards the windows, trying to give Wrench a minute to recover, desperately hoping to do the same thing. "So them being here means what, exactly?" He knew his voice was hoarser than normal but hoped Wrench didn't know him well enough to catch the change. "Keister—fuck me, what a fuckin' name—if he's the stupid one, he was talkin' more smack than the other. But Royal shut him down pretty fast and hard. What bugs the hell outta me is they felt comfortable enough to just show up here." Shuffling his feet, he used every movement to telegraph his intention as he turned around to face Wrench. The extra distance helped because he couldn't sniff the air trying to catch a whiff of Wrench's scent. "Got any thoughts on that?"

Wrench's voice was quiet, and his tone serious when he said, "I think we should start our investigation at the source."

"You think they're still hangin' out 'round the fire?" Po'Boy stared at Wrench, feeling a twist in his gut when the man grinned again. "Do they know you can recognize 'em?"

"Only one way to find out." Wrench gestured to the door, and said, "Let's go see."

***

"Twisted's party." Po'Boy angled his head towards Wrench as they stood side by side, watching the two men in a group clustered around one of the coolers filled with beer. "Man, you don't know the shit I went through for this. Penny's gonna have our asses if we fuck it up."

Once outside, it hadn't taken long to find the VWMC members they were looking for. When Po'Boy indicated them with a tip of his chin, Wrench had nodded. The two of them had made their way through the crowd to a position near the men, but out of their line of sight.

"Penny's harmless." With a shake of his head, Wrench dismissed Po'Boy's statement. "But we would be better off if we had less in the way of observers."

"Fewer witnesses, check." Po'Boy pulled his phone out and tapped a message, then shoved the device deep in his pocket. A vibration a minute later made him grin. "Handled," was all he said.

"Handled?" Now Wrench's snort of disbelief was aimed at him, and Po'Boy looked at him, one eyebrow lifted.

"You doubt me?" Wrench shook his head. Po'Boy stood, waiting for things to start happening. The tension between them felt like it was pulling him sideways towards Wrench; he needed to break the silence. "Penny's harmless?" When he repeated the words from Wrench's previous statement, the man grinned yet a-fucking-gain and then tipped his chin down to hide the expression. "We both know that's a flat-out lie."

"Sometimes she's harmless." Wrench spoke to the toes of their boots, and Po'Boy looked down, too, not seeing anything fascinating enough to hold his attention like it was Wrench's. "When she's sleeping."

"Give you that one." He lifted his head when Penny yelled across the field, angling his head closer to Wrench as he said, "Told you, handled. She fuckin' made a cake out of cupcakes. Long as she don't tell these fuckers that tidbit, they'll all be fallin' on the cake in about a minute. Fuck, they'll eat it even if she told 'em it was stuffed with crawdads."

"She ain't gonna make 'em sing 'Happy Birthday,' is she?" Wrench laughed outright, and Po'Boy turned to grin at him, surprised when Wrench's smile faded away. "Looks like Royal is allergic to larger gatherings. Prolly someone here he knows."

"No doubt. You and me both know it's a small world here along the coast. Mean's it's time, then. Which do you want?" It went without saying they expected both men would put up a struggle. Po'Boy cracked his knuckles, shaking out his arms. It also went without saying he would be enjoying the next few minutes as long as they did try and struggle.

"You take the short guy. I wanna see you kick Keister." Po'Boy snorted and nodded as Wrench continued, "On three?" Po'Boy nodded again, tensing and getting ready to move. "One—"

He jumped, hearing Wrench's soft cursing from behind him. "Shoulda told you I cain't count," he called over his shoulder as he barreled into his target, knocking the air out of the man as they landed on the gravel together, Po'Boy's knee firmly in Keister's gut. The meaty sound of a fist meeting flesh came from behind him, and then the solid thud of a heavy object hitting the ground. Po'Boy twisted to look back and saw Wrench standing over a motionless body in the dirt, having taken down his target. "Let's get 'em outta the light." He took a moment and pulled back, driving a short, hard punch to the side of his guy's head, rattling him even more than the sudden airless state had. Po'Boy stood and gripped the man's wrists, yanking his arms over his head and tugging him back towards the line of cars and trucks in the driveway.

Once out of sight from the rest of the party, he and Wrench made quick work of hauling their targets behind a truck. The sight of the blanket pallet in the back made him laugh, and he opened the door, pulling the lever to unlock the seatback. Digging in the space exposed, he came up with a handful of bungee cords and lifted them, waggling his eyebrows at Wrench who laughed quietly and asked, "Whose truck is this?" Wrench moved to the other side of the truck and shifted trash around, then stepped back when a noise came from the back of the truck. Po'Boy pulled in a heavy sigh of relief knowing the man's hand had been about to encounter something it would have been hard to explain. Lunging across the space, Po'Boy grabbed the silk boxers, wadding them up and shoving them deep under the seat.

"My truck," he called, slamming the seat back into place and closing the door with a bump of his hip. "Help me get them ready to transport." They worked efficiently, lifting the men to the bed of the truck and then quickly securing wrists to ankles. Po'Boy held up one finger and walked to the car he'd seen them shove their cuts in, opening the door and pulling out the bag to toss it into the bed of the truck. It landed with a loud clunk that sounded heavy and metallic. "You can check that out while we hit the Mandeville clubhouse."

Without a word, Wrench climbed over the now-closed tailgate, resting his back against the cab of the truck. He reached out a long arm and grabbed the bag, dragging it closer to him. Royal was awake now, his eyes flickering madly between Po'Boy and Wrench. Then when he recognized the bag Wrench was digging through, he struggled in earnest.

"You sure you're okay back here with them?" Po'Boy asked before he could stop his mouth, glad when Wrench didn't even look up, just grunted. Climbing into the truck's cab, Po'Boy glanced across at the crowd gathered near Twisted's house. With a silent apology to Penny for ditching the rest of the party, he jammed the key into the ignition and turned. In a short time, they were off the country roads and onto the highway, and Po'Boy made good time, pulling into the deserted clubhouse and wheeling the truck in a tight circle, backing up to the building in front of a sliding metal dock door. "Gimme a second," he yelled and grabbed his keys. There was a thud followed by a groan, and from where he stood next to the door, he flicked a glance over his shoulder. Wrench stood, staring down, bag in one hand, a gun in his other. "They give you shit on the way over here?" Wrench shook his head as Po'Boy slid the key home into the lock. Unlocking the door, he slid it wide and turned around. "What's the pissy look for then, man?"

Without responding, Wrench held out the bag, and Po'Boy took it, staring down into the darkness. Something shiny moved, and he reached in and pulled out what looked like two lengths of pipe. "Fuckin' pipe bombs?" Wrench made a noise of agreement as he bent his knees and jumped out of the back of the truck, landing softly beside Po'Boy. "What the fuck you think they were planning on blowing up?" He reached into the bag again and came out with a piece of paper. Glancing at the paper, he stopped in his tracks. "Are you fuckin' kiddin' me?" Whirling, he lunged towards the back of the truck, pulled to a halt by Wrench's hand on his arm. He turned in place, jaw clenched as he crowded Wrench against the building. "Did you fuckin' see this?" Brandishing the paper, he waved it back and forth. "Huh? Did you? Did you fuckin' see this? It's a fuckin' map to my fuckin' suite. *My fuckin' suite.* Did you see this? What these motherfuckers have?"

"I saw it," Wrench spoke quietly, and his eyes held Po'Boy's gaze. "It's just a place in New Orleans." He shrugged, and Po'Boy saw the lie when he said, "Just any other place. Nothing important."

Breathing hard through his nose, Po'Boy struggled to hold onto control. "They were gonna blow it up."

"Just any other place." Wrench's voice was still quiet and even, his gaze steady. In a soft whisper, he said, "As far as they know. Don't fuck it up, Po'Boy."

Ripping his gaze from Wrench's, Po'Boy stared down at the paper again. The building circled on the map was his club. Not the MC, but his *club*, where he'd spent the weekend. Where he spent most weekends. He wrestled with himself for a moment, then dared a glance back up into Wrench's face. He saw compassion and knowledge there, a softness he didn't expect. His voice was hoarse when he repeated Wrench's words. "Just any other place." He nodded, building steam on this, knowing he'd already burned bridges with this man as with the look on Wrench's face, he had to know. "Not a fuckin' thing important about that address. These motherfuckers though—" He turned towards the truck, not able to bear the sympathy in Wrench's look another single moment. "—got some 'splainin' to do."

Chapter Six
Wrench

Tyler Sawyer stood in an empty parking lot beside the truck of a good man, watching as that man pulled himself back together after losing his shit over a piece of paper. *What the hell is it about this dude?* Po'Boy had a way of getting under his skin, back from the first time they'd met at a party. One comment too many from the big man and he'd been ready to skin *him*. Slowly. Bagger, Penny's uncle, had talked Wrench off the ledge that day. Then the day they'd ridden together to rescue Twisted, Po'Boy's borderline abusive treatment of Penny had yanked his leash again. He'd gotten his ass handed to him, Po'Boy absently taking him down on his way to get in Penny's face. It was only later when he'd realized the emotion he'd felt rolling off the man had been terror. Not at what they were riding towards, but that something would happen to Twisted.

Extreme emotion like that couldn't be faked, and Po'Boy's distress when Twisted was missing had been real and palpable. Once things were back to a semi-normal state, it had made Wrench look closer than he would have otherwise. That looking? He'd gotten more than he planned on, as some things can't be unseen, once they're seen. Like those pictures which need a person to unfocus their eyes in order to see. Or in this case, refocus.

Po'Boy loved Twisted. Not in a "got your back, bro" kind of way, but a soul deep love. They'd been friends since grade school, and Wrench knew it probably had started out as a friendship, but the things they'd been through together since had pulled it sideways into a segment of the relationship diagram he didn't think Twisted recognized. Penny did. Wrench had seen her watching Po'Boy more than once, pity and regret on her face. And now, Wrench did.

That recognizing had tugged something inside him sideways, too. He'd gone from seeing how Po'Boy loved Twisted, to wondering what it would be like to inspire that kind of love. And then tonight had jumped from that straight to wondering what it would be like to consummate that kind of love. Had looked at Po'Boy sleeping and wanted to have the right to crawl up beside him.

He watched now, as with a grunt, Po'Boy hefted the final guy out of the truck, and tipped his head towards the vehicle. "Get the tailgate on your way past, Wrench?"

He'd felt that same terror as before boiling off Po'Boy a moment ago because of an anonymous address circled on a map. His own distress had been the existence of the explosives, but Po'Boy had glanced at them and known they weren't armed, something it had taken Wrench longer to suss out. Po'Boy had lost his shit about the address, however, and then pulled things sideways yet again when he got up in Wrench's face like he did. *And I liked it.*

He nodded, watching the play of muscles under Po'Boy's skin. *Fuck, no. I'm totally into chicks.* Po'Boy bent over slightly as he slung the man to the floor. "And this guy, apparently." Before Po'Boy could turn around and ask him what the fuck he meant by that, Wrench slammed the tailgate closed, and then stepped into the room, sliding the door into place with a soft click. This was a room without an interior door, the only openings were the one through which they'd entered, and a small window set high in the outside wall. "How you wanna play this,

Po'Boy? Your house, your rules." They were in an Incoherent clubhouse, just outside Mandeville, and Po'Boy was a national officer.

"I'm in a mood," Po'Boy shared, and Wrench chuckled. "And that mood is both ass-kickin' some keister—" They both chuckled. "—and getting someone royally jacked up." Po'Boy straightened and then bent backwards, his deep stretch sweeping the edges of his cut open across his defined chest. *Fuck, now I'm noticing this guy's chest.* Wrench reflexively closed his eyes and shook his head in short, sweeping arcs. "Let's start with the smart one." Wrench opened his eyes to see Po'Boy stepping towards Keister and tipped his head to the side in question because that man was the opposite of smart. Po'Boy grinned and held a finger to his lips. "The smartest one is more likely to know everything, so we might not even have to kill the other one."

Royal made a noise and Po'Boy looked over at him. "Hold on. Are you the smart one?" At the rapid headshake, Po'Boy nodded. "Didn't think so. Course, neither of you assclowns are smart, coming to Twisted's house like you did. You don't invade a man's property. Invasion of the assclowns." He snorted a laugh. "Might as well make a movie outta it." Tossing his phone to Wrench, he said, "Keep track 'o that for me?"

* * *

Wrench lay in the back of the truck, staring up at the stars. A tinge of light had begun to creep along the eastern edge of the sky as dawn threatened. He smelled bleach, and there was a noise, then the springs of the truck sagged as Po'Boy settled on the tailgate. "You at least get cleaned up before you flopped on my blanket?"

Tilting his head slightly to the side, Wrench squinted until Po'Boy's profile came into focus against the darkness. Even in this limited light, the fatigue on his face was clear to see. Back bowed, the big man stared down at his hands and Wrench watched as they clenched into fists and tightened until his forearms shook, then released, and then tightened

44

again. The repetitive movement seemed to soothe Po'Boy which was odd because Wrench knew from experience how his hands had to be hurting after the workout he'd had tonight. Po'Boy had insisted on being the main interrogator, which meant he was the one dealing out the pain. Wrench's role had been delegated to holding the men and securing whichever of the two that wasn't actively being questioned.

Without thinking he reached out and laid his hand on top of Po'Boy's fist as it tightened back into a hard ball. The heat coming off the man's flesh was enough to bake through the chill of the nighttime, and Wrench jerked his hand back abruptly. He'd had a flash, wondering what it would feel like to have Po'Boy touch him, hard and calloused fingers instead of the soft and delicate ones of a woman. *Jesus.*

"Yeah, I cleaned up." He belatedly answered Po'Boy's question. "Need me to do anything inside?" He'd come out when Po'Boy left the room to get a couple of barrels for disposal, but that had been at least an hour ago. "Need help loading 'em up?"

"Naw, all covered." Po'Boy's voice was hoarse, rasping and low as his exhaustion bled through. "Just gotta throw the barrels into the truck. I've already sprayed the room down." That explained the strong scent of bleach which had followed the man out of the room. "Just needed to sit a spell."

"Hear ya." Wrench straightened his neck, staring once more at the ceiling of stars overhead. "Deuces has a backer." That was the main bit of intelligence they'd garnered from tonight's work. "That's big, because whoever this Diego is, he isn't local, which means somehow Deuces garnered widespread attention. Bombs aren't this group's style. You and I both know they're mostly good old boys, which would mean they'd lean towards shotguns and fists."

"Diego. What the fuck kind of name is Diego? Is it the city?" Po'Boy yawned loudly. "The artist? Maybe he meant Dingo, because that would make more sense."

"Why you need to have people's names make sense?" This was something he'd noticed about Po'Boy, how he dissected people's names and motives, at times tangling the two into an unrecognizable mess, but other times making so much sense Wrench had wondered how he'd missed the obvious.

"Duh, because names matter. We all get tagged with a bunch of shit until something sticks. Names are deep, and who they come from matter. Take your name, Wrench. It's deep." Po'Boy shifted and leaned back on his elbows, then lay flat on his back, his shoulder nearly brushing Wrench's. "Fuck you taking the whole blanket. This bed is cold and hard, man."

"Should it be hot and hard?" Wrench squeezed his eyes shut tightly, closing out the stars. He quickly followed with a segue to the topic Po'Boy had been on, trying to make it all casual when it felt anything but. "Wrench isn't deep. I work on bikes."

"Who named you?" The question came so quickly he wondered if Po'Boy was avoiding the same topic he was.

"Bagger." This was a source of pride for Wrench. He had loved the old man like a father. Wrench had grown up around the CoBos like Penny had, and having been part of the club his entire life meant he revered the founders like her uncle, Bagger.

"So a mentor and officer named you. Means it's deep. How long had you been patched when you got the name?"

Wrench thought back. "It wasn't right away. Probies aren't given names. They're just probe or scrub."

Po'Boy murmured, "Smart. We should do that. Make it so the failouts don't become so personal."

"Yeah, but I think for us it was tied back to 'Nam. They'd call the first tour guys scrubs or just 'new guy,' so it stuck. For me, I think I'd been a member for a year or more before Bagger tagged me. I'd just gotten in off a run nearly gone sideways. Salvageable, but only as long as you worked it. You know how it is." Po'Boy made a noise Wrench took as agreement. "Rolled in and there's this party." Penny had been there, flirting with one of the new prospects. Something she used to do a lot before her shit happened. Something that used to chap his ass, back when he loved her. *I still love her, just now I understand she'll never be mine*. "Big fucking party. The whole club was there, standing around, jawing. Old ladies and kids addin' to the racket. Bagger brought me a beer." Wrench laughed, the movement accompanying the sound jarring the knobs of his backbone against the metal of the truck bed and making him wince. "Brought me a beer, like it was normal for an officer to schlep for a member."

"You weren't just a member, though. Not then, and not now." Po'Boy's words made Wrench tense up, waiting. "You were Penny's best friend, and so in love with his niece, you couldn't see straight. Plus by the time you patched in, I'd already heard you were the fixer for the CoBos. Man to see if you needed shit straightened."

"Not sure where you're going with this, Po'Boy." He swallowed, aware the sound was audible. "Not sure I like it, either."

"Truth spoken, though. Cain't deny it. You were the fixer, the tool pusher for the CoBos' rig." Po'Boy sighed. "Wrench. Even before you knew it was your calling, so named by Bagger." Wrench tilted his head so he could look at Po'Boy, meeting the man's gaze across the foot separating them. Stunned at the idea, he thought, *Jesus*, because he'd never put it all together. Po'Boy stared at him, repeating, "Truth."

"Who named you?" Not something you'd normally ever ask a member of your own club, much less a high-ranking officer in another. Questioning the origin of someone's name in the life was taboo. Something about tonight, however, seemed to say things previously forbidden were off-limits no longer. "Twisted?"

"Jimbo," Po'Boy named a former member of Incoherent, a man who was also Twisted's grandfather. Dead now, killed in an opening salvo to a years-long war between IMC and the VWMC. "Founder of my tribe in more ways than one. All the important ways."

"Is it deep?" Wrench had a sudden flash back to being in Twisted's den, not last night, but a year ago, when he had stood beside Penny as she worked to convince this man she knew where to find Twisted and deserved a spot in the line of bikes set to ride to his rescue. "Jimbo was a good man. Bagger was tight with him."

"Jimbo was the shit," Po'Boy readily agreed, his voice quiet and low, respect reverberating in his tone. "And yeah, for a nineteen-year-old kid to be named before he even finished his prospect period was deep." Po'Boy snorted a soft laugh. "Jimbo'd be the first to tell you it was deep shit got me into the position to be so named. I'm always in the shit, man." He pulled in a hard breath. "Much the same kinda shit I found myself wadin' in tonight. Thanks for the assist, brother."

"Anytime, man." Wrench was intensely aware of how close Po'Boy was to him, felt the heat still rolling off the man, a result of his earlier exertions. "Not just words, either." He swallowed, trying to clear a knot from the middle of his throat. "I mean that. Call on me anytime, for anything, brother."

The truck jolted and moved as he pushed up from the bed into a sitting position. Hands on either side of his thighs, he gripped the tailgate hard. Po'Boy moved to sit up beside him, adopting nearly the same position, and the side of his hand brushed Wrench's. He shivered, muscles twisting fiercely under his skin.

He leaned back, digging in his pocket for the phone. Over the course of the evening, he'd seen several texts pop-up. Some were expected, from Penny, labeled as Yousa, and Twisted. Some had been from names he didn't know, couldn't make sense of. And a couple of them had been from what looked like hookups, the labeling so blatantly sexualized it'd made him grin. Po'Boy took the device and thumbed through the list, sucking in air like he'd been hit in the gut. It was his stillness first caught Wrench's attention, so when Po'Boy asked, "What are you gonna tell Twisted?" he was already on high alert.

His voice had been so guarded Wrench wasn't sure how to respond, and he turned to look into the man's face, hoping for a clue. Fear had taken up residence there. He saw a fear and grief so intense it tore at Wrench's gut. "Tell him? About VWMC?"

"About me." Those words didn't have any weight to them. Had no heft that was tangible, but Wrench had an acute feeling a misstep now would topple whatever it was about this fledgling friendship he had with Po'Boy. Fear was the dominant emotion that had clawed its way to the surface in Po'Boy's features, and his expression told a story of a betrayal which hadn't yet happened. "About what I am."

"What are you, brother?" When he said those words, he could nearly hear the gate slamming on Po'Boy's thoughts, and the shuttered expression on his face now was a disappointment. "I got nothing to tell him, Po'Boy. Who you are is your business." The address that had flipped him out earlier was something to consider, and he vividly recalled Po'Boy's vicious reaction when he'd seen the paper. Just another street to Wrench, but it was something a lot more to Po'Boy. "Where you go, who you call, that's also your business." He might have expected relief at his words, but if anything, the angles in Po'Boy's face got tighter, and Wrench watched as his arms bulged, muscles taut with strain and his knuckles were white where he gripped the tailgate. He tried for reassurance, "We all go where we want, brother. No judgment here."

"Fuck you." Po'Boy exploded from the tailgate, stalking towards the building. "Fuck you." Disappearing into the darkness inside the open door, Po'Boy called out a final response, his last words of the night. "You say anything to Twisted, I'll fuckin' kill you dead. Anything at all. I'll handle it, but he don't deserve to find out from you."

Find out what? Wrench wanted to say those words aloud, not just scream them in his head, but the rapid withdrawal executed by Po'Boy had shaken him. Had stung, too, because for a few minutes there he thought they'd been verging on being friends. *Maybe something different from friends.* Shaking his head, he silently climbed out of the truck and went inside, wordlessly lifting the other end of the first barrel to haul it out to the truck.

Chapter Seven

Crissy

Pulling the last bag of groceries out of her trunk, Crissy tried to get her elbow over the top of the lid, muttering a brusque, "Fuck," when the bags swung from the handles she had looped over her wrist, getting in the way. She tried a different angle with the same result and then stood there, glaring at the still-open trunk. "Fuck. You."

Sticking her tongue out at the offending vehicle, she was turning to place the laden bags on the ground when a hand appeared, wrapping familiarly around the curve of the trunk lid. A male voice, raspy and filled with gravel asked, "Need some help?"

Crissy stumbled sideways, tripping over the curb, coming up short of falling when an iron band gripped her upper arm. "Easy, honey. I didn't mean to scare ya." She twisted and pulled, yanking her arm out of his grip, turning to face whoever this was. Her gaze hit him midchest, and without thinking she took another step backwards as her chin lifted, raising her eyes to his face. He lunged forwards and gripped her arm again just as she stumbled over the curb, again. "Jesus." He was frowning down at her, and Crissy instinctively lifted her arms between them, the grocery bags swinging and thumping him right in the crotch. The man released her and bent over with a grunt, one hand covering his groin, the other pressing hard on the edge of the car's frame. "Fuck." The expletive was a second grunt, forcefully pushed from between what she had seen were full lips, curved just the right amount to make a cupid's bow. She was only seeing the top of his head now, since he was staring at the ground.

"Oh, Jesus. I'm so—" Moving abruptly, Crissy became aware of the bags still dangling from her arms, so she turned to put them down, straightening up just as he began to unbend.

Both hands on her car now, he was leaning forwards, elbows locked. Eyes closed, he licked his lips and then grunted again. "Umm. Fuck."

"—sorry," she finished. "Is there anything I can do?"

"Nope." His voice was hoarse now, not gravelly, and he definitely sounded in pain. "Take a hit like that, just gotta wait it out."

"I'm so sorry," she repeated and was rewarded by glittering eyes that opened a slit as he glared at her. "I don't even know what happened."

"You clocked me in the dick with your groceries," he said helpfully, his voice losing a little of its hoarseness. "Pretty fuckin' hard. What'd you buy, rolls of quarters?"

"No." Crissy shook her head, hating how high-pitched her voice sounded. "Just food. Bags and boxes, some butter." She lifted her hand, waving it towards the car he was still leaning against. "Thanks for offering to help with the thing."

"Trunk." The guy stood straight. "You get everything out of there? Got any other dangerous groceries to retrieve?" When she shook her head again, he gently closed the lid. "You nutted me with butter? Fuck. Do me a favor and don't tell anyone that part, yeah?"

"Oh," she cried, whirling to dig into the bags, pulling out a package. "I bought batteries, too. They're heavy." They were, too. It was a large package of AA batteries; she'd bought the economy pack.

"Jesus, honey. That's a lotta batteries." The corners of his mouth curved up, cheeks losing their angular planes as he smiled. "You need a boyfriend."

"What?" She stared at him, confused by his statement.

"Never mind, gorgeous. And you're welcome for the—" he waved a hand towards the car, "—help. Are you the new tenant?"

Crissy looked over her shoulder at the single-story condo, nodding. "Yeah. I moved in last week." It felt stupid to keep staring at her home, but anything was easier than looking at this man and imagining where she'd hit him with her batteries. "It's a nice neighborhood. Quiet."

He laughed, and she glanced back at him. "Yeah, quiet." He shoved a hand towards her, palm perpendicular. "I'm Ty, your neighbor." Crissy lifted her hand, placing her palm against his, feeling a thrill as his large hand engulfed hers. "And you are?"

"Crissy, um Christine Emmerson. I just moved in." Entranced at how the muscles in his forearm moved, she didn't notice at first when he didn't release her hand, only realizing his hold hadn't relaxed when she had to tug a third time, trying to escape.

"Yeah, last week. Saw the car. Did not see you." Ty tipped his head to one side. "I'd have remembered seeing you."

"Wrench," the shout came from across the cul-de-sac, and Crissy looked to see a big man walking towards them. "Need a chat, brother."

"No worries, Pony." Ty dug into a pocket with his free hand, coming out with keys he tossed towards the man. "I'll be inside in a minute."

"Ma'am," Pony said as he strode past them and to the front door of the condo next to hers. She stared at him for a moment, noting he wore a black leather vest like Ty's.

"Ty Wrench?" She finally succeeded in squirming her hand free of his and Crissy bent to pick up the bags of groceries, more than ready to bring this awkward encounter to an end. "It's good to meet—"

The deep peals of laughter startled her, and she scarcely stopped herself from retreating, remembering about the curb in time to avoid a reenactment of the previous near spill.

"Ty Sawyer. That's me—" He jerked a thumb towards his chest, then pointed to a motorcycle parked nearby, backed into a narrowly lined spot which seemed designed for that kind of vehicle. "—but when I'm on the bike, I'm Wrench." He took a step towards Crissy, and she again barely suppressed the instinct to retreat. "And I'm very glad to meet you, Crissy Christine Emmerson."

His playful misunderstanding made her smile as she corrected him, "Christine Rene, but my family and friends call me Crissy."

"And you already count me in that group? I'm honored, Crissy." He gestured towards the condo, then reached out and efficiently stripped most of the bags from her hands. "Unlock the door, honey."

"I can do this, Ty. Thank you." She tried to take the bags back, but he lifted them to the sides, arching his hips back exaggeratedly.

"Unlock the door, honey." Arms outstretched, he took a step towards her, forcing her to take a step back and up onto the sidewalk. "I got a guest to get to. Lemme get your butter in out of the sun." He pushed at something on the cement, and she looked down, seeing the battery box lying on its side. "Don't forget your weapon."

"Oh, shoot." She stooped and grabbed them, then juggled everything in her hands to swap things around to put the key into the lock. It stuck, and she pushed the door open, still struggling to extract the key, startled when Ty walked past her as if he lived here, making his way directly to the kitchen. *His condo's the same layout, idiot*, she told herself, and then found him back in her space, deftly withdrawing the key from the lock to hand it to her, and then quickly divesting her of the other bags. She was left with the keys in one hand, cradling the batteries in her other as he walked back towards her from the kitchen. "Thank you," she said, feeling strange as his eyes blatantly traveled down and then back up her frame. "It was kind of you to help."

"I'm the neighborly sort," he explained, coming to a halt a bit too close, but her only path of retreat was back outside, which would leave him in her condo. "Good to meet you, Crissy. I—" He shifted to squeeze past her through the doorway, his groin brushing against her belly, her breasts grazing his stomach. "—will definitely be seeing you around."

***

Wrench

He stood for a moment after the door clicked into place behind him, listening for and not hearing the sounds of Crissy applying the deadbolt or chain locks on the inside of her door. He shook his head, knowing it probably meant she hadn't engaged the alarm, either. *Baby chick just leaving the nest*, he thought. He'd known he was getting a new neighbor. Owning the complex gave him a head start on making certain his neighbors would be palatable. Crissy was wholly palatable, delicious looking, in fact. Curved in every place he liked, she'd been cute and sweet, with a mouth entirely made for kissing.

Until now, he hadn't felt a need to know more about this particular neighbor, but he would be making his way to the network of company servers the first chance he got and looking up all the info he could on this Christine "Crissy" Emmerson. Cute, and a little helpless, all wrapped up in a version of pretty he liked. *Woman needs a keeper, she's a danger to herself.* He grinned and reached down, gingerly adjusting his still-aching dick in his jeans. *And others.*

Inside his condo, he found Pony lounging on the couch, beer in hand, game on the large TV mounted on the wall. They'd known each other a long time. The CoBos, Wrench's club, and Pony's previous club, the Vicar's Wrath, hadn't been enemies as such. That meant they'd seen each other around rallies and parties, finding a cautious friendship before all the shit went down. Pony was one of several VW who had admitted it was a relief to drop his patch from Vicar's and take up the center for Incoherent. Leswayne had been a bastard, and not just to those he claimed to despise.

"You get me a beer?" Pony shook his head in response, not looking away from the TV. "You need something in particular, neighbor?" Pony lived in the condo opposite Wrench's. In fact, there were a number of CoBo and Incoherent members who lived in the complex, one of the reasons Wrench had the parking spaces re-lined, ensuring there was always parking for the bikes.

"You look like shit. Like you're running on about zero sleep," Pony said as he glanced up as Wrench walked back from the kitchen, three beers in his hands. Setting two of them on the coffee table, he flopped down onto the other end of the couch. "You bailed on the party early. Penny was looking for you."

"Yeah, had breakfast with her and Twisted this morning. She had her chance to chew on me already. I told her to get over herself." Wrench twisted the lid off his beer, tossed it to the table and looked up at the TV. "Who's playing?"

"No clue. Least it's football."

Wrench angled his head, tipping his chin to one side. "Football?" It looked more like rugby than football, but he wasn't certain. The uniforms didn't look at all like football. The sound was turned low so he couldn't hear the commentary, but the names displayed on the screen weren't familiar. "You sure it's football?"

"Jesus, you're picky." Pony huffed out a laugh. "Okay, how's this. Least it ain't golf."

Laughing loudly, Wrench agreed with his brother, "True that."

The second beers were polished off, and Pony had gone to the kitchen for more before he spoke again. Wrench had been letting him approach the topic at his own pace, knowing from experience trying to push or rush Pony would result in both of them being frustrated.

"What do you think his deal is?" Pony lifted his beer and took a long pull of the cold liquid. "Po'Boy, I mean. What do you think his deal is?"

"Deal with what? You gotta elaborate a bit, brother." Wrench took a breath. "And you already know I ain't gonna say shit about anything IMC. Ain't my way to trash talk a member of another MC, much less a fuckin' officer. Shit for IMC to deal with ain't my business. Be wary with your questions, yeah?"

"Oh, I'll be wary with 'em. I'll fuckin' hold 'em in until I can't anymore. Which is why I'm on your couch right now, instead of bustin' down Po'Boy's door. Twisted is all about IMC and Penny, and I get that. I dig it. Brother has a family in the club and then found himself a righteous ole lady. Cannot go wrong in such a scenario. What I'm asking is what's Po'Boy's deal with hatin' on Twisted these days. Those brothers were tight. Saw that before I patched in. Hell, I saw that years ago, the night all the shit went down at Trudette's, my first taste of the duo I'd heard of for so long. Ride or dies, no doubt. See one, see the other. Tight and right, honor-bound closer than blood. I dig that." Pony reached out and grabbed the remote, muting the TV. "Penny changed the equation." He cocked his head, shaking it side to side. "And it ain't in a good way. Boys are talkin' about it. Used to be Po'Boy spoke with Twisted's voice and wrought change with Twisted's hands. Now, half the time he's bailing on fuckin' church, and he's not nearly the first to know any-fuckin-thing. He seems half surprised about shit. Boys are talkin'."

"What are they sayin'? Exactly what are they sayin'? You got specifics in mind with this shit? Huh?" He could almost hear Po'Boy in his words, the quick-to-attack version of the man, at least, and he attempted to dial back his irritation. "Tell me what you want to know, Pony, but Christ on a stick, man—this, all of this? Not my beeswax. IMC biz to the core."

"When we first rolled into IMC, back then, the leadership seemed solid. So tight you could see the ship sway with every shift. One mind, one voice, one direction." Pony grimaced when he took a drink, then tipped the bottle up to finish off the lukewarm beer. "Now they seem as splintered as an old paddle. Nothing smooth about anything. I'm an officer, and if I do shit, I for sure don't get called on *any* of my shit. I've been callin' guys out from other chapters for doing shit that should get called out. I get looks but ain't no one telling me not to. And they fuckin' should. I shouldn't be up in their shit, that's a national job, but national seems to have stepped back. Seems like each chapter is runnin' their own gig, and except Ragman, ain't nobody tryin' to hold shit together. Po'Boy pullin' back has left a wake, man. Huge waves still rollin' around, and I'm not seein' how things are going to settle without him coming back to the fold. You spent some time with him last night, how do you see things shakin' out?"

Fuck.

Everything in what Pony said was concerning. IMC had grown fast, so fast Twisted had known he had to lock shit down. He'd stepped down from local, focusing on national, and Po'Boy had done the same. That meant the two men were in different places more often than they were together. If the members were feeling the change, it meant it had to be significant. Weak leadership led to weak clubs, where things could go sideways faster than anyone had a right to expect. Weak leadership at any level was bad. Weak leadership at the national level of a large, influential club? Disastrous.

Considering for a moment, he decided to lay it out there, expecting Twisted to bring it to his chapter officers shortly anyway. "What went down last night, not my beeswax either. I was there, Po'Boy needed a hand. Discreet assistance, ya know? Reformed VWMC were at Twisted's blowout. They were talking shit, and Po'Boy overheard, decided he needed to know the extent of what they had. Turns out, they didn't have anything. They didn't have anything and only gave a little. You heard of a dude named Deuces?" Pony nodded. "Kin to Leswayne somehow, don't know, don't care. Inbred motherfuckers. But he's the relaunch point. The thing is, he's not the one driving things forwards." Pony's expression grew more alert, and Wrench watched as his lips thinned when he suppressed a response. "Uh, uh. Not gonna cut it, you want me to talk, but you put a clamp on your tongue? Fuck that. Spit it, man."

"Deuces has someone flogging him forwards? Know who?"

"Diego. That's all we got." Wrench shook his head. "A name and some pipe bombs the assholes didn't realize weren't toss-and-go models." He snorted. "They thought the sticks were like Molotov cocktails, I guess. No detonators, no boomie. But they brought them to Penny and Twisted's house."

"Fuck. I'm betting Po'Boy didn't much care for that shit." Pony made a clucking noise with his tongue. "Man's still got a short fuse where Twisted's concerned. I suspect the shit hit the fan."

"You'd suspect correctly. They were dealt with, though, so there's comfort. This Diego shit? I got no fucking clue." Wrench drained his beer, leaning forwards to place it on the coffee table near the forest of empties they'd left there today. "As far as what's going on with Twisted and the rest of it, you need to take your concerns about leadership to the leadership you're concerned with. Talking around things won't fix shit. You're smart enough to know that, brother." He gestured towards the TV where the previous game had ended, a new show starting. "Unmute, brother. I like this show."

Pony glanced at the TV and laughed, thumbing the button on the remote. "Fuck, yeah. Gator huntin' for the fuckin' win." Without looking at Wrench, he said, "Opinion noted. I'm guessing you're gonna call Twisted and let him know you told me about the shitfest from last night?"

"Yeah. I'm not IMC, but CoBos and IMC been friendly for a lot longer than I've been around. I won't be the one fucking shit up." He yawned. "You said I look like shit, I feel worse. Fuck." He adjusted his cock, wincing at the twinge of soreness remaining. "Bitch next door bagged me, man. Fuckin' hit me in the dick with her bag of groceries."

"Groceries? The fuck?" Pony chuckled. "She's hot as hell, though. You see the rack on her? The little bitty thing, still got those great big tits. Hell of an ass, too. Round and begging to be bitten."

"Oh, yeah. I got an eyeful of that. She seems sweet, in a confused sorta way."

"Dick punched you with groceries."

"Yeah, guess she had a big tub of butter or some shit." He leaned back, adjusting himself again because at the thought of Crissy's breasts brushing across his belly he'd started to harden.

"Fuck." Laughing loudly, Pony bent forwards and tossed the remote back to the table. "Nutted you with butter? Priceless. Butternut."

"Fuck you."

Chapter Eight
Po'Boy

Idling the boat the last few feet to the dock, Po'Boy wasn't watching for danger. Didn't expect to find anyone or anything waiting on him. It had been nearly sunrise when he jumped over the gunwale from terra firma to head out, and it was full dark now. He'd run with muted lights, navigating by instinct as much as anything else. Raised on these bayous, he'd had grown up knowing them like the back of his hand. Still, things changed. The Gulf and Mississippi were in constant battle over these grounds, and sediment or storms could swap familiar with unfamiliar in a matter of hours. Didn't pay to take the skiff too fast, not with a load like he'd gone out with, so it had been slow going to the channel he had been aiming towards.

On the way back, he'd opened the engine up in the clear spots, going a bit quicker while staying alert for debris floating on the surface. Watchful, because at night a boat going even hardly faster than an idle still carried a distinct sense of danger. He knew hitting a submerged log or a gator could flip the boat in a heartbeat and wasn't always something you could spot, even in ideal conditions.

He'd cut the motor and climbed to the front of the boat, stiff-armed the post on the dock's corner to bleed off additional velocity, and then looped his rope around the next post, tying the front of the boat to the dock. He was clambering towards the back when he heard footsteps on the dock, echoing sounds of leather a shock in the quiet darkness. Flipping to his back in the bottom of the boat, he ignored the chill of water seeping into his jeans and yanked his gun from its holster under his arm, pointing it towards the outline advancing towards him. His finger was already squeezing down on the trigger when he recognized his visitor.

"Twisted, what the fuck you doin' out here?" Sagging in relief, he laughed harshly. "Got my fuckin' pants wet, motherfucker."

"You done out here?" Twisted slapped at a mosquito, and Po'Boy became aware of them. A constant on the shores, the wind of the boat kept them at bay while you were moving. "Fuckin' skeeters been eatin' me alive."

"Yeah, I'm done." He turned off the fuel to the engine, and then palmed the boat's key, shoving it into his pocket as he climbed out of the boat and onto the dock. His vest was still in his truck, locked up, and those keys were in a box nailed to a nearby tree, a lesson learned long ago. Sucked to get back to dry land only to find you'd dropped your car keys somewhere out there in the lake. Retrieving his keys, he glanced around, reseating his gun into the holster. "Where's your ride, man?"

"Got a drop-off. Wanted to hitch back with you." Po'Boy shook his head and turned to see Twisted's teeth flashing in a grin. "Didn't know your keys was in there, or I'd have been sitting in comfort, at least."

They climbed into the cab of the truck in silence, Twisted not saying a word while Po'Boy got the engine cranked. With the air conditioning going at full blast, Po'Boy sat for a moment, letting the cool air blow across his sweaty skin. Still quiet, Twisted pushed back in the seat, propped a boot heel against the dashboard, and leaned one elbow on his lifted knee. He seemed content to sit for however long it took Po'Boy to ask why he was there, something Po'Boy was trying not to do.

Fuckin' Wrench, he thought, reaching over to twist the volume knob on the radio. Scanning up and down the frequency got him nothing but static, which he already knew he'd find, was just looking for something to occupy his hands.

He pushed in the clutch and bumped the gearshift into reverse, turning to look over his shoulder as he backed up. With his attention so engaged, it made it safer to ask what he wanted to know. "The fuck you doin' here, man?" Facing front, he steered the truck around the worst of the potholes in the dirt road leading back to the local highway. They were rocking through the ditch and up onto the pavement before Twisted answered.

"You cut out of the party you helped Penny plan awful early. Vid showed you at the CH, brother. You and someone who's not a brother. Wanted to make sure everything was chill." Twisted's voice was quiet, smooth, a tone Po'Boy recognized was normally reserved for talking to combatants Twisted was still trying to sort out. "That's all."

"How'd you know I'd be here?" Turning the wheel towards the nearest crossroad which offered a route to the interstate, Po'Boy decided to take the direct path, instead of the circuitous one he would normally follow. "I didn't leave a fuckin' callin' card, did I?"

"Naw. Shit was spick and span; nothing less than I'd expect. I got a gander at what you loaded up, figured you'd need to do a drop-off tonight. Saw you in the drive at the house this morning. Woulda invited you in for breakfast with Penny and me, but you dumped Wrench and then peeled outta there." Twisted shifted, reaching for the air vent and angling the vanes so the air blew more directly on his face. "He likes cheese on his eggs."

"The fuck would I care about what he likes on his eggs, asshole?" It felt as if Po'Boy's chest had frozen, his heart stuttering to a stop at what Twisted might be implying. "His ride was there. That's all."

"How'd he wind up with you at the CH, brother?" Po'Boy didn't look, but he felt the weight of Twisted's gaze on him. He knew if he did turn, the glare would be filled with disgust and betrayal. He was asking all the right questions, but Po'Boy wasn't ready to answer them yet. "He was torqued over when he got to the house. Y'all cool?"

"Yeah, we're cool. Had a bump in the road last night. Was headed to your place to clue you in after I finished up with cleanup on the water." Po'Boy stomped on the gas a little hard taking off from the next intersection, and the tires barked as they spun and then caught traction. "He was in a position to assist last night, that's all."

"Nothing else?"

Fucking hell. Chin angled towards the side window, Po'Boy shook his head. "Nothing." He pulled in a hard breath, then as was his norm, went on the attack. "You even fuckin' want to know what happened? Or you just tied up in your pussy's friend leavin' the party early? Huh? You wanna know what I did, motherfucker?" He didn't pause, didn't give Twisted time to respond. "I was savin' your ass yet a-fuckin-gain, that's what I was doin'. You heard VWMC was on the move again. At least I hope you heard that, or maybe your head was so far up your own ass you didn't hear shit about it. Looks like Deuces dropped a couple hundred on patches and started slappin' 'em on anyone with a ride and the balls to wear a vest. Balls or stupidity, that's up for debate. Whatever it was, he's partnering with someone big. Had two reformed VWMC at your goddamned birthday party last night, and I fuckin' took care of it. Like I always do. Took 'em to the CH, chatted 'em up, and found out what the motherfuckers knew. Which wasn't a fuck of a lot, I'll tell you what. They were dumber than a box 'o rocks, but between Wrench and me, we got a story outta 'em."

"What story?" Twisted broke in, and Po'Boy chanced a glance his direction to find a laser stare aimed his way.

"Story of how they're partnering with a group. A big group with a fuckin' lot of leverage. The only name they know, the only thing they heard Deuces drop, was Diego. I ain't heard of anyone flyin' that name on our patch of grass, but just 'cause I ain't heard it don't mean he wasn't zoomin' through. Wrench hadn't heard shit, either, so it ain't just me in the wind on this one." On the highway now, he settled into the center lane, letting faster traffic roll past on the left, and passing slower traffic traveling in the right-hand lane. "I got some diggin' to do. Hey, you want me to drop you at home, or at the CH?"

"Home." Twisted's response was quiet, and when Po'Boy glanced his direction this time, he was staring out the window on his side of the truck. "What do you think it means, brother?"

"Not a fuckin' clue." Po'Boy finished passing a semi, then maneuvered into the right lane, waiting for the exit that would put them off the interstate near Twisted's house. They were both silent the rest of the drive, and when Po'Boy pulled into the driveway, he was not surprised at the invitation offered.

"Come in, have a beer. Penny's probably still out. She had shit to do in town." Po'Boy was already shaking his head before Twisted stopped speaking.

"Cain't. Need to get my ass home and fall into bed. I done been up for more than two days, brother."

"Fuck, I shoulda drove home then. Shoulda said something, Po'Boy." Twisted stood in the open truck door, hand on the frame and one on the edge of the door. "Come in and sleep here. We can talk more when you get up."

"Rather hit my own bed, man. No offense." Even as the phrase rolled off his tongue, he knew the half-assed apology was useless. Before Penny, it was a given he'd stay here as often as he was in his tiny apartment, more often, if he were being real. Before Penny, it was seldom anyone saw one of them without the other close, and the silence in the truck this afternoon would have been comfortable, not filled with tension. Before Penny, he would have never given up a chance to spend more time with Twisted. Now, even looking at his friend and brother as he stood there, what Po'Boy wanted to see was different. Scruffy instead of bearded, sharp cheekbones set under brilliant hazel eyes instead of the dark brown ones. Wrench, instead of Twisted. "You done, man? I'm wiped." He shoved the gearshift into reverse and made it plain he was waiting on Twisted to close the door.

With narrowed eyes, Twisted stared at him for a moment longer, then stepped back and quietly shut the truck door. Po'Boy backed out of the driveway and then drove off, not giving himself permission to look back, afraid he'd see his brother standing in the driveway, busily puzzling out the secrets Po'Boy was still holding close to his chest.

***

Wrench

Gaze locked on the figure sauntering down the sidewalk, Wrench reminded himself why this was a bad idea. *If Po'Boy sees me, after the way he freaked over an address on a piece of paper, he's going to come un-fucking-hinged.*

He'd stayed at Penny and Twisted's house for a couple of hours before heading home. Exhausted, he'd expected to fall into his bed and sleep for a day at least, instead finding himself dealing with Pony, and then tossing and turning, unable to find a comfortable position on the mattress or within his own head.

Wrench had learned early on that girls and women liked him. And he liked everything about a woman. Their soft curves, the ample pillows of their breasts, and how their cushioned thighs cradled him while he fucked their hot pussy. Liked it in a way no one would ever mistake since he'd always been happy with what he found. Didn't always get what he wanted. That was a sad fact of life, because if he'd had his way, he and Penny would have been together years ago. Cockblocked by her uncle, that action starting when they were barely teens, and carrying on until after Bagger got diagnosed with cancer.

Wrench had been out of town for a few months, and her uncle had called him, brought him up to speed because they had to line out succession plans for the club. Bagger's last words to Wrench had been as memorable as everything else the man had ever said. "Ain't no mistakin' me, Ty. You hear me, and open your fuckin' ears, because you needa hear me good. Penny ain't for you. She's gonna need comfortin', but that's all you do. She's my china doll, and she ain't for you. She needs careful handlin' from a man who's gonna have nothing but her in his head. Ain't for you."

Bagger hadn't died from cancer. He'd been gunned down sitting outside a store down by the VA in Alexandria, an old grudge coming home to roost. Hadn't mattered, because like Bagger had known would happen, Penny needed comforting. And that was exactly the limits of what Wrench had allowed himself, because in his gut he'd always known Bagger was right. Penny needed more, needed someone who hadn't tied their string to a club, who was guaranteed a longer lifespan and more stability. She needed a good man, one who hadn't done the kind of shit Wrench had.

In the darkness of his bedroom, he'd lifted his hands, studying them in the light filtering through the curtains. Had muttered, hearing the exhaustion in his own voice, "Bagger was right. These hands never had a right to her."

Unrequited love was a bitch.

That was how he'd recognized it in Po'Boy. Seen himself in the man's face, spotted a match to his own pain and agony over seeing the one person he'd ever loved become consumed with someone. In his case, it was being a captive spectator to Penny falling in love with Twisted. She'd already been halfway there by the time the man had knocked on her truck's door at a truck stop. Wrench and Twisted had gone at each other on sight, knowing instinctively they were battling for the woman. Twisted had been preoccupied, proven by his covetous nature after having only spent a single night with her. She was the same person, only more, because Twisted was her soul mate, finally paired with her in life.

For Po'Boy though, his trial had been watching Twisted change because of his love for Penny. Not becoming less, but instead becoming more. More of a leader, more of a strategist, more of a friend and brother. Penny brought out the best in the man and seeing Po'Boy track that was hard. Then noting how the man reacted to his first introduction to Penny, the first time he'd seen the competition in the flesh, there'd been no mistaking things.

Oh, yeah. Unrequited love was a huge bitch.

No way anyone understood or saw what he had, though. *No fucking way*, he thought now, as he trailed the man up the sidewalk and towards a nearby bar. They'd be up in arms, and Po'Boy'd be out on his ass in less time than you could say words to call him to the floor during church. It'd be only a heartbeat later he'd be takin' his beatout, and then he'd be out bad. The worst thing that could happen to a true brother, someone who loved the club and brotherhood like Po'Boy did.

Out bad meant other clubs wouldn't entertain the idea of patching you. Out bad meant everyone would know whatever had happened, it was the worst of the worst. Betrayal not quite enough for death. Being shunned and running lone. *Fuck.* Even if what he suspected was true, he'd never say a word. Never breathe anything to bring question to Po'Boy. *Be a fuckin' hypocrite if I did.*

Wrench had been staking out the address for most of a day, about to give up and try to find a different route to figure out what was going on when he'd heard the unmistakable sound of a motorcycle exhaust. He'd watched Po'Boy drive into the courtyard of the building, sitting on his bike for a minute while the gates opened, then he rode the bike into the darkness of the parking area. Thirty minutes had passed before Po'Boy stalked out the main doors, and Wrench nearly hadn't recognized him. Po'Boy wasn't wearing his cut, and when Wrench tried to figure out what else was different about him he was stymied, it was as if Po'Boy even moved differently.

Po'Boy paused to check his phone, leaving Wrench to duck into the recessed door of a storefront, where he angled his head around the corner to keep an eye on him. Po'Boy had always been a big man, imposing, but over the past year, he'd lost some of his mass. Wrench studied how the streetlights cast shadows across his face, accenting the angular planes of his cheekbones and forehead. He sucked in a breath when Po'Boy smiled, the expression changing the shadowing in a way that was attractive, and nearly erotic. Then he watched as the smile turned so sly he nearly forgot to blow the air back out. Po'Boy had stopped walking directly in front of a bar, and with a yank on the handle, he was gone, the door settling back into place behind him, shutting him in and closing Wrench out.

What was different? Wrench replayed everything he'd seen, small as it was, and finally thought he'd put his finger on it. The clue was in that smile. As sly and roguish as it was, the look on Po'Boy's face had been...playful. Wicked yet mischievous. Out of character for what he knew of Po'Boy. There'd been an ease to his movements, too, like he was relaxed. Maybe for the first time Wrench had ever seen him, which would be why it looked so odd on the man.

Nondescript building, ordinary upscale bar with an unremarkable name. Very different Po'Boy.

Standing with his thumbs hooked into his front pockets, Wrench waited for a few minutes, growing more restless with each passing second. No Po'Boy tumbling back out of this place where a wild man like him normally wouldn't belong. Not a lot of foot traffic in or out, and when the door did open, there wasn't a blare of raucous music. *Fuck it. I just wanna see what's going on.*

In front of the door, he paused, suddenly unsure of his actions, the decision taken out of his hands when it shoved open, and he sidestepped to avoid two men walking out, arm in arm. *Oh, fuck.* Slipping through the opening, he sidled along the wall for a moment until he came to a clear place where he could stand and survey the crowd. Quiet murmurs of conversation, clinking ice and glasses, quiet music playing through the speakers. It only took a second for his eyes to land on Po'Boy, seated on the only occupied stool at the bar. Fortunately, his face was angled down to check his phone, and by the time Po'Boy looked up, Wrench was in tune, tipping his head to the side. He kept his eye on Po'Boy through a mirror strategically placed across the bar, and as soon as the man looked back down at his phone, Wrench turned to stare at him again.

A waitress strolled past and asked the expected questions. Wrench absently ordered a draft, anything cold and wet to keep his hands busy. He felt out of place here, having placed his back to the wall and protected his cut, but just wearing the vest felt like it was shining a spotlight on him. This was not a biker bar, more of a neighborhood gathering place. Friends and coworkers might come here after work. Not a place Wrench felt comfortable, and not a place he would have ever expected Po'Boy to seek out.

A woman came through the door to Wrench's left, fingers twined with the ones of the man following her. From the corner of his eye, Wrench saw her smile, and then she turned her head to speak to her companion, saying, "There he is. Lewis is already at the bar." *The fuck?*

Sure enough, the couple went directly to where Po'Boy sat, and the look on his face when he saw her was open, welcoming, and heated. The corners of his lips quirked up, the middle of his full bottom lip bowed down, and he smiled knowingly at her. It looked as if she introduced him to her companion, and then—*fucking hell*—the trio turned towards the door. There was no physical way Po'Boy could miss him standing there, not ten feet from the exit. Wrench immediately cocked his head to the side as if the waitress standing near his elbow again had suddenly become engrossing, angling his shoulder so his nameplate was hidden in the wrinkles of the leather, and waited for the explosion.

He'd silently counted to twenty before the air cylinder finally made a sighing sound as it allowed the door to settle back into place gently.

***

Po'Boy

Fucking hell.

He couldn't go back inside to be certain, not without bringing attention to himself, and if he hadn't been seen, then bringing that attention could be the ending of him.

Shoulda figured Wrench wouldn't give it up.

After his meltdown over the VW members having this address, something Wrench couldn't help but notice, it shouldn't have been a surprise the man pursued what it meant. Thank God the bastard had been chatting up the fucking waitress as he walked out the door. Po'Boy had steered Denise and the guy she'd brought at his request down the street and Po'Boy hustled all of them into the side door of the building. Even then he didn't take a free breath until they were off the elevator and into the suite.

All the way down today, it had felt off. He'd taken the long way around, and nearly called it before getting on the bridge that led across the mouth of Lake Pontchartrain. Finally down into New Orleans proper, he'd turned around once, circling the block before getting back on track to finish the journey. *Shoulda listened to my gut.* His intuition had never steered him wrong, and not listening to that little voice had gotten him into more shit than most people would ever believe. His gut now was telling him to ditch the bitch and her partner, go back to the bar, and see what Wrench wanted. Or an alternative solution was to park the bitch and the dude, go back to the bar, and then pound the shit out of the asshole for nearly fucking up what had promised to be a spectacular night of uncomplicated sexing. *I'd at least get my nut off then.*

Shaking his head, he stepped to the side of the door, catching Denise's arm as she walked past, hand in hand with her friend. "Denise," he started, but the tilt of her head stopped him cold.

A slow, sweet smile spread across her face, and she told him, "Don't worry, Lewis. I saw him. Want us to clear out?"

"Saw who?" He couldn't help the bite in his voice, and he belatedly tried to soften it with a smile, knowing it didn't hit his eyes. "Who'd you think you saw?"

Proving herself the discreet partner he had expected, she gave lip service to his lie. "I didn't see anyone, Lewis." Getting close, she crowded his space, and he had to lock his muscles to keep from pulling away. Mouth next to his ear, she whispered, "I hope you have a good time, honey." Lips to his cheek, then a trailing slide along his jaw to the corner of his mouth to press a soft kiss there. "Don't lose my number." Turning away, she gave his hand an absent squeeze, calling, "Tony, we're going to head over to the Quarter. Come with me, honey."

The man, having spoken not a single word, turned and walked ahead of her to the door. Po'Boy reached out to grip her arm again, pausing her retreat for a moment while he told her, "Word to the wise? Not my type. I like a little feist."

That slow smile again, and she lifted up to put her mouth next to his ear, her whisper this time seductive, "So noted, Lewis. I hope to see you again soon." The door closed behind the pair, and Po'Boy took in a deep breath. He gave it a ten count, waited another ten, and then pulled his phone out. He didn't bother texting, didn't hesitate before he dialed, and then stood with his eyes closed, waiting.

A moment later the call connected, and he gave out the building address, added the suite number, and then disconnected and stood glaring at the door, waiting. Proving his gut had been right, it was less than ten minutes before the knock sounded on his door. Not tentative, this was three short, confident raps with hard knuckles. Po'Boy stood and stared at the door for another moment, knowing the end of his world might be standing on the other side. Lifting his hand, he slowly reached for the knob, turning it and pulling the door open to see Wrench waiting there. Hands shoved into his back pockets, he closely resembled an awkward teen showing at his date's door. Turning his threatening smile into a sneer, Po'Boy stepped to the side, giving Wrench ample room and time to walk inside.

The door closed, he leaned his shoulders against it, making it clear Wrench would only be exiting the suite when, and if, Po'Boy allowed. They stood like that for a long minute, silent and still. Po'Boy couldn't tear his gaze from Wrench, seeing as if for the first time the strength and character in the man's face. His broad shoulders and the way muscles rippled under his skin were proof of the physical strength, but what had captured Po'Boy's imagination right now was the struggle going on behind the man's features. It was as if he could see the cost it took Wrench to be here. What he couldn't understand was why.

For his part, Wrench couldn't seem to look at Po'Boy, which gave his fears firmer footing. If the man didn't have a problem with him, then why wouldn't he look Po'Boy in the face? Instead, his gaze skated around the room, seeming to take in every detail. From the kitschy flocked wallpaper that somehow managed to pull off classy to the sleek appliances in the kitchenette, Po'Boy knew it was a total departure from his normal living space but also knew Wrench had never seen the inside of that place, so it wasn't as if he had anything to compare this against.

After a second, and then a third minute had passed in silence, Po'Boy cleared his throat. "Get yer looking done. You ain't gonna see the inside of here again. What the fuck are you doing in Orleans anyway, Wrench?"

73

At the instant his voice hit the air, he saw Wrench jolt and sway, as if from a physical hit, then the man's gaze cut over to him. He didn't turn to face him, just cut his eyes like it hurt him to be in the same room. *Fuck.* He must have gotten more of an eyeful than Po'Boy knew, as he was acting like a man who either had a secret, or knew one.

"Hey."

Po'Boy waited, but that was it. The sum total of everything Wrench had to say and now, off balance and unsure, he did what was most comfortable. He went on the attack. "Fucking 'hey'? That's it? All you fuckin' got to say to me? Hey? Fuck you, man. What the fuck am I supposed to do with a goddamned, fuckin' 'hey'? You ain't got more? Nothing more in you?" As he spoke, he pushed away from the door, taking two aggressive strides into the room. "All you got, boy?"

"Ain't your boy, and you know it." Now Wrench's shoulders moved back, and he squared up to where Po'Boy stood, lifting his gaze to stare fully into Po'Boy's face. Hands at his sides, they balled into tight fists. "Didn't know you had a place in New Orleans, is all." The expression on his face rippled, then fell back into the same stoic lines Po'Boy knew were on his features, too. "It's nice."

"The fuck you talkin' about? 'It's nice.' It's fuckin' cush, is what it is." Now he was defending his fuck suite? *Jesus, I'm a fuckin' moron.* "The fuck you doin' here, Wrench? Saw the goddamned address, couldn't stand not knowing? You that hung up on me, motherfucker?" At the accusation, another ripple passed over Wrench's face, but this one got stuck somewhere between pissed and guilty. *What the fuck?* Shaking off his confusion, Po'Boy continued. "You got more on VW, you got my fuckin' number. You fuckin' text me to set-up a goddamned chat. You ain't got business, then I don't know what fuckin' business me bein' here is of yours. You pushed your fuckin' way into IMC business a few nights ago, mostly because it was a right place, motherfuckin' right time, and you ain't a pussy. Everybody knows what a hardass Wrench is. Oh, yeah. Everybody knows that about you. Just like they know the same about me. So what the fuck you doin' playin' find-the-fuckin'-Po'Boy to chat about business when you got a motherfuckin' phone, and I made it crystal-fuckin'-clear this address wasn't anything. You said it yourself, don't nobody know nothin'. It's just a fuckin' address." Even Po'Boy was having trouble following his own arguments and decided this was a good place to put a plug in it.

After his tirade, Po'Boy would have expected Wrench to blow or react, anything really, but he didn't. He simply stood and stared, locked on Po'Boy's face in a way that was unsettling.

Shaking his head, Wrench took a step back, and Po'Boy did not miss the gesture when he lifted his hands and shoved them into his back pockets again, intentionally making himself vulnerable. Instead of reacting to any of the posturings Po'Boy had spewed, he said the one thing Po'Boy didn't expect. "It is cush."

He couldn't help himself, Po'Boy snorted a laugh, and then let a real one out, liking how it rang through the air in these rooms. He retraced his couple of steps to lean against the door again, feeling the muscles in his arms relaxing, felt his shoulders lower a couple of inches as he took a deep breath. "It is, ain't it?"

Shrugging a shoulder at one of the chairs in the sitting area, Wrench asked, "Mind if I cop a squat? I don't have an agenda here, Po'Boy. Was curious was all. And you're right, I've had absolutely no right to be digging into your personal business." At his nod, Wrench turned and gave Po'Boy his back, and the implied trust hit Po'Boy hard. That was something a man worked for his whole life, getting a trust like that from someone who mattered. *When did Wrench turn into someone who mattered?* He reached back and flipped the deadbolt as he moved across the room to take a seat in the matching chair.

"You got a good memory. It ain't a…" Po'Boy huffed a laugh and then eased back, getting comfortable as he lifted one ankle to rest on his knee. "You've got a good memory," he repeated but dropped the patois he used around the club. "This isn't an address that would stand out." He looked around the rooms, marveling again this was his. "But here you are. You found me." Gaze back to Wrench, he asked, "What were you expecting?"

"I don't know. A skank flop over a tattoo parlor? That's what I'd probably have." Wrench showed exactly how much he understood because that would be the exact opposite of what he had across the lake. His condo was nice, in an upscale neighborhood in Slidell.

"Yeah, well. You know me. I'm nothing if not extreme." Po'Boy offered him a grin he knew was crooked since he was fighting hard against having it spread into a smile. "So you were curious about the place that caused me to freak out, so you decided to…what? Stake it out? See what I had going on?"

"Well, kinda. I cruised past and couldn't decide what it was. High-end pad to crash, or a place to run a stable out of." That cut a little close to the truth, and Po'Boy felt his gut clench. *Follow your gut.* "Then I saw you roll in. I was—" Wrench's eyes focused intently on Po'Boy's face, and he knew that stare. *That is a "dare you to call me a liar" face.* He knew because he wore it so often. "—curious. I tried to catch up to you at the bar, but you left with your friends."

"Nope. Try again." He didn't let any of his anxiety show, kept the same semi-amused smirk in place, waiting. Wrench didn't blink.

"Saw you hit the bar, so I followed you inside. Then I saw you meet your friends, Lewis." At that name, only used here, and most often in intense sexual situations, Po'Boy couldn't help his flinch and knew Wrench didn't miss it, knew how deeply he'd scored. "They left really quick. You selling out of this place?"

His mind frantically tried to assimilate what Wrench might have heard. This was an unexpected out, but one that made total sense, given the short time he'd had Denise and her partner up here. "If I am, then it's IMC business and nothing to do with CoBos." Talking about the club pulled him back into character, the mask so comfortable on his skin he could have sighed in relief. "Ain't nothin' to do with you, and that's a for sure truth. You done stepped into it, Wrench, and if it's what I'm doin', I can tell you me sellin' dope ain't nothing to do with you." Leaning forwards, he propped his elbows on his knees, keeping his gaze pinned on Wrench.

"Do you a favor, let you walk out of here without a limp or a lump. Appreciate your assistance the other night, and you got a personal marker to call with me." He'd give him that, and should have already done so. The assistance Wrench had provided would actually rate a club marker, but with his connection to Penny and who she was to Twisted, it would be a given anyway. This was him giving to Wrench, and the man wouldn't mistake the intent. "Been a nice chat." He stayed in the same position, his gaze unwavering as Wrench stared at him. "That's your fuckin' cue, man. Get your goddamned fuckin' ass outta my pad."

Wrench tipped his head to one side but didn't make any move to rise from the chair, and Po'Boy felt his muscles tense. Then with a smirk that said he might have gotten more than Po'Boy wanted to give away, Wrench corrected him, "Outta your *cush* pad." Pushing to his feet, he strode to the door, turning back to Po'Boy once he had it open. "We're not as different as you think, *Lewis*." With that zinger, he was out the door, and it pulled gently closed behind him.

Po'Boy asked the air in the room, "What in fucking hell was that?" The room had no answer.

***

Crissy

She was standing at the kitchen sink when she heard the noise. It sounded like a herd of buffalo racing down the street, the rumble shaking up from her feet through her bones. Jogging towards the front windows, she stopped a few feet back from the sheer curtains, taking in what was going on in the cul-de-sac. What looked like hundreds of motorcycles were pulling in and parking along the sides, stacking the bikes two and three deep as men and women dismounted to stand and look around.

Glancing across the room, she eyed the drawer that held her pistol, immediately discarding the idea of arming herself to look out her window.

From the joint sidewalk leading up to the condo unit, she saw Ty walking out to greet what had to be his guests. Although, she couldn't fathom where he would be putting so many people in the two-bedroom condo next to hers. Then she realized none of the riders or their passengers were approaching Ty. They were maintaining their distance, and from the tension she saw in Ty's frame, she wondered if these weren't welcome visitors after all.

That was settled for her when he leaned forwards from the waist and yelled, "The fuck you think you're doing coming here, bitch? You even thinking?"

A tall woman with long, dark hair took a step up onto the sidewalk and screamed back at him, "I think I'm done with you pulling your fade bullshit, Wrench." *Oh, yeah. He said when he was on the motorcycle he was called Wrench.* Crissy had forgotten for a minute. "I'm here to deliver a message, motherfucker." That was the brunette again as she took another step forwards. A man behind her put his hand on her arm, trying to hold her in place. She tried to shrug him off, but his fingers tightened until Crissy knew there would be bruises circling the woman's thin bicep tomorrow. Crissy frowned, not liking this guy, and not liking the woman much, either. "You fucked with the wrong bitch. Done messed yourself up, big time." The woman slung her free arm out behind her, indicating the full breadth of her support. "Nobody fucks and runs with me."

"Jesus, Sam. You think you got some kind of golden pussy?" *Ah, okay.* Now she knew what this was about, at least. "Fuck, woman. Any man who's a man wants someone who'll do more than just lay there. Hell, half the time when I finally got myself off, I'd climb off you and check for a fuckin' pulse." Wrench shook his head, fists to his hips. "You're not even as good as my goddamned hand. Least it don't bitch and raise a stink with me."

"Oh, no, you did not!" The woman was screaming now. She gestured crudely at her crotch, and screeched, "Best you ever had, right here. Right fuckin' here, motherfucker." *Jesus, give it up already.* The idea of Ty with this woman made her cringe, but a little bit of "how dare she" had started to stir in her gut. When a man dumped a woman, it hurt and usually sucked, but the right way to deal wasn't by coming to his home to declare yourself the best he'd ever had.

"Get over your fuckin' self, bitch. And as for you,"—it looked like Wrench was staring beyond the woman now, at the man who was still making a show of holding her back—"you value her, you'll keep her away. To me, she's nothing but a goddamned discard, man. You want that shit, fine. But you keep that shit *in line*."

The woman finally tore her arm loose from the man and started up the sidewalk towards Wrench at a run, her intentions clear. *When did I start calling him that in my head?* Without another thought, Crissy flung open her door and stepped out. At her entrance, the woman abruptly halted in place and glared at her, barking a laugh and asking, "You his new pussy?" Crissy felt her body jolt at the words, not wanting to admit she'd been thinking about Wrench in that way ever since she'd met him. "Come out to take your man's back?"

Wrench didn't turn around, just stepped to the side to put himself more firmly between the woman and Crissy. Then he said, his voice quiet and vibrating with fury, "Crossin' a line, Sam. Not a fan of putting hands on a woman in anger, but you're seriously pushing me to reconsider my stance, and you fucking know it. You came to *my* fucking house. A place I never even brought you to fuck." To the man behind Sam, he said, "Thorne, get your goddamned bitch off my property, and get your motherfucking skank bastards of an RC out of my complex. Do not come back, or there'll be hell to pay, and it won't pay out easy. If you want to stay healthy, you will not mistake me."

Crissy took a step forwards, and Sam's gaze moved from Wrench back to Crissy as she angled her shoulders aggressively. Sam shouted, her voice shrill with frustration as her fists lifted to either side of her head, fingers twisting in her hair, "Bitch, you want a piece of me?"

Pulling out her best graduate school attitude, the one she used when presenting an argument in class, pretending nothing mattered except what she wanted, Crissy said, "I've never been in a cat fight. But from the look of him—" She pointed at an enraged Thorne who was rapidly advancing on where Sam stood. "—you've just been declawed. So I—" She gestured to the side. "—have nothing to worry about." It was time to sell it, the optimal moment to sway people to her point of view because every set of eyes was staring at her. "Wrench, baby," she called with a smile, "want a beer?"

Without turning, he said, "Sure, honey. I'll be right there. Put it on the table next to the bed, yeah?" At the implied intimacy, Sam started fighting the grip Thorne had on her arms. "I'm ready to get me some more of the good stuff." He paused, and when he spoke again, his voice was filled with gravel, rough as it stroked along the bare skin of Crissy's arms, raising gooseflesh in its wake, "Mmhmm. So ready for you, honey."

"You got it," she called softly, turning and swaying back into her condo, leaving the door open in silent invitation behind her. A few moments later the roaring started again, and she listened as over the next few minutes the sound gradually diminished in volume, finally trailing off and disappearing entirely. After another minute had gone by without an appearance, she thought Wrench must have returned to his own condo and Crissy had started to walk around the corner from the kitchen to the living room when she heard the front door close. Then she heard the deadbolt lock slip into place, followed by the unmistakable sound of the chain being latched. *Odd. Why would he lock himself in here?*

Wrench stalked around the corner, headed straight towards her, and she was surprised at the anger on his face. He looked furious. At her.

"What in the fuck do you think you were doing out there, Crissy? I don't know you, and you sure as fuck don't know me. What made you want to put yourself into that situation?" He was aggressively crowding her, coming close, so she backed up until her butt hit the counter behind her and she stared up into his face. Nostrils flaring, he was glaring down at her. "You have any fucking idea what you just did?"

"Um. I…uh." Crissy rolled her lips nervously, then whispered, "I'm thinking maybe…no?"

Lifting his hands, he covered his face, fingertips pressing against his closed eyes. Muffled by his hands, his words still came through loud and clear. "I do not need this shit." That didn't feel good, and she tried to draw back farther. Dropping his hands, he stared at her again. "Look, honey. I get you were trying to help. I appreciate it, more than you know. I didn't have anyone close enough to call when they rolled up, and while I doubt you're carrying, it was good to know someone was watching in case I got my ass kicked. That's sweet."

His tone didn't sound like he thought it was sweet, and she flinched at the bitterness coating his words. "I'm sorry." Her instinctive response to so much, the need to immediately apologize was something Rhoda had tried to rid her of. Unsuccessfully, clearly.

"No, you are what you are. Sweet and so fucking innocent it burns." He shook his head, taking a half step towards her, his legs brushing against hers. "That setdown you just gave Sam? She isn't the forgiving sort. Means on top of every other fucking thing I got going down, now I need to keep an eye on her and you. I'll do that. You won't have to worry, honey. I'd have done it anyway, just to make sure my shit didn't leak your way, but since you opened the faucet by setting yourself at my side like you just did, I'll just have to work harder."

"I don't understand."

"I get that, Crissy." He swallowed, and his eyes dipped closed in a slow blink. "Oh, baby, do I ever get you don't have a fucking clue." Leaning backwards, he glanced down her torso and back up, blinked again, and then abruptly changed topics. "Where's that beer?"

Startled, she stared up at him, trying to read his expression. He'd closed down, shutters drawn so tightly across his features she couldn't get anything from him. "I don't have any beer."

Shaking his head, he chuckled. "Of course not. Are you always one to make promises you can't keep, honey?"

"Um. No?" Crissy stayed still, frozen in place as he lifted a hand to cup the back of her neck. "I don't think so."

"Seems to me you might be guilty, honey." His fingers squeezed her neck and tugged her an inch closer to him. "Might have made another promise outside. Gonna pony up and pay the piper on that one?"

Crissy rolled her lips again and watched as his expression grew heated when his gaze dropped to her mouth, lips pursing while he stared at her. They were frozen in time for a moment, and it felt like she was on the brink of something.

"Fuck it," he muttered, then pulled her close again, covering her mouth with his, lips working, pressing and caressing. "Open for me, honey," he murmured, lips grazing against hers, his mint-scented breath heated as it coasted across her lips. The rough pad of his thumb moved up to her chin and brushed across her skin, urging her mouth open. His tongue swept in, slicking alongside hers, pushing and thrusting as his head moved and his hips pressed against her belly.

She responded, couldn't have stopped the instinctive reaction if she'd tried, his mouth felt so good on hers. Abandoning reason, forgetting he was a virtual stranger, she relaxed into the kiss, into his caressing strokes along her skin. Every nerve ending tingling, it felt as if she were awake for the first time in eons, and she never wanted it to end.

The heat from his hand on her neck was nothing to the heat from his erection against her belly, and he groaned, thrusting gently when her hands rose to rest on the hard wall of his chest. The kiss seemed to go on forever, and Crissy was focused on the sensuality of Ty's hands and mouth on her. She was gone, lost in a world of heat and soft noises, hard hands cupping her ass to pull her close.

Then she was left standing alone, back against the counter, elbows bent as her hands propped her up. The chill she felt was intensified when she realized Ty was five feet away, turning to the side as he ground out a harsh, "*Fuck.*"

He pulled in a hard breath, and then without looking at her muttered, "I gotta go." Eyes to the floor, she didn't watch him walk away. The chain and lock rattled and clicked, and then the door closed quietly, leaving her standing alone in her condo.

"I...what?"

***

Wrench

Slinging a leg over his bike, Wrench shoved his helmet into place and took a short moment to breathe before he started the engine, punching the transmission into gear and roaring out of the cul-de-sac, climbing gears before he even hit the road. Kissing Crissy had never been part of his plan. Not that he'd had a plan when he went into the woman's condo, but she'd left her goddamned door standing wide open. If Thorne had taken him down, she'd have been defenseless against Sam.

That's what had been running through his head when he stalked through her door, locking it to make a point.

Then he'd rounded the corner and seen her looking at him, happy to see him, red lips glistening with a gloss he'd found tasted as good as it looked. Blonde hair tucked behind her ear, she'd looked pleased as punch with herself for the play she'd just made outside—there hadn't been much thinking going on at all. Not with his big head, at least.

Out on the highway, he cranked the throttle and thumbed the knob for his cruise, propping his wrist on the handlebar. He'd checked into her. Checked and found nearly nothing on the surface. Just enough of something to be sure she was who she claimed, but not enough to get a read on her. Graduated from university with honors in three years, went on to graduate school and finished that in record time, too. Then she'd dropped out of sight. It bugged him, so he'd left the surface behind and dug until he found something, an online posting listed her in the survived-by section of an obituary. This gave him a new location and another set of names, and from there he'd found out more than he wanted.

No wonder she seemed a little fragile. Her parents died early, she'd barely been a teen. Then her sister, the only family she had left, passed only weeks ago. The last thing Crissy needed was a horny bastard of a neighbor barging in and kissing her so thoroughly her lips would be bruised for a week. "I'm an asshole." His words were torn from his lips by the wind, scattered in the wake of his speeding bike.

She wouldn't have to deal with him for a week or so. Before Thorne had rolled up with Sam riding bitch, Wrench had gotten a dispatch text from his president. He'd been headed out to strap his bag on the back of his bike, ready to roll north to Kentucky when he'd heard the motorcycles incoming. CoBos had been dealing with assholes trying to horn in on their pot business for years, typically handling it by sending in a member to find the source of the trouble and bargain face-to-face. This was different. The report was another storage unit had been hit last night, and expectation suggested it had been the same stupid set of brothers as the last time. CoBos tried hard to keep the peace, but they'd finally had enough. Enter Wrench, who was their ultimate solution.

At least I have a ton of shit to think about on my ride. Between Po'Boy and whatever it was Wrench had fucking with his head there, and now knowing how sweet Crissy tasted, he had ample subject matter to cover the hours before he would park the bike and hop in a cage for the last stretch of miles, running incognito.

Po'Boy, as he seemed down in New Orleans, appeared to have turned into a different beast. Even in the apartment, the man had been far different than Wrench had ever seen him. Still confident, but less of an ass. Attitude, speech patterns, laughter, posture—all changed from the norm for him. A good look on the man. Wrench frowned, reaching down to press on his dick with the heel of a hand. *Fuck*. It didn't matter what story he'd tried to spin to Wrench, what was happening in that space wasn't dealing drugs. Po'Boy and the IMC might be as dirty as Wrench or any of the CoBos when it came to pot and recreational drugs, but whatever his lies might be, the use of that apartment was for dirty of a far different sort.

Wrench liked what he knew about the man. After he'd got past his initial issues, he'd liked what he'd seen, every time there'd been an opportunity to be around him. Po'Boy was a good brother to his club. He was ride or die when he had your back, and he held that position unwavering once he'd staked his place there. Now if Wrench could just wrap his head around what he thought he'd seen...and what he'd felt.

Nope. Time for another topic. He checked his mirrors and then the speedo, looking to verify the miles remaining on this tank of gas. *Too many*.

IMC was in a tough place if what Pony inferred was true. If what he'd come right out and said was true, too. In addition to the pressures from outside, in the normal forms of LE and Feds, they had the outside pressure of the fake club pushing at their borders. Twisted needed to get a handle on that like yesterday and deal with whoever was behind it all. In some ways, it seemed as tough a spot as the clubs had been back in the 80s when the drug cartels started their plays for territory. Wrench knew Jimbo and Bagger had partnered on more than one campaign to rid the area of the threats. Maybe it was time to renew that kind of bond and bring IMC and CoBos to the table again.

They'd virtually done that during the short-lived war between IMC and VWMC, fighting alongside Retro's 'Bama Bastards to ensure the right club came out on top. Bloody work, but worth it, in Wrench's opinion. *Maybe I needa drop a line to Ace*. Ace was the president for the CoBos and had been for decades. He had lived through the fight against the cartel, and knew the cost as well as the benefit. *Time I bring him up to speed, anyway.*

Ace was another topic Wrench knew he couldn't shy away from forever. The man had made no bones about whose name he intended to put in the hat next year when it came time to vote in a new president. CoBos followed a strict two-year cycle for officer seats. For the last twelve elections, Ace had been the one with a unanimous tally of votes. He'd nearly refused the last election results, speaking eloquently about bringing new blood to keep up with changing times. That refusal had been vetoed, and in the end, he had acquiesced. For the last few months, though, he'd made it crystal clear his name shouldn't come up. He'd also made it crystal he expected Wrench to be taking up the gavel at the end of that day.

Not something I ever aimed for, Wrench thought. *And he fucking knows it.* He grinned. *Ace just don't fucking care.* Wrench knew he could do a good job, had sure knowledge in his gut because Ace had been grooming him for this since Wrench had first put the prospect vest on his back. He'd become the go-to guy for all the club members. When they had shit happening, he was who they called. No questions and no holding back, he was all-in with every man who wore the CoBos patch. That was something he'd learned from Twisted. Not from talking, but from observing. It was one of the memorable ways Twisted had made his name, because no matter the need, he was there for his members. No need too deep, no ask too big. "Got your back" was more than something Twisted said for show, it was the way he lived. Something Wrench still felt he stretched towards some days.

Still, it'd be nice to delegate shit like this run. The two men in Kentucky weren't bad guys, they were just stupid. Or they never thought it would get to this point, being as the people they were fucking over—namely the CoBos—were hundreds of miles away. Hopefully, this visit would pound the point home in a final way. Before he had to take care of things in a different final way.

Sam was another problem he'd have to work and put in his rearview sooner rather than later. Bitch had to be high if she thought pulling that kind of stunt was going to get him back in her pants. Back when he started fucking Samantha Rotain, she'd seemed sweet. He'd gone along, talked sweet while he was inside her, wasn't cruel when he turned her away at club events. He didn't mind screwing her, just didn't want her in his face every moment. It wasn't until she realized he wasn't coming close to putting a ring on it she had shown her true face. She was flat crazy, and now Wrench believed Thorne had to be even crazier for taking her ass on, after seeing all the shit Sam had pulled over the past few months with Wrench.

Which brought him right back full-circle and thinking about Crissy. A woman who was as sweet as she seemed, inside and out. A woman who'd put herself out there for someone she thought was a decent neighbor and guy. The chick was pretty, and a fucking phenomenal kisser. Made a man long to try out other activities, those fun horizontal ones and see how good she was at those, too.

Chapter Nine
Po'Boy

He sat on an upturned bucket, boots stretched towards the fire pit in the middle of the back lot behind the Mandeville clubhouse for Incoherent. Eyes turned towards the dancing flames, Po'Boy ignored all movement around him, knowing only members and trusted friends would be here tonight. He didn't even flinch when a hand landed on his shoulder, the familiar grip pressing heavily as the person maneuvered around the stump to his left. Tipping his head back, he looked up to see Twisted stretch, his shirt hiking up to show belly flesh and an angular hipbone. A month ago just that would have made him insane, and would likely have sent him home to stew about it until he rolled across the causeway looking for relief from the demons in his own head.

Tonight he found himself able to simply note it and then glance away. It wasn't he didn't feel for Twisted, but whatever the emotion was that'd been stoking his fires for so many years had banked back to barely a smolder. Sucking in a hard breath of relief, he caught a strong scent of sweet pot smoke that typically hovered over an IMC party and glanced to his other side. Feet firmly apart, Wildman stood just behind the ring of seating around the fire pit, critically eyeing the ember at the end of the twist he was holding. Without speaking, Po'Boy held out his hand and curled his fingers impatiently, and Wildman grinned, leaning over to pass off the hand-rolled smoke.

Po'Boy took a long toke, then a second one, and held his breath as he offered it to Twisted, laughing soundlessly as he shook his head, turning down a hit. *Sweet dreams tonight.* Lips pursed in a slow, controlled exhale, Po'Boy gave it back to Wildman, the entire exercise conducted silently. With a quiet sigh, Po'Boy faced the fire again, recrossing his ankles so the other boot sole was nearest the flames.

It had been a month since he'd seen Wrench down in New Orleans. A month of wondering. Of expecting things to go sideways any moment. For the first week, not knowing when the accusations would be leveled, waiting for the shoe to drop had been exhausting, constant expectation a sentence would be handed down. The second week had seen him asking around quietly to find Wrench had gone out of town, the CoBos having sent him on a run up East. The third week had been filled with relief as if he'd escaped judgment, thanking his lucky stars Denise and her partner hadn't been demonstrative in the few minutes Wrench had his eyeballs on them, or things could have been entirely different.

This past week had been a mix of emotions because first, Wrench still wasn't back, and Po'Boy couldn't relax and put it behind him until he knew for certain if the man was going to instigate a play to have an IMC officer call him to the floor or not. And second, it'd been a shitty few weeks because Po'Boy was missing New Orleans. He hadn't stayed away for an entire month ever, not since he'd first rented the suite, and this self-imposed restriction was killing him. So the past seven days had seen him swinging from paranoid as fuck and afraid to look anyone in the eye, to horny as hell and wanting to hump anything.

Yesterday he'd found a distraction at least. One of the information trolling lines he'd set following the night of Twisted's party had begun to pay out. He wasn't certain yet what he'd hooked, but the line was leading him into open water, where the currents were deep. Deuces had been seen in Slidell headed east, which would have him going into

Vicar's territory. Not a surprise, but the man riding in style was, and the pictures Po'Boy had seen put the asshole in a huge SUV all tricked out with gold everything and lighted anything. *Pimp-mobile*, he snorted at the thought. Definitely wasn't hard to track and follow. Po'Boy had laughed at the reports received because it seemed it'd be harder to lose the man in such a ride.

Now to wait, because Deuces had gone beyond where Po'Boy could safely send his brothers.

Staring at the flames, he remembered the call he'd made a few days ago to the president of another club, a man he liked but didn't fully trust. Mostly because the man, Retro, had something like X-Ray vision, but for bullshit. His freakish ability meant being as Po'Boy was always on his guard around any MC, he was doubly so around Retro. The 'Bama Bastards, Retro's club, were based out of Birmingham, Alabama, a little further east than Po'Boy expected Deuces to go, but still the only asset he could put into play that direction.

"Retro," he said as soon as the call connected, *"Po'Boy here, man. How ya doin'?"*

Silence, then over shouts in the background he heard, "Po'Boy. Good to hear from you. I'm good, man. Good. Gimme a minute to get private." Noise in the background swelled and then quietened, and Retro said, "I'm where I can hear ya now. What's up, man?"

"Need some info on a man rolling east towards your plot." Po'Boy didn't flinch from diving straight in, knowing Retro would appreciate the no-nonsense approach. "He's still a bit west o' you, but close enough to sound the alert. Dude's rebuilding Vicar's Wrath and has strolled way to fuckin' close to too many of us for comfort."

"Shiiiiit." Drawing the single word out slow, Retro effectively communicated his dismay and the disquiet he felt at this knowledge.

"Yeah, all of that right there…I'm feelin' it, too, man." Rude to ask if he was private enough to speak openly, so Po'Boy started paddling along the edges of the stream, hoping to give enough info to entice Retro's assistance. *"He dropped a couple of friends off a few weeks ago. We scooped 'em up just in time to realize they'd brought some go-bang fireworks to a birthday party for our friend."* He paused and chewed on his lip for a moment, selecting his words with care. *"Old school VWMC was never a friend of yours and sure ain't friends of ours. This version is more zombie than alive, but still gonna be a fuckin' pain in the ass."*

"Whatcha needin', Po'Boy? Lay it out plain." Retro snorted and then chuckled. *"Plain as you ever do, man."*

"Momma didn't raise no fool, man. Deuces comes to you, I'll take anything you can find." He chewed his lip again, ignoring the sharp pain and only wincing when he tasted the bitterness of blood. *"Whatcha need?"*

"Marker." Noise swelled in the background and then cut off abruptly, and Retro confirmed what Po'Boy thought, that he'd called someone into wherever he was. *"I got Mudd here, I'll fill him in."* That was good. Mudd was Retro's VP, which meant the club would be on the case, not just Retro alone. *"And Po'Boy?"* Retro called the question, then went quiet, waiting for confirmation Po'Boy was listening.

"Yeah?" Pushing up from the chair where he'd been seated, Po'Boy stalked around the desk, ready to be out of the enclosed office behind the clubhouse bar. *"What?"*

"Personal, not club."

The demand made Po'Boy's stride stutter awkwardly and halt as he barked, *"The fuck? Say again, man?"*

"Personal marker."

"Uh." Shaking his head, Po'Boy squinted at the wall in front of him, brows drawn sharply down into a frown. He struggled to dial back his initial reaction, trying hard to keep from saying something to fuck up the fact Retro was willing to take this on at all. He lifted a hand and scrubbed across the skin of his jaw for a minute straight before he felt in control. Finally, he forced out a clipped, "Done," and then heard Retro's laughter. "You fuckin' with me?"

"Hell, yeah. You're an easy mark, man. Can't do it in person, you'll rip my head off."

"And shit down your fuckin' neck," Po'Boy agreed, not hiding the fact he was more than half ticked off Retro would have pulled that shit.

"Still, good to know you'd be willin' to give me that. Thanks for the info, man." And that was Retro all over, because the man dealt in information and knowledge more than anything else. Lived to work his network, which was exactly why Retro had been the only man Po'Boy had considered calling. "Talk soon as I got anything."

"Roger, that. Have a day, fuckwad." Po'Boy disconnected the call and then shoved the phone deep into his pocket, finishing making his way to and through the door to the bar where he poured three fingers of whiskey. Fucking Retro.

"So you'll help, right?" The question came from his right, and Po'Boy twisted around to see Ragman sitting on a stump he'd pulled close. "Fuck, brother. You hear anything I said?"

With a sigh, Po'Boy shook his head. "Beat, man. Sorry." He crossed his ankles again, swapping positions with his feet. "Twisted bring you up to speed?" Ragman was the only son of the previous president of the VWMC, and had disbanded the club when his old man was killed. One of Twisted's main concerns about what Deuces was doing had been about what Ragman would think. He didn't have any loyalty to the old club, nor any ounce of regret for what he'd done a year ago. Still didn't mean he wouldn't feel something.

"Yeah." Scowling, Ragman shook his head. "I made some calls. Put the word out. All patch sightings are gonna be reported. You can bet your ass on that. I'm not best pleased this bullshit popped up again, brother."

The word "again" caused Po'Boy to narrow his eyes, staring at Ragman for a moment. "Any idea where they got the patches?" He was shocked when Ragman flinched, face scrunched up as in pain. "The fuck's wrong, man?"

"You remember Trudette's?"

Now it was Po'Boy's turn to flinch because that bar had been the scene of the worst massacre in recent memory. One resulting in the death of Twisted's grandfather, Jimbo, along with several other Incoherent members and officers. The loss from that night had reverberated through the club for years following, and had been the ignition point for a fire which burned in Po'Boy and Twisted still. In a coup facilitated by fucking Sabrina—the gash might be dead but still had the power to roil Po'Boy's gut and not only in his dreams—men who owed time and dime to Leswayne, Ragman's old man, had popped up out of nowhere wearing fake VWMC patches, carving a path through the IMC to get to Jimbo.

There'd been a gathering of original Vicar's in the place that night, too, and they'd been the first to point out the dead and fled imposters. That group had been led by Pony, the VW SAA from the 9th ward chapter, who now wore an IMC patch. *Good man*. Po'Boy shook his head, realizing he hadn't answered Ragman, and the silence had grown around them, soaking into the group in an expanding ring, like gasoline spilled on a rug. Pregnant quiet, it felt like they were all waiting for his words to start up the talk again.

"The fuck you mean, do I remember goddamned fucking Trudette's? Ain't an IMC member who don't remember that shit, even the ones patched after the piece of fuckery went down. We pound it into their heads as lore and history. Come on, Ragman, whatever you got, just spit it the fuck out." Po'Boy cleared his throat and cast around, realizing he'd sat down all those minutes ago without a beer. Between the fire, the pot, and the emotions, he was dry as the desert. *Fuck*. "You sayin' you think these patches are part of that batch? Same fuckin' lot as the ones took out our leadership, rocked our world? You sayin' that's bad boomerang mojo at work, or what? What the fuck you sayin', man?"

"I'm not saying that. Jesus, you get wound up. I'm just saying we all know Leswayne's down-south partners were behind those patches, and who knows how many they had made up. We don't know the numbers. Fuck, man. We don't even know where those masters are." Ragman frowned. "If I can get my hands on a set of these patches, I'll know in a minute if they're the same. Cartel worked a figure into the edge, a tell, so they'll stand out to someone who knows better."

"Are you sayin' the Columbians were the ones who threw these patches out there? Shit." Po'Boy thought furiously. That actually lined up with everything they knew so far. "Shit *fire*. You're too smart for your own fuckin' good, man. *Jesus*." He raised his voice to a shout. "Wildman, 'mere, brother." A minute later the big man had made his way back around the fire and stood close, one crooked eyebrow lifted in a question. Po'Boy leaned forwards and pulled the man's half-empty bottle from his unresisting hand, upending and draining it in a few swallows. Handing him back the empty, Po'Boy said, "Need a beer, brother. While you're inside, bring me the bag from behind the bar." Wildman looked at a nearby cooler, filled to overflowing with bottles and cans and Po'Boy shook his head. "Bar, brother. Bring me the bag."

As he walked away, Po'Boy heard quiet laughter from his other side and turned to see Twisted's head tipped back, curved lips aimed at the stars overhead. "One of these days he's gonna realize he don't have to do your probie shit anymore, you know that, brother."

"Oh, yeah. I know. Don't mean I won't push it 'til he pushes back." Po'Boy grinned. "Not sure he'll ever ditch me, though." Waggling his eyebrows, he laughed. "Quack, quack."

Twisted repeated the phrase, slightly different, still with a laugh. "Quack, fuckin' quack."

That was their shorthand for a preferred method of bringing new members into the club, pulling them close and folding them into the club in a way which meant they were immersed in everything good for so long they couldn't see any other way. Like just-hatched ducklings imprinted on the first thing they laid eyes on, those members were tight for life. Wildman had been Po'Boy's prospect, pulled in from another club that'd had just enough fuckery so he saw the difference in the IMC, and liked what he saw. Po'Boy cackled, laughing hard, the green relaxing him enough to play a little bit. "Hell, yeah. Got us a lifer, brother."

Wildman dropped off the bag and two cold beers, one for Po'Boy and one for Twisted, which made both men burst into more laughter, pulling a confused "What?" from the man.

"Nothin'," Twisted grunted, shaking his head. "Whatchu got there, Po'Boy?" There was an edge to Twisted's voice he didn't recognize, tension in his tone at odds with the ease of their company.

"Patches," Po'Boy said, and pulled out a piece of fabric, tossing it to Ragman, "and toys." He brought out a long knife, the two unarmed pipe bombs he and Wrench had taken off the two VW, and a phone. "Knife showed up on the hip of a guy a few weeks ago. Divested him of said possession, I did. Educated him how it wasn't healthy to pretend to be somethin' he ain't." He glanced around, lips pulled to the side. "In case you're wonderin', it's entirely unhealthy." Ragman's eyes narrowed and Po'Boy nodded, confirming his apparent suspicion. "Crater makers came off the two dudes I told y'all about. The phone"—he held it up between thumb and fingers—"was lifted off a bitch we both know." Twisted raised an eyebrow, waiting patiently, and Po'Boy grimaced at the memories he knew would be stirred with the name he was about to give. "Sam Rotain."

Twisted's back straightened, and he snarled the name back at Po'Boy. "Samantha Rotain? What the fuck does Sam have to do with anything? Ain't she over west somewhere, fucking her way through social clubs?" Twisted's eyes narrowed, staring at Po'Boy. "Last I heard, she wasn't much to look at anymore. Didn't have a tight hole left, either."

"Truth to everything you just said, brother, except direction. She's east, and the bitch gots a serious hard-on for Wrench." He shrugged. "I happened to be in a position to see what I could get for him." That had been Retro's ask, called in yesterday. Po'Boy didn't understand the timing, but had been quick to clear the marker, finding out what Retro needed. The phone had been extra, and not something he'd disclosed in his report, holding it close for his own club. "Bitch hates his ass. Blind hatred. So, seein' as he's your ole lady's bestie, ya know, thought I'd do what I could." Po'Boy felt his lips pull to the side and tried to battle the sneer. "Got a little more than I expected."

Twisted shook his head. "Sam's been a pain in our asses for years. Bitch surfaces occasionally to try and stir shit between clubs, never as successfully as her sister, thanks be to God." He stared at Po'Boy. "Where the hell'd you run across her?"

"She crashed at a party where I'd been lurkin'." It was the truth, and following a lead for information he'd had good reason to be there, and not just to have one of the locals suck his dick. *I wasn't averse to the action, though*. Po'Boy shrugged at the thought, flicked the screen with his thumb and lifted it up, showing off the lighted screen. "Unlocked."

Raising his voice, he told the crowd gathered around the three men seated in a row: him, Twisted, and Ragman. "Lesson time, baby boys. When pussy figures shit out—and they *will* figure shit out, because sharing a pillow means they're going to know more than you ever fuckin' want them to know. But, pussy also means they're gonna be oversharing with *their* bitches, so if you give that pussy you're sleepin' with a little too much info, it just might mean oversharing with whoever picks up that pussy's or their bitches' shit."

He held the phone over his head. "Exhibit number one," he said with an exaggerated drawl, "is the fact the pussy who owned this phone knows a whole lot of shit about a whole lot of people. She's got notes on routes and even got fuckin' names. Her newest old man's RC is verging on outlaw. They want it so bad they done gone cross-eyed trying to find it. What they did find is cartel. And cartel likes to move all kinds of shit. This little phone here"—he shook the phone again—"has probably three million dollars' worth of info on it. And I got it, right here."

Ragman interjected, "Same patches, man. Cartel here, too."

"Oh, yeah. We got those fuckin' Columbians alllll up in our shit." Po'Boy turned to Twisted. "Got word about CoBos. They found the same goddamned group was jacking up their shit in Kentucky."

"Word about, or from?" Twisted asked for clarification, clearly wanting to know the source.

"About. Via Alabama." That'd tell everyone the who without having to put Retro's name out there. "I'm digging through every ditch I can think of to pull info together, boss. Tryin' to find the breach lettin' shit through. Now—" He looked around at the circle of faces, grown by double handfuls in the few minutes they'd been talking. "—the question is, what are we gonna do about all this shit?" He tipped his head over and stared at Twisted, who was glaring at him. Po'Boy felt a trickle of unease biting through the haze of the pot. *Maybe woulda been better to do this quietly. Private like. Fuck.*

"Church. Tomorrow." Twisted paused between each clipped word and then lifted his chin slightly, and Po'Boy knew Twisted was about to make a point or an example out of him. "Open church. Our man Po'Boy's makin' eggs and bacon, feedin' the entire membership. Better line up your helpers, brother. You got a lotta pork belly to fry."

Fuck. Stone sober now, without looking away, Po'Boy lifted his voice and shouted, "Wildman, 'mere, brother."

Loud laughter chased away the unease from the men's faces as Wildman tipped his chin up and asked the heavens, "Lord, why me?"

***

Po'Boy lifted a hand to the bartender, asking for another overpriced bourbon. He sighed and drained the drink in front of him, placing the empty glass with the rattling cubes of barely melted ice close to the bar rail. He woke his phone to confirm there were no messages and made a face, sighing again. He'd downloaded the app and used their system to send texts to a half a dozen people, hoping to find one of his regular hookups free and with company in tow. No such luck tonight.

Perfume tickled his nose, light and sweet, and he turned in time to see a pretty blonde woman in the process of perching on the stool next to him. The chick took her time arranging a big portfolio bag between her feet, hooking the strap over one knee. He eyed what he could see of her legs, appreciating the curvy view as her skirt slipped higher on her thighs. No skinny Winnie, this pretty thing had some meat to her bones, which met a lot of the need in Po'Boy when it came to women.

He quickly checked his phone again, hoping perhaps she was there as a result of his messaging, but there were no responses waiting for him. The bartender wandered down, rag in hand and a predatory smile on his face. Po'Boy lifted his chin, scowling. Fucker could see she wasn't his normal clientele and had poised to swoop in and scalp her. Po'Boy wasn't about to see a woman taken advantage of just because she was out of her element. "Hi," she spoke quietly to the bartender, softly enough Po'Boy had to strain to hear her over the background music, "I'd like an Amaretto sour, please."

"ID please." The bartender held his hand out in a demand and damned if she didn't have to undo everything she'd just worked on with her bag. In the process, her skirt hiked even farther up those glorious legs, and Po'Boy saw the lacy top edge of what had to be a pair of thigh-high hose. *Jesus, fuck me*. She fumbled the retrieval of her ID, and it flipped out of her hand in an arc, headed towards the floor. As much as he'd like to see her climb down and bend over—*oh, fuck yeah, I would*—Po'Boy reached out and deftly snagged the rectangle. He eyed the picture, nearly as pretty as she was in real life, and made a note of her name and age, and then saw her address. Same condo complex as Wrench over in Slidell. *Hmmm*.

"Christine Emmerson, it's a pleasure to meet you." Smoothly Po'Boy flashed it at the bartender and then held out her ID with one hand, reaching across with the other to shake. He held her hand longer than necessary, not enough to make her uncomfortable, but just enough to send a clear impression of interest. "I'm Lewis." Without turning from her or breaking their gaze, he spoke to the bartender, "Put that sour on my tab, yeah?"

"Hi. Uh, Lewis." Her musical voice fumbling for words was cute. There was a lot of cute to this gal, which meant she wasn't at all like what he normally went for. Still, cute was sexy as fuck in the right setting. "That's not necessary, but thank you." Hand still In his, she glanced up the bar to where her drink was being mixed by a slyly smiling bartender. "I can buy my own drinks."

"I expect you can, seeing as you came into a bar by your lonesome." He squeezed her hand, liking the eye flare he got as her fingers twitched in response. She was looking at him again, which was his intent. "But Joey there—" He tipped his head towards the bartender, already not his favorite who worked at the bar, and even less so now. "—was about to mix cheap and charge top shelf. I'm just keeping him honest." This earned him another eye flare, this one shocked instead of intrigued, and he chuckled. "It's one drink, Christine." Tightening his grip for a moment, he reluctantly released her hand, gaze following its retreat to her lap, noting how her fingers immediately set to twisting around the strap of her bag. "Nothing more."

"Well, then. You're doing me two favors. Your next drink can be on me?" Po'Boy gritted his teeth, fighting against going hard at the thought of being on her. *Fuck, yeah*, his dick said, fattening with a pulsing throb. She needed to consider her words with more caution. "And, it's Crissy. That's what my friends call me."

Pitching his voice low, creating a feeling of intimacy, he leaned closer and repeated her name, letting it drip off his lips like honey. "Crissy." A slow breath in, and he saw he'd captured her attention, her gaze locked on his mouth. *Awww, yeah.* "Beautiful." A smile curved her lips, and she turned her head to try and hide it. Shy, sweet, cute, and fucking hella sexy. Po'Boy heard his phone buzz with an incoming message from the app. Without shifting his gaze, he reached out and grabbed the phone, thumbing the button to silence it as he shoved it deep into the front pocket of his jeans.

Three hours later he knew a lot about Miss Christine "Crissy" Emmerson. She was twenty-six years old, recently moved home to Louisiana after a stint away at college and then helping care for her dying sister. She was working a new job she loved, adored her niece to distraction and missed her terribly, seeing as the little girl was in Minnesota. He also knew Crissy was a lightweight and didn't know it, and the woman was into Po'Boy in a big way.

He hadn't set out to get her drunk. That had been the furthest thing from his mind actually, because other than passarounds at an MC party sometimes, he didn't fuck drunks. Never down here in New Orleans. Not even once, because consensual was the only way to rock his normal encounters. Drunk dudes couldn't get it up, or couldn't manage to keep it up long enough to work for him, and drunk women made bad decisions.

Crissy was quiet. So quiet he had to work to pull things out of her at first. So quiet it had masked the level of inebriation very well for a while. Too well. It wasn't until she had started talking freely he realized it was alcohol making her mouth loose. He still hadn't realized just how drunk she was until she abruptly slid off her stool and stood, weaving, the strap of her bag falling to the floor unnoticed as she announced, "I need to piddle."

Piddle. Fucking cute.

He bent, grabbed her bag, threw some money on the bar and gave Joey a tip of his chin as he escorted Crissy towards the back of the bar. In the short hallway outside the women's room, he stood and stared, considering her. Too drunk to manage on her own. Shoving the door open, he led her into the little room, glad it wasn't a communal facility. "You do your thing, honey. I'll just make sure you don't fall."

"You're so nice." Even now it was hard to hear the level of drunkenness in her voice. She wasn't slurring, wasn't stumbling over her words. They were soft and sweet, and she stared up at him with wide eyes, blinking slowly. "And pretty. You're very pretty."

"Yeah, every guy likes to be told he's pretty. Thanks, Crissy." He waited. "I thought you had to pee?"

"False alarm." Her open-mouthed grin gave him a glimpse of her tongue, trapped behind her pretty, pink lips. "I should go home, huh?"

"Did you take a cab from Slidell this morning?" She shook her head. "You drove?" A nod. *Fuck.* "Honey, you got any friends in town you can stay with?" She shook her head again. "Nobody? No coworker you can call?"

Her voice was hushed when she whispered, "There's so many of them. I don't know who to trust. One wrong step and *blooey*. New jobs suck balls."

He could relate. Trust was hard in most situations. That was why earned trust was so precious. "If I send you home in a cab, can you get back here to get your car?"

Her brow wrinkled as she considered his question. "Are we in a bathroom?"

"Crissy, focus, honey. If I send you home in a cab, can you get back here to retrieve your car?"

She looked around. "It's a nice bathroom."

"And that would be a no. Got it. There's a hotel near here, what if I drop you there, get you a room?" Crissy made a face. "Do you have money to cover a night in the hotel, honey?" She shook her head. Not surprising if she hadn't worked for a long time, and then had the expenses of moving and setting up house while starting a new job. A lotta dough went into that kind of change. "Then I guess you're stuck with me."

"How am I stuck with you?" She looked around again, and her face paled. "Are we locked in?" Lunging at the door, she pounded on it with her palm. Her voice squeaked when she whisper-shouted, "Help!"

"Jesus," he grunted as he captured her arms down at her sides, pulling her back against him, his dick liking the close contact more than it should. "Crissy, stop it. We're not locked in. I'm going to take you to my place, okay?"

"Okie day." Head tipped to the side and looking up trustingly, she smiled at him, her open expression sweet. "You're a nice man, Lewis."

"Oh, yeah. I'm a fuckin' peach."

He steered her out the door and then through the bar, holding her close to his side to help mask her more obvious staggers. The two blocks to his building went past uneventfully. Wrapping his arm around her tighter, he pulled her against his front as he worked the keycard, and was unprepared when she looped her arms around his neck, rolling far up on her toes to press her lips against his. He tasted her, a mix of sweet fruit, liqueur, and something undefinable, something he wanted more of. A lot more. Bending deep, he leaned her over his arm and took her mouth, thrusting inside to stroke against her tongue, eating down her moans, aware he was making similar sounds, going from nice guy to a fucking sex monster in the space of a kiss.

He heard her sobbing, heard her whispered *"Please,"* and thought it was a plea for him to stop. Po'Boy tried to pull back and sucked in air as she clung to him, leg hooked around his hip, open to him in a way that was invitation and demand rolled into one. That single breath brought him back to his senses, made him realize where he was, and what he wouldn't do because this woman was not sober. She might be horny, but not straight in her head, which was the only way it would work for him.

After running his keycard through the reader, he swept her into his arms and took her into the building and up the elevator. Once in his suite, he unwound her arms from around his neck and lay her gently on the bed. "Please." Her whisper was soft and vibrating with need. As he straightened, he watched her hips undulate side to side, movements as unconscious as breathing. "Please love me." Her eyes were closed, mouth slightly open so her tongue could sweep along the curve of her bottom lip. "Please love me."

She's fucking drunk, he reminded himself and then lost the train of thought when her fingers tugged at the hem of her skirt, dragging it up and up her thighs. Her hand darted underneath the fabric, and he had a clear view of her sheer, black panties, then her fingers were underneath that material, too, and he watched as she worked herself by turns hard and fast, and slowly caressing, her moans and sighs a musical torture to hear.

Hands fisted at his sides, he restlessly shifted from foot to foot, eagerly watching every movement. He could smell her arousal, could hear the wet sounds of her fingers moving, see the shifting of the fabric. His cock ached, and when he clenched his ass, he got a zap of desire straight up his spine. "Fuck it," he muttered, and unfastened his pants, shoving them down and out of the way. He wouldn't take advantage, but didn't mean he couldn't enjoy the show. One hand wrapped around his dick and stroking hard, the other cupping and tugging on his sac. His dick was weeping, and he used the slick fluid to lubricate his hand, thrusting through his clenched fist.

He must have made a noise because Crissy's eyes opened and as she stared up at him her fingers worked faster, frantically pushing towards orgasm, raw and needy sounds pouring from her throat. It only took him a dozen strokes to be there with her, and he caught his semen in his hand, palming the heat around the head of his cock. She whispered, "Lewis," proving she at least knew who he was. Her hand had nearly stilled, moving lazily now, he imagined her fingers slipping unhurriedly through her folds like his palm slicked gently around and over the sensitive crown of his cock. She gradually slowed then stopped, and he glanced up to see her eyes were closed, face tipped slightly to the side. She was asleep.

He reached out and grabbed a handful of tissues to clean up, every movement deliberate and thoughtful as his breathing slowly returned to normal. He stared for a long time then bent over her, getting close enough to feel the heat from her skin. Gently tugging her hand out of her panties, one at a time he sucked her fingers into his mouth, slowly wrapping his tongue around each, savoring, his first taste of her heady and sweet. *Mmmm. Not enough.* "Gonna be seeing a lot more of you, Miss Crissy." Po'Boy straightened and stared down at her. "A lot more."

***

Crissy

She woke when the form beside her stretched and groaned, something heavy moving and sliding across her upper chest, nearly a caress. Hot mouth nuzzling against her breast, her companion hummed and sighed, then stretched again, wrapping one long arm around her middle and pulling her close to his torso as if she were a favorite stuffed animal. Startled, she jerked her arms up and away from where they'd been cradling his head and shoulders, holding him against her.

Eyes wide, ignoring the pounding in her head, she stared down at the man who lay half on her shoulder, half on her breast. She couldn't see his face but heard him hum again as he nuzzled the fabric of her blouse. "So pretty," he said, the word coming out mumbled and muffled, sounding more like "purdy" which was almost funny.

Okay. Time to regroup. First to figure out what I did.

Squeezing her eyes closed, she clawed through her memories, trying to find the right ones.

A bar.

She'd gone to a bar after closing a deal, the presentation happening at the client's offices in downtown New Orleans. They'd loved the campaign she'd put together for their products, and her boss had been so pleased with the effort he'd given her the rest of the day off. She'd gone to a bar to celebrate, hoping a single drink would calm her buzzing nerves, still on fire with adrenaline from standing in front of a room full of judgmental clients, not quite believing they hadn't kicked her out the door as a fraud.

A drink.

Her still-shaking fingers had betrayed her, dropping the ID demanded by the bartender. That had opened the door for the man next to her to strike up a conversation. Not a typical pick-up move, but he had seemed genuinely interested in getting to know her. She looked down at the head on her shoulder again, finding a name in her memories. "Lewis." An answering hum told her he wasn't sleeping, either. "Hi."

"Hey, doll baby." His arm squeezed her, the touch somehow familiar and comforting. *How? He's a stranger.* "How's the head this morning?"

"Pretty achy," she admitted, still holding her arms awkwardly in the air, avoiding any unnecessary contact. Something which seemed silly to do when he was still nuzzling her breast, the scruff of his beard rough even through the fabric of her blouse. "You?" *Stupidest conversation ever.*

"My big head's fine, honey." He drawled the words and then chuckled, the tone dark and knowing. "You can put your arms down, Crissy. This ain't a stick up. Ain't nothin' up. I already dealt with my mornin' wood, so there ain't even a pup tent to be worried about."

Oh, Jesus.

When she didn't move, he rocked his head, shifting around so he could look up into her face. Whatever he saw there made him chuckle again, and she watched as his plump lips curved into a smile. "Relax, Crissy. Nothing happened except two people sharing the same bed to sleep." His voice dipped an octave. "Not that you didn't entice me, mmhmm. Nuh huh, believe you me, I am *totally* fucking enticed." He reached up, fingers clasping loosely around one of her wrists, bringing her arm back down, resting her hand on her belly. He shifted to grip her other arm and drew it across so it settled comfortably around his shoulders. Once he had her arranged to his satisfaction, he sighed and draped his arm across her hips, his massive hand curling around her side and ass, fingers clamping down firmly as if to hold her in place. "Relax," he said again. "It's Saturday, and you said you didn't have to work today. Lemme snuggle a lil' bit. Least you can do, honey."

"The least I can do?" She hadn't meant to say anything, hadn't meant to ask anything, and certainly not in such a breathy voice, but the weight of him all along her side was something she liked. The way he held her possessively, as if he had a right to do so, she liked that, too.

Her heart pounded fast, something she was certain he had to notice since his ear was directly over her chest.

"Mmhmm. Yeah. You probably don't remember last night at all, do you? Not a single thing?" His slyly worded question made her stomach clench, and fear roiled through her because she didn't remember much. Nothing past a certain point at the bar, and not a bit of whatever journey had brought her here to his apartment. Deciding silence was her best option, she said nothing, and her silence made him chuckle again, rough and dark, the sound stroking along her skin to raise goose bumps everywhere. "You put on quite a show, doll face. You beg so pretty. So fuckin' gorgeous, rolling those naughty words around in that pretty mouth of yours. I can't wait to have you in a place where I can make everything you want happen." He moved restlessly, fingers flexing and releasing in a pulsing pattern on her hip. "Give you everything you desire." The fabric of her blouse shifted, and she realized he was plucking at it with his lips, each movement grazing across her taut nipple. "Begged me to love you. Made me watch you get yourself off. Hottest thing I've seen in a long time, Crissy. So letting me snuggle…least you can do."

Lips trapped between her teeth, she chewed for a moment, then whispered, "Oh." *Understatement much?*

"Yeah." His voice rasped and something stirred along her thigh, heat radiating from a central point of growing pressure she realized was his hardening cock. "Oh." His repeat of her word was sultry and hot, and blood rose to the surface of her skin, flushing hotly. "Now—" He pushed up, propping himself on an elbow and she got a good look at his face, distracted from his words by the beauty of the man hovering over her. Full lips moving, she ignored his words, losing herself in his eyes, unaware her hand had slipped from his shoulder to the sleek skin of his back, stroking slowly up and down. He wasn't classically handsome; the evidence of a hard-lived life had stolen that away. What was left though was an entirely masculine man. His high brow lent strength to his features, framing his extraordinary eyes over angled cheekbones and a wide mouth.

***

Po'Boy

She's gone for it, he thought and suppressed a grin. *And now, I'm gonna go for it.* No longer inebriated, Crissy was clearly turned on by whatever she saw on his face. Her hand on his back was hot, sensual. Flattened on his spine, it made its presence known with an insistent *come here* pressure downwards that was hard to resist. He licked his lips, and she mirrored the motion, bitable bottom lip glistening in the low light from the open door of the bathroom.

He'd stood over her again when he'd woke up earlier, not needing a naked body to imagine the delights hidden underneath her clothing. His mouth and fingers had mapped much of it, any far-from-innocent positioning of his head and hands intentional. The scent from her dizzying as she shifted next to him, cuddling into him in her sleep, a heady mix of spice and musk that made him a drunkard.

So he'd stood over her and denied the touch he'd wanted, cock rigid and straining at the air, slapping his stomach insistently, offering itself up for her enjoyment. *Pick me, pick me.* Large breasts held in place by her bra, enough cleavage for a good fuck, more than enough to motorboat with gusto. Pretty titties, the deep rose of her nipples showing through the sheer fabric of her shirt promised a mouthful of suckle waited for any man lucky enough to get her naked. Waist narrower than her hips, gave him vivid thoughts of having her on her hands and knees. In his head, he could imagine the give of her flesh as he buried his fingers and dragged her pussy back on his cock, impaling her over and over. An ass which was made to be spanked, or eaten until she screamed in frustration and pleasure, begging for his cock inside her. He'd scarcely come up for air if she'd let him have her like that.

Last night, after long minutes of self-torture, he'd padded to the bathroom and stripped down. Leaning on a forearm against the back wall of the shower, he'd spread his legs wide, alternating between stroking his cock with brutal strength and tugging on his sac, with a rough finger pressed against his hole, tracing the entrance with a delicate touch. Edging himself twice, he'd turned the water on and let it slick his cock, fist moving in a blur as he jacked hard. When he'd come in his hand, the force of his orgasm had bowed his back, shooting white streamers high on the tile. Breath coming fast and hard, he'd sagged against the wall.

Dark need curled inside him now, staring down at her face as she looked up at him. Crissy wore a look of innocent arousal, and if her neediness last night hadn't been an act, then he'd bet money she hadn't been fucked in a long time. *I can fix that for her. Be a kindness, really.* He curled his tongue behind his teeth, waiting. Her gaze dipped from his mouth to his throat, and her lips pursed slightly. Po'Boy felt her gaze like a weight on his skin. "Wanna fuck." He'd intended it as a question but knew she heard the command in the words instead. Her mouth fell open as she panted out a breath. "Yeah, I wanna fuck. Wanna fuck you, beautiful. Make you come with my mouth. I'll eat you. Make a meal outta what you'll give me. Wanna hear you moan my name."

She shifted, and he felt the scrape of material along his naked torso. Except for her shoes, she was still fully dressed, and he remembered her thigh-high hose and the tiny scrap of fabric between her legs. Remembered her taste. *Want me some more of that.* "I'm just gonna shove your panties to the side, bury my face between your thighs. Crissy—" He leaned close, lips to her ear, feeling her shiver as he whispered slowly, putting a pause between each word to ensure she understood. "I...wanna...fuck...you. Unless you tell me no, I'm gonna."

He didn't wait for a response, didn't expect one, and he wasn't disappointed because instead of "no," what he got instead was a soft moan of desire when his hand landed on her thigh below her skirt. Pushing it up, he made quick work of getting it out of the way, gripping the hem and tugging it up underneath her ass, lifting it to her waist. Hand under her back, he found the zipper to her blouse and whispered, "Arch up, beautiful. Don't wanna snag your flawless skin." She did, and he unzipped it, then worked the clasp on her bra. He pulled her bra and shirt down and freed her breasts, wasting not a second before he had his mouth on her. Sucking and nipping, feeding her nipple between his lips, he drew her deep into his mouth and worked her with his tongue. One hand landed on his head, cradling him closer as her other hand stroked along his shoulders, fingers working their way into his hair.

Frantic to get his hands on her, he abandoned finesse, shoving between her legs as they fell open to his advance. He pushed up to his elbow again, fingers tweaking her wet nipple, feeling the surface pebble and tighten when he blew a stream of air across. Tipping his head to look down her body, a lock of hair fell across his face as he stared at his hand delving into her pussy. He shoved her panties out of the way with the edge of his hand and dipped a finger in, then two, finding her wet and ready, pumping deep as her hips rose instinctively.

Pulling out he brought his hand up and licked, then turned to face her and painted her juices on her nipple, opening his mouth and falling on her again, growling and sucking hard while he returned those slick fingers to her core, fucking her hard and fast. She mewled and strained, and he lunged to take her mouth again, forcing his tongue into her mouth to stroke along hers. "Gotta fuck you. Jesus, fuck. Hot as a firecracker, Crissy." Her channel was sleek and hot, tight around his fingers and he groaned when her muscles contracted around him.

"Condom." The first word she'd said since he started was breathy, and once the dam was broken, the sounds burst from her. "Please." All the words he remembered from last night, this time offering something he could take, something he could give her in return. "Please, love me." Her hands cupped his cheeks, and she drew him down for a hard kiss, aligning their bodies as he shifted over her. "Please, Lewis." Then the naughty parts he'd wanted to know about. "I remember. I saw it. Your cock. So big. I want that. Please." Her hips pumped up in time with his fingers in her pussy. "You're so strong. So big all over. Like you could crush me, but you won't. Strong enough to keep me safe. Fuck me, please." Another gasping pant as her neck arched, breaking their kiss. "Lewis, please."

"Not yet, Crissy. I'm gonna eat you first." At his words, her muscles clenched around him again. "Oh, yeah. You like that. Want my mouth on you." Arms around her, he rolled them, stretching out on the mattress underneath her. He shoved the pillows off, making room, then told her, "Crawl up here, baby. Fuck my face." She stared down at him, expression confused. "Hands on the headboard. Knees by my head. I'm eatin' you now." He watched her swallow and then she shifted. Too slowly for him, and a loud crack of his palm against her ass had her scrambling faster while he grinned. "Don't be shy. I like pussy. I wanna hear you, honey. Wanna feel you get off on my tongue."

"What if I smother you?" The muttered question seemed to slip out unintentionally, and she bit her lip as her fingers found the top of the headboard, curling over the rail. He didn't answer, just flexed and lifted her by the hips into place over his face, illustrating his point without having to say a word. She stifled a laugh. "Okay, I won't worry about that, then."

After that, the only sounds she made were groaned versions of his name, and raw stuttering moans as he lashed her with his tongue, fingers of one hand holding her open for easy access while he pressed deep inside with his thumb. Fingertips slicked with her juices, he rimmed her ass again and again, feeling the tight pucker loosen to let him in. The second time she tried to climb off his face and escape his mouth, he cracked her ass again, and she settled down, whimpering. He knew her thighs had to be burning from his beard and decided to give her a break. He used her hips to pull her down his body, slipping her down his chest until he could reach her titties with his mouth, moving back and forth between each nipple, sucking and lapping at them, playing tag-a-titty with an alternating suck and pull on each one.

Stretched out like she was, arms supporting her weight, he felt her tremble with the strain.

"Let go. I got you." He tugged on her hips, and as her hands came free, he found himself buried in the softest and most delicious pillows a man could ever ask for. Licking his lips, he rolled his face back and forth as she struggled to lift off him, stymied by his hand between her shoulder blades, holding her in place for his mouth. Then, he motorboated. *As any red-blooded American man would*, he thought, smiling at her surprised laughter ringing through the room.

I like that, he thought with surprise, wrapping his arms around her when she buried her face in his shoulder. *That sense of ease she's got.* There was an air of gentle surprise and exploration in her actions which belied her uninhibited show from last night. Her shoulders shook, and the dampness on his skin told him she was no longer laughing.

"Hey." He shook her tenderly and tried to pull back to see her face, but she burrowed against him. "I can't fuck you if you're crying. I got rules. No fuckin' if the other party's wasted, and no cryin' chicks." He slipped a hand up her neck, cradling the back of her head. "You gonna let me fuck you?" She nodded, and he grinned, then turned his head to kiss the side of her face. "Want your mouth, Crissy. And, serious as a fuckin' heart attack, I really do wanna fuck you. Kiss me, darlin'." She sniffed, and he kissed her again, trailing his tongue up and tracing along the shell of her ear. He whispered, his tone urgent, feeling the rumble in his chest, "I want you. I'm not lookin' at anyone else but you right now, and I see you. I really do, darlin'. *I see you.* Every inch of you is gorgeous. Gimme a chance, beautiful. I'll rock your world." Her muscles relaxed, and she melted against him. "Now," in a voice barely audible, he ordered her, "kiss me."

Her head turned, and he saw the tears gleaming like diamonds on her lashes as her eyes dipped closed, her mouth seeking his. In this position, he couldn't control the kiss as he wanted, but he worked at it, angling across her lips with his, kissing side to side, pausing to nibble on the edges of her bottom lip. He groaned when she sucked his lip into her mouth, teeth grazing across in a barely-there threat that made him chuckle. Her tongue slipped past his lips, stroking delicately along his, the tip swirling cautiously. He didn't quite understand what had brought on the waterworks, but they seemed to be over with, and she was definitely getting back into the game. He closed the gap between them, hand to the back of her head, sucking and dueling with her tongue. He kissed her deep and wet, keeping at it until she wriggled around on top of him, looking for friction or a fuck, and he'd happily give her both in just a minute.

Arm across her back, the other hand buried in her hair, he rolled them so she was underneath him. Hips aligned, the fabric of her skirt and blouse became an annoyance, when all he wanted to feel was slippery skin. "Let's get you naked," he suggested, and she moaned. A sound he took for agreement. He pushed up, straddling her hips, fingers seeking along her waistband, pausing for a moment when her belly jumped underneath his fingertips. "Is someone ticklish?" He tested the theory, was rewarded by a laughing shove at his hands and tucked the information away for future use. "Where's the fuckin' button?"

"It's a hook in the back," she gasped, and he realized his dick was wedged between her legs, the head poking at her drenched panties. He tightened his ass, and she gasped again when the action shoved his cock against her again. "Lewis." Her voice came out in a whisper, and he grinned down at her.

"Little more than a pup tent now, ain't it?" That pulled a true laugh from her, and he stilled, letting the music of her laughter settle in the air around him.

"It's definitely more along the lines of an excursion tent." She grinned up. "Not a little one, this is a deluxe model."

"Hell yeah, it's a deluxe model. Fuckin' de-luxe. I'm huge, you seen my dick?" Reaching down, he gripped the base and swept the head of his cock up and down the fabric of her panties. "He's friendly, though. Always wantin' to come out and say hello."

"Hello," she echoed sweetly, and he noticed her shirt and bra were still concealing important parts of her anatomy.

"Naked," he reminded her. "As the day you were born. Now, honey. Deal with the top if you want to wear it out of here later." She pretended to gawp at him, and he snorted. "I'll send you home flat naked, Crissy. That's not a promise you want to collect on, honey. Guarantee." He grinned savagely and bent deep, nipping at her jumping belly, enjoying her tiny cries of surprise. "But these bottoms? They are all mine. I'm keepin' those panties. Gonna lick and suck them for days, keepin' the taste of you in my mouth. Sleep with 'em under my pillow, wake up with the scent of you in my head. You can go home bare under your skirt, I don't care. Gonna keep you wet and needy, so you'll have to work hard not to get a big ole wet spot on it drivin' home." He found the clasp and unfastened the skirt, slipping to one side to skate it down her hips and legs, panties going with it. "Leavin' those fuckin' stockings on. Fuckin' you just like this. Hell yeah, I'm a lucky bastard you climbed on the stool next to me last night. You are hot as hell, Crissy."

Condom retrieved from the nightstand, he watched as she divested herself of her top, folding it in half before she dropped it on the floor, following it with a bundled-up bra. Lying back on the bed, she stared up at him, unease warring with arousal on her expression. He caught her trying to suck in her tummy and shook his head. *Bitch needs some real talk*, he thought. "Can I tell you something without you gettin' pissy?"

Her head jerked to the side and shook in short arcs, not a no, just in confusion. "Wha—what?"

"You're worried. That's gonna jack with me. If I'm worried about you being worried, I can't bring my best to the table. I want to…Jesus." He shook his head, deciding to just dive in. "Okay, here it is. Gonna piss you off but hold out until the end. I'll make it right, okay?"

He waited until she nodded, her movements hesitant.

Cock in hand, he rolled the condom on as he talked. "You think you're heavy. In my head, I call it healthy or just that you're not a skinny chick. I don't like skinny chicks. Most real men don't. Fuckin' bones and shit, like dickin' a board. No fun. You can't tickle them, might break a fuckin' rib. Can't make motorboat noises on their boobs, either. And I fuckin' like that shit. I like to have fun in bed." He grinned. "Fuckin' is supposed to be fun. A good time. For everyone. So—" He shrugged. "—I don't like skinny chicks. I've fucked 'em, found it not to my likin'. So I dig you. Your body?" He bit his bottom lip as he allowed his gaze to roam her curves. "Everything I like, right there on display for me. I see you don't believe me." Shaking his head, he stared at her face, willing her to understand. "I don't know what kind of dudes you've been dickin', but they put shit in your head. Fuck that noise." He ran a hand up her leg, tracing along the tender flesh where it joined her body. Spreading his hand flat, he ran it up over her belly, taking care to keep his touch firm. *No ticklin' during the serious talk*. Moving so he knelt between her legs, he gripped her hips and tugged, bringing her down the bed towards him. "I don't worry I'm gonna hurt you. And you see my dick?" He gestured towards his groin. "He likes you, too. A fuck of a lot, if I'm honest. That skirt you had on? Sexy as hell, showed off all your curves." Hand on each thigh, he let his fingertips roam the top of her stockings. "Fucking. Mmmm. Hell yeah. I like these.

"So don't get jacked in your head about what you look like. I'm seein' alla you, and I like what I see." With a grin, she shook her head and then shocked him by lifting her arms and tucking her hands behind her head, showcasing her phenomenal tits. "Oh, hell yeah. Baby, you were made for fucking."

He leaned over her, fingers to her core as he tested the waters, making sure she was still turned on. He groaned. "Wet, Jesus. Slick as satin, honey. Made for fuckin'."

Elbow to the mattress beside her head, he lined his cock up with her entrance. With his forehead pushed into the pillow beside her head, he shifted so his mouth was next to her ear. "Here I come," he muttered, and then sucked in air with a gasp, letting her hear how good she felt as he slid inside her. "Oh, fuck, baby. Yeah, that's it. Hot and tight. Jesus. You want this as much as I want this. Slick and sleek, takin' every inch I got for you." He slotted his hips deep between her legs, grinding in with a twist of his hips. "Every inch of you is perfect. Lovin' this, baby." She clenched down, and he gave her an audible reaction, a groan that had her hands dropping to cup his ass, slide up his back and back down, pulling so he'd grind in again. "Gonna fuck you slow. You ready for some lovin'?"

"Please," she whispered, and her back bowed, hips tipping up to meet his every thrust. After a few moments, she dug her heels into the mattress, lifting to fuck him back, taking his cock as he moved. "So good, Lewis."

"Fuck yeah, it's good. You're good, baby. So fuckin' good." Sweat prickled along his upper back as her nails dug into his biceps. He slipped one hand under her, reaching down to grab her ass, anchoring her in the bed. "Give it to me. All you got, all you want. Take it, honey."

She moved in undulating waves, rubbing her nipples against his chest one instant, slipping their bellies together the next. Pussy clenching with each gasp of breath, she telegraphed her orgasm when she wrapped her arms around him, burying her face in his neck. "Lewis," she breathed, "I'm close."

"Fuck yeah," he repeated, pounding into her harder, faster, feeling his sac slapping against her ass with each thrust. Molten pussy surrounded his cock, the heat intense, sensation around the head of his dick exquisite. Tight and hot, so wet, each glide inside her was heaven. "Gonna blow, baby. I'm right there with you."

Her muscles tightened, tensing around him, gripping and milking him as she came. Voice lifted in a cry of his name, she shook and arched up. Teeth to his neck, her nails were tiny scores of pain in his back as she climaxed hard, and every reaction of her body ratcheted up his own until he was coming, the lightning strike of lust crashing into his spine, shooting sensations everywhere. With shaky legs, he plunged deep inside her again and again, all rhythm lost, primal need taking over. In the back of his mind, he recognized this felt different, hotter all along his cock, but changed in an undefinable way.

He pushed deep and stayed there, riding out the last pulses of his orgasm, feeling her tremble underneath him and they lay like that for a few minutes. Catching their breath, hands stroking each other, soothing as the languorous aftermath settled on them. Heavy limbs made for slow movements, as their short and fast breaths gusted over sweat-dampened skin. When he slid out and off Crissy, he settled into the bed next to her with a chuckle. "You're good at that. I liked it."

Her voice was soft, words slurring as if she were already half asleep. "I liked it too. No slouch." A flail of a hand slapped his belly gently. "Good job, Lewis."

"Thanks." Another chuckle. He reached to remove the condom and touched the head of his dick instead. *What the hell?* Lifting his head, he looked down to see the condom had split along the length of it and was wadded in a bunch around the base of his cock. "Crissy, any chance you're on birth control?"

"What?" Her voice was even sleepier, as if she were on the verge of dozing off.

"You on the pill?" With brusque movements, he removed the remains of the failed prophylactic, tossing it to the floor in disgust. "Condom blew out."

Movement beside him and he glanced over to see she'd lifted on a propped elbow. Her expression was soft, but not alarmed, which made his belly slow the roll it had started as soon as he'd realized what happened. "Yeah, I'm on the pill. I'm covered. Are you clean?"

"Yeah, you're safe with me." Rolling to his side, he bent over her, brushing her swollen lips with a gentle kiss. "No worries, doll."

She made a face and moved towards the edge of the bed with a sigh. "I need to go clean up." When he realized what she meant, Po'Boy's heart started pounding. *Oh, no you don't*. He lifted a leg across hers, anchoring her in place beside him, hand curved around her hip. She laughed and pushed at his chest. "Let me up. There'll be a wet spot, Lewis."

"No there won't be," he promised her and began moving down her body, keeping his gaze locked with hers. He licked his lips in anticipation and saw the instant she realized his intent and was rewarded with a slow blink which left her eyes hooded, again aroused. "I'll take care of everything."

Chapter Ten

"Gonna remind you I'm here with permission." Po'Boy's voice was intentionally flat, lacking inflection. "Your president gave me a token which I've shown you in good faith." He tried to keep his anger tamped down, knowing it would solve nothing if he reacted as he wanted. He was in El Paso, had been for four endless days, pending approval of IMC's request for assistance. "Smoke," he referenced the Silent Deaths' president, "said you'd be available to accompany me on my little side trip. If that's no longer in play, then someone should lemme know. Like now." He glanced at the man's nameplate and then scowled at the Silent Deaths' SAA. "Zipline," Po'Boy kept a sneer off his lips through sheer willpower at this point, "can you confirm we're a go?"

This little trip wasn't his idea. *No fuckin' way I'd raise my fuckin' hand for this bullshit*, he thought. After his two-day interlude with Miss Crissy in New Orleans, he'd seen her back to her car in time for her to drive across the long bridge Monday morning to go home before heading into work. The memory of her rounded ass in that skirt, topped by one of his T-shirts was enough to help keep his current level of anger down to a simmer. True to his word he retained possession of her panties, and those were tucked under his pillow in the suite.

They'd made tentative plans to hook up the following weekend, plans which were flushed down the toilet as soon as he'd turned on his phone, the ceaseless pings and vibrations of missed calls, voice mails, and texts had made him roll his eyes all the way back to the garage. By the time he got on his bike and sorted out what was going down, he didn't like a fuckin' bit of it.

"Seriously, if you can't give us what your president promised, then we'll look elsewhere to source what we need." Po'Boy twisted his neck and scowled at his companion, this person's identity being the biggest reason he wasn't happy about this trip. Wrench lounged at the bar, an elbow propped on the dull surface, uncaring of the greasy grime covering the bar top. The man looked like he had not a care in the world, and something about his attitude chapped Po'Boy's ass even more than normal. The entire trip across Louisiana and Texas had been conducted mostly in silence. The two nights spent in roadside parking areas Po'Boy had rolled into his sleeping bag without acknowledging the man lying on the next table over.

Bad enough Twisted sent me on this fuckin' wild goose chase. Then he had to fuckin' saddle me with this asshole.

At night, though, that asshole turned into a turn-on in his dreams, causing him to wake with a groan in the middle of the night. Silently unzipping the sleeping bag, he'd rolled until his back was towards Wrench and jerked off, all the time imagining the hand on his cock belonged to the other man.

Now, stalled in El Paso for days with no resolution, he'd come to the end of his patience. Shooting a glare at Wrench, Po'Boy said, "I'm thinkin' we're done here, brother." The need to show an unshakable solidarity went without saying, and to the outside observer, especially one who didn't know either of them well, they'd clearly pulled it off. "Time to call my man Retro, pull the trigger on him hooking us up with the Las Cruces folks." That would be the newly drafted chapter of a Chicago club, filled with men who walked the line and lived the life, but stayed a little farther away from the outlaw side than either Incoherent or CoBos.

"No, man. I got you. No need to go so far." Zipline unlocked his lips at last, presenting Po'Boy what he needed in just a few words. "I got you. We'll head back to the office, go over the map and my notes. This time tomorrow, I'll have you where you need to be down in Mexico. No worries."

Po'Boy hadn't looked away from Wrench, hadn't given Zipline anything in response to his proclamation. Rewarded for his scrutiny by seeing tiny crinkles of amusement appear next to Wrench's eyes, he knew a look of satisfaction crossed his face. Wrench glanced at him, and the line of his lips tightened slightly, something Po'Boy instinctively knew was him suppressing a grin. *Fuck, why in the hell do I think I know this man so well?* Still without turning, Po'Boy gave Zipline the first real inkling of who he was with his gritted words, "Lead the fuckin' way."

He turned and heard Wrench moving behind him, but wasn't ready for the arm that came down across his shoulders, nearly flinching in his surprise. "Yeah, Zippy," Wrench's voice was jovial as he agreed with Po'Boy. "Lead the fuckin' way."

Three hours later they'd hammered out a plan. They'd spend one more night in the cheap motel and Zipline would meet them in the morning with two men. One would be his, and one a member of the Mexican club that ruled Juarez, right across the river from where they sat. Zipline offered a room in the clubhouse, but even without consulting the other, Po'Boy and Wrench both declined, their responses in sync and seeming nearly practiced. Zipline recommended they travel light tomorrow as they crossed the bridge, promising to get them enough iron to roll heavy once they were deeper into the foreign territory. That didn't sit well with Po'Boy, even if he saw the wisdom because the last thing any of them wanted was to have any bumps in the road that could be avoided, and getting stopped with guns on them by border agents was a bad idea.

Strolling out of the office, Wrench's shoulder bumped and jostled him, and Po'Boy looked over to see Wrench cutting his eyes in a telling way. Following the direction of his gaze, it took every ounce of concentration to continue walking because standing at the bar in the back of the clubhouse's main room, in exactly the same spot Wrench had been earlier, was Deuces. He nearly swallowed his tongue in an effort to stop the shout wanting to erupt from his body. They hadn't specifically named the man to Zipline, but the implication based on the club's name they'd thrown around shouldn't have been hard to follow. *Fucking assholes.*

Outside, Po'Boy angled towards where their bikes were parked, hearing Wrench's footfalls behind him. Beside his bike, head down, he fiddled with his bag as he asked quietly, "The fuck you think that bastard's doing out here?"

Voice low, matching Po'Boy's tone, Wrench said, "No idea, but I surely do not believe in coincidences as big as this. There are no odds big enough to cover him being here at the same time we're out here looking for his bosses."

"Yeah," Po'Boy said, squatting so he could stare over the seat of the bike back towards the clubhouse, surprised when the door remained closed. *Time to go.* "Skin's crawling, brother. Let's get the fuck outta Dodge."

"Motel?" Wrench threw a leg across his bike, settling onto the seat as he shoved his key into the ignition. "Not recommended, man."

"Gotta be two hundred motels in El Paso. I'm thinking we can't trust Zipshit as far as we can throw him. I'm also thinking we know the exact reason we've been strung along as far as we have been. Fucker can eat my ass, man. I'll call Retro soon as we get private." Po'Boy pushed up with a groan, climbing on his bike and thumbing the starter switch. Voice raised over the rumbling of two sets of exhaust, he asked, "Ready to roll?" At Wrench's lifted thumb, Po'Boy twisted his throttle and led the way off the clubhouse's lot, onto the highway.

***

"Call Opie." After only two brusque words, Retro disconnected the call, and Po'Boy wrinkled his nose. Retro wasn't wrong, but it wasn't a call he wanted to make. Not tonight at least.

"What'd he say?" Wrench spoke from the other bed, back against the headboard, legs extended towards the TV. Po'Boy used the mirror fixed to the wall to watch the other man, his mouth watering when Wrench stretched and put his arms behind his head. *Gorgeous arm porn*, he thought, spending a moment to wish Wrench had taken his shirt off before stretching out on the bed. "Well?" Impatient now, Wrench looked away from the TV screen and towards Po'Boy, catching his gaze in the mirror. *Busted*, he thought, seeing the blank expression Wrench schooled his features towards when he realized Po'Boy was watching him.

"Told me to make the call we were talking about earlier. Didn't fuckin' hesitate, which makes me mad I wasted time callin' his ass."

"Hmm. Retro's a good one to bounce ideas off. I've never regretted asking his opinion." Wrench rolled his head back, the cords on his neck standing out as he stretched with a soft grunt, chin tipped towards the ceiling, fabric of his clothing rustling against the bed's comforter. "Beds are better here than the last place."

"Yeah." Every movement seemed choreographed to highlight another perfect aspect of Wrench's anatomy until Po'Boy couldn't tear his eyes off him. Knew he needed to before the man caught him eyeballing him again, but couldn't stop watching the undulating movements of the man. "You hungry?" This was the most they'd spoken since leaving Mandeville six days ago, and Po'Boy kept wanting to hear Wrench's voice again. "I'm starved. I could order pizza or some shit."

"Pizza's good." Wrench lifted his head, and Po'Boy immediately stared down at his phone, pulling up a browser to search for a restaurant nearby that delivered. "I like meat. Lots of meat." *Me, too*, Po'Boy thought, glad his lips only twitched but stayed closed.

Clearing his throat Po'Boy nodded, saying only, "Sounds good." He'd just finished ordering their dinner and disconnected from the call when his phone chimed. Looking down he saw a text from Crissy. With a grin, he opened the app and read, **You sure the weekend is out? :pouty face: I was looking forward to seeing you again.**

Shaking his head, he responded, **Yeah, sorry. Soon as I get back, it's on. We'll let your freak out to play again.**

Her return text had him chuckling. An emoji of a jumping cheerleader and a simple, **Yay**, still managed to convey her anticipation.

"Got something to smile about?" Wrench's voice came from nearby, and Po'Boy looked up to see he'd shifted to the edge of the mattress, feet on the floor between the beds, his head angled to look into Po'Boy's face.

"Yeah, the chick I hooked up with last weekend was looking for a round two. Havin' to let her down easy." He shook his head, leaning back to shove the phone into his pocket. "Pretty? Oh, yeah. Man, she's pretty. And just kinky enough to get off on my shit. A rare combination, man."

"You and Twisted used to share women." Not a question, the statement came from left field, startling him into staring at Wrench's face. "Caught the show a couple of times. Hot as hell." As he spoke, a flush crept up Wrench's cheeks, and Po'Boy wondered if the words were intentional or a slip.

He nodded. "Yeah, we'd double team any chance we got. Good times. Yousa put a stop to that. I can't imagine going there with her. Fuck, Twisted would kick my ass if he thought I was suggesting it."

"You got a partner lined up? You know, if it's something you liked and wanted to keep doing? You could find someone else to screw around with."

What the hell? Was Wrench offering to be Po'Boy's wingman in a fuck fest?

"Not something I think about much." *I'm a fuckin' liar because hooking up is all I think about.* "If you're offering, I'll give you a buzz next time I find a two-hole piece of fun." *That will never happen.*

"How about this one? You said she's kinky, yeah? Would she be down for some fun?" Wrench persisted, the red in his face more pronounced.

"Yeah, she's kinky enough to be fun. Not sure she'd be into two dudes, but I can sure as fuck ask her, see what she says. Crissy didn't seem to be afraid of much. I bet I can talk her into it." The idea of doubling up on her with Wrench was more than enticing, it was damned exciting. Exciting and terrifying, with the thrill of possible exposure buzzing in his gut.

"Crissy?" Wrench's head tipped to one side, surprise clear in the motion, his eyes narrowing suspiciously. "That the chick's name?"

"Yeah, and get this, she lives up by you. Saw her license, noted the address. She's a fuckin' looker, man." He reached down and adjusted his cock. "Tore me up in a good way."

"Jesus. She's my next-door neighbor. You're right, she's drop-dead gorgeous, and a hella kisser. Where'd you meet her?" At Wrench's admission, Po'Boy felt another thrilling buzz. Not of jealousy, not of possession, but at the idea maybe he and Wrench had already shared her however remotely.

"Mmmm. You fuck her?" There was no hiding the fact his slow, rolling tone was hopeful, and his cock fattened more just considering the implications.

"No, never got so far. I had a run-in with Thorne and Sam that involved her, then had to head straight up to Kentucky. I was gone for a couple of weeks, and when I got back, she was out, didn't come home until right before I got the call from Ace to meet you. I'm guessing she was with you last weekend?" Wrench sighed. "Now that'd be a show."

"You want that? Wanna see that? Oh, fuck, man. No hidin' the fact I like the idea." Po'Boy stroked his cock through his jeans, fingernails dragging across the fabric. "We get back, I'll give her a call, see if she's up for more kink than I threw at her so far."

Can I do this again? Be around someone I want and can't have, in the kind of setting which forces intimacy? One fuckup. That was all it would take. One goddamned fuckup and everything he had worked for would be toast. He looked at Wrench, locking on the sensual expression of arousal and intense interest on his face as he nodded eagerly. The idea of having that staring at him across Crissy's body was a thrill he wouldn't be able to pass up.

He considered again the dangers of having his activities exposed.

I don't care.

***

Wrench

Jesus. Crissy and Po'Boy. His mind was going wild with images pulled from parties where he'd watched Po'Boy and Twisted share women, superimposing Crissy's face and body on the activities. The sound of the TV blaring to life jerked his attention back to the room, and he watched as Po'Boy idly flipped through several channels before settling on one showing the weather. *Thank God.* If he'd found porn and put it on,

Wrench wasn't certain what he'd have done. He'd already popped wood watching Po'Boy stroking himself through his pants, the size and length of the man's large cock clearly defined.

What would it be like to have him touch me like that?

Fuck.

"Ask her now." He almost didn't recognize his voice, gravelly and rough. His balls drew up, and he couldn't suppress a full-body shiver of anticipation. "Give her a nudge, at least, man. Won't lie, the idea more than interests me."

"Tell me about the kiss." Po'Boy seemed to want to negotiate, and Wrench found himself willing.

"You spent time with her enough to see her sassy side? She's got one, no doubt. I was about to strap my bag on the bike to head out when Thorne rolled up with his crew. Sam, fuckin' asshole she is, bailed off his bitch seat and wanted to push me. Still not sure what she expected to get outta the deal, except a set down in public." He grinned, tipping his chin up. "Bitch was screaming and yelling. Thorne just looked stunned, like he didn't know what he'd unleashed by bringing her to my door. Over her bullshit I hear the door behind me open and next thing I know Crissy's laying Sam out about her shit. Tore her down and pissed Sam off. That woman's got balls like you wouldn't believe."

Po'Boy muttered, "Oh, I'd believe."

Wrench grinned. "Thorne contained and then rolled off with Sam, and I went inside to explain to Crissy she might want to know something about a situation before she throws down. She's so...cute. Standing there all flummoxed by why I was pissed. I just went for it. Hella good, man." He swallowed, sweat stinging along his skin thinking about Po'Boy kissing her like he had. "You know how she is. As if there's no end to the sweet you'll find inside her."

"Be happy to look all day long, though." Po'Boy grinned lasciviously, one corner of his mouth quirking sideways. "All you did was kiss?"

"Yeah, had me hard as a rock in under five seconds. She looked so confused when I stopped, but Jesus, I *had* to get out of there, or I'd never have gone to Kentucky." He shook his head. "Sweet. She's *so* sweet. *Jesus.*"

"You fuckin' missed the boat, man. Missed out on so much." Po'Boy stretched his neck, hands lifting to slide down his chest. "Fuckin' phenomenal lay, man. The woman has moves and hellacious stamina." Wrench watched without blinking as Po'Boy gripped his cock again and gave the smallest of tugs. Heat on his own hand made him aware he had palmed his hard-on through his jeans, too. "You want me to give her a nudge?"

"Yes." Wrench knew he would cringe at his tone later, but for now, he didn't try to hide the excitement and need in his voice. "Fuck yes."

With a sly grin, Po'Boy lifted his phone and started tapping at the screen. After a moment, he cut his eyes towards Wrench again, then began narrating what he was sending her. "When I get back, I got something I want to do with you. Turn up the heat, Miss Crissy. You wanna get hot with me?" He paused, staring down at his phone, and Wrench realized he was waiting for a response.

His phone chimed, and he grinned as he read, "Your place or mine?" Laughing softly, Po'Boy typed out his answer, "We could meet in the middle." He lifted his gaze and stared directly at Wrench. "She thinks I'm living in New Orleans." A chime and he cut his eyes down to the phone, his grin turning wolfish. "A new location for playtime? I'm intrigued." Lifting his chin, he offered Wrench a smirk. "She's intrigued. Now to set the hook. You said she had your back, right?" Wrench nodded. "Think she was into you?" With a small shrug, Wrench nodded again. "Go big or go home, right?" Without waiting for a response, he typed and then read, "Second thought, my place. Gonna need privacy for all the things we're going to do to you."

Wrench's cock pulsed, and he palmed it again. *Why does this do it for me?*

A chime.

"We?" The wolfish grin was back, and Po'Boy turned his full attention to the phone. "Yes, baby. We. You and me got friends in common and *we*"—the emphasis was clear—"have a hundred ideas of the fun things we can all do together." Chime. "Who's your friend?" Po'Boy winked at him. "Want a pic pic, or a dick pic?" Pause. Chime. "Both."

Wrench groaned as Po'Boy laughed, moving to sit on the side of his mattress, legs in the small space between their beds. Within touching distance. Wrench shifted to match his pose, putting one foot between Po'Boy's, one foot on the outside. Close enough to feel the heat from Po'Boy's leg.

"Okay, time to go all in. Whatcha packin'? Can't have you comin' up short, man." Po'Boy stood and unbuckled his belt, staring down at Wrench, his hands working at eye level. "You hard, man?" Wrench swallowed. This had suddenly become real.

He stood and unfastened his jeans, letting them gape open and droop slightly around his hips. "I'm packing plenty. If she likes 'em big, we're good." *In for a penny*, he thought and shoved his pants down his legs, his erection springing out, rebounding up to lightly slap his belly. Hand circling the base, he angled it down and turned his hips slightly to the side, pulling his foreskin back to expose the crown. "I got your cock right here." A moment later Po'Boy had also shucked his jeans, leaving them tight around his thighs. His skin was darker than Wrench's, the contrast stark. His cock was thick and long, cut, the head nearly purple and weeping.

Wrench couldn't stop the gasp from escaping his lips when Po'Boy's hand gripped his cock, a slight tug pulling him into alignment. Then there was a blazing heat all along his length when Po'Boy pressed their erections together, holding them in one hand. Their hips and shoulders jostled for space, but Wrench didn't look up to see what Po'Boy was doing, his attention entirely captured by the sight of his dick, something so well-known and memorized suddenly foreign because another man's hand was holding it tightly. A click, and movement, then another click. "Got it. Good one."

The iron bands of Po'Boy's fingers disappeared, as did the silken slide of his dick and Wrench heard a sound of frustration in the room, realizing it came from his throat. Then heat along his shoulders, and Po'Boy whispered in his ear, hot breath gusting along his skin, "Look up." Blindly following instructions, he stared up at the phone held in a ubiquitous selfie pose. The camera was reversed and he could see their faces, side by side, Po'Boy's grin again wolfish, the look on his own face stunned and bewildered. Click. "Smile, Wrench," another whisper and the arm around his shoulders squeezed. "Smile," Po'Boy reminded him, and he must have complied because he heard a click. "Handsome boy. She ain't gonna turn this shit down."

Po'Boy abandoned him, reclaiming a seat on the edge of the mattress, head bent over the phone, "Sending the dick pic first, because that's some impressive shit. You're a fuckin' bull, man. She's gonna lose her mind." His tone changed, and Wrench knew it was because he'd shifted to narration mode again. As Po'Boy moved, his hair brushed Wrench's erection, each tiny touch a seismic quake of sensation.

All it would take is for him to turn his head.

An image of Po'Boy's mouth on his dick overwhelmed him, ghost heat snaking down his spine to curl around his hole and balls, causing him to clench every muscle in his thighs and ass, each movement giving him a much larger curl of desire. "Don't share this with anyone. It's only for your viewing pleasure, baby."

A pause.

A chime.

At the sound, Wrench watched, riveted by the sight of Po'Boy's cock jerking. Whatever she said was good. His voice had a lilting falsetto tone when he said, "Jesus H. Christ. I nearly choked on my tongue."

Po'Boy lifted his head to look up into Wrench's face, ignoring the cock nearly touching his cheek. "I'd say we're a hit, man." Po'Boy's head tipped to the side, and now Wrench's dick did touch him, slipping along the edge of his jaw, the rasping grind of stubble nearly too much against the sensitive head of his cock. Wrench watched in fascination as the unexpected contact left a shining smear of fluid on Po'Boy's face. "Moment of truth." Seemingly oblivious, head tipped back down to the phone, Po'Boy worked the keyboard. "And now our smiling faces."

Pause. Chime.

Po'Boy didn't say anything for a moment, and Wrench's gut clenched. He roughly yanked up his pants as his legs gave out, so he sat heavily on the side of his bed, mostly clothed, hard cock buried from view by the loose fabric. "What? What's she saying?" He hadn't realized how much he had invested in this little bit of play, but if she turned them down, he didn't know what he'd do. *I want this*, he thought and gritted his teeth waiting on the inevitable letdown. "What'd she say?"

Po'Boy's lips spread in a slow, grin, looking self-satisfied and predatory. Intense. "Hell, yeah."

***

Crissy

She stared down at her phone for a moment, then flipped back to the text app. Scrolling down, she found the conversation she wanted and started typing.

Don't laugh. I got another dick pic today. The difference was, I wanted this one.

She picked up her glass and twisted to sit sideways on the sofa, staring out the front window. Drinking deeply, the iced water was blessedly cool as she swallowed. Lewis knew Ty. Lewis alone was almost more than she could handle. They hadn't done anything she didn't want last weekend, not at all. In fact, she'd enjoyed everything to a level she hadn't ever before experienced. Under his gentle urging, she felt free to explore all the things she'd wondered about. Books and movies built sex up to such a frenzy, she had come to believe the lackluster activities of her past were normal. Not disillusioned, just accepting.

Then Lewis had blown in and torn down every preexisting expectation, shoving aside her past boyfriends and hookups in a blaze of fulfilled passion. Crissy felt a rise of heat in her cheeks. They'd done so much, so many things in the hours spent together. Her thighs clamped together, and she squirmed on the couch, gulping another big mouthful of water. *He was a mouthful*, she thought, and nearly spit the water back out.

Lewis and Ty.

Am I going to jump in with both feet?

She looked at her phone, changing conversation views with a slide of her thumb. Stopping on the picture of their cocks, she stared for a long moment. The two men's erections were nearly the same length, Lewis' was slightly more slender, the exposed crown flush with color. The cock she assumed was Ty's had more breadth to it, Lewis' fingers cupping it alongside his own. Ty's foreskin was stretched tight, pulled back to show her the streak of fluid along the flesh. She licked her lips. From the angle, she could see Lewis' sac hung low and heavy, and she remembered pulling it into her mouth, rolling his balls with her tongue, two lubed fingers stroking inside him while he groaned loudly and complained about holding still as she'd ordered him. She squirmed again, lifting the glass to roll the chilled surface against her cheeks.

Is it possible to like two guys at once and not have it be a disaster?

Crissy sighed, staring through the sheer curtains. Lewis had said it would be Wednesday before he was home. That was four days away. "You're assuming they don't have anything better to do than you when they get home." Shaking her head at the absurdity of talking to herself, she concentrated on keeping her dialogue internal. *Even if they don't have jobs, I do.* Saturday. The absolute soonest they could explore this idea Lewis had.

I told you I was with the one guy, Lewis. He was … is amazing.

Tipping her head back, she let her mind wander back to those hours spent in New Orleans with Lewis. *Sometimes you can know a body forever, and yet not know them at all.* She conjured up an image of his eyes as he moved over her, moved in her. He'd been staring down to where they were connected, and when he lifted his head to look at her, he let every feeling show on his face. Desire was there, of course, and lust. *So hot. Everything we did.* Pupils dilated, his enjoyment of the act was undeniable. What she hadn't expected was how much he'd like how into it she was.

Unselfish in bed. Not that he didn't know, and demand, what he wanted. Rhoda, it was more that it mattered more to him that I find mine than he get his. You know?

The way his arms had framed her face, not letting her hide anything, that had been his demand for emotional access. Someone who studied a person that intently did so for a reason, and his was to take care of her. For the space of a day or more, he had taken very good care of her. *He'd never hurt me.* She knew that with certainty, deep in her belly. Could that extend to others, though? Ty had been pretty brutal to the woman, Sam. *She deserved every word, coming at him like she did.* In fact, Crissy remembered Ty containing himself and giving advice to

Sam's boyfriend. Even with not liking the woman, and really not liking how she was behaving, he'd still taken care.

The other guy, Ty, he's not just hot, but he's kind.

In the aftermath of the shouting match, when he'd come into her home, even then every word he'd said was taking care. That time it had been of her. *I don't think he'd hurt me, either.* Pulling in a deep breath, she looked down at the phone again.

I miss you. So much. Every day, honey. I know what you'd say, though. Go for it. If it's what you want, don't be afraid to reach for it.

Friday night, maybe. Crissy shivered as her mind returned to her previous thoughts, and she looked at her phone, changing conversations again. Lewis had sent her three pictures total, the first one of their erections had taken much of her attention. This time she looked at the other two images, surprised all over again to recognize Ty's handsome face alongside Lewis' striking features. In the first picture, both men were smiling, standing shoulder to shoulder, leaning in so they were in the frame. Lewis' grin held a naughty promise she already knew he could deliver on. *Yes, he surely can.* Ty's smile was softer, his gaze into the camera intense and focused. He looked a lot like the last time she'd seen him, right after he'd kissed her senseless. He appeared aroused and ready to act on it.

She flipped to the third picture. It had come in after her and Lewis' final discussion about possible details for their meeting, but the pose was so similar to the other one it had to have been taken at the same time. Angled differently, this one had their faces and shoulders across the breadth of the image and framed in the mirror behind them, their bare asses. In this picture the expression on Ty's face was different, he looked almost stunned, and the reflection showed his hands were clenched into fists. Lewis' arm was around his shoulders, holding him close, providing support that looked necessary. *Maybe I won't be the only one new to the idea*, she thought.

Unable to help herself, she flipped back to the first picture, staring at their erections cupped in Lewis' hand, thinking she understood the look on Ty's face all too well. *I probably looked just as stupefied the first time Lewis laid a hand on me, too.* Lifting the glass, she drained the cold water, gasping for air.

* * *

Wrench

He and Po'Boy had rolled through Deridder about an hour prior, which meant he had about three hours before he pulled into the condo parking lot. In another forty-five minutes, they'd stop for fuel in Opelousas, and he'd try to sort out how Po'Boy wanted to handle this whole thing. There was no doubt in either of their minds who was in charge of the planned encounter. *What should I call it?* He wondered, worrying various words through his head. Threesome. Ménage a trois. Nothing sounded right, and as he followed Po'Boy around another semi, shifting lanes effortlessly behind the man, he made a conscious decision to set it aside. *Doesn't matter, anyway. If it works, it'll work. No need to classify something like this.*

Half of him hoped it wouldn't work out. That Crissy would get cold feet at the last minute. It would be worth it to hear Po'Boy grumble about it without having to try and perform in front of the man. The other half? Quivering with anticipation, he'd gotten off the bike at each stop with the head of his dick sitting in a sticky puddle in his jeans. Possible scenarios running through his mind constantly, and from the knowing grins Po'Boy gave him, it must have been plain on his face at times.

He'd seen enough brothers double-team bitches at parties to have some familiarity with the concept. Pussy and mouth were popular targets, but he remembered one party in particular where Twisted had lifted a girl so her legs were around his waist, and impaled her on his dick. Standing up while fucking wasn't new to Wrench, but he'd been mesmerized when Po'Boy had come up behind her…he sucked in a hard breath flavored with diesel and the dense scent of rotting vegetation so peculiar to southern Louisiana, shaking his head to rid himself of the memory.

Ever since the night of Twisted's party, it seemed as if fate had conspired to throw Po'Boy in his path. After that moment of insight where he had realized something in the man was appealing, the only time they'd not been together was when he'd run to Kentucky. Even then, Po'Boy followed him, never knowing how he'd haunted every dream Wrench had. On this trip out to El Paso and back, the awareness of Po'Boy had been a thrumming vibration barely under the surface of his skin. The nights sharing a motel room torture. *For me at least.* He snorted. Po'Boy didn't seem to be disturbed in the least. He was calm to the point Wrench had wondered if he had imagined the desire he'd seen in Po'Boy's face.

Then, last night they'd again avoided paying for a room by staying in a rest area, and Wrench had gotten a show. Bright moonlight shining down had kept him up later than normal, so when Po'Boy rustled around, adjusting his position in the thin sleeping bag, Wrench was still awake. Awake and watching as Po'Boy released his cock into the nighttime air, working himself over in a frenzy, then slowing with a groan before jacking his dick faster again. That groan, however, was Wrench's undoing, sending his cock harder than a steel rod, wedged between his hip and the cement tabletop beneath him. The groan that contained his name.

Pulsing lights ahead of him snagged his attention, and he followed Po'Boy into the left lane, slowing slightly as they rolled past a group of bikes stopped on the side of the road by two state patrol cars and what looked like at least three sheriff trucks and SUVs. The bikers' heads swiveled as one to watch him and Po'Boy ride past. He knew it'd be a tossup if one of those trucks would pull out after the two of them since they were proudly wearing their colors. Things had changed in the past decade and a half, and every club knew it was bullshit like Deuces had been pulling which made the police turn their eyes towards the clubs. Pretend clubs kept popping up everywhere, wanna-bes who felt putting a set of patches on their back gave a license to do anything they desired. Then there were the groups like Thorne's riding club who had an idea in their head about what the biker lifestyle was all about, never really understanding it was a way to live, not a lifestyle.

He kept one eye on his mirror, breathing a relieved sigh when they rounded the first curve without any sign of lit up bubblelights behind them. A few miles farther up the road, Po'Boy signaled a stop and they pulled into a small, country gas station and convenience store. Po'Boy halted at the first pump, and Wrench pulled around him, shaking his head as he idled up next to the next set of pumps. *Asshole*.

Crissy's mouth kept intruding on his thoughts. How hungry she'd seemed, how responsive. The bereft look in her eyes when he tore his mouth off hers. *I coulda fucked her right there*. He licked his lips. *I shoulda*. The muscles in his stomach jerked. *Mouth that sweet. What Po'Boy said about her? Woman's gonna fucking kill me when we get together*.

He killed his engine and heeled down his kickstand, then was in the process of easing backwards into a long-needed stretch of his muscles when he felt a hand on his neck. Jerking sideways, he looked up into Po'Boy's grinning face. He barked, "The fuck you want, asshole?"

"You deaf, man? You sat here and idled for a longass time. Fuck, man. I called you like five times. They got a hot buffet bar with a couple of tables inside. I need something to eat. I know we're nearly home, but it'd be better if we stuck together, I think. You see the shit on the highway back there?" Po'Boy shook his head, reaching down between Wrench's legs and twisting the gas cap off his tank. Wrench stared as the man grabbed the handle from the pump, wedging it into the open hole and swiping his card to authorize the pump. He turned back to the bike, engaging the handle lock so the gas would start to flow. As he did, his hand grazed Wrench's crotch, waking his dick up even more.

Another seemingly honest miscalculation had Po'Boy's fingers slipping down Wrench's thigh, causing his ass to clench. Po'Boy spoke as if nothing had happened, as if he hadn't noticed what he was doing, "That was a crew from down by Terrebonne. They were tight with VWMC back in the day. I ain't heard shit about 'em since Ragman did his thang. Wonder what they did to crawl up po-po's ass?" Po'Boy stepped back, crossing his arms across his chest as he surveyed the store and parking lot, head swiveling back and forth.

"The fuck are you doing, Po'Boy?" Wrench hadn't even dismounted his bike and had no idea if Po'Boy had already finished fueling his own bike.

"Gettin' your ass in gear, man. I done tole you, I'm hungry." The gas pump clicked off and Po'Boy's fingers wrapped around the handle, expertly topping the tank off. Wrench grabbed the cap back from him, feeling an electric zing as their fingers touched. The smile faded from Po'Boy's face, and Wrench knew he couldn't be the only one feeling whatever this was.

"I got it. Go park, I'll see you inside."

Without looking up, he started his engine and punched the shifter into first, idling away from the pump and around to the front of the store. By the time he had parked, Po'Boy was backing in beside him. Tipping his chin, he tried to analyze the expression on Po'Boy's face, unsure if the entire thing at the pumps had been a way to get him off center, or if it was how Po'Boy was with his friends. *Am I his friend?* He gave a short headshake. *We're gonna be fucking the same woman. We should be friends before we start down that path, shouldn't we?*

Inside, he nodded at the woman behind the register and grabbed a plastic tray, standing in the line for the cafeteria-style hot food bar. Another woman was working there, quickly moving from spoon to spoon, ladling each customer's selections onto a plate that was delivered at the register, money exchanging hands there along with rolled silverware and packages of condiments. An efficient system, with accessible buckets filled with packages of chips or iced soft drinks along the way. Po'Boy was behind him, crowding Wrench, leaning over his shoulder to look at this entrée or that one, poking his arm to bring his attention to the pulled pork, bumping him to get a look at the peach cobbler. Wrench was excruciatingly aware of each touch, each brush, the heat along his side from where Po'Boy had gotten close. It felt as if every eye were on them, and he didn't understand how no one seemed to notice the way Po'Boy had invaded his space. A hand on his arm startled him, and he jerked around to see Po'Boy right there.

"Relax, brother." That's all Po'Boy had to say. A squeeze of his bicep was there and then gone, and then he heard Po'Boy repeat himself softly, "Relax, man."

Three men were rising from a table as they approached, and Wrench took possession of the bench facing the front of the store. Po'Boy wrinkled his nose but didn't say anything, seating himself on the other bench, back to the door. The two men ate in silence, and Wrench realized this was normal for them. They didn't need to fill the silence with posturing or bullshit. Somewhere along the way, the silence of avoidance had simply become what they did. If there were something worth saying, one or the other would say it. If there wasn't, then both of them were comfortable with quiet.

He glanced around and saw a decent buffer of emptiness between them and the next occupied table. "Crissy give you any indication when she's gonna want to see us?" He shoved the last bite of his self-assembled sandwich in his mouth, trying to hide the eagerness thrumming through his veins at the idea of what they were planning.

Po'Boy lifted his bottle of water and took a drink, then grinned at him over the open mouth of the bottle. "Brother, she lives next door to you. Why in the hell would you think we'd be waiting? I'm tagging along with you tonight, we roll in, she hears the bikes, comes to the door—then it's seriously just a question of who's got the biggest bed."

"I figured we'd go to your place in New Orleans." Wrench was surprised, not sure what to think about this going down in his condo. "You know I got hardly any neighbors who aren't patches of some brand, right?"

"Two dudes, one chick." Po'Boy shook his head. "If—and brother, that's a big fuckin' if—someone sees her coming to your place, not a single man is going to look at this and think anything except we're lucky bastards. If they see us going into hers, they're going to think the same. Be easy, Wrench. We're just a couple of guys who belong to clubs who are friendly. We just had a longass run shoved on us by our presidents. Tonight we gather our thoughts and get ready to present them at the joint church Ace and Twisted called for tomorrow. Or—" He winked. "—that's my story, at least. What one you gonna spin?"

He stared at Po'Boy for a moment, taking in the confident smirk on his lips, the way his frame filled the seat on his side of the table. He remembered the sandpaper grasp of Po'Boy's fingers around his cock again. *Be honest*, he thought. *You want this with him as much as you do Crissy*. Wrench's hard swallow made a clicking sound in his throat. His voice shook when he said, voice low and rumbling in his chest, "Text her. Tell her the door will be unlocked as soon as we hit the condo. Tell her we can't wait."

Po'Boy's lips slid sideways, and his grin grew into a broad smile. He dug out his phone and unlocked it, then held it up for Wrench to see the screen. Crissy was captured in midair-kiss, red lips pursed and blowing across her fingertips. "That, my friend, is what we are riding towards." Phone back in his hand, he typed for a moment and then cut another look up at Wrench. "What we got, three hours?" Wrench nodded, gathering and crumpling the trash left behind from their meal. A chime—and by now just the sound was enough to make Wrench's cock twitch in anticipation. Po'Boy chuckled and said softly, "Oh, man. She's ready."

Lifting his phone again, he showed Wrench the new picture of Crissy he'd received. Wrench could see the upper swells of her breasts pressed behind her arms which were folded across on the top of a chair. It looked as if she were in her bedroom. In the background, he could see a closet door with a full-length mirror. In the mirror, her legs, ass, and back were bare, and he traced the curves of her naked body with his gaze. "Jesus," he muttered as he pushed up from the bench. "Two hours, max. Let's ride."

Chapter Eleven
Po'Boy

Po'Boy trailed Wrench into the complex, following behind and just to the side as they rode through the curving streets to the back units where Wrench and Crissy lived. Mentally he compared his apartment in Mandeville to this and curled his lip at the idea of bringing either Wrench or Crissy back to that place. His suite, sure, because it was just ritzy enough to make him proud, but his apartment? *Fuck, no.* He idled in the street, waiting for Wrench to back into a space, and then maneuvered his bike into the small parking spot next to him. Neither man spoke as they killed the engines and dismounted their bikes, the soft ticking sounds of metal cooling coming from their hot exhaust systems. They'd covered a lot of miles in a short period of time. Wrench unhooked the netting he used to hold his belongings to the second seat on his bike while Po'Boy retrieved his own bag. Still wordless, they walked towards Wrench's front door and were inside within moments. Po'Boy made a point to verify the door was unlocked, and then stood looking around the condo, taking everything in.

A big couch in front of a wide TV. A dark wooden table at one end held remotes and an open book, turned facedown. Without asking permission, he stalked across the room and yanked open the refrigerator door, scanning the contents until he found bottles of water.

Grabbing one for himself, he retrieved another bottle and grunted to ensure Wrench's attention, tossing it towards him. Prowling through the rooms, he located a small half-bath next to a closet, and then the door to the master bedroom. There was a king-size bed centered in the space, and across the room, a door was open to the master bath where he saw the edge of what had to be a huge bathtub. Making a guess as to which side Wrench slept on, he pulled open the drawer of the nightstand and grinned at the contents. Lube and condoms, and what looked to be a vibrating dildo still in the retail packaging. A sound caught his attention, and he looked to see Wrench standing in the doorway, glaring at him. "Just acclimating myself." He picked up a condom and tossed it to the top of the nightstand. "I'm like a fuckin' scout, man. Always wantin' to be prepared."

Wrench didn't say anything, but his eyes were blazing with anger or frustrated passion, Po'Boy wasn't sure which. Gaze locked on Wrench, he stared, watching as the man's jaw ground side to side, lip curling. Po'Boy dropped his chin and eyed Wrench from underneath his brows. "We're both wantin' the same thing, Ty." Using that name was intentional, he wanted to give Wrench space to separate this from the biker life they lived. "Ain't nothing wrong with takin' what we want. Not hurtin' anyone. Surely not hurtin' Crissy, and I'll be damned if I hurt you."

Wrench's Adam's apple bobbed as he swallowed, and then he nodded and gave verbal indication he was still on board. "Lewis. What if we want different things?"

Po'Boy huffed out a soft laugh and shook his head. "I'm pretty sure we absolutely want the same thing, Ty. I want you in bed with Crissy. I'm not confused about what I want." Aware his palms were smoothing down his thighs, he stopped and propped a hand on each hip. "Outside of this condo, I'll deny everything. But inside? Anything goes."

"Anything?" Wrench's voice was a deep, growling rumble Po'Boy felt as much as heard, the vibrations setting up a resonance inside him.

Without moving anything but his lips, he answered firmly. "Anything." By the time he heard the front door open and Crissy's careful "hello," he was already more than half hard. "Moment of truth, Ty. This what you want, too?"

Without waiting for a response, he pushed past the larger man and into the living room of the apartment, long strides taking him across the space to where Crissy stood in front of the closed door. He didn't give her a chance to retreat or demur, stalking up to her without a word and gripping an arm in each hand. He turned and pulled her towards him, putting them at an angle to Wrench, ensuring he had a good view of everything that was about to happen.

Po'Boy bent his head and covered her mouth with his, needing the physical connection in a bone-deep way. As she had the last time he'd kissed her, she melted into him, meeting every advance with her own, their tongues sliding and dancing as he drew the breath from her mouth. Her shoulders hitched, and he pulled back to allow a sliver of room between them, but she clung to him, fingers wrapped in the shirt underneath his cut, breathing hard. "Hey, baby." Leaning close again, he kissed her softly, nibbling on her bottom lip, feeling the velvet touch of her tongue across his mouth. "I missed you."

"I missed you, too." Her voice was quiet, but vibrating with need. It was no wonder she sounded like that, if their text exchanges had kept her as on edge as he had been. Already his cock strained at the front of his jeans, climbing his hip in small movements, arching towards her.

Hand to her back, he held her tight, the giving touch of her breasts against his chest making him groan silently. He stepped back and slipped his hand down her arm, tracing along delicate veins underneath her skin to her wrist, winding his fingers between hers. With a tug, he pulled her along behind him as he strode towards where Wrench stood, the expression on his face uncertain. Po'Boy got close, as he'd done with Crissy, nearly chest to chest with Wrench and reached up with his free hand, cupping the angle of Wrench's jaw. Rough scruff scraped at his fingers and palm, and he traced the curve of Wrench's mouth with the pad of his thumb. Without making a sound, he pushed the tip of his thumb between Wrench's lips, his own mouth falling open when Wrench willingly took it deep, rolling it with his tongue.

"Fuck, that's hot," Po'Boy muttered, leaning in slowly, giving Wrench every chance to pull back. No longer hesitant, eyes open, his fierce stare dared Po'Boy to deliver on what he'd started. Wrench let Po'Boy press their lips together around his thumb, the erotic feel of Wrench's mouth everything he'd wanted. It was all Po'Boy could do to strangle a groan, and he pulled his hand out of the way. Wrench must have heard or felt it because in the next instant his tongue thrust into Po'Boy's mouth and his taste flooded Po'Boy's senses. Raw and ardent, the sense of possession was immediate and overwhelming and need raced up his spine. He tugged Crissy closer, and felt her hand light on his arm, stroking up and down in a way he knew telegraphed a growing arousal driven by what she was seeing. By them. Fisting Wrench's hair roughly, he pulled the man's head backwards, breaking their kiss and saw hooded eyes dark with lust, pupils dilated.

"Crissy thinks you're hot, too," Po'Boy whispered, his lips brushing across Wrench's as he spoke. "Show her how hot you can be." He used his grip to angle Wrench's head down and arched backwards to better watch when the man wrapped his arms around Crissy, more confident since he was back in familiar territory as he crushed her against him. *It's a start*, Po'Boy thought, watching their tongues dance delicately.

***

Crissy

After Lewis had thoroughly claimed her with his hands and mouth, and then led her on weak knees across the room, she'd stood there dazed while she watched him and Ty, trying to ignore the buzzing arousal pulsing in her core. Intense and heavy, the feeling coiled and grew until she was tingling, wanton.

Seeing the two men kiss had been the single hottest thing she'd ever experienced, driving her need to a throbbing demand.

Their muscular jaws clenched and flexed as their mouths worked together. Lewis' knuckles were white with the tight grip he had in Ty's hair, and she drank in the sight of how he dominated the embrace for the first few seconds. Then it seemed as if Ty had become unleashed, pent-up desire taking over as the men kissed hard. There was nothing soft about the moment, pure masculinity in play. Lewis' fingers had gripped hers tightly, his hold nearly painful as he gave way to Ty's mastery.

Then, just that fast, the dynamic had shifted again, Ty's hair held in an unbreakable grip as Lewis brought the attention of both men back to her. Lewis handed her off to Ty without releasing his hold on her hand, and Crissy was glad he knew she needed a grounding touch. Ty kissed her hard, without finesse, teeth clashing and tongue lashing along her lips. So different from Lewis' kiss. It was like and yet unlike the one other kiss she had shared with Ty, and she got the sense he was holding back.

She leaned into Ty, feeling him take her weight, his arms around her solid and secure. His tongue delved into her mouth, tangling with her own and she moaned as the intensity of the kiss surged and swelled, then broke abruptly. Lips brushed her ear and her eyes jerked open in response, gaze meeting Ty's as Lewis' teeth nipped sharply at her skin.

"Couch, or bed?" Lewis whispered the question and at the sound of his voice, Ty's eyes closed.

Hands stroked her shoulders while Lewis' fingers slowly released her hand, his touch trailing up her arm until he encountered her breast, cupping and plumping it. Ty's mouth left hers, and he nuzzled down her throat slowly. She felt his breath against her skin when he spoke, the puffs of air rolling across sweat-damp skin causing a fresh wave of goose bumps to form. "Bed. I want y'all in my bed."

Heat surrounded her and Ty rubbed his cheek against hers, stroking like a cat. Lewis fit himself against her back, his mouth to her ear. "Can you walk, honey?" She made a confused noise, and Ty's laughing response was almost soundless. Without giving her a chance to respond, Ty shifted and cupped her butt with his hands, lifting her off the floor. Instinctively she wrapped her legs around his waist but then gasped when, behind her, Lewis pushed close enough for her to feel his rigid erection against her ass. Sandwiched between the two men, she angled her head sideways in response to a nudge from Ty, and Lewis' mouth covered hers. Ty's breath caressed her face, and his tiny kisses trailed along her jaw, nearing her and Lewis' mouths with each motion. Crissy's fingers twisted in Ty's shirt, holding tight. She let her head fall back on Lewis' shoulder, gasping again when two different sets of lips touched hers.

She angled her head slowly from side to side, allowing each man time to take over the kiss, waiting for Ty and Lewis to possess her mouth in turn. Each transition painted a clearer image in her mind of the men and how different they were from the other. Panting, Ty was the first to break the caress, and she watched as he pressed his forehead against Lewis'. "Bed." Voice shaking, the single word was all Lewis needed. He moved, and Crissy missed the heat and pressure from his hard chest. She must have made a sound because Ty's mouth was at her ear instantly, his voice low and comforting, "Shhhh. Nearly there."

Beside the bed, Ty let her slide down his body until her feet were back on the floor, and then she was swept away with the sensation of hands and fingers and lips. Undressing her down to her skin, the two men led her to the bed, stretching out beside her. They took their time, Lewis rediscovering all the places he'd enjoyed before, teaching Ty every secret until they worked in tandem, seeming to read each other's mind, bringing her to the edge again and again without letting her fall over. Breathing hard, Crissy was on her back, elbows bent, a palm flattened against each man's chest. The heat rolling off the men on either side of her brought a sheen of sweat to her body, making every connection between them slippery, giving her the feeling they were on the verge of losing control.

Ty ghosted his lips across hers again and again, the barely-there touches driving her mad with need. "Ty," she whispered, "please. More. Let me come."

Lewis' mouth was on her breast, sucking hard and drawing deep. Fingers pinched her other nipple sharply, pain flaring as he tugged the hardened nub and then stroked slowly, soothing it away with a gentle caress. A rough hand slid up the inside of her thigh and a demanding pressure pulled at the back of her knee until she acquiesced, bending her leg, draping her calf over Ty's hip. Opened to his touch, she called out on a whimper, "Lewis," hips pumping up as his palm settled on her pussy. Heat from his hand baked into her, frustratingly gentle fingers tracing either side of her opening. "Please." He stroked and played, pulling a gasp from her as he dipped a fingertip inside, painting her labia with evidence of her desire, creating a slippery surface for each teasing glide.

Lewis nuzzled her breast, sucking deep again and again before releasing her nipple with a pop. The change in pressure made her hips lunge against his hand, and he chuckled. She lost his hand on her pussy, felt the scrape of his forearm between her thighs and rocked her hips again, seeking a return of what she needed. "So fuckin' responsive. Goddamn love that. One touch and you're gone. Makes me feel like a fuckin' king."

Ty groaned, a note of surprise sounding in his deep voice and she tipped her head to look down along their bodies, seeing Lewis' hand rolling a condom down Ty's cock. The muscles in Lewis' arm tensed as he stroked and pulled, and Ty shifted down in the bed in response, his hips fitting against hers at an effortless angle. Lewis' arm moved again, and Ty rocked against her, the tip of his cock slipping through her wetness and up over her clit where the pressure made her groan, every sensation intensifying as her eyes slipped closed.

"I want you." Ty's words were quiet, but the strain in his voice was matched by the one in every muscle in his body. "Wanted you since I saw you, baby. Fucking gorgeous." She glided her hand up and down his arm, over his shoulder, and behind his neck, blindly pulling him down for a deep, wet kiss, breaking apart only to hear him gasp her name again.

"Oh, yeah. I'm gonna watch you, Ty," Lewis gritted out the words, and Crissy opened her eyes to see him staring down to where his hand still cupped and stroked Ty's cock. "Gonna watch you fuck her. Our Crissy. She's gonna take every fuckin' inch, man. Aren't you, Crissy?"

"Yes," she panted against Ty's lips, pleading again, "Please."

Ty shifted, slowly pressing into her on a smooth glide, filling her. Welcome pain blazed through her while she took him in. He kissed her hard as he seated himself deep, tongue stroking along hers. He pulled his cock out until only the head stayed inside her, plunging forward hard, jolting her body against Lewis' as he filled her. Again, he drew back slowly before pumping deep and fast, his thick cock stretching her with a delicious burn. His mouth hovered over hers, his harsh breaths sharing space with her quick pants. Her scalp stung as a hand fisted in her hair and she turned her head when it tugged, Lewis possessing her mouth as powerfully as Ty was possessing her body. Heat touched her belly, prodding insistently and she reached down, encountering Lewis' cock, cupping it in her palm. He was leaking, the head streaked with fluid and she slicked her fingers through it, stroking his length.

He groaned into her mouth, back arching and bowing as he took over and fucked her fist when she lost the rhythm. Ty had wrapped an arm around her hips, pulling her down hard while he pistoned into her, slapping sounds of each collision of their bodies echoing around the room. It was on her in an instant, the build from before crashing around her, and every muscle in her body stiffened, pleasure rolling through her. She was aware when Ty came with a breathless shout, burying his face against her neck while his cock deep inside her jerked and pulsed as he filled the condom, drawing a final shudder from her.

Lewis' hand covered hers on his cock, and he gripped tight, pressing hard against her fingers. "Make me come, Crissy." She slipped two fingers up to where their mouths were joined, coating them with saliva. He lifted his leg, propping his heel against the mattress to give her access. Eyes open and locked with his, she watched his pupils dilate when she circled his hole. His eyelids dropped closed when she dipped and pressed, then made a strangled sound into her mouth when she pushed both fingers inside. His fingers clutched hers around his cock, ass flexing as he fucked forwards and back. She changed the angle and pushed deeper, and he erupted between them, stripes of heat covering her belly and breasts, coating Ty's arm where it was still wrapped around her waist.

***

Po'Boy

Soft sounds of movement in the room woke him. Po'Boy opened his eyes a slit, frowning as he recognized the feminine form standing near the bed, twisting and struggling to pull a shirt on. "Shit," he heard Crissy whisper, the single muttered word muffled by folds of fabric wrapped around her head. Glancing over, he saw Wrench lay on his back, his arm flung wide, fingers curved around Po'Boy's wrist, the hold possessive even in his sleep.

Carefully rolling his arm free from Wrench's grip, he slipped off the bed and approached Crissy. "Hey," he whispered softly, not wanting to startle her, suppressing a chuckle when she froze in place at his voice. "Might as well not bother, honey. I'm just gonna take it back off you. Come back to bed."

They'd collapsed earlier, both men curving around the woman connecting them, and Crissy had gone to sleep with her head resting on Wrench's shoulder, her arm thrown behind her, curved over Po'Boy's waist, holding tight to him as if he were her anchor. Po'Boy glanced at the bed as he reached out to grip the hem of her shirt, seeing Wrench still sleeping peacefully. He brought his gaze back to Crissy when she started fighting his efforts to undress her. "What, honey?" She managed to pull the shirt down, head finally popping out of the top, hair a mussed halo around her head. Face angled to one side, she refused to meet his eyes.

Nope, not happening, he thought, knowing if she permanently backed away from what they'd done he'd never get Wrench to try again. *She's the glue*. He wrapped an arm around her waist, and cupped her chin in his hand, forcing her to look at him. *Plus, I fuckin' like her*.

It took a moment, but she shook off whatever hesitation she'd been feeling, straightening her shoulders and tilting her chin as she stared in his face. "I'm not like that." Quiet, but not a whisper, her words told him everything.

Buyer's guilt, he thought. Crissy wasn't innocent, she told him she'd lost her virginity in college and had run through a couple of boyfriends before going to Wisconsin to help her sister. He knew she'd enjoyed pushing her boundaries when with him before, but even with everything they'd done, it had been nothing like tonight. In the heat and rush of the moment, high on anticipation and desire, they'd slammed right past anything she might have predicted could happen. Then she'd woken in a strange place, sandwiched between two men she scarcely knew, and unsure of herself or her place in this bed, she'd thought to retreat to the known, probably intending to head home once she got dressed.

"No," he reassured her, stroking across her jaw with his thumb. "You're not like anything I've ever experienced, honey." A slow back-and-forth glide across her lips made her eyes brighten. He remembered, *She likes sweet*. "Did I do or say anything to make you think otherwise? Make you feel cheap? If I said anything, tell me, and I'll set things right. If I did anything, tell me so I can make it up to you. You're a lot of things,

Crissy, but if 'like that' means cheap or a whore, then 'like that' for sure isn't one of them." He slipped his hand down and cupped the back of her neck with a firm grip, holding steady. She quivered in his hands, not shivering like she was cold, but vibrating like a just-tapped tuning fork. He glanced down and saw twin peaks in her shirt, a deep rose shadowing behind the light-colored fabric covering her breasts. *Turned on.* Watching closely, he tightened his arm around her waist and saw her eyes widen. *Aww, yeah.* "I want you to stay, honey. I want to sleep next to you and know you've got a good thing on the other side, too. I want to know Ty has a sweet lover curled up next to him. I want you to want this, but it's on you."

He leaned closer. "Not to make light of your nerves, but if you're just freaking out, let me settle you. Let me love on you a little bit and remind you how good it can be. If you can't sleep for another reason—" He chuckled again. "—then let me tire you out so you can sleep, baby. I can't change how you feel, but I want you to know this wasn't something spur of the moment. I'd thought about you and me *and* him since I walked you to your car. Ty and I were working, but I couldn't stop myself from talking about you. Tell ya a secret, though, you need to know you weren't the only first timer tonight—" He tipped his head towards the bed. "—and if anyone's going to leave to prevent a freakout, it should probably be me. That means if you bail and head home, I'll be on the couch, for sure."

Squeezing the back of her neck lightly, he pulled her up to meet his mouth, stroking between her lips with his tongue. Crissy leaned against him, her arms lifting to wrap around his neck as she kissed him back, soft lips lingering on his. "Beautiful," he whispered, dusting kisses up her jaw, pleading with both actions and words. "Stay."

She snorted a soft laugh, resting her cheek against his chest. This was her trusting him, and knowing he held that trust caused a bloom of warmth inside his chest. Her words were murmured, but clear, "Well, I wouldn't wanna be the reason you get a crick in your neck. I'll stay."

Settling her between them on the mattress, he rolled to press his chest against her back, one arm wedged underneath his head. She shifted and nestled hers against Wrench's shoulder, then reached back and gripped Po'Boy's hand, pulling it up between her breasts. It took a while, but before long, she was back asleep, her breathing evening out as her body relaxed.

Wrench surprised him when he spoke, his voice slow and drawling, thick with sleep. Po'Boy tensed involuntarily until the meaning of the words sunk in. "Wouldn't have made you leave." Movement, and then he felt Wrench's hand at his hip. Calloused fingers slowly stroked up and down his flank, finally gripping his ass firmly and tugging until Po'Boy angled deeper over Crissy's back, rolling towards Wrench's side of the bed to give him better access for the continued caress. "My bed, my rules. You sleep here." Wrench's voice rumbled low and deep when he finished, "But, thanks for getting her to stay, Lewis."

"My pleasure, Ty."

Chapter Twelve
Wrench

"Sure, come on over. I'm home." Penny's voice was bright and cheery, and she sounded like just the medicine he needed to take his mind away from the events of the past week. Studiously not looking at the still rumpled bed, he dressed with efficient movements and walked out, locking the door automatically behind him and slinging a leg over his bike. A moment later he was on his way out of the complex and headed on the highway towards Mandeville.

Rolling carefully down Twisted's gravel driveway, Wrench took stock of the vehicles he could see, recognizing most of them, including Penny's semi. A pickup truck with Alabama license plates caught his eye, and he grinned. Few doubts about who that would be and he killed his engine, heeling down his kickstand as he took off his helmet. Sure enough, the grassy twang he'd expected to hear rolled out of the open windows. "Damn, boy, you lookin' distinctly unfancy these days." Squinting against the glare, he strained to look through the glass, making out the silhouette of a man with long hair, striding towards the back door.

"Retro," he called, swinging off the bike and approaching the house with a hand already outstretched. Fingers wrapped around the other man's thumb, he allowed himself to be hauled into a close clinch, the reassuring drumming of a closed fist pounding against his shoulder. "How the hell are you? When did you get here?"

Leaning back, Retro looked him up and down. "I'll repeat myself, damn, boy." He shook his head. "You look like shit."

"Gee thanks." Wrench released his grip, letting go of Retro's hand and looked around the man to see Penny standing in the doorway, hand on her hip and a fond smile on her face. "Hey, Penny girl. You didn't say you already had company. Want me to skedaddle?"

Shaking her head, with quick strides she crossed the distance to where he stood and pulled him into a tight hug. "Not a chance, Ty. We're all going to sit a meal." Stepping away, she gripped his hand and tugged, dragging him towards the house. "Come on inside."

Scrubbing across his face with his palm, he noted the rough scruff of his beard and suspected Retro had the right of it with his comment. He hadn't bothered to look in a mirror this morning before leaving the condo. In fact, he might not have looked in a mirror since he and Po'Boy were in West Texas. And he'd mostly used that one to watch Po'Boy. With a sigh, he followed Penny, putting aside the topic he'd intended to discuss. *Maybe this is a sign I should keep my mouth shut*, he thought. It sure wasn't anything he would be willing to talk about where Retro could hear.

Penny was already in front of the range by the time he got inside, and Wrench walked past with a quick slap of her ass on his way to the refrigerator to get a beer. The sizzle of bacon competed with the sound of her squeal, and she danced aside while laughing. Retro chuckled and then asked, "How was Kentucky?"

"Kentucky was there, man." *Jesus.* Club meant club, and Retro knew that. Surely the man didn't expect to get more out of him. "You know how it is." Maybe he didn't. Maybe the reason for Wrench being in

Kentucky wasn't known outside of the CoBos. *Give him an inch.* "Club. Just another run."

"And then you went to El Paso." *And he takes a mile.* "How was that?"

Turning with three beers in his hands, he shook his head at the older man. "Retro," he let the edge of a little scold slide into his tone, "don't go there. It's club, man." Handing one bottle off to Retro who was now grinning broadly, Wrench stepped to Penny, setting hers to one side of the stove. "What's for breakfast?"

"Everythin' me could find in the fridge. Got me a dab of dis, a little of dat, scobit o' sumthin else." She laughed up at him as she spoke, and Penny's intentionally thickened Cajon patois made him smile. "We gonna have ourselves a *fais-dodo*, man."

"Aw, hell naw. I'm not gonna dance this early in the morning." Wrench twisted and leaned against the countertop, looking across to where Retro had hiked himself up to sit on the counter opposite. "Not a dancin' man."

"We used to dance," Penny disagreed. "And you liked it." She pointed to the open cabinet behind him. "Get some plates out, wouldja?"

"How many we need?" He set his bottle down and grabbed four, anticipating their little party would be joined by Twisted, surprised when she said, "Three" instead. He put one plate back and handed her the stack. "Hell of a lotta food for three, darlin'."

Penny shrugged and looked over her shoulder at him, grinning as she answered what she'd do with the leftovers with one word, "Jambalaya." That grin, the position—faster than a thought he was back in bed with Lewis and Crissy this morning.

He'd woken to the mattress moving gently and had known from hearing the soft sounds what was happening on the bed beside him.

Rolling to his side, Ty opened his eyes to see Crissy kneeling over Lewis, her body rhythmically rising and falling as she rode his cock. Eyes closed, she had gathered the long ends of her hair on top of her head with one hand, strands of it draping around her face, swaying with each motion. Her other hand cupped a breast, fingers alternately twisting and stroking the stiffening nipple.

Lewis' had a hand on her thigh up near the crease where it joined her body, his thumb buried between her legs, the rolling movement of his wrist illustrating what he was doing. His other hand was high on her ribs; that thumb gliding in a smooth motion across the underside of her breast, back and forth.

Lewis' mouth was open, and Ty heard the same soft flow of praise and profanities as from last night falling from his lips.

"Fucking beautiful, honey. Lawd, you're hot." Lewis sucked in a breath and groaned. "Ridin' my dick like you was born to it. Made for me. Fit me like a glove, baby." He groaned again, and Ty watched as his chin rose, head pressing backwards into the pillow in response to the sensations he was experiencing. "Fucking perfect fit, being inside you like this. Hot and sleek, you got the finest pussy I've ever fucked."

His hand moved to cover her breast, gripping tight, fingers pressing deep into her flesh. "Your tits are so gorgeous. Look at you, perfection. Ride me, baby. Take what you need." Another deep groan, more a rumbling than vocalization. "Goddammit, my cock loves bein' inside you. Found my happy place right there."

Each sentence, each phrase was punctuated by an upwards thrust of his hips, the jolt and jar setting Crissy's breasts swaying even more, the gasping sound of her pleasure musical. The muscles in Lewis' legs flexed and tightened, keeping perfect time with Crissy. Their coupling so exquisite, Ty couldn't stand it, had to be involved in some way, even just as a voyeur. He reached down and gripped his cock, stroking root to tip and back again, and again, remembering how tight Crissy had been last night. His breathing came faster, grew irregular, and then changed again to a stuttering pant when Lewis rolled his head to stare at him, the man's softly spoken commentary never faltering.

"Fucking gorgeous. Look at you. Hard as a fucking rock. Like what you see, man? Me, too. I like what I see, mmhmm." Lewis slipped his hand down Crissy's side, resting on her hip and Ty could see how reddened her nipple was, puckered and tight from Lewis' attention.

"So fuckin' long and hard, and that's perfection, too. God, look at you. You're leaking like a sieve, use that to slick yourself up, Ty. Fuck your fist while you watch me fuck our Crissy." Ty did as ordered, shifting his hips to slide his dick faster through his firm hold on the shaft. Crissy gasped and moved, leaning forwards slightly, both palms resting on Lewis' chest as he groaned and wrapped an arm around her shoulders, holding her in place. Ty tore his eyes away from the movement of her breasts and up, seeing her gaze locked on his hand. He gripped tighter, moving it slowly and steadily over his cock. Ty shivered at the hungry expression on her face, shivered again when she licked her bottom lip and then caught it between her teeth, her gaze never leaving his cock.

"Feel your clit gettin' hard, Crissy. You like what you see, don't you, honey. Me, too. I like everything I see in front of me. Fuck yeah, like it hard, like it wet, like it thick, like it tight. Get it, baby. Get it for yourself. Got you under my thumb, baby. Working for it, you're so fuckin' beautiful. Come for me, darlin'. Come for me while you're watching our Ty. He wants you, baby. Loved being inside you last night, wants you again. What's that say about how desirable you are? Got two hard cocks up for anything first thing in the morning, just from how gorgeous you are takin' your pleasure. Fuck me with that sleek pussy. Hard as you want. Aw, yeah, you're gonna come for me, aren't you? Crissy, come for me, honey. Fuck my cock, baby."

She gasped, and Ty watched her eyes become unfocused as she panted, "Lewis. Please."

Lewis shifted his grip to her hips, and Ty saw the muscles in his arms flex as he raised her high, thrusting up into her hard and fast. "Fuck," he grunted. Through gritted teeth, Lewis coaxed her, "Come for me, darlin'. Come on, come. Come all over my cock." She cried out again and stretched an arm towards Ty, waving her hand until he grasped it, then she clamped her fingers down on his, holding tightly. He could feel Lewis' movements by extension, through her, feel how powerfully she was being slammed by his cock. Ty lifted the hand that had been stroking his dick to her mouth, groaning when she let go her hold on his hand to grab his wrist. Sucking hard, she pulled his wet fingers into her mouth, drawing fiercely and rolling her tongue across them before she shook her head, strands of hair clinging to her sweat-dampened cheeks.

"Ty," Crissy breathed, gaze locked with his. "I'm gonna—" Her eyes squeezed shut as her head dropped forwards, and she buried her face in Lewis' neck with a vibrating moan.

"Fuck yeah, come all over me, baby." Lewis' face was red, cords standing out in his neck as he powered up into her, holding her full weight suspended by her hips while she came. "Fuck," he gasped, "need. Jesus." Lewis pulled her tight to his crotch, tugging and shoving her back and forth, grinding up into her from his prone position. "Fuck." With a surge of movement, Lewis was on his knees, Ty's hands falling away as Crissy's legs wrapped around his waist, and then Lewis slammed her onto her back on the mattress, his ass clenching as he drove into her.

Ty grabbed his cock again, using tight, short strokes over the head, fingers bumping past the swollen rim, each movement sending little short-circuited shocks through him. He climbed to his knees, moving towards the head of the bed, away from where Lewis had Crissy pinned beneath him. The sounds of fucking filled the room, musk, and sweat riding the motionless air until he was breathing in the two of them. The idea they were now part of him was thrilling, and his palm collected the steady stream of fluid rolling from the head of his dick, stroking hard and fast.

Then Lewis moved, shifting with a groan, gathering his legs under him so he was powering down into Crissy. No longer fucking missionary style, but on his knees with his weight coming to bear, her hips canted up to catch him. Each time Lewis slammed into her, Ty felt his asshole clench, and that involuntary movement caused more stuttering shocks to ripple through him, his balls drawing up tight to his body.

Then Lewis moved again, and Ty saw his hole framed by his ass cheeks. It was there and then gone, and then there again, the glimpses of it somehow as erotic as the vision of the thickly veined cock disappearing into Crissy's pussy. Then—and this was what caused Ty to come, ejaculating so forcefully stripes of white decorated Lewis' ass and back, dripping onto Crissy's legs—Lewis looked over his shoulder at Ty with a grin and winked. That fucking wink told Ty he knew exactly where Ty's focus had been, and the exposure of that part of Lewis' anatomy hadn't been a mistake, hadn't been on accident, but had been fucking purposeful. Knowing Lewis wanted him to look at his hole, wanted him to look at it and want it so fucking bad, that had been what drove Ty to the best orgasm he'd ever had.

"Earth to Ty," Penny said, still smiling at him over her shoulder. "Penny for your thoughts?"

He shook his head, instinctively glancing down to see a telling bulge in his crotch. *Shit.* "No thoughts, Penny. Just hungry. You ever gonna get done cooking?"

After the meal, Retro said his goodbyes and Wrench stood beside Penny on the front porch as she waved him down the driveway. Without turning around, she asked, "You gonna tell me what's eating you up inside?"

"What?" The one-word question came out harsher than he intended, and he coughed, clearing his throat. Still on the defensive, he ignored her sidelong look and asked, "What do you mean?"

"I mean you've been nervous as a rabbit on opening day." She walked to the porch swing and sat, holding the swing still with her feet wedged against the boards of the porch. "Sit down and talk to me. You know I know what I'm talking about, so don't even try to deny it. Something's wrong, and I get to help you sort it out." She patted the seat next to her. "Come on, sit." He heard an echo of Lewis' voice, "*Come on, come*," and shivered.

"Jesus, you're pushy," he grumbled as he settled onto the seat next to her. His legs were longer than hers, and he started pushing, causing the swing to move in a slow arc. "What'd Retro want, anyway?" The man's visit had seemed random, and the conversation during breakfast was all surface talk, nothing deep or necessary. "He come visiting from 'Bama often?"

"He's looking to foster his daughter out for the summer." He must have made a surprised sound because she laughed softly. "She just turned 15 and thinks the sun rises and sets on a prospect in the Bastards. He's just looking to broaden her horizons. I know Nelda, watched her grow up, and Twisted and I have plenty of room. It'll be fun, like having a little sister for a while."

"Having a houseguest is gonna make life interesting." Wrench stretched, laying his arm across the back of the swing, curling his fingers around her shoulder. "She coming soon as school's out?" Penny nodded, leaning her head on his shoulder. He bent his neck to press a kiss to the top of her head, surprised for a moment he didn't smell coconut, and then realized that was the kind of shampoo Crissy used. Clearing his throat, he straightened his legs, pushing them a little faster. "You ready?"

Without hesitation, she answered, "Lay it on me."

Shit, I'm not sure I'm ready.

When he didn't respond, she urged him, "Give it to me, Ty. Let me help."

"I don't...it's hard to decide where to start." Fingers dug into his side and he squirmed away, the swing jarring to a stop as he complained, "Stop it. It's not easy to put the words together, that's all." She relaxed against him, and he slowly started the swinging motion again. "I don't do unconventional, you know? Everything Daddy and Ace wanted from me, I've done. Straight and narrow. Even things I wanted, if they warned me off, I didn't go there."

Her hand landed on his knee, and she squeezed, letting him know she understood without him spelling it out he was talking about her. He'd loved her since they were kids. He'd been even younger than Nelda, and yet Ty had known what he felt for Penny was real. Her uncle, Bagger, had waved him off more than once, in addition to his father's words of warning. Every time it looked like Ty might be getting close to her in a way that wasn't brotherly, they'd all called him on it. Finally giving in at about age seventeen, Ty had launched himself into the brother role, forcing every emotion down a black hole, living for the moments when they could be together. Taking what he could get.

"It's been a long time since I felt like this. Maybe..." He glanced at her, hoping he wouldn't hurt her with his words. "Maybe it's the first time I've had feelings like *this* for someone. But..." He trailed off and sat quietly for a moment, wondering how to explain. "You know how you meet someone and you either like 'em, or you don't? There can only be any kind of middle ground after you get to know them a bit. And sometimes, after getting to know them, you'll change places and make it all the way to the other side of the line. Like you move from the don't like to the like side of things. I..." He shook his head. "If I were to be in a relationship, I'm so fucking clueless. Penny, how do you even make it work?"

Wrench's phone chimed, and he leaned back to pull it out of his pocket, expecting it to be a summons from Ace. Instead, he saw a selfie from Po'Boy, mugging for the camera, a photo filter giving him google eyes and circling his head with cartoon birds and hearts. The caption asked, "Missing me yet?" Rolling his eyes, he shoved the phone back into his pocket, realizing too late he should have angled it away. Penny was still, and her very stillness was concerning. *Fuck.* Glancing down, he could only see part of her face, but from this position, it almost looked like she was smiling. Lifting his chin, he squeezed his eyes closed tightly. *Anything I say at this point will be defensive, and a lie.* Choosing silence, he pushed against the floor, moving the swing back and forth.

"Are you happy?" Of all the things she could have asked, Wrench wouldn't have put money down on that one.

This was something he could answer, so he did. "I, uh. Yeah, I think so."

Penny's hand squeezed his knee again, tight. "Good. You deserve happy, Ty." Her voice was thick when she said, "You've always deserved happy." They sat in silence for a moment, the motion of the swing soothing. "So how long have you known you were gay?"

Wrench couldn't have stopped his reaction if he'd wanted to. Instinctive and raw, he flinched and felt a hot flush climbing his neck, coloring his cheeks as he barked, "I'm not fucking gay." *Fuck.*

"But I thought..." Now Penny's voice was the one to trail off, and Wrench wasn't sure how to answer the confusion in her voice when she asked, "Wasn't that Po'Boy's picture on your phone?"

"Well, yeah." *Fucking asshole.* As if on cue, his phone chimed again, and then again, and Wrench gritted his teeth, ignoring it for now. "But I'm not, you know. I've slept with plenty of women." He had, too. When he'd been ordered to stay away from Penny, he'd tried hard to fuck her out of his thoughts and memories. Over the years he'd had dozens of one-night stands. *Dozens. Fuck, I'm a man whore.* "I just never found anyone."

"Until now." She supplied this rationale as if it were logical. "So it's not because he's a man?"

"No, I've never..." He sucked in a breath. "I think it's just...him. It's Lewis. But I'm definitely not...you know. Because we've got Crissy, too."

"Who's Crissy?" Penny cut her gaze up at his face, eyes wide in surprise. "You've got a girlfriend, too?"

"Well, we do. Kinda. I think." His muscles twitched with the need to move, to get up and be gone from there. *This wasn't the talk I wanted to have.* With a sigh, he tried to regain control over the conversation. "She lives next door to me. Cute and sweet. You'll like her."

"I get to meet her? This not-girlfriend who is sleeping with...what, one at a time, or do y'all just puppy pile in the bed at night?" Now she was definitely grinning, and he frowned at her, trying to understand how she could be so comfortable with the idea of something he couldn't even clearly articulate. "I'm just messin' with you. But I'm curious, too. So, are you bi?"

"Fuck, Penny." Wrench stood, his rushed movements leaving the swing bouncing side to side behind him. "Why you need a label for everything? I just...I don't know what I'm doing, okay? I've never had anything I wanted to keep before. You have—" He spread his hands wide. "—everything you want. Right here. You have what you always needed. I thought I could come here and...shit. I don't know what I thought, okay? Just never mind. You're my best friend, and I—" He stuttered to a stop. "I don't know what I'm doing."

"How long?"

"How long what?" He couldn't bring himself to turn and look at her, not wanting to see that fucking amusement in her eyes.

"How long have you been seeing Po'Boy?"

Swallowing hard, Wrench considered her question, shocked at the answer because the shift in his life seemed to have happened decades ago. "Uh, I guess, maybe a couple of days?" He shook his head. "But it's not like that. It's not like that's all there is. Really, if I had to put a date on it—" His phone buzzed again, cutting him off. He yanked it out of his pocket to see two texts from Po'Boy and the expected summons from Ace.

"Twisted's birthday?" His head jerked around, and he stared at her. She grinned. "What? I notice things." Her words caused terror to twist in his gut, because while he trusted Penny not to say anything, if anyone else had noticed, it could be— "Stop, Ty. It wasn't obvious. And this is just me here. You're only talking to *me* right now. And, I'd never, ever do anything to hurt you." Clearly frustrated, she repeated herself, tone sharp, "*Stop it.*" Pulling in a deep breath, she patted the swing beside her again, and with a sigh, he settled back down. She leaned over, putting her head on his shoulder and with that single gesture, Penny told him nothing would ever change for them. Then, in a soft voice, she said, "If you can't talk to me about Po'Boy, then tell me about Crissy."

Wrench huffed out a laugh. "I gotta go, doll. IMC and CoBos have a meeting in thirty minutes."

"Well, it's ten minutes to the clubhouse from here. So—" Penny squeezed his knee. "—you have at least fifteen to tell me everything."

***

Po'Boy

"Not gonna put up with his brand of bullshit today." Po'Boy was muttering to himself as he dialed, waiting on the ringing call to connect. "Man always tries to make me believe he's got some fuckin' ace up his goddamned sleeve. I'll rip the fuckin' sleeve right the fuck off and shit down his shirt." When the phone continued to ring, he tipped his head back, squinting at the darkening sky. "*Fuck.*"

The call connected finally, and he heard Retro's voice mail message, the man's tone of voice self-satisfied and amused, "Ain't callin' you back. Ain't listenin' to nothing, either. Try me 'til you find me."

"Jesus," Po'Boy muttered, thumb slashing across the icon to terminate the call. He was staring at the phone trying to decide what to do next when it rang in his hand. A glance at the name showing made him grunt, and he answered with an angry, "Fuckin' liar. Said you didn't call people back."

"For you, I'll always make an exception," Retro said. "What's up, man?"

"Why you always think something's up when I call you? That your standard response to everybody? 'What's up' like you're ready for anything. I don't get you, Retro. I don't get you at all." Po'Boy glared without seeing the scene in front of him, ignoring the background hum of activity as cars pulled up to the gas pumps and people went in and out of the store. He was at the edge of a tiny convenience store's parking lot, sitting at a highway junction just south of Ponchatoula, waiting on a connection who didn't seem to be showing up today. The heat, the people, the frustration at a missed opportunity all conspired to put Po'Boy in a foul mood. "I don't even know why I call you, man. You fuckin' piss me off like nobody's business. Fuck you." He jabbed at the screen, disconnecting the call, then stared at the phone again, running through his options.

His lip lifted and he snarled at the phone when it rang again, Retro's name back on the screen. "What?" His question was loud enough to pull a half dozen heads his direction, his anger ringing through the air.

"Po'Boy," Retro's voice was patient and calm, "tell me what you need."

"I don't know what I fuckin' need. If I knew what I needed, I wouldn't be calling you, that's for damn sure." His hand slipped across his cheeks and chin, the skin sweat-slick and bristling with a rough three days' worth of beard. "Did Twisted or Ace talk to you?" Po'Boy knew he couldn't ask straight out because the 'Bama Bastards were friendly, but they were not aligned with any club. No support patch on their vests, which meant help at the level he needed would have to be called in by leadership. *Forget the fact I wear an officer patch*, he thought, *I ain't the shot caller for any-fuckin-thing and glad of it*. "Anybody call you 'cept me?"

"Yes." Po'Boy waited silently, because a straight affirmative response wasn't enough. He needed names, and Retro supplied. "I got one call, both men. The two clubs are in agreement on what needs to be done, Po'Boy. I have an all-clear to provide whatever you need, man. Tell me. Gimme somethin' to work from. I need a point of entry."

At those words Po'Boy pulled in a deep breath, blowing it back out as a steady stream of air. "Thank fuck. Okay, you got what happened in Texas, yeah? Best begin there, if you haven't." Retro's grunt was enough response. "So you know who we fuckin' saw there, and it was definitely a planned encounter. Fuckin' slap in the face. Assholes. Deuces though, I can't get it out of my head that he wants this too hard. Wants it too much. So we've got him lording over IMC and CoBos how he's got the El Paso club in his pocket. I think it's a lie. I can't...ain't no way people would follow that douchebag. And I'm not talking about the way the VWMC followed Leswayne, that was mostly culture and loyalty to a known entity. A founder. The Silent Deaths, man, they got no loyalty to him. Something that's been bothering me is the level of fear we got off the men there. Every breath was like walking on eggshells. I think whoever or whatever is behind the reboot of VWMC is what ties that same bullshit club to the El Paso one. I can't find a toehold though, brother. Can't find where things cross. I know they do. I just can't see it. You get me?" He finally ran out of air, slamming his lips closed, shutting off his words abruptly.

Retro's question was quiet but intense. "Do you know who Deuces is?"

"Like, his lineage? His blood? No, should I?" Po'Boy's tone gave away his confusion.

"Yeah, it's key, brother. Fiddler had a sister." Fiddler had been president of the Guanyan's Shield MC, the CoBos' rivals for years until he and his son incurred the wrath of Twisted, pulling the IMC into the fight. Gollum, his son, had made an arrangement with Penny which had cost her dearly. Just thinking about all the things he'd heard pissed Po'Boy off even more. He knew Retro had stood behind Twisted's takedown of the Shield. Po'Boy had been on the field the day it happened and seen Retro and his men appear through the woods like vengeful wraiths. "That sister had a boy."

"No shit? You sayin' Deuces was cousins with that fuckwit Gollum? Jesus fuck me now, please. That's bullshit, man. Deuces is Fiddler's nephew? Jesus fuck." His snarl returned, and it felt as if his teeth could break and splinter in his head from how hard his jaws ground together. "Where does the fucking cartel come in, man? I don't get that at all."

"Me, either. At least, not yet. I've got rumblings of things, but my net's shockingly empty where it comes to the connection. I'm working everything I have, man. I'll feed you what I get." Retro paused, then his voice returned but sounded different. Quiet, guarded. "My auth only extends to you, Po'Boy. This is do-not-share territory." He paused again, then said, "That's my authorization, man. Who you share with is your business or club business, however you look at it. That means I can't tell someone who needs to know, even if I know they need to know."

"Fuckin' talkin' in riddles, man. What the fuck do you mean?" Po'Boy shook his head, eyeballing two men in plain, white T-shirts who had climbed out the side door of a van parked in front of the building. The front of their shirts had been tucked into the waistband of their black cargo pants, but the backs billowed free, covering everything down to their ass. Without waiting for the door on the vehicle to close, the driver reversed out of the space, maneuvering around the side lot to the back. "Fuck, I got shit going down here." Shouting from inside the store confirmed his instincts. "Gonna have to go. If I'm not avail for a convo, what other means you got to get me what you find?" The sound of gunshots inside the building caused his back to straighten, and he whipped his head sideways to see people pouring out of the front doors.

A young woman in a pink shirt—short and blonde, probably cute— came running through the shattered doors, but lost her footing just as another shot rang out. She was carrying something, and he watched while she managed a slow-motion twist as she was falling to protect what he now saw was a child. A toddler who clung to her neck with wiry strength. The woman finished her tumble, an act that seemed to take minutes and not the fraction of a second he knew actually passed. Then she lay in the gravel and dirt, still as death, head angled to one side, arms slowly slipping away from their cradling hold on the child.

Retro's voice buzzed and hummed in his ear, shouting questions and demands but Po'Boy couldn't focus on him. "Get up." His throat hurt. "Get the fuck up. Get the *fuck* up."

For a moment he was that child, but older, almost a teen. Not carried out of a conflict, but abandoned in the middle of a firefight. Huddled beside his mother's body in a pharmacy, listening to the screams all around him, staring as her eyes looked at nothing. Even in death, they angled up and away from him as if he were disgusting. The blonde lay still, color leaching from her face and onto the fabric of her clothing. His repeated words were hoarse, scarcely audible over the revving engines of those escaping the scene. "Get the fuck up." Two men stooped beside the woman, and when they stood, she lay there alone. A moment later the van roared past Po'Boy, a glancing view of the scuffed soles of a man's shoes the only thing visible as the door was pulled closed.

He wasn't aware of shoving the phone in his pocket, didn't see the people he threaded his bike around and between, only noting a few faces of the brave ones, the ones who ran towards the noise and chaos and not away. Then he was on the highway and in third gear, eyes locked on the back end of the van already a half a mile up the road. Fourth and fifth, jamming his foot up to catch the next gear, hands working in thought-free harmony, the back doors of the van growing larger and larger until he was directly behind the vehicle. He swooped towards the line, angling for a view of coming traffic, knowing the road ran straight for several miles. Seeing a semi in the distance, he fell back behind the van, waiting.

Before the truck drove past in the other lane, the van's brake lights came on. It slowed, then turned right onto a small country road. Po'Boy grinned, thinking, *Perfect*. Reaching to the small of his back, he pulled his pistol out, letting his arm drop until the gun rested on one thigh, keeping his grip loose but steady. His thumb twirled the throttle set, aiming for just slower than he was running right now. Then he shifted the gun to his right hand, left on the handlebars keeping the bike straight, waiting to lift the gun until he angled out into oncoming to see nothing. *Perfect*. He leaned a little further left, and then lined things up, taking out the front tire on the driver side with a single shot. Still rolling at speed, the van weaved, the driver fighting for control. Po'Boy jammed the gun between his leg and the seat, thumb again working the throttle set on the bike, letting his speed slowly bleed off. Waiting. Half a mile, no more, before the van pulled to a stop, the shredded tire gone, bare rim grinding on the chip seal surface of the road, digging furrows, gouging deep. Po'Boy put the bike in neutral and stopped before the van did, letting it gain a few dozen yards on his position.

He was ready when the men appeared, gun in hand, each of his shots hitting the intended mark, the entire encounter over in moments. "Fuckin' liked this gun," he muttered, ejecting the magazine and shoving it in his pocket. Kickstand down, he dismounted the bike, stalking towards the inoperable van where even over the ringing in his ears he could hear the child screaming. Po'Boy wiped his gun clean with the inside of his shirt before swapping it for a similar make one of the men had in hand, taking that magazine with him, too.

He approached the van and peered in through the open side door. The child was a little girl, blonde and desperately cute, if you overlooked the blood coating the front of her outfit where she'd been pressed up against her mother.

"Hey now," he crooned, lifting her into his arms, bouncing her gently. "Hey now, little one. It's okay."

I'm a fucking liar.

"It's gonna be okay." Her screams trailed off into hiccups as she stared up into his face.

It'll never be okay again.

"Hey now, I got you." Blinking at him, her eyes framed by impossibly long eyelashes clumped with tears.

Please, God, let her have a decent family.

"You're gonna be all right." She pulled in a deep breath, her tiny body shuddering in the aftermath of her screaming terror.

Please, God, let her be all right.

He turned to walk back to his bike, still bouncing the shuddering toddler against his chest, leaving the unmoving men sprawled in the glaring sun, van doors wide open to the elements. "Those bad men won't hurt you." Straddling the bike, he reached behind him and opened a bag one-handed, pulling out a long sleeve shirt. Tying it like a makeshift sling, he anchored the compliant child to his body. She was so small he could fasten his vest over the top of her, cocooning her safely. "I got you, darlin'." She rested her cheek against his chest, every breath coming easier.

"Retro," he said as soon as the call connected. "Need a safe place in Tangipahoa Parish to drop a kid." Silence greeted his statement, and Po'Boy rolled his eyes. "Fuck, man. I got a kid here and need somewhere to drop her. You got a place to gimme or not?"

"How did we go from that—" Retro paused, clearly having problems putting words to his thoughts for once. "—to this?" Po'Boy sighed, hoping it was audible. "Tangipahoa. Okay. Gimme a minute."

Po'Boy stared at the bodies, seeing a cloud of flies already starting to gather. *Nature is efficient, even if people are assholes.* "Anytime here, man. Gonna say it's kinda urgent. Dude, I'm sittin' on the side of the road. Not even callin' a service for this one. Fuckers can rot."

"You got something else you need me to finesse, brother?" Retro cleared his throat. "You cut me off in the middle of what sounded like an interesting situation. I looked it up, so I got you. And I get what you've got. That package? I get it. Can you get to Ponchatoula?" Po'Boy grunted, tipping his chin down as the child squirmed against him, seeing those wide, blue eyes staring up at him. "Okay, go there and stop at the car wash on the south side of town. Trevarborn's is the name on the sign. I'll have someone waiting." He grunted again, and Retro continued. "Are you okay, brother?"

"As okay as I've ever been, man. Trevarborn car wash. Copy. I'll be there in probably twenty. You got me covered?"

"I got you. Already rolling the pickup. Where are they going?" Retro's voice was low and steady, calming in a way Po'Boy knew was intentional.

"Fuck, I don't know. Hospital?" Po'Boy shook his head. "Morgue? No fuckin' idea. Just know I can't roll like this for long."

"I'll sort it out, brother. You get there, you hear me?" Retro sounded so certain, so convinced he would have Po'Boy covered, it never occurred to him to doubt the man.

"I hear you." Phone back in his pocket, he started the bike and then swung in a tight turn, heading back the way he had come. Thirty minutes later he stood beside his bike, blood-caked clothing sticking to his torso, watching as a pretty brunette buckled the sleeping child into a car seat in the back of a small sedan.

"She's not hurt, right?"

He'd already asked the same question three times and hated the warm sympathy he saw in the woman's eyes when she looked at him and answered for the third time. "She's fine, physically." The woman, whose name he'd never know, said, "Don't worry. I'll get her to her family. The news is blowing up over this. Sounds like her father's a good man. He's going to be sure she gets everything she needs." The brunette smiled at him, the edges of her mouth soft with an emotion he didn't understand. "You saved the day, but no one will ever know. That's the measure of a true hero, isn't it?"

Po'Boy snorted. "Not hardly. Just saw something needed fixing. Kids don't deserve most of what happens to them. I'm glad her daddy's decent. It'll go a long way." Stripping off his cut, he removed the shirt and crude sling and passed the bloody garments to her, slipping the vest back onto his shoulders. She stuffed them into a grocery store bag, tying the top and placing it behind her seat. He didn't wait for her to pull away, just climbed back on his bike and kicked it into gear. He did keep watch in his mirrors, seeing when the sedan finally left the carwash headed the other way, deeper into downtown. Safe. *Coulda used a daddy.*

Picking up speed, he rode past the convenience store, seeing official cars parked at every angle in the parking lot. *Instead, I got Grover.*

Grover had been his stepfather, and after his mother's death had become the monster a twelve-year-old Ralphie feared more than death. Shoving thoughts of those years from his mind, he focused on the road in front of him, running through the things Retro had told him before everything went sideways.

***

Wrench

"Y'all good?" Wrench narrowed his eyes, casting his gaze around the large room. The pole barn at the back of Ace's place outside Baton Rouge had stood as the CoBos clubhouse for decades. For prospects and members who happened to be between living quarters, there were bunk beds lining the walls of the open upstairs loft, stretching half the length of the building. The space was equipped with a full kitchen inside for the winter, as well as a standard southern summer kitchen on the screened-in porch along the back. With a full bath both upstairs and down among the amenities the building boasted, it served the club well.

Ace had deeded the building and two acres surrounding it to the club a few years ago, shortly after Bagger was murdered. He'd told the officers he didn't want any confusion about what he wanted to be done after he was gone. Not that there were problems about the things Bagger had which were club. No, Penny's aunt had held her head high and handed over everything they'd needed, no matter the pain visible on her features as item by item, everything that represented the club Bagger had helped found was removed from her house, leaving conspicuous empty spaces along the walls and shelves. It hadn't taken any discussion at all for the club to let her keep her rags.

Some of the newer members hadn't understood how everything club belonged to the club, which gave Ace time to fall into teaching mode about protocol. Something he well understood and appreciated, being an adjunct professor at a private Christian college.

They were preparing for a big fish fry tonight, and Wrench had spent half the day directing the prospects on how to hook up and set the fry rings and gas tanks to minimize the danger of an accident. Some of them were backwoods bayou boys and already held such knowledge, but a troubling number of them were from the city. He didn't know why he found the fact troubling, just that the ones who had less self-reliance and survival skills seemed to be the ones most often pulling dramatic shit.

His phone had been annoying, dozens of calls and texts coming in with questions. They were to host the IMC tonight, and until a few minutes ago, only Wrench and the CoBos officers knew Retro was bringing some of his Bastards over from Alabama for the party, too. Now the announcement had been made, every member was scrambling to do those last-minute things which shouldn't be last-minute, but other shit always got in the way.

Dismal, a member recently promoted from prospect, drove a truck up the dirt track reserved for the cages, dust sifting through the air in his wake. He wheeled the vehicle in a circle and backed up to the porch door. Swinging out the door, he lifted a hand to Wrench in greeting, then pulled the handle on the tailgate, letting it fall with a bounce. Without speaking or asking for help, Dismal reached in and grabbed one of the coolers stacked in the bed of the truck, pulling it to the edge and strained, lifting it in both arms with a grunt.

Wrench's phone vibrated in his pocket, and he yanked it out as he yelled across the yard for one of the prospects. He pointed to the truck and got a chin lift in response, then glanced down at his phone. Po'Boy. A text, not a playful selfie.

Something happened yesterday, and Wrench had a glimmer of what it was, but he wasn't certain he had the full picture. He'd come home from the extended dual club meeting to find Po'Boy sitting on his back deck, ass to the boards, leaning against the outside wall of the condo. Lewis—and Ty wasn't sure how it came to be that their names reverted to government when they went into his condo, but he didn't really care, just went with it—hadn't said much, just stared at the TV screen regardless of what was on. Sat and stared until Crissy got home. They'd first heard her car, then had listened as her door opened and shut,

175

which left them glancing at each other. Ty wasn't sure what his expression had said, but Lewis' had been inscrutable.

"She coming over?" Ty hated the way his voice sounded when he asked that. He'd fought against showing need for so long about Penny, hearing it in his words now sounded wrong. Weak.

"How the fuck should I know?" Lewis' barked response didn't sound any less needy to him, and at that moment Ty knew whatever had happened to Lewis today, he'd been barely holding it together. His hold was unraveling quickly, seemingly in direct correlation with the stretching moments without the sound of Crissy at the door.

He studied Lewis. Not directly, not in a way which would challenge the man, but sidelong. Since he'd been watching Lewis for weeks and was so familiar with him, the how didn't matter. He could have been using the reflection on the curve of a chrome tailpipe and would still have seen the shaking hands, the shallow breaths. All signs of distress being brutally suppressed.

He ran every encounter through his head. Lewis had been careful not to touch him unless Crissy was within reach. Even with the first nonsexual incident in West Texas, Crissy had been the catalyst. Would Lewis push him away if she weren't part of the equation? Pulling his phone out, he texted her a brief message and placed the phone on the wooden coffee table where they'd both hear if there was a response. Ty slipped down to the cushions from the arm of the couch where he'd been perched, awkwardly wanting to be close to Lewis, but stupidly afraid of sitting too close to him. How do people do this, *he wondered.* With women it was easy. You looked, and if they looked back, you approached to do a little verbal sparring. If the sparring stirred sparks, then you followed those to see where they led. *He didn't go to Crissy's condo and wait for her, he came to mine. Sat on my back deck until I got home.* Might be a spark to follow.

Ty considered his options, eyes on the TV screen, only half listening to the commentary of the game. Lewis liked to take care of both Ty and Crissy. He liked to touch and comfort. Seemed to enjoy the tactile sensation a lot. In bed and out of it, in the privacy of the condo, his hands had stroked and glanced off Ty's arms and shoulders. That's my in. *Ty rolled his neck, shrugging with a groaning sigh. Making a fist, he flexed his arm, drawing it across his chest, stretching out his deltoid and triceps muscles. He groaned and did it again, then stretched his arm up over his head.*

"You stiff?" Lewis' voice had a ragged edge to it, a bleeding rawness which made Ty flinch.

"Yeah, man. Just a bit." Ty flexed and repeated the motions with his other arm. Even ready for it, the moment Lewis' hand skated up the bicep of the arm closest to where he sat, still startled him and sent a thrill arrowing straight to his dick. "Just tight. Long day, ya know?"

"Come here," Lewis said, spreading his feet wide apart. "Get down there on the floor. Lemme see if I can help out." Ty moved and settled between Lewis' knees, leaning back. Lewis tugged Ty's shirt over his head and off, tossing it on the coffee table beside the phone as Ty smoothed his ruffled hair back from his face.

At the first touch of Lewis' hands on him, Ty's breathing sped up, then as moments passed and there was only the pain and pleasure that came from a strong massage working tense muscles, he relaxed. Lewis rubbed deep with his thumbs and the heels of his hands, then stroked Ty's neck and up into his scalp firmly. His fingers drew tiny circles along Ty's jaw and in front of his ears, and with each touch Ty felt...better. Not that he'd felt bad before. It was just he'd been carrying tension he didn't even recognize until it was gone. It almost seemed as if Lewis' skin on his transferred something more than the massage. He remembered the night of Twisted's party, when he'd lain side by side with Lewis, their shoulders touching. I felt a little bit of this that night, *he realized.*

Ty started to feel like an ass. He'd started this charade with the hopes of helping Lewis let go of whatever had him twisted up in knots, and here he was getting the most benefit out of it. "Lewis, why don't I—"

"Shhhh." Sharp and irritated, Lewis shushed him. "I like this." Thumbs dug into his lats, deep, setting up an aching release of muscles grown tense again with his worrying. "I had a shit day. Didn't know where I was headed until I wound up here." Lewis' tone softened, gentled as his fingers stroked up the back of Ty's neck. When the tug came on his chin, he went with the demanding touch, turning his head sideways, tilting up. As Lewis' lips brushed against his, he was eager for it, feeling the prickling scrub of scruff across his skin. Another soft caress of Lewis' mouth trailed to the side of Ty's, and then along his jaw to the skin just behind his ear. The threatening edge of teeth gripped his earlobe, tugging gently, heated breath gusting across his skin as Lewis released some of the tension he'd been carrying, too. Then the hands on Ty's neck pushed until he was facing front again, thumbs digging into the long muscles running on either side of his spine.

Several minutes had passed before Lewis asked, "You hear about the gas station thing over in Ponchatoula?" Ty nodded. It had been on the radio all day. "What'd you hear?"

"Kidnapping gone bad. Three dead, little girl missing." He tried to twist around and look at Lewis' face, but the hands held him steady. "Were you there?" Ty wasn't sure where Lewis had gone after they finished debriefing the IMC and CoBos. Not surprising, since they weren't in the same club, and both clubs' officers were keeping a lot of what they were finding out close to the vest. There was some sharing, of course. They had to if they were going to collaborate on taking down the VWMC. Less than Ty wanted, but asking after the whereabouts of any member of the other club would have been noted. Given who Lewis was in the IMC, Ty asking about him would have been a flashing neon sign of oddness. "It sounded ugly."

"It was fuckin' ugly. Shit like that always is, ya know? Little girl's okay at least. They talking yet about the shooters?" Lewis' hands stilled, becoming two stationary islands of heat on Ty's shoulders. "You know, about finding 'em? Where they found 'em, and how?"

"Not that I know of. The little girl's been located? That's good, I hadn't heard that." The fingers squeezed tight, contracting in a painful grip. "I won't ask why you were there, but are you okay?"

"They didn't find her? What do you mean? She's fine." The cracks in Lewis' composure resonated in his words, and Ty twisted against the hold on his shoulders to look up at him. Eyes locked in a blank stare, Lewis didn't see the TV across the room. His vision was turned inwards. "She's fuckin' fine."

Lewis startled and grabbed the remote, keying in the numbers for a local news station. He tossed the remote back to the coffee table, and his hands returned to Ty, one on his shoulder, fingers gripping, thumb rubbing circles. Lewis' other hand settled on Ty's head, threading through his hair over and over, sweeping it back from his face. Ty watched the screen, waiting as Lewis seemed to need him to do.

A minute passed with a weather radar on the screen showing storms to the west, headed their direction. Both men knew from experience the bulk of the storms would pass to the north, bending around the massive inland lake Slidell sheltered behind.

Another minute with local sports scores and information.

Then the talking heads were back, neutral accents in place, the woman and man staring solemnly at the camera in turn, reading their cues. "The sheriff in Tangipahoa Parish announced just moments ago baby Abigail has been found, unharmed. A local business owner claims to have found the child at the back door of Espressed Illusions, a coffee shop on East Pine Street. She immediately called the authorities, who determined the toddler was indeed baby Abigail, missing since the shootout that killed her mother earlier in the day. Little Abigail was taken to the hospital where her father was waiting. Reports indicate the child was not injured by her kidnappers." Here the camera shifted to the man. "The sheriff's department also reports they've located a vehicle matching the description of the van seen fleeing the scene. Several suspected fugitives were also found dead in what seems to be a disagreement among their outlaw band. In other news…"

With each word, Ty could feel Lewis relaxing, hear his breathing come more freely. After a moment, Ty picked up the remote and returned the TV to the game. He asked, "You good?"

Lewis didn't answer right away, then his fingers tightened in Ty's hair, the grip inexorable as it tilted Ty's head back. The men stared at each other for a moment, then Lewis bent to press his lips to the corner of Ty's jaw, the scruff on his cheek a rough scrape. Lewis pulled back with a muttered, "Yeah, I'm good." A pause, then he kissed the edge of Ty's mouth. "Was shit, you know? When I got here? But now, I'm good." A gliding touch was followed by the hot tracing along Ty's bottom lip with the tip of Lewis' tongue. "So fuckin' good." The next kiss didn't start slow, the combination of Lewis' grip in Ty's hair and the way he possessed Ty's mouth a heady acknowledgment of why he'd come to Ty's condo.

That's what Crissy had seen when she walked in the door, her appearance in response to Ty's earlier texted plea. That second night the three of them slept together had been as hot and sensual as the first, culminating with breakfast sex on Ty's dining room table this morning. Crissy laid across a corner of the wooden surface, Ty between her legs, buried deep while Lewis fed his dick into her eager mouth. The erotic sight of her taking the thick cock deep into her throat, hands over her head holding onto Lewis' hips, had been nearly enough to make Ty lose it and come right then.

His phone vibrated again, and Wrench looked down to see he'd received two texts from Po'Boy. Keying the screen open, he read the first one. **Meant to say something last night, want you and Crissy at**

the suite this weekend. The second text was shorter but just as bossy. **Don't even fuckin think of bailin.** Wrench's gut clenched with anticipation of what was to come. Then he grinned and touched an icon on the screen, waiting as the image app loaded. He swiped until he found the filter he wanted and snapped a selfie, then saved it to his phone. Without adding anything other than a three-word caption, he sent the image to Po'Boy. A moment later he got it back, with a hand-drawn **U R** on top of the picture of him with a fake full beard and a cigar, his text below it read, "Who's your daddy?"

***

Crissy

Walking through her front door, Crissy toed her shoes off and nudged them to the side as she set the alarm. She sighed and smiled. *Was a good night.* She'd gone out with her coworkers for a drink that turned into a late dinner, listening to them regale the group with stories of their families, previous jobs, college hijinks, and in general all the things that friends talked about. She'd even contributed a story or two, earning laughter for an impersonation of her college advisor, doing her best to explain his cockney slang.

Bedtime rituals complete, she stared at herself in the bathroom mirror. *I'm doing a little bit of all right,* she thought, grinning. Tugging her nightgown down, she smoothed fingertips across two overlapping bruises on the swell of one breast, one from Lewis and the other from Ty. She knew when the marks faded her men would renew their visible claim. *Maybe I'm doing a lot of all right.* Her grin flashed in the mirror again as she turned off the light.

Seated on the edge of the mattress, she texted Bob to set-up a time to video call Missy the next day. He responded right away, reassured her she wasn't bothering him, and they settled on early afternoon. That would put the call post-nap for Missy, and predinner preparations for

Bob. It also put the call right before she left the office, which worked out just fine for Crissy.

Since moving back to Louisiana, she had tried to find a healthy balance between giving them space to establish their forever changed family unit with his folks, and her longing to see and talk to them every day. She wasn't homesick, not really, because Louisiana was home and each day that passed cemented the feeling more. No, she was peoplesick, and missing the hours of playtime she would spend with Missy. *It's healthy*, she reminded herself, *for them and for me*.

Leaning into the pillows, she grabbed her phone, thumbing the screen until she got the text app open. The string with her sister was long, and most of the recent texts were filled with commentary about Ty and Lewis. Nothing too personal, nothing like the kind of giggling rundown she would have given Rhoda before. Crissy had tried to keep it PG-13, keeping the details to herself, but still she'd poured out her hopes and fears in text.

I miss my Missy Prissy.

Tapping the photo icon, she opened the folder of images she'd captured as stills from video chats. Her niece's face was so expressive, and that slightly crooked smile was enough to make her want to fly to Minnesota tonight just to hug her. Crissy sighed, tracing her fingertip along the curve of Missy's cheek.

Look how beautiful she is. Just like her momma.

Back to the images, she found a picture that had been misfiled, this a photo of Ty and Lewis on Ty's couch. Captured in nearly identical poses, beer bottles cradled in their laps, bare feet resting on the coffee table, they were staring at something out of frame. Because she'd taken the picture, she knew it was the TV and a ball game that had captured their attention. She also knew that the moment she'd stepped out of Ty's bedroom, their eyes had swung to her. And being as she was only wearing a towel, it had only been a moment later the TV was off, and her men had her sandwiched between their heat. Ty's fingers had teased the towel away from her body, dropping it to the floor as he'd kissed her. Then Lewis' hands had cupped her breasts, lifted and offered them to Ty with a growled, "Our Crissy's needy tonight, brother." That had been an offer Ty had eagerly accepted, wrapping his lips around her nipple and drawing deep.

I'm so lucky, Rhoda. I can't even tell you.

Smoothing the cotton covering the pillow next to her, she rolled her head and sniffed, finding the scent of Lewis lingering in a telling way. He'd surprised her last night, coming in sometime after midnight and crawling into bed. He'd curled around her, shoving his leg between hers and pulling her tight against him with a muttered, "Sleep."

This morning had found him cursing and covering his head with the pillow when her alarm went off, mumbling about torture devices. Then he'd surfaced and kissed her hard, rolling into her and pressing close so she felt his erection, one long arm outstretched to silence the alarm. "Mornin', baby," he'd murmured against her lips, leaving her dazed as he'd exited the bed. Turning to look at her, Lewis had shaken his head, a soft look on his face. "You're fuckin' gorgeous, darlin'. I'm a lucky bastard, gettin' to see this first thing." Crissy had pulled the sheets to her chest, smiling up at him. "Tomorrow night, my suite in Orleans," he'd ordered as he bent deep, kissing her gently.

"Bossy Lewis is back." Resting her head on the pillow, she'd stuck her tongue out at him.

"You get your shower in," he'd responded, and she'd been caught off guard, his knowledge of her morning routine warming her belly. "I'll get the coffee going, honey."

So very lucky.

Chapter Thirteen
Po'Boy

Easing his bike off the bridge and onto the tangle of surface streets, Po'Boy wove between the cars on his way to the building housing his suite. According to Twisted, the fish fry had been a success, generating the exact feeling of comradery and support the officers from all three clubs had hoped. Where normally his mind would be filled with the plans he and Twisted had talked through last night, his ride today had his mind consumed with one scene from the previous evening.

Beer in hand, Po'Boy stalked across the field behind Twisted, both men headed to the bonfire nearest the small dock. They'd been directed this way by no less than three prospects, each man pointing to the group around the fire, mute mouths not speaking so they could give no offense, arms lifted to point out Ace. Felt good to know they could count on the CoBos to offer up respect in fair measure. That had a warm burn in his belly as he trailed his president towards the large group of men gathered around the fire.

What Po'Boy hadn't counted on was how it'd feel to see Wrench standing next to the CoBos president. He'd never fucked around with someone he knew. Never fucked around with someone in the life. A cavern-deep line he'd not ever been tempted to cross, and now he was so far on the other side of that line, he didn't know what to think. He'd stood there, silently flanking Twisted as was his place, carefully maintaining a neutral expression. Protect and support were his watchwords as VP and even though he and Twisted were surrounded by brothers and friendlies at the moment, from long experience his gaze remained in constant motion, cataloging body language, assessing everyone and everything for hidden threats.

Wrench had much the same role, but in this setting, the CoBos were more laid back, understandable since the place was their clubhouse. Still, Wrench appeared visibly aware of every man in the group, his eyes flicking from one to the other in an unending cycle. Every man except Po'Boy. The way Wrench's gaze seemed repelled by him felt like a spotlight shining down on him, even if he knew it wasn't. Knew not a single man would think anything about their public conduct with each other. Once he saw how Wrench was reacting, Po'Boy became hyperaware of his own behavior, determined to leave no room for questioning. Still, it was his first experience of seeing Wrench and not being able to acknowledge anything, not letting himself even go so close as to touch Wrench in passing, and it stung painfully. Ain't like we're goin' steady, *he scolded himself.* Just fuckin'.

Rolling to a stop in the garage, he killed the engine and backed the bike into his parking space. From the way Wrench ignored him, it might have been easy to take offense, but Po'Boy knew what was going on underneath the surface. Made him glad he'd already ordered the man to come to New Orleans. They needed to set some ground rules for future encounters, get shit straight, so no one learned anything the two of them wanted to be kept secret. *Do I want him to be a secret? What about Crissy?* He wanted to take her out, but the idea of her appearing to be only Wrench's gal pulled at Po'Boy's gut. *And vice versa*, he thought, knowing Wrench would most likely have the same reaction to a night on the town where Po'Boy got to show her off, but Wrench's touch would be forbidden. *How in the fuck did it get so goddamned complicated?*

He unstrapped the small bag from the back of the bike and prowled towards the elevator. They'd be here soon, and he wanted to be ready. Leaning on the back wall of the car on the way up to the suite, he let his mind wander back to the rest of the previous night.

From across the flames, he heard the hiss of a name that pulled his focused attention: Deuces.

Ace said, "Got word a delivery was coming in for him, and the product got diverted. Heard the man was hot to trot about missing shit." Beside him, even though Twisted didn't speak, Po'Boy knew he had been surprised by the announcement. It was likely no one else in the group would be able to read the tension flooding his brother's frame as they listened to Ace, but he knew him so well it could have been shouted. "Shoulda known better than to try and run shit through territory what didn't belong to him." He paused, and Po'Boy watched as his gaze ran across the circle of faces, gauging his next words. "Redirected Houston way." Three words said a lot, because none of the three clubs here tonight had tight connections with any groups in Houston, which meant unlike Po'Boy had immediately assumed, it hadn't been the CoBos who jacked Deuces shipment. Houston meant they were looking towards a new player in the game, and changing the dynamics within the region was dangerous.

His words underscoring Po'Boy's unease, Twisted asked, "You sure? Houston?"

"Houston," a voice confirmed from behind them, and Po'Boy swung around to see Retro walking the same path he and Twisted had just followed, paced closely by his VP, Mudd. "I'm gonna need presidents and their officers only for what I got." The pronouncement meant Retro had intelligence none of them would want to hear, but he'd give it to them anyway, letting them control how far down the ranks the information ran.

The CoBos members who were standing nearby quickly scattered at a gesture from Wrench, while Po'Boy glanced around to ensure there weren't any IMC he needed to shoo away. Their group of six formed a ring not far from the fire, Ace and Wrench with backs to the blaze, which left their features in shadow and made them hard to read. Retro studied each of them in turn and then began.

"Mexi cartel in Houston jacked the VWMC shit. I got a name and not much more from my—" He paused, tellingly. "—source. But you know me—" His lips twisted as he grinned at Twisted and Po'Boy. "—I always got another source up my sleeve. Found a trail. That phone you lifted"— he nodded at Po'Boy—"has come in handy in more than one way. Even if it took a few days to make it to me," he looked at Po'Boy in a meaningful way, making it clear that as usual, Retro knew everything that was going on, "I'd have considered the trail tainted just because it was fucking Rotain and we all know the kind of bitch she's turned out to be. But after a couple of days the phone rang, and when I answered it, there was a wealth of information to be had. Seems her 'sponsor'"—he made air quotes with his fingers when he said the word, and Po'Boy snorted a laugh—"is highly disappointed in her ability to come through with what she promised." He paused again and turned to look at Wrench, head cocked to one side, waiting.

"What'd she promise?"

The question was asked by Ace, not Wrench, but Retro's stare didn't waver as he answered, "Bitch promised an in with the CoBos. Claimed golden pussy." Wrench's head snapped back and, for the first time, his eyes met Po'Boy's, every line in his face accentuated and taut. "Said her pussy was so golden, she'd serve the VP up on a platter." Po'Boy couldn't blink, couldn't look away, the expression of disgust on Wrench's face disconcerting for a moment because Po'Boy assumed it was aimed at him.

Wrench's outburst put that fear to rest, and Po'Boy took a deep breath even as Wrench swore. "Fucking bitch! She did not offer to fuck her way into my ear, did she?"

Retro nodded, and Po'Boy's gut twisted as the man looked between Po'Boy and Wrench, a look of amusement mixed with interest on his face. That was wiped away as soon as Retro started to speak. "She absolutely did promise, man. Had a tight deadline, too. You fucked it when you headed to Kentucky, but the word is that fucking up happened just before you left. Something about a little front yard showdown which turned into a smackdown for Sam." He tipped his head to the other side, offering a slight smile. "Care to fill in the gaps there?"

Without hesitating, Wrench said, "Sam rolled up ridin' bitch on an RC leader's bike. Wasn't looking for anything from me but bullshit, hit the ground humming her lies. Didn't take but a minute for me to set her straight, and she left with her man." Po'Boy noticed he left out the part about Crissy dipping her toe into the bullshit and set aside his unease at this, deciding it wasn't an omission that mattered. "Thorne knows what he's got in his bed, and you gotta know I'm not interested in having her back in mine." Shaking his head, Wrench muttered, "Bitch wasn't worth the effort the first time. Fuck."

Twisted snorted and asked, "Anyone here hadn't banged Sam Rotain?" Retro's hand was the only one raised, and they all chuckled. Twisted said, "Rotains have been a blight on the parish for decades. Her big sister"—Po'Boy's stomach rolled at his last memory of Sabrina Rotain, huddled against the wall in a holding room at the IMC clubhouse, her ruined face blindly tracking Twisted as he stalked back and forth, coming to grips with what he knew had to be done—"caused my family and club no end of pain before she went missing. Sam knew the score every time she climbed a man's cock. This is just her trying to hook a bigger fish." He made a noise far back in his throat and spat to the side, Po'Boy fought the urge to do the same, the memory of the smell of blood and lime, the taste of shit mixing with old rust coating his throat. "Mexi cartel had put their feelers in this neck o' the woods *before. We always chop those motherfuckers off. Won't be any different this go around." The certainty in his voice lent confidence to every man except Retro, and Po'Boy watched as the man eyed Twisted's face in the flickering light from the flames.*

"I hope you're right, brother." The tight line of Retro's shoulders eased as he visibly relaxed. Then in a sing-song he asked, "Po'Boy, wanna tell me about the beauty you snagged down at Plaisirs Caches?"

Retro's question had pulled Po'Boy tight as gut on a crossbow and he glared at Retro. "Want a beer?" Turning on his heel, he stalked away from the fire, ignoring the four men laughing behind him, knowing the silent mouth belonged to Wrench, who was probably just as freaked out as he was right now. Plaisirs Caches was the bar he'd met Crissy in, the bar where Po'Boy picked up his hookups, the bar where he'd seen Wrench that first night. The fact Retro knew about the bar didn't surprise him, but him knowing about Crissy? Buckets of cold water wouldn't have caused a bigger chill down his spine.

Inside the suite, Po'Boy slung the bag to the floor at the foot of the bed. He kicked off his boots on the way to the bathroom, and after a quick shower toweled off, each movement brusque, rough. Tugging on clothes from the dresser in the bedroom, he found himself impatient with the way the fabric clung to his still-damp skin. Phone in hand, he paused when he saw he'd missed a pair of texts. Thumbing open the app, he stared at an image he'd received. It was one of him on the bike, feet up on the highway bars, head tilted back with a big smile as he rolled into the parking garage about twenty minutes ago. The second image was a selfie of Wrench touching his pursed lips with the extended tip of his middle finger, posed in front of none other than Plaisirs Caches, the bar only half a block away. That had come with a message. **I'll be waiting.**

Shrugging into his cut with automatic movements, he was already stalking towards the door as he tapped out a response. Slowing, he turned, studying the room for a moment. Flipping back to the selfie, he looked again, seeing Wrench was wearing a plain T-shirt. He removed and folded his cut, laying it on the dresser then headed through the door, pulling it tight behind him.

***

Wrench

He leaned along the short side of the bar, back to the wall, keeping his eyes on the front door. It opened in a flood of light just as his phone vibrated in his pocket, and he didn't have to check the device to know who had texted him. Po'Boy stood in the doorway, highlighted by the sunshine behind him, scanning the interior of the bar for a moment before his gaze landed on Wrench.

Those eyes stayed on him with a weight which was palpable, goose bumps raising on his arms as he shivered. Not angry, but intense, and filled with a promise Wrench wasn't sure he was ready for. *What the fuck am I doing here?* That thought had run through his head a dozen times on the ride over, and a dozen more as he waited. Crissy wasn't here, and the fact he didn't care confused him. Without her as a buffer, what did it mean that he couldn't wait to be alone with Po'Boy? *What? Am I suddenly gay?* That thought winding through his brain didn't leave the residue behind he'd expected. Nothing bad, nothing frightening, just knowledge if that was how things were, then he was okay with it.

Before he could complete the thought, Po'Boy had leaned against the wall, standing so close the heat from his arm felt like a touch. The fine hairs on Wrench's arm raised and he shivered. Low and quiet, Po'Boy asked, "You been here long?" As if they'd planned on this meeting, as if Wrench hadn't surprised him by showing early, and his easy acceptance was a balm.

"Not long." He paused, lifting two fingers in response to the bartender's questioning look and receiving a nod in response. "Want to eat something?"

"Nah, I'm good." Po'Boy shifted as he spoke and his shoulder lightly brushed against Wrench's, pulling another shiver from him as sudden desire plumped his cock. When he glanced over, Po'Boy's knowing smirk had pulled his lips to the side, and he stared at Wrench, the corners of his hooded eyes crinkling in amusement. Without looking away, Po'Boy called out, "Truman, gimme those two to go, add four more." The bartender made quick work of putting a cardboard holder with six beers on the counter, and Po'Boy flipped out a bill as he twisted to look at Wrench. "You comin'?"

God, I hope so. Startled, he checked himself to make sure those words stayed in his head. "Yeah," he muttered, watching Po'Boy lift the beers and offer the bartender a two-finger salute. The man's eyes flicked to Wrench, looking down and then up before aiming back at Po'Boy as he returned the gesture. Even though he seemed to have an easy and familiar attitude, Wrench saw a flash of irritation cross the man's face. Once they were outside, unable to stop his mind from turning over the expression, Wrench looked at Po'Boy, and asked, "You know him well?"

"Who?" His stride loose and long, Po'Boy glanced towards Wrench and then back down the block towards the bar. He tipped his head with a grin, sidling sideways to bump into Wrench's shoulder. "Truman?" Po'Boy shrugged. "He's been working there for a long time."

"You know him, don't you?" Wrench mentally compared himself to the man, coming up unaccustomedly short. Truman was clean shaven, hair styled over the collar of his pressed button-down shirt. Even under the clothing Wrench could tell his body was fit and sleek, like a swimmer. Definitely an athlete. Wrench ran the past couple of minutes back through his head, again seeing the expression of frustration on Truman's face, marking how the bartender's eyes had tracked Po'Boy moving through the door before angling to determine his destination and landing on Wrench. A single look from the bartender which judged and found him wanting. "He sure knows you."

"What? Truman? Oh, hell naw, man." Po'Boy jostled his shoulder again, the bottles clinking softly in their carrier. "He don't do it for me." Wrench sipped at the air, trying not to let his breathing accelerate audibly. Everything they'd done so far had been bridged by Crissy's presence, and this might be the first out and out statement by Po'Boy that he was open to something more than sharing a woman. Ignorant of the tremor caused by his words, Po'Boy continued, "Tru is a pretty boy, and nothing wrong with such a thing once in a while. Each his own, I always say. Just don't do it for me. I like..." Po'Boy's voice trailed off as he punched in the code to get into his building.

By unspoken agreement, the silence stretched as they waited for the elevator, and by the time they'd entered the suite, Wrench knew the moment had passed for him to question anything. Po'Boy had withdrawn, saying nothing as he set the six-pack on the kitchenette's counter, taking four of the bottles out to put in the refrigerator, then opening the remaining two. He was fussily folding the cardboard container, and Wrench watched as he tucked it between the backsplash and the microwave, the action so practiced he would have known just from that how much time Po'Boy spent here, in New Orleans, where few people knew him.

Testing the waters, Wrench walked to stand beside Po'Boy, accepting the bottle slid across the counter to him, cupping the cold glass with his fingers. Po'Boy stood, stared at the blank cabinet door as he mechanically lifted his beer and took a deep drink. Quietly, Wrench asked, "What's going on in your head?"

"Trying to figure out how this is going to end up." Po'Boy's words dropped into the air between them with a bleak finality, as if whatever they were doing had an inevitable bad end. "I figure if I can map out the ways I can fuck something up, I can at least avoid those." He lifted the beer and drank, muscles in his jaw moving with each swallow, Adam's apple bobbing up and down, the cords on his neck stood out briefly, highlighting the hollow of his throat. "This place—" He tilted his head, looking at Wrench from the corner of his eye as he gestured around them. "—has been my sanity for a while now. There's a fetish club in the penthouse. That's why I got the place, figured easy access would help me find what I wanted. Then it just was a place I could come without dealing with all the bullshit it'd bring down on me back across the causeway." His cheek lifted in a grimace as his eye narrowed, the corner of his mouth curling down. "I always kept shit separate. Never wanted to break the rules, man."

"Why are you now?" Wrench shifted, leaning against the countertop, crossing his arms while still holding the beer, the cold and wet of the bottle surprising him when it hit his bare arm. "Why'd you open the door, Lewis?" He used the name intentionally, knowing any regret or misgiving Po'Boy had were tied up in the clubs and members. "I've been wondering."

Lewis turned to face him, fingers sliding the empty bottle away from the edge of the countertop. They were standing close, less distance between them than might be comfortable in public, but it wasn't close enough for Ty. Unfolding his arms, he reached out, losing his confidence at the last minute, letting his hand dangle at his side. Lewis smiled, the teasing expression spreading slowly across his face and he took the bottle from Ty's other hand, lifting it to his mouth and draining it. Letting it clatter to the countertop, he finally responded to Ty's question. "I don't rightly know, but I know I wanna. There's something...just something different here, you know?"

Ty dipped his chin in agreement. "What happens...what do you...how do you know what...?" He shook his head in frustration. "Behind closed doors, right?" He'd meant to imply they depended on each other to keep the secrets they had to hold close. "But how did you know I'd...?" His voice wavered because he didn't know what he'd be willing to do anymore. Every single thing they'd done so far had been out of this world hot, but everything had also been outside his range of experience. The idea Lewis had been confident enough to approach him was boggling. "I'd never expected to be here."

Lewis took a step, then another one, erasing the small distance between them, stopping only when his firm chest brushed against Ty's pecs. Firm, not soft. Steel wrapped in strength.

Ty felt disoriented, lightheaded, as if he'd been playing with fire and narrowly escaped being burned. Dizzy, he closed his eyes for a moment then reached out to find something to hold to, and his hand encountered Lewis. Fingers sliding along his hip, Ty gripped and held tight, digging in.

The scent drifting to his nose warned him, musky and clean, not filled with oil and gasoline residue. It smelled like Lewis had showered off the stink of the road before coming to the bar, and Ty wondered at the preparation. *Was that a way of setting aside his club persona? Should I have...done something?* Distracted by his thoughts, Ty startled when he felt the heat radiating from Lewis against the skin of his cheek, his neck, his arm. Strands of hair brushed across his face, that the only contact between them for the longest time, seconds stretching as if in a wormhole.

Everything snapped back into focus when Lewis nuzzled against his neck, for an instant the rough scrape of his short beard as startling as it had been the first time, but now a known touch. Known and desired, and Ty found his fingers gripping tighter, winding into the belt loop at Lewis' waist. A hot mouth tugged at his earlobe, then teased Ty with a sharp bite immediately soothed by gentle sucking. Lewis' hand landed on his arm just above his elbow, fingers digging in fiercely, pulling them even closer so Ty felt the first touch of Lewis' erection against his hip.

God, I missed this, he thought, angling his chin so Lewis could kiss along his jawbone. *How can I miss something I never had?* He shook his head, dislodging the thought, and Lewis chuckled, deep and rasping in his throat as he said, "I don't know what happens, Ty. I just wanna fuckin' feel for a while. You make my head quiet when it's fuckin' loud all the time. Help me find the quiet?"

He felt Lewis' lips moving against the skin on his neck. Then Lewis' hair was back in his face, teeth gripping firmly at the top of his shoulder. Lewis' hand slipped down his arm to his side, then around to the small of Ty's back, pulling him closer. A clever flick of Lewis' fingers earned entrance underneath Ty's shirt, and then a hard hand had slid into the back of Ty's pants, beneath his briefs to palm his ass, gripping and tugging him forwards, the pressure against his erection exactly what he needed. He pumped once, then a second time against Lewis' crotch, spreading his feet wider and not giving a shit if things were lining up because he just needed another couple of moments of this and he'd come.

Lewis shoved his hand down further, his fingers curling under Ty's ass, sliding in until fingertips were stroking his balls. Ty groaned when they tightened in response to the caress and let his head drop forwards, twisting and pressing close as he sought access to Lewis' skin. His mouth skidded along Lewis' neck and Ty bit firmly, his other hand lifting so he could grip Lewis' arm. He breathed a quiet warning, "Gonna come."

"Fuck yeah, gonna get you off, Ty." Once the silence was broken, Lewis seemed to gain momentum, and from that moment his voice flowed over Ty, pulling him along as it always did, his filthy words exactly what Ty wanted. "Gonna get you to blow so hard. Bust a nut for me, gonna blow the top of your head off, man." Lewis moved, one leg slipping between Ty's, and he ground firmly, pulling Ty's ass cheeks apart with the strength of his grip. "Your dick's so fuckin' hot. Feel it through my jeans. Scorchin', like you." Ty's hips moved again, and he felt his orgasm building.

"Fuck," Ty gritted, turning his head to look down between them, the tented evidence of Lewis' arousal appearing as he pulled back. Ty watched as their bodies crashed together again, the rough fabric of their jeans making a hissing sound as the material moved with them.

"Want my mouth on you. I'm a greedy bastard." Together, apart, sliding up and down Lewis' leg, he watched, the sensation of rubbing against Lewis amplified by the visual. "Gimme your goddamned fuckin' mouth." Hard fingers tightened in his hair, and Lewis lifted his head with a strength Ty couldn't fight, covering Ty's mouth with his own. Perfectly timed with the thrusts of their hips, he stroked into Ty's mouth, teasing his tongue until Ty was drowning in sensation. Ty flicked his tongue in response to a playful lick, their gasped breaths mingling, Lewis' mumbled words vibrating against his lips.

Lewis' grip was certain, and Ty fought only a moment before he gave himself over to the feeling of being controlled, held, his mouth fucked hard. Fluid wept from the tip of his cock as Lewis' grip on his ass shifted, fingers wedged in the cleft of his ass holding him close, fingertips glancing across his hole raising sparks of sensation. More a rubbing than a thrusting now, he ground against Lewis' leg, grunting deep in his throat when he came, the swiftness of it overtaking him in an instant. Ripping his hair free from Lewis' grip to break the kiss, he pressed his forehead to Lewis' throat, the pulsing heat from his cock all consuming, thrumming through him.

They stood like that for a moment, the sound of Ty's harsh, panted breaths filling the air. Slowly, Lewis untangled them, giving Ty's ass a final squeeze as he slid his hand up and out. Chill settled in all along Ty's front, accentuating in his mind how hot Lewis had felt against him. With a shaking hand, he picked up his beer, forgetting Lewis had drained it, laughing awkwardly when the tilted bottle failed to deliver more than a drop or two. "Can I shower?" he asked, abruptly feeling uncomfortably sticky from the semen soaking into his underwear.

When Lewis didn't answer, he glanced up to see the other man looking steadily at him. Without a word, Lewis turned and walked towards the bathroom and disappeared inside. A moment later he heard water running, and a now shirtless Lewis appeared in the doorway, gesturing impatiently at him with a wave of curled fingers. "'Mere," Lewis called, then turned and disappeared again.

***

Po'Boy

Lewis grinned at the reflection of himself in the bathroom mirror, pausing to admire his physique for a moment. *No wonder the guy looked stunned*, he thought, flexing to watch his muscles bunch and slide. He felt the smile fade from his lips as he stood there alone longer than expected. Ty hadn't followed him. *Fuck. Too far, too fast*. An uncertain Ty was a freaked-out Ty, and that wasn't what Lewis wanted. Not at all.

Discarding his vague idea of showering with Ty, Lewis adjusted the heat of the water again, nodding with satisfaction when hot steam started rolling out of the enclosure. He left the bathroom to find Ty still standing in the same spot, frozen in place. *Fuck*. As casually as he could, Lewis strode to the dresser and pulled out another clean shirt, yanking it over his head. His actions seemed to pull Ty out of his thoughts, and he spoke, his words quiet. "You're not...?" Ty made a vague gesture towards the bathroom, where steam had begun to wisp out the top of the door.

"I ain't eat yet." Lewis deliberately used the cadence and tone he would if he were north of the lake, slipping into the dialect as comfortably as an old pair of jeans. "Figured you ain't either. Gonna hit the bar, get us somethin' for supper." He let his voice dip to a lower range. "Crissy'll be here soon." He grinned, aiming for a leer and figuring he hit the mark when Ty grinned back. "Gotta keep up my strength." With a gesture towards the bathroom, Lewis said, "Go. Shower. We're of a size, and I got shit here." He thumbed over his shoulder at the dresser. "Extra key to the suite is in the top right drawer if you need to step out for somethin'. I'll be back in thirty, mebbe forty-five minutes. Take your time, man. It's all good."

He pulled the door closed behind him, leaning back on it for a moment while he blew out an unsteady breath. For a moment there, it seemed things were riding the edge of disaster, no matter Ty had shown up early, and forget the fact the man had been openly jealous of Truman. The idea they'd had a moment like that one with just the two of them had nearly sent Ty's barely-bi ass back to straight town.

Seated on a stool at the bar, order placed, he pulled out his phone to call Crissy, seeing she'd texted him earlier. **On my way!** It had been followed by a series of repeated eggplant emoji, and he snorted a laugh. *Our Crissy's got a little raunch in her.* He tapped out, **Come to the bar**, and set the phone face down on the bar in front of him, reaching out to pull the glass of beer closer.

Eyes on the TV over the cash register, he didn't pay attention when the back door opened and jerked in surprise when the stool next to him scraped back. Crissy's jeans-clad ass settled on the cushion, and she leaned close, pressing her cheek against his shoulder before sitting back upright. "Hey," she greeted him, her voice soft and affectionate as she reached for his nearly empty glass. She drained the rest of his beer, flicking a finger at Truman as she set the glass back on the bar.

Lewis wrapped an arm around her back as she settled in, tugging her close again and pressing a kiss to her temple before relaxing his arm. "Mmmmh." He breathed in her scent, then slipped his hand down to her ass, gripping and giving her a squeeze as he responded, "Hey, baby. You got here fast."

"I was waiting for the elevator when you texted." She lifted slightly, and he pushed his fingers under her ass, swiping across the seam of her jeans with a firm glide. *Fuck, hot.* Settling back on the stool, she glanced up at him and winked. "I expected you to be in the apartment. Whatcha doin' over here?"

Tugging his trapped hand free, he shoved his fingers into the back pocket of her jeans, not wanting to relinquish his hold on her yet. "Ty's showerin'." Her eyelids lowered at his words, and the tip of her tongue slipped out to glide across her bottom lip. Her reaction was instinctive, and hot as hell, revealing her desire for their partner. "Yeah, it's exactly like that. He showed early and I already nearly fucked up. I figured if I didn't want to screw the pooch for this weekend with y'all, I'd better get my ass out of there. Put temptation at a distance, at least."

He hadn't spoken to her again about Ty's lack of threesome experience. Didn't want to highlight the breadth of his own as a contrast, and surely didn't want to know about what unvoiced experiences Crissy had in her past, either. Silence had served him well before, he expected the same would work with the three of them.

She wrinkled her nose and grinned at him, slipping her bottom lip between her teeth, letting it slowly slide free, glistening wet and plumping from the pressure and friction. "Crissy, baby. Your sass is showing." He grinned and leaned in, brushing his lips across hers.

She sat back, returning his smile, then shared her thoughts. "If Ty showed up early, don't you think whatever happened might have been what he was after? He knows how this thing"—Lewis frowned at her word, but then realized he didn't have a better replacement—"works between the three of us. Maybe he's looking to stretch his boundaries? His favorite bedtime story is the first time you and I hooked up." Lewis frowned again, thinking, *It wasn't a hookup.* "Did he show you his tests?" Lewis shook his head slowly. "He went to a clinic over in Biloxi. Said he wanted to make sure, just in case." She shrugged. "I've carried mine in my purse since you and I met, so I get it." She glanced around, seeming to make sure no one was close. "If you are both good with it, I was hoping to change the game a little." So focused was Lewis on Crissy that he startled when a hand hit his back; he hadn't heard the back door open. Twice in one night he'd been inattentive. *Fuck.*

Ty leaned in between them, and Lewis saw only the back of his head for a moment, but the position combined with the way Crissy squirmed under his hand told him what was going on. Ty's body pressed against his arm where it crossed the space between him and Crissy, and heat from Ty's palm on Lewis' waist was scorching. Then Ty turned his head to face Lewis, and for a split-second Lewis hesitated, unsure how to react because Ty's face was getting closer and then his mouth was on Lewis', covering his lips. It was a soft, closed-mouth kiss, but every atom of his being fired molten at the public acknowledgment by Ty that Lewis was as much in whatever this was with the three of them as Crissy or Ty.

Ty pulled back a fraction of an inch, the stir of air from his words ghosting across Lewis' lips when he said, "You didn't come back." Lewis saw the corners of Ty's eyes crinkle and knew the movement he felt was a smile when Ty continued, "Decided to hunt you down."

Without moving, Lewis responded, "Wasn't runnin'." Crissy moved, and he spread his fingers in her pocket, holding her in place. There was a thump from the bar in front of them, and Lewis turned his head to see Truman had deposited two plastic bags filled with take-out containers. The bartender's mouth was pulled sideways, brows drawn together in a scowl, and he grunted before turning away. Lewis glanced back at Ty to see a broad grin on his face, and he smiled in response. "Let's get going." Lewis grabbed one bag, and Ty grabbed the other, Crissy walking between them as they made their way out the back of the bar.

In the suite, the three of them bustled around the kitchen as Crissy pulled plates from the cabinets and Ty unloaded the bags, leaving Lewis to gather the flatware and napkins. By unspoken agreement they moved to the bed, the two men sliding onto the edges at the head, while Crissy sat cross-legged on the foot. She managed to keep the atmosphere light as she engaged the two men in quick question and answer exchanges about their days since they'd last been together, and regaled them with stories about her clients and how frustrating they could sometimes be.

After the easy affection between himself and Crissy, and then Ty's approach in the bar, Lewis found himself relaxing back against the headboard, bottle of beer in hand, watching as Ty tipped his head back laughing at one of Crissy's stories. That was when it hit him. How different this was from everything he had before. Probably the closest he'd ever come to having an easy friendship relationship was with Penny. Which was entirely fucked up because she belonged to Twisted, and what Lewis had with her had never been about sex. But this thing with Crissy and Ty had started being all about sex and then somewhere along the way it segued into more. Now it was something he'd never experienced, something he wanted, and something he feared losing.

Ty slipped off the bed and stood, stretching his arms over his head before he leaned back and gathered their empty dishes. The hem of his shirt rode up on his back, and Lewis eyed the exposed strip of skin, wishing he could trace the path with his tongue. Before he could reconsider what a bad idea it could be to try and command Ty, Lewis demanded, "Kiss me." Ty grinned and leaned in, scarcely brushing his lips across Lewis' before he straightened. Lewis sucked in a breath at the tease, then narrowed his eyes as he told Ty, "You come right back, you hear?"

Crissy laughed and muttered under her breath, "Lewis is feeling bossy again tonight."

Lewis turned to look at her as Ty carried the plates to the sink, and shook his head. "You are sassy tonight." He grinned. "Come 'mere, woman." He stretched out on his side, parallel to the pillows, and patted the mattress in front of him. "I want you right here, right now."

She took her time, inching forwards on hands and knees. Lewis felt the mattress shift, and her head lifted, surprise flashing across her features when Ty settled himself behind her, sandwiching her between them.

"Ty, wanna give me a hand, man?" A fumbling grip at his crotch had him laughing as he swatted Crissy's hand away. "Not you, woman. Tonight, honey, you take what we give you." Her eyes flashed, pupils dilating with either arousal or a wave of sudden fear, and he soothed her. "You trust me; you trust us. You know you do. We aren't going to do anything you aren't a hundred percent in on, honey. You know that. I also—" he edged closer, reaching up to tug her shirt over her head. "—know you like having control taken away sometimes."

He leaned up and kissed her, nibbling softly on her bottom lip.

On a whisper, he offered, "Let's explore that tonight." She nodded and then her hair was swept to the side, draping over one shoulder as Ty's head appeared over the other, mouth to the skin of her back. He moved up, bracing himself over Crissy and leaned closer, licking his lips as his gaze dropped to stare at Lewis' mouth. Clamping a hand around the back of Ty's neck, Lewis pulled him down, collapsing Crissy on top of him as he kissed Ty hard, forcing his mouth open when he plunged deep inside with his tongue, Ty's groan filling his mouth at the assault. He pulled back to allow a breath of distance between them and stared into Ty's eyes when he said, "Crissy said you had some blood tests done."

"Yeah." Ty's voice was husky with desire, his words quivering with need. "Wanna see it?"

"You wanna see mine? Is this a show-me moment?" Ty's jaw clenched shut as he shook his head. Lewis gave voice to every doubt in his barrage of questions, knowing Ty would have the same underlying fears. "Trusting me on this? It's a big fuckin' deal, man. Life or death. You trustin' me? Me?" Ty nodded, and Lewis responded with a shake of his head. "Tyler,"—the man's full name felt strange in his mouth, he didn't think he'd ever said it before, but he tossed the oddity aside to focus on the issue at hand—"be honest." Crissy made a noise, and he shushed her without looking away from Ty's eyes. "You been with another man before?"

"No." Short and clipped, the answer wasn't unexpected, but Lewis felt a burn of desire bolt through him with the knowledge no other man had ever touched Ty the way he would tonight. "This, though...I don't think it's because you're a dude, Lewis." Ty shrugged, looking a little lost for a moment before his jaw firmed with determination. "It's just you." Pulling back, he twisted to look at Crissy. "And you. It's like y'all are a package deal. I'd felt—" He stumbled for a moment and then bulled through. "—something towards you, Lewis. The night of the party shone a big spotlight on what I'd been trying to ignore for the past year. But I would have never acted on it. Crissy is the glue." His words echoed Lewis' thoughts of a few days ago, and he grinned. "I want her…" Ty looked at Crissy and rephrased, "you. I want you. But I want you with him. And I want you"—gaze back to Lewis' face, he smiled—"with her. We…"

When Ty's trailed off narrative showed no signs of continuing, Lewis picked up the thread. "Yeah. We just fit. There's a dynamic between the three of us that's unique. Never felt the like. And I get you, man. I totally get you. Crissy's got her piece of me, and you got yours, but when you're both on top of me like this—" He stroked up Crissy's side, his fingertips glancing across Ty's ribs. "—it's amplified. Addictive."

"Can't get enough of it," Crissy agreed, rolling her head so her lips grazed his jaw. "Not just in bed, though."

"All the time," Ty filled in. "Like a need, but deeper."

"So, back to the tests." Lewis prepared himself for whatever response would be coming his way. "I'm clean, and I got the papers. I've been with men, but my HIV is negative." He shook his head. "Never went bareback." He pressed backwards into the pillow so he could better see Ty's face. "Never wanted to before. Crissy and I had a condom fail, and you've heard all about that. She's clean, you're clean, I'm clean. Are we sayin' we're done with condoms? I ain't tryin' to fuck with your head, but if we do that, then to me it's a statement. We makin' a statement right here, right now?"

"Does it have to be a statement?" Crissy's voice quavered and he looked at her, seeing welling tears in her eyes. "Does it have to be all of one thing or another?"

"Naw, darlin'." Ty bent his neck, pressing his lips to her cheek before he tilted his head to slant his mouth across hers. "Don't gotta be a statement. Nothing has to change."

"But you want it to," Lewis pressed, knowing he was right. "So does Crissy, or she wouldn't have brought it up at the bar." He hesitated, then took a breath, blowing it out slowly. "Gonna go out on a limb here and say we're all of the same mind on this. We do this, we can change our minds and come back to zero and go back to usin' condoms. No problems because we all gotta be comfortable with it. But if we're on the same page and doing this, then I expect to be the only other dick in the mix. One of two for you—" He flashed a grin at Crissy who cuddled closer, then looked at Ty. "—and other than your own, mine better be the only D you're touchin'."

"So now I'm touching your dick?" Ty smirked and tilted his head. "You sure I wanna?"

"You tellin' me you don't?" Ty shook his head, lips spread in a broad smile and Lewis laughed aloud, confident for the first time all night. He let that shine through, adopting a teasing tone as he told them, "Alla y'all gots too many clothes on. Includin' me. Shuck 'em now, gimme some skin, baby."

Between them, they stripped Crissy, and then Lewis got to watch as Ty removed the clothes he'd put on after his shower, and Lewis realized he liked seeing his clothing on Ty. The jeans fit well, but the shirt was about a size too small, so tight it outlined every ridge of muscle on the man's stomach and chest. It didn't take Lewis but a couple of seconds to drop his own jeans, toeing off his socks as he yanked his shirt over his head. He crawled up the bed, feeling his hardening cock swinging back and forth, plump shaft brushing against the bristle of hair on his thighs as he moved. Stretching out on one side of Crissy, he kissed her slowly, Ty's hand coasting up and down his bare back as he pushed aside the covers Crissy had pulled up to their waists, cupping Lewis' ass. Ty's thumb rubbed and slid across his skin, every stroke tantalizingly close to the crease, barely dipping inside before the touch was gone again.

Crissy's lips plucked at Lewis' and she teased him with a sliding grip of her teeth on his tongue when he dipped inside, causing him to growl fiercely as she giggled. As he had in the past, Lewis took up the reins of control, knowing his partners still needed guidance, at least in the beginning. "Ty, on your back, man. I want our sweet Crissy ridin' you." Her heated gasp against his lips shared the excitement with him, and he crushed his lips to hers for a moment. "Fuck him for me, baby girl. Fuck him good." Mouth to her ear, he whispered loud enough for Ty to hear, "Gimme a show. I wanna see you and hear you, and I'm for sure gonna taste you. Fuck him for me."

The mattress bounced, Ty's hand shifting off his back to glide up his side, fingers circling his bicep and tugging. As Crissy positioned herself, Lewis kissed Ty, then scraped his teeth down Ty's throat to his chest, tonguing and sucking on the flat disks of Ty's nipples, each touch causing a startled breath to huff out of Ty. The tense iron of his muscles gave under Lewis' mouth, and he longed for a thousand days like this, knowing he could explore every inch and still find more to learn.

Angling himself down the bed, he draped his arm over Ty's thigh, voice rasping as he told Crissy, "Hump him, wanna tongue you while you torture our boy." She shifted and rocked, sliding her hips back and forth and Lewis could smell her arousal, see the glistening, slick fluid gathering in her folds. *Hot as fuck.* He pushed closer, then closer yet, wedging his face to where Crissy and Ty were nearly joined, lapping at her pussy. Each taste of her was torture; he would never get enough of this, her sweet mixing with Ty's musk. From this angle every stroke of his tongue skated along Ty's cock, and he heard a throaty groan, knowing it came from Ty's lips.

Without a word, he buried his tongue deep inside Crissy, thrusting fast. *Gimme everything, baby.* She whined, a high sound far back in her throat and froze in place, causing Ty to groan again, this time with an edge of frustration in his voice. Crissy moved, shifting and bending, and Lewis heard the sounds of them kissing, sloppy and wet, passion driving them both forwards. He saw them in his mind, lips fused together, eyes closed as they focused on each other, and him. *God, yes.*

He slipped a hand between them and cupped Ty's cock, gratified when his fingers glided in Crissy's juices while he stroked once, root to tip, then back down. She was hot and ready, hungry for Ty to be inside her, her body leading the way. Still eating her pussy hard and fast, he urged her ass up as he angled Ty's dick, eagerly tonguing the tip until it lined up to her entrance. Then Crissy shifted again, and he sucked in a breath, watching Ty slip inside her, veins throbbing all along his cock's thick length. Crissy moaned, the vibrato of the sound making Lewis' rigid cock pulse as more fluid leaked out of him.

Tonguing and sucking the length of Ty's cock as it moved in and out of Crissy, Lewis shifted so he was crouched between Ty's legs, balancing on his knees as he gripped Crissy's ass, a cheek in each hand. *Baby, I'm home.* Tugging gently, he opened her and then dived deep again, lapping and licking at her entrance and Ty's cock, then he drew the flat of his tongue up and over her hole, smearing her own fluids on her. *God, I want in there.*

Alternating between her pussy and ass, he stroked with fingers and tongue, teasing her open with the tip of his tongue, groaning at the deep shiver she gave, shifting back towards him in encouragement. Leaning over her, he bent and took Ty's mouth in a hard kiss, relenting for a moment to let Ty into his mouth so Lewis could suck his tongue. Then he offered a finger to Ty while he shifted to kiss Crissy, telling him, "Suck it, get it good and slick for our Crissy."

She panted, pressing her cheek to his and he felt goose bumps chasing his fingertips as he drew tiny circles on her hip and back. Heat surrounded his finger, and he twisted to see Ty's cheeks hollowing as he sucked hard, then felt the rolling caress of his tongue as he licked along all sides of Lewis' finger. Withdrawing his finger, he closed the distance between them to kiss Ty again, then trailed caresses over Crissy's shoulder and down her back, Ty's fingers smoothing through his hair and across his cheek.

Finger to her hole, he licked all around again, teasing her open before he pressed slowly. One knuckle deep, and he knew she liked it when she pushed back against him. Two knuckles and he could feel the shifting thrusts of Ty's cock inside her pussy. *Fucking hot.* Lewis reached down with his other hand to palm his own cock, slick fluid trailing down the crown. A slow thrusting movement and he slid a second finger inside her, pushing deep so she got the full thickness of his digits, tongue flicking and working around her rim, keeping everything slippery so he could glide in and out easily, scissoring them inside her, working her asshole.

She hissed and clamped down hard, and he heard Ty groan, knowing he felt the same pressure inside her pussy.

"Too much?" His voice sounded gruff, unused, and Lewis realized he'd been nearly silent when his lovers were more accustomed to a flow of thoughts and reactions, commands. "Too much, then all you gotta do is say so, Crissy. Gonna pleasure you, and I wanna fuck you in the ass, wanna fuck you slow and sweet while Ty does the same to your pussy. Fill you right up, back and front, knowing you're the thing holding all of us together in so many ways. It's just symbolic of everything that's us, honey. And I want it. Fuck yeah, your pretty asshole clamped around my fingers. Opening for my mouth. Am I the first to taste you here, honey? God, I hope so, claiming a first with a beauty like you is rare, and I want this so fuckin' bad."

He didn't stop moving, interrupted himself every few words to pause and lick or suck, dipping down between Ty's legs to slurp at his cock, tasting her pussy mixed with the dark flavor of the other. Ty gave a shout when Lewis lapped at his balls, his thighs spreading wide as he shoved his ass backwards into the mattress, giving Lewis more room while trying to escape the sensation at the same time. Lewis catalogued it for later, returning to preparing Crissy for what he wanted to do. "Wanna fuck your ass, honey. Make love to you with our Ty. It's a first for him, too, and I want that. Want it to be with you. You ready, baby?" Fingers moving patiently, he licked and laved saliva on them, then shifted and gave her a third, entering her with small thrusts, increasing the depth gradually but steadily. "Ty, you want this?"

"Fuck. Jesus." Angling his head to look around Crissy's body, spread out over Ty's, he saw Ty had his lip gripped between his teeth, biting down hard. "Yeah, I can't imagine...been thinking about it ever since I saw her riding you."

"Liar," Lewis taunted, bending to suck Ty's balls back into his mouth, rolling them gently with his tongue, feeling them contract and draw up. "You've been thinking about takin' my ass." Ty gave another shout as his hips punched up and, quick as a snake, Lewis wrapped a finger and thumb tight around the base of Ty's cock before commanding, "Do *not* come, man. Crissy hold up, be still, baby. Let him edge back."

It took a minute, but he gradually turned loose of Ty's dick, picking up the pace of his fingers in Crissy's ass again. "You want that, Ty? Want to bust in my ass? Best thing in the world, getting a dick that knows what you need. Me buried in our Crissy, you buried in me? You want it, we'll get there. Takes a confident man to take it up the ass, and I'm the guy for you. Promise you, motherfucker, I promise you I'm the guy for you." He palmed his cock again, slicking the leaking fluid across the crown. "For now, we're gonna share our Crissy a different way. It's amazing. I promise you that, too. Crissy—" He rose to his knees behind her, withdrawing his fingers as he angled the head of his cock into place. "—push back against me, honey. Push out. Nice and loose." She did, and he felt the initial resistance, then it gave way slowly, and he let her take the head inside, heat and pressure surrounding him. Caressing her ass, with a knuckle he traced the edge of her hole stretched around his cock. "Holy shit, you're tight. Fucking tight, baby. Love that. So fucking hot inside you. Fuckin' perfect. You okay?"

"Yeah." Her response was breathy, head lying on Ty's shoulder, face buried in his neck. "It's different. Not bad different. Just, different. Y'all are so big." Lewis stroked her back and hips, fingertips drawing random circles. "It's good, Lewis. I like." Ty kissed the side of her face. "I can take more."

"Your pace, baby. You want more, you take it. Ty, baby, you wanna move a little, keep our girl's fire stoked up?" A shiver rippled Crissy's skin, and he felt her tighten around him as Ty gave a hesitant pump of his hips. "You like that? That nice?"

"Yeah, very nice." The tip of her tongue appeared, and she lapped at Ty's throat, teeth making tiny indents in his skin as she nibbled on him. "More, Lewis. Please."

With Ty moving, he knew it wasn't as easy for Crissy to come back to him, so he unlocked his muscles, held in the same position with a brutal control so he wouldn't hurt her, and thrust forwards slowly. She groaned, but the sound was filled with pleasure, so he eased forwards again, heat and pressure all around him. His balls grazed against Ty's cock, bouncing in place with a jangled rhythm set by Ty's shallow thrusts up into her pussy. "Fuck, baby. So good."

Lewis skated his hands up her back, circling one around to cup her breast where it was smashed against Ty's chest, his other hand traveled farther up, fingers winding in her hair and tugging her head up. "Kiss him, baby." She did, lips coasting along Ty's, then he saw the movement in their mouths as Ty licked and thrust. Lewis pulled back slightly, then pushed deeper inside, groaning as his cock encountered Ty's. "Feel me, Ty? You feel that? That's us and Crissy, that's perfection, man. Fuckin' love this. I could fuckin' die a happy man right now, buried balls deep inside our woman, knowing you're lovin' her too."

Crissy giggled, and he felt that in his dick, too. Just in a different way, knowing she was confident enough to laugh in their bed. "Don't die yet, you still haven't made me come."

"Mmmm." He grinned as he bent down, teeth gripping the muscle in the middle of her back, tugging and growling to pull another laugh from her. "Lemme remedy that immediately, baby." Pulling back, he undulated his back, pressing deep again, angling differently so the head of his cock skated alongside Ty's inside her.

"Ungh." The sound Ty made wasn't a word but conveyed how much he liked what Lewis was doing. His arms wrapped around Crissy, holding her in place as he pumped up with his hips, increasing the pace. Lewis matched him, trying to alternate the pattern so Ty thrust in as Lewis withdrew, ensuring Crissy was always filled with one of them.

"Still doin' okay, Crissy?" Lewis bared his teeth as she twisted under him, angling her chin to look over her shoulder into his face. Mouth open, she was breathing hard, face flushed as she nodded. "All right, then. Gonna make you come so fuckin' hard, honey. Wanna hear our names when you do. Gimme that, baby. Gimme you calling out how much you like it. Fucking hot and tight, and I'm bumping up against Ty every fuckin' stroke."

Faster now, sweat coated their skin, making every contact slippery. "Come for me, honey," Lewis said, slipping a hand between her and Ty, hearing Ty's gasp as his fingers glanced along her clit, coasting past to stroke the base of Ty's cock before circling back around. Lewis rubbed side to side, and Crissy groaned. "Fuck, I'm close, honey. Come for me." Tight circles of his fingertip over her clit, he caught it between his fingers and pinched lightly, feeling the pulsing firmness of her arousal. "Fuck." Ty's pace increased, and Lewis tried to match it again, seeing how big Ty's pupils were, knowing he was close, too.

Crissy gave a whimper, then she tightened around him, a smooth-walled vise that was blistering hot, the pulsing of her clit changing to a hammering. A moment later she whispered something he couldn't hear. Then she was coming, and all he could hear were their names. "Ty, please. God, Lewis, yes. Please. Please."

Radiating throbs of heat hit his cock, and he watched Ty's face twist, mouth opening on a silent cry, features warped in pleasure. Pounding into her now, it was a half a dozen strokes later, and he was coming, semen bathing her ass, heat surrounding his cock inside her and he grunted through it, rocking and groaning until he was wrung dry. He turned his head to press his cheek to her spine and draped himself across her back in the aftermath.

He rested there a moment, then lifted, hands framing her ass as he stroked down to her thighs, thumbs and fingers digging in, massaging muscles he knew had to be strained. Pulling back, he eased out of her, a fingertip circling her hole as it flared and clenched, then flared again at the renewed pressure. Bending, he licked her crease, teasing the tip of his tongue back inside to taste himself before he trailed down to where Ty was still buried, bottomed out inside her.

Using broad, flat strokes, he lapped at Ty, nudging Crissy's ass with his fingers, getting her to slide forwards and off Ty's cock. Still straddling Ty, she shifted up a couple of inches, just enough for Lewis to pull Ty's softening dick into his mouth, rolling and sucking him clean. Swallowing down every trace of Crissy's taste, he chased up Ty's belly, abandoning his cock to lie coiled in a thatch of dark blond hair.

Lapping at Crissy's pussy, he sucked and licked, suppressing a groan at the taste of musky salt, evidence of Ty's enjoyment. Exploring every fold and dip of her flesh, he teased her clit out from its hood until she squirmed. Throughout all of this they were silent, and it wasn't until he was done that he gave a thought to how Ty might have taken it. Kneeling, he pushed back on his heels, staring down at his lovers, Crissy's profile showing her lips curled into a sated smile.

Ty blinked at him over Crissy's shoulder, then the corners of his mouth tipped up as he said, "I was gonna offer to get a washcloth since you did most of the work. But you took care of it for me." His eyes slipped closed, and he bent his neck to press a kiss to the top of Crissy's head. Not a single ounce of disgust or awkwardness, and Lewis breathed a shallow sigh of relief.

"My dick still needs cleanin' up." He rocked back, settling on the mattress between Ty's legs, draping his calves over one of Ty's thighs. "If you're offering."

"I'll get it," Crissy said, stretching, her breasts lifting and arching out until Ty clearly couldn't help himself; he reached up and cupped them, the muscles in his arms flexing as his thumbs worked across her nipples while she moaned. Voice more breathless than before, she murmured, "Y'all did all the work, that's for sure."

"The fuck was it you called us?" Lewis watched her walk across the room with appreciation, her naked, round ass shimmying back and forth with each step.

"What did you...?" The sound of water running in the bathroom covered the rest of her question, and he waited until she reappeared, wet cloth in hand.

"You called us something. Right as you came. What the fuck was that?" Knee to the bed, she settled onto her ass beside his hip, using the warm cloth to bathe his cock and balls, then she turned to Ty, performing the same duty there. "Lewty? You made up some kind of fucked up couples' name or something. Called us Lewty. Right as you came." He affected a falsetto tone. "Oh, Lewty, that's so good. Please. Don't stop, Lewty." He leaned forwards, wrapping one arm around her shoulders, pulling her down across Ty's lap with him. Ty pushed up on his elbows, looking down his body to where Crissy lay tangled with Lewis. "Oh, Lewty." He kissed her softly, nuzzling along her cheek. "Lewty." Her body shook with laughter, and he froze when her fingers threatened to dig in at his ribs.

Sighing, he levered a heel against the mattress, shoving them across the bed slightly, letting Ty extricate his legs. A moment later he felt heat along his arm around Crissy's back, and then a large, rough hand settled on his hip. Lifting his head, he saw Ty looking at him from behind Crissy. "Sleep," Ty said firmly. Crissy's palm cupped Lewis' cheek, and she angled his face down for another kiss.

"Sleep," she echoed Ty's command, wiggling as she snuggled down between the two men.

Lewis lifted on an elbow and leaned forwards, a final, fluttering uncertainty knotting his stomach. Then Ty wedged himself up, too, bending towards him. Their mouths met in a soft kiss, more a caress than anything else, comforting and reassuring. "Sleep," Lewis agreed, collapsing down to bury his face in Crissy's neck.

Chapter Fourteen
Po'Boy

Po'Boy squinted in disbelief as the man spoke to him over a scarred table near the back of a bar deep in Plaquemines Parish. "Gonna need more than that." A broken fingernail caked with engine grease tipped the finger sliding the envelope back over in front of Po'Boy.

"You ain't got no idea what's on the table." Po'Boy ignored the envelope, which he knew was respectably thick, and leaned back in his chair, hooking one elbow over the seat next to him. "Certain you can afford to turn down a sure thing without even knowing what's what?" The unstated but implied question, was if the man, who'd been a reliable source of information in the past, could afford to piss off the IMC and Po'Boy.

"Yeah, seein' as if I take it and you're wantin' to know what I think you're wantin' to know, I'm fucked either way." The man shook his head, greasy strands of hair falling across his face. "I cain't help ya, not this time, Po'Boy."

Po'Boy didn't respond. He didn't stop the man as he began to push to his feet. Didn't even stop the man when he turned to walk away. After a few moments, he called out one word, "Tessimine." As he'd expected, the man reacted. Whirling to face Po'Boy, his face had gone pale, accentuating his gaunt features. Po'Boy glanced down and up, shaking his head at everything he saw. Receding gums, unkempt appearance beyond what one would expect for a backwoods boy, at least twenty pounds of weight gone as evidenced by his sagging jeans and too-large T-shirt. "You're cookin' over in Sun. CoBos frown on someone shittin' on their plot. Prolly thought you was far enough to go unnoticed." He sighed, holding his hands out in a "what do you want" gesture. "Jeff Tessimine is a fuckin' idiot. Man don't know when not to run his fuckin' mouth. You didn't count on that. Need to pick your partners better, dude. Sucks he jacked you like that."

He used one booted foot to kick the leg of the recently vacated chair, moving it away from the table. "Come on back here. Sit down. You give me what I want, for what I want, I'll overlook telling the CoBos about your meth lab until sundown. Gives you at least half a day to shut it down and shift it." He leaned forwards as the man sat down, wrinkling his nose when he caught a whiff of unwashed body. "What you don't wanna do is shift east into Bastards' territory, and you for fuckin' sure do not want to shift west into mine."

Po'Boy settled back as the man grabbed the envelope and shoved it into the back pocket of his jeans without even opening it. "Now we've settled the question about what you are willin' to take on, I do believe it's time for you to ask me what I need."

"What..." The man swallowed hard, and angled his head down, trying to hide his anger. "What do you need?"

"What do I need, what?" Now he was just taunting the man, and he mentally chided himself for it.

"What do you need, Po'Boy?"

"Got that right in one, boy. Good job. I need—" He settled his elbows on the table, palms laid flat on the surface. "—Deuces. Plain and simple. I need Deuces. Gimme everything you got on him."

An hour later he walked out of the bar with a broad grin, glancing overhead at the dark clouds. As usual, he'd picked his source well. Seemed the man had everything he needed after all. Thunder rumbled in the distance, and he slung a leg over his bike, thumbing a text to Twisted. **Got everything we need.** Without waiting on a response, he shoved the phone deep into his pocket and headed onto the highway rolling north.

The man had more than he'd expected. Not only did he offer proof Deuces was dealing with Columbia, but he had a dozen routes that'd been opened up since they'd gotten Sam's phone. Po'Boy was pondering the implications when he realized he was rolling into the south side of Ponchatoula, passing the carwash where he'd last set eyes on baby Abigail.

His mind immediately went to her and how fast the news had dropped her story. As soon as they knew she was safe and had family, gotten their weeping sound clips from a daddy grateful she was safe and alive, even as he mourned her mother's death, the news stations had moved on to greener pastures.

Mebbe redder ones, he thought, reaching up to tug on his earlobe, fingers catching on the scar there as they always did, spending a second or two tracing it back to his scalp. His mind replayed the soundtrack to that day, hearing Jimbo say, "Poor boy, you done good," adding in the unexpected belly drop when he realized it was Po'Boy the old man was saying. *Named.*

Seemed the news was full of tales of woe, something southern Louisiana had in plenty. There'd been a string of multiple murders, bodies left in plain sight as a clear warning, the only question was who was warning who. Other than disposal, there weren't any clear similarities between the victims, at least that the news could put together. *Hell, they can't wipe their own asses most days. Sure as shit the po-po know more. Wish like fuck we still had an inside with the state boys.* Incoherent had lost their inside man when he passed unexpectedly, and as hard as Twisted had worked his magic, they hadn't been able to find another amenable person placed in the right position. *Yet*, he thought, snorting as he eased to a stop at a red light.

He glanced around, scanning left to right, and his heart stuttered when he saw a familiar silhouette in the front window of a diner. Staring closer, he realized his mistake, the man seated at the table was about three decades too young to be the one he'd feared seeing.

As he pulled away from the light, working his way up through the gears, Po'Boy shook his head. *Grover. Motherfucker*.

As much as he'd talked to Twisted through the years, his childhood had been one secret he'd held close to the vest. As far as Twisted knew, Ralphie Lewis had sprung full-grown onto the school playground that day. No reason to tell him any differently. Lewis let his thoughts slide to last night with Crissy and Ty and his mouth twisted sideways wryly. *Two secrets*. The expression faded.

Lewis' father had run off before he was born, leaving his mother to birth him alone in the hospital in Hammond. Lewis didn't even know the man's name, or where he was from. Didn't care either. His mother, Shirley, was destitute, her family, angry at her for being pregnant out of wedlock, had disowned her for deciding to keep the baby. One of the nurses at the hospital had told her about a job cleaning house down in Ponchatoula, for slim wages, but the job could include room and board for her and her baby. She'd never had to work for a living, but within days they were installed on the estate owned by Archie Grover, and those wide, expansive grounds were where Lewis had learned to walk and talk, ever conscious his real place in the house was up the back stairs to the dark and stuffy bedrooms reserved for staff.

When Lewis was five, Mrs. Grover had died from an unspecified ailment. It killed her slowly, eating at her from the inside, and by the end, he had sensed everyone's relief she was finally gone. It wasn't long after when Grover, the man who owned the estate, had turned his eyes towards Shirley. Two years later she and Grover were married, filing paperwork at the local courthouse with no fanfare.

To the outside world they probably appeared happy, a perfectly blended family, little Ralphie babied by Grover's two older children. The only thing that changed for Shirley was she shared a bed with the man, her duties unchanging regardless of any papers. In reality, for Ralphie, the estate quickly became hell on earth, Grover's children resentful of Shirley's place in their father's bed, their deep resentment taken out on Ralphie. Grover and Shirley turned a blind eye on any scrapes or bruises he collected, and Shirley continued to blame Ralphie for most things. After all, he was the reason her own family shunned her.

For five years, things rocked along, until Shirley was caught in the crossfire between police and robbers, falling dead on the floor beside where Ralph knelt.

Not long afterwards was when the nighttime visits began. Grover seeking his pleasure wherever he desired, and no one left in the house to tell him no.

Po'Boy pulled in an unsteady breath. *Ain't that kid no more.* That was a promise to himself. *He ain't the reason I like what I like, either.* Something it had taken him longer to figure out, and a fear which could still trip him up at times.

The curtains at the window stirred in the nighttime breeze, curling ripples of cooler air passing through and into his bedroom. With hesitant movements, he prodded and explored the edges of the bruising on his jaw and around his eye, mapping a discomfort that had far less sting than what he'd experienced on the playground today.

His every thought circled those moments. The taunting yells, faces all around, mouths open wide in anticipation of seeing someone get hurt. The sudden, brutal pain in his face. Two hits, then a third, and then everything tilted sideways as the earth moved away from underneath his feet, dumping him flat of his back. Ralph, *he thought, stepping carefully along the line in his head. A grown-up name, given to him by a boy he thought would be an enemy, but who just might be a friend instead.*

Ralph knew George, knew of him anyway. Knew where he lived, mostly, and that he was somehow tied up in the mysteries laying behind the red door of the house at the end of Nondall Lane. Parents talk, and kids listen, then discuss whatever adult tidbits they've overheard. Gossip was the currency for popularity in school, and Ralph had tried to pay his dues, never catching along more than the edges of the in-crowd.

Gossip said George's mother was a whore. Gossip also said he'd whup the ass of anyone daring to say that to his face.

Ralph tested the bruises on his face again, pressure from his fingertips finding them just as uncomfortable as before. The boy could whup ass, that was for sure. *These weren't the first bruises Ralph had sported, not by a long shot. Just the first ones given to him by someone not kin or near-kin.*

A creaking floorboard in the hallway exposed the approach of the monster in the house, his stepfather, Grover. The man's full name was Archibald Jefferson Grover, but Ralph—he held onto that tiny change in his head, shifting from Ralphie to Ralph with a liquid twist—had never heard anyone outside the family call the man anything except Grover, or Mr. Grover. Another creak, and Ralph waited to see if he would pass by tonight, see if the man moved on to the next door in the hallway. That one belonged to his daughter's room, Genevieve. It made Ralph sick to hope for reprieve when he knew his relief would mean suffering for another, but Ralph did like he always did. He prayed.

Please, baby Jesus, don't let him open the door. Please, sweet baby Jesus.

The doorknob rattled and hinges made a coarse grinding sound, so loud it echoed up the hallway. Ralph knew the noise would make it to

Genevieve and Jeff, her brother, giving them assurance they could breathe freely tonight, owning the relief he'd longed for.

Denied.

Again.

Grover's breathing sounded in his room, and Ralph closed his eyes tightly, hoping against hope the man would go away if he believed Ralph asleep. Hoping, even as he knew slumber wasn't a real deterrent. He'd been woken more than once by hands and fingers digging and prodding at him. Memories curdled his stomach, and he swallowed hard, fighting the bitterness threatening to flood his throat.

A bare sole twisted against the flooring, giving a faint squeak, telling him Grover must be fresh from his bath. A clue to the night's activities, because if he'd intended to get messy Grover would have visited before bathing.

Nearer his bed, a muffled thud as something was kicked, shifting and moving, propelled out of Grover's way. No impediment in this house registered when Grover wanted something. He wanted it, he took it, complaining and ranting about how the outside world didn't fall into line as he demanded. He had to negotiate for his desires out there, work for what he wanted. Here, anything at all was available at a word. Without labor involved, it was cheapened, made worthless by its very accessibility. People as playthings; pawns in games played within these walls that trapped so much more than sounds.

"Boy." When Grover spoke in the night, he never used anything else. Always "boy" or "son," never names, as if uttering a designation so personal was abhorrent in the act. Impersonal in word, very personal in deed. "Belly down. Knees to the floor."

Ralphie squeezed his eyes tighter, tiny starbursts of light flaring in the darkness behind his lids. Even in his mind he abandoned the name granted him today by George, wanting no part of their fledging friendship here. No taint, *he thought, flinching from the idea George could ever learn what happened in the dark.*

From the time of his mother's marriage to Grover, Ralphie had been subject to his whims. At first it had been gentle touches, Grover's excitement hidden in a façade of teaching pleasure to a child too young to understand. After Ralphie's mother's death things had altered and as months passed, Grover changed the way he played with Ralphie. The last time Grover so commanded him, Ralphie had something carefully inserted into his anus, burning caused by the probing finally fading away to a dull throbbing that lingered, and stayed with him for days.

"Boy, best be moving your ass, now." In the few seconds since he'd told Ralph what he expected, Grover's patience had slipped, and his words were clipped, brusque. Without pause Ralph complied, slithering to the side of the bed as he flipped to his belly, letting his legs drape over the edge of the mattress. "Good, boy." A hand slipped up the back of his leg, hard fingers moving to his crotch, flicking at his ballsac. "Good."

The waistband of his pajama bottoms was gripped and tugged, pulled inexorably downwards. Air from the open window gusted cool across his exposed skin, the curtains flapping in the sudden wind. Crickets chirping their version of a love song swelled for a moment then faded back, overwhelmed by his ears registering the sound of clothing hitting the floor behind him.

Po'Boy shook free from the memories as he leaned hard, angling the bike around the turn which would take him up onto the interstate. *Not something I'll be sharing with Ty or Crissy, either.* Some secrets needed to remain buried and as long as Grover stayed away, Lewis could hold his silence close. *Least Abigail's gonna be all right.* Twisting the throttle, he gunned the bike up the ramp and into traffic, recklessly weaving through and between traffic in his way, aiming his wheels straight towards Slidell.

***

Crissy

When she heard a bike driving into the parking lot, Crissy was standing in her kitchen, cold glass of sweet tea held in hand, e-reader in the other. Since so many bikers lived in the complex, it was a common sound, drawing her to the windows at all hours to eye the bikes, and try to get a glimpse of who was coming or going. Hoping to see one of two bikes she'd come to know very well.

This time the sounds of the bike's exhaust grew louder, and she knew it had pulled into the cul-de-sac her and Ty's condos shared with two other residences. One belonged to Pony, a man she'd only met a couple of times, but he seemed nice. He was in the same gang as Lewis. She knew because she'd seen the back of his vest more than once.

Neither Lewis nor Ty had made a big deal about what their affiliations were. Ty was in a different gang, and her in-depth searches online had shown her both were old organizations, established in the wake of so many disenfranchised soldiers returning to the country after the Vietnam War. Each gang was as feared or respected as the other, depending on which reporter wrote the news article. There were other gangs—*clubs*, she reminded herself, having noted that was what the members preferred to be called—in the area, many of them seeming so much worse than either the Incoherent or Caddo Hobos.

The easy friendship between Pony and Ty—Crissy sipped her tea, e-reader ignored for the moment, mentally converting the name to Wrench—was echoed in the interactions she'd seen between other members of the clubs, including between Wrench and Po'Boy. Lewis hadn't given her that name, but it was one she'd heard Wrench call him more than once when he'd slip up. Usually it was right after they got home, and Po'Boy would occasionally call him Wrench, too. Like it was a persona or something they could leave at the door.

Crissy knew better.

Having shared a bed with each man, and then together with them both, she knew even in sleep they carried a tension she hadn't been aware could even exist. In Ty's condo—Crissy laughed at how she reverted to his normal name in her thoughts of the inside of his home—nearly every drawer held a weapon of some sort, and there were knives balanced in many of the windows, tucked alongside the sills in case of...what? The zombie apocalypse?

Lewis' apartment in New Orleans wasn't as well stocked with guns, but the ones she'd caught sight of were placed in easily accessed locations, and loaded. He'd only asked her once if she'd shot guns before, and when she told him about going hunting with her daddy as she grew up just outside of Baton Rouge, he laughed and told her to make certain the safety was back on before she put it up.

The sound of the bike grew closer still and Crissy set her glass on the countertop, putting the e-reader to sleep as she lay it down. Making her way to the front door, she opened it in time to see Pony headed up the sidewalk towards Wrench's condo. When he saw Crissy, he veered her direction, tramping across the grass, boots leaving flattened patches in his wake. "Where's Wrench?" The question was barked, angry, and she didn't know what to do with it for a moment. "Bitch, where's Wrench?"

"I...uh, don't know?" Fingers holding tight to the doorframe, she still took a stumbling step backwards when he pulled to a stop directly in front of her, about three feet closer than Crissy found comfortable. "Sorry?"

"Jesus," he clipped, eyes raking down and then back up her frame before he arrowed a look over her shoulder into the living area. "You sure he ain't with you?"

"Uh...no?" She shook her head. "I mean, yes, I'm sure he's not here." She gestured behind her, taking another small step backwards. "I'm sure." Biting her lip, she tried to instill certainty into her last response, knowing she'd missed the mark when he rolled his eyes.

"Huh." Pony's grunt was accompanied by another blatant perusal of her body. "You're fuckin' tight, baby." His hand rose, and she stumbled in her haste to put more distance between them, a pained look appearing on his face at her movement. "Honey, no. I ain't gonna hurt you. Just sayin', you're a walkin', talkin' heart attack."

Crissy felt her brows draw together, confused. "A heart attack?"

Pony chuckled. "Nothing, honey." He smiled, the expression warm and inviting, as if she were a trusted friend, leaving her even more confused. "Let Wrench know I'm after him, yeah? I texted, but he might be ridin'. Figure he'll check you before he checks his phone."

"Oh. Okay." She hesitated, then asked, "How about Po'Boy?" The club name for Lewis felt odd in her mouth, foreign, a part of him she hadn't been granted access to, stolen by her claim to a stranger.

Pony's features sharpened, a look of alertness there which hadn't been present a moment before. "What about Po'Boy?"

"Well, he…uh. Sometimes he comes…" Her voice trailed off as his expression changed, transforming into a sexually aware look, filled with predatory hunger.

"Sometimes Po'Boy comes? Oh, honey. You're gettin' the best of it, ain't you." Pony took a step backwards, deliberately putting distance between them when before he had been crowding her. "Bitches all over Louisiana gonna be gunnin' for your head, them boys let it be known they're taken by a pretty thing like you."

"Well, I kinda already made a statement with Wrench." She didn't know where the admission came from, heard it falling from her lips at the same time he did. "Some girl named Sam was over, and she was just so rude to him. So I pretended—it was still pretend then," she rushed to explain, "—that he and I were together."

At Sam's name, his features alerted again, this a frightening change as he shook his head. "Not a good enemy to make—" He paused, then grinned broadly before finishing absurdly. "—Butternut. I got you, honey." Pulling his phone out, he messed with it for a minute before looking up at her expectantly. "Well?"

"Well, what?" The sound of several bikes in the distance pulled her attention towards the entrance from the road and she saw a half dozen unfamiliar bikes driving in, angling towards the other side of the complex. "What?"

"Your number, honey. So I can get you in my phone. I'll text you so you've got my number." He shook his head, his smile easy and affectionate. "Number, honey. What is it?"

"Uh…"

Pony glanced over his shoulder, then swore, "Fuck. Don't got time." Before she knew what was happening, he'd turned her around and she felt fingers at the back pocket of her jeans, then the absence of her phone which had been tucked inside there. Crissy whirled to face him in time to see Pony grinning down at the screen. Her background was one of the first pictures Lewis had sent her, weeks ago. Him and Ty smiling at the camera. "Jesus," Pony muttered, opening the phone app and pulling up a new contact form. A moment later his phone chimed, and he sighed. "You need me," handing her phone back with a confident, pleased smile, he instructed, "you call me. Any time, butternut."

After saying that strange word again, he was striding across the grass, headed towards the adjacent cul-de-sac, one hand lifted in a wave he didn't look to see if she returned.

* * *

Wrench

The thinly padded seat on the stool had become uncomfortable over the past two hours, and Wrench shifted irritably. Truman stalked to stand in front of him again, third time in the past fifteen minutes and stared pointedly down at the nearly empty beer glass on the bar. Licking his lips, Wrench nodded, earning a sneer for his reorder.

The fuck did you expect? You think Po'Boy's just sitting around and waiting for you to want to be around him? Wrench winced and pulled out his phone, hoping for an electronic distraction from the thoughts inside his head. He unlocked it and saw he'd received four text messages. Looking through them, he saw the first was one from Ace, asking for a callback. Phone to his ear, he waited through two rings then the call connected. He greeted his president with a grunted, "Yeah, boss? You rang, man?"

Focused on Ace, he absently watched Truman sauntering back towards him, noting the glass was full to the top, hardly any head on the beer at all. The oddity drew his attention, and he saw the moment the man decided to follow through with what he'd clearly been planning, dropping the glass too low for the bar top and clipping the bottom against the surface, tipping it towards where Wrench sat. With a curse, he jumped backwards, letting the stool topple to the floor behind him, narrowly avoiding taking a lapful of beer. A mess as it was, splashing on his boots, but if he hadn't been attentive, he would have had a long, wet, sticky ride back across the bridge.

"Sec," he said into the phone and shoved it in his pocket as he moved towards the dripping bar and a wide-eyed Truman. "Fucker, you wanna think twice before you pull that kinda shit again." Wrench reached across and gripped the man by the front of his shirt, pulling him half across the bar, sliding him back and forth slightly, mopping the beer up. "Stupid motherfucker."

Wrench released his hold, and Truman stumbled backwards, bracing himself against the back bar, face twisting with hate as he opened his mouth. "You think you're all kinds of special, don't you?" Brushing one palm down the front of his shirt, Truman grimaced. "You think being an asshole makes you someone he's going to want to keep around?"

"The fuck are you talking about, idiot?" Wrench bent slightly, hooking the stool with the fingers of one hand and setting it back upright. His belly felt scooped hollow, like he was just reaching the peak before the first big downslide on a roller coaster.

"Lewis." Truman had his full attention again with one word. "Do you—" He gestured towards Wrench, mouth pulled into an ugly slash across his face. "—think he is going to want someone like you around long term? He doesn't keep anyone long term. He only keeps them until they get attached."

"Is that a threat of some kind? You think you're gonna jack me around?" Wrench had known in his gut Truman had his eyes set on Po'Boy, or Lewis as he knew him. Feeling superior because Truman didn't know the half of the man Wrench had begun to think of as his, he scoffed and said, "You think you're something he'd ever want in his bed?"

"I've been in his bed, baby." Truman seemed to be finding his confidence in sparring with Wrench, and he advanced towards the bar again, leaning his palms against the flat surface. "He told me I was the best he'd ever had. For about six weeks. Then—" He pointed towards a muscular man standing nearby, who, like several patrons, had abandoned their seats when Truman spilled the drink. "—he took Greg to his bed, and no doubt told him the same thing."

Wrench swung to stare at the man who was glaring at Truman. "Shut up, Tru."

Wrench stared, because something about the man seemed familiar. *The set of his eyes, maybe?* His thoughts were interrupted when Truman got loud, shouting, "No, I think pretty boy deserves to know what he's sleeping with."

Greg shook his head. "Lewis' business, not yours." He turned to look at Wrench, his expression pitying. "And not mine, even if Truman's right. But—" Greg glared at Truman again. "—I lasted a fuck of a lot longer than six weeks." The sinking feeling had turned into a full-on express elevator to the basement, and Wrench gripped the back of the stool tightly, masking the tremors in his hands. Greg slapped a bill on the bar, then with a nod towards Wrench made his way to the door.

Wrench followed him, ignoring Truman's shout about payment, thinking the fucker could take it out of tips if he needed to pay for the one beer Wrench had consumed. On the sidewalk in front of Plaisirs Caches he caught up with Greg and stopped the man with a hand on his shoulder. "So you and..." He didn't have breath to finish the sentence, but Greg handled that for him.

Looking Wrench up and down, Greg said, "I suspect you know him better as Po'Boy, but yeah, I was with him. Truman was lying about him and Po'Boy, but for all he's an ass, Tru is right. Po'Boy doesn't do relationships. It's just sex to him. Never been anything but, and at least he never made any bones about the fact that's all it is...was."

Wrench dropped his hand, leaving Greg to turn and walk away. Sounds from his pocket snagged his attention, and he pulled his phone out, seeing the call to Ace was in the process of disconnecting. A moment later he got a text which said only, **Clubhouse. Church.**

Chin down, feet stuck to the sidewalk while staring at the phone he tried desperately to ignore the fear bubbling in his gut, he flipped to the other texts that had come in. One from Po'Boy, the message a selfie of him on his bike, erection in hand, grinning down at the phone with a caption, "All yours."

Two were from Pony, and he read them in order. **Need to talk to you.** That had been a half an hour earlier, then five minutes ago a cryptic, **Damn. You and Po'Boy? Fuck man.**

The fear overwhelmed him and in an instant, he was back at a backyard *fais-dodo*, listening to Bagger as he said, "Ain't for you. Gotta watch your p's and q's, son. Ever vigilant, that's a motto to live by." The old man had been talking about Penny, of course, but Wrench had turned the advice on its ear through the years, using it as a mantra to keep his head down as much as possible, working the club so it was everything he wanted or needed.

"Fuck." *I fucked up.*

With quick strides, he went to his bike and climbed on, shoving the key into the ignition so viciously it was a wonder it didn't break off. Ten minutes later he was on the bridge headed to Baton Rouge and the clubhouse to learn his fate.

***

Po'Boy

Idling into the condo parking lot, Po'Boy steered the truck towards a spot at the rear of the lot, backing in and killing the engine. After leaving Ponchatoula, he'd swung by the IMC clubhouse in Mandeville, pleased to run into Wildman. "Been too long, brother," had been the steady greeting from members as they came and went while he drank with his former prospect. Middle of the day when he arrived, he'd finally gotten a ride to his apartment about midnight, deciding to sleep it off there.

The dreams had woken him not three hours later, and he had wrestled with those demons for longer than he should have. Finally giving up on getting any more rest, sitting on the tiny balcony and smoking half of the smallest joint he'd rolled in a long time. That had taken him into thoughtful considerations of how long it had been since he'd smoked any green, something which was normally a constant. He tracked it back to the weekend spent with Crissy, before introducing Wrench into the mix. "Fuckin' weeks," he muttered now, eyeing the ashtray in the truck, knowing there'd probably be a joint in there. "Be stale as shit. Fucking junk weed now."

Leaving his cut on the seat as he swung out of the truck, he stretched, feeling the pull in his muscles from fighting the dreams earlier, tendons popping like snapped chicken bones as he pushed his joints to the limit. Not only hadn't he been smoking, he hadn't been working out, either. Or partying with his brothers, as had been pointed out many times tonight.

Po'Boy eyeballed Pony's condo across the street, thumbing the key in the door to lock the truck. The man had come into the clubhouse at one point, offering a quick shoulder bump and one-armed clinch. He confused Po'Boy with a muttered, "Fucking lucky asshole. You get all the best ass, man." But when asked what he meant, he just laughed, bending over to slap his knees before shouting to a prospect for a beer.

Turning towards Wrench's condo, Po'Boy saw Crissy's front light was on and her door open. Standing in the doorway, her frame was backlit from within her living room, sleep pants and tank top turning sheer in the lighting. "Hey, baby," he greeted, moving to her and putting a palm on her belly, pushing her back into the condo. "Ty in your bed tonight?" That would be unusual, even if it had just been the two of them. They always went to Ty's place, or Lewis' suite in New Orleans. Crissy's place was a stopover, a place to pick her up from in order to bring her over to Ty's, her arms around the neck of whoever came to get her. He gently kicked the door closed, bending to brush his mouth across hers, burying his hands into her hair, pinned precariously to the top of her head. "Missed you."

"Hey, Lewis." Her belated greeting was off, and he pulled back, staring down into her face and seeing clear signs of distress. She'd been crying recently, and a lot.

"What's wrong?" Po'Boy scanned her apartment, seeing the things that told him she was by herself. No boots on the floor, no cut draped over a chair. A single wineglass on the cabinet next to the sink. When she was with them, she drank beer, only consuming wine when alone. "Where's Ty?"

"He's home." He studied her, noting the lines of strain on her face. "Got home a while ago."

"Why aren't you there?" Lip between her teeth, she worried at it, chewing hard enough to make him wince. "Crissy, honey. What's wrong?"

"He...uh. He's...he said he's..." Fingertips pressing against her lips, she tried to hide the quiver of her chin. "He said he's done." Cupping her elbow in her other hand, she looked to be holding herself together by will alone. "He said *we're* done."

"What the fuck happened?" Reaching out, he wrapped his arms around her shoulders, pulling her close as the first sob broke free. "Oh, honey. What the fuck happened?"

"I think I messed up today," she whispered, words hard to make out muffled as they were against his chest. "Pony came over, and I didn't deny I was with Ty." She squirmed, burrowing closer, her voice softer when she said, "And I kinda said I was with you, too."

Po'Boy let his eyes slip closed. The one thing he had been most afraid of. Right there. Even so, Pony's admiring words and attitude didn't ring true, not to what she had said, so he pressed, asking, "What did you say?"

"I said I told Pony I was with both of you. That we were all together."

Jesus.

Gonna take my patch.

Why would Wrench...how would Wrench even know?

"Where'd Pony go after you told him?"

"He...uh. He got my number, put his number in my phone and texted himself, then he walked next door." She twisted, pushing back so she could look up into his face. Eyes swollen, she looked miserable. "Not to Ty's obviously, because he wasn't home, that's why Pony came over here in the first place. He went to the other next door."

The next set of condos held three IMC members. And one CoBos. *That's how Wrench knew what Crissy had done.*

"Pony got your number? Why?"

"He told me to call him if I needed anything." Her chin trembled, bouncing up and down as she tried to regain her composure. "I'm sorry, Lewis."

"Yeah, I bet he wants that call." *Fucker.* Even if it were the case, Pony's behavior still didn't ring true. "I'll go over, see what's up."

"He's probably sleeping." Tears welled in her eyes again, and she sniffed softly.

"Were you sleeping, honey?" She shook her head, the movement dislodging the pin holding her hair in place, causing it to cascade down around her shoulders. "Then neither is he." He bent, pressing his lips to hers, the kiss soft, meant to be reassuring. "I'll find out what's going on and let you know. It's fine, honey. I guarantee you there ain't nothing wrong other than Ty's havin' himself a bad day. I'll figure it out, and fix it."

"Promise?" She breathed the question, sounding full of hope and he nodded.

"Promise."

He lied.

***

Wrench

The lock made a forced grinding sound as the key was shoved in from the outside, and Wrench pushed so he was sitting a little more upright in the chair pulled around to face the door. He'd been waiting for this all night. Had expected it sooner. Surely hadn't expected to have to wait all night to have this particular scene. It had been easy enough to shut Crissy down, because she didn't argue. Didn't raise any kind of fuss, the only indication he'd hurt her had been written in her eyes, sculpted by the tear tracks raining down each cheek. Leaning sideways, he put the empty beer he'd been cradling for the last two hours on the floor, the glass bottle making a hollow thump against the wood.

Po'Boy entered, moving quickly to one side and pushing the door closed as he scanned the room, gaze coming to rest on Wrench. He didn't approach, which told Wrench absolutely nothing, because if he hadn't talked to Crissy, he might not know anything. Wrench remembered the look on Ace's face and revised his thinking. Po'Boy might know everything that had happened.

When Po'Boy spoke, his voice was soft and quiet, sounding nearly exactly how he'd sounded the nights they'd laid in bed with Crissy. Time spent talking about inconsequential things before falling asleep, voices pitched low so as not to wake her. "Sittin' in the dark?" Wrench ground his teeth, clenching his jaw, not responding. "Mind if I turn on a light?" Wrench maintained his silence, and Po'Boy reached out, fingers finding the switch on a nearby lamp and twisting to turn it on.

In the sudden illumination, he saw Po'Boy looked tired, exhausted. Lines of fatigue on his face, hair mussed like he'd climbed off a bike after a two-day run. As if he'd run a marathon today to get back to Slidell. *Back to Crissy and me*. Wrench squashed the thought, stuffing the emotions accompanying it as far down as he could. Po'Boy squatted

233

on his haunches, feet flat on the floor, folding in half, making himself small and giving Wrench the physical advantage. From there, arms wrapped around his knees, one hand dangling from a loosely clasped wrist, he appeared to study Wrench.

He's lost weight, Wrench thought, *a year ago he wouldn't have been able to squat like that*. "You have a nightmare?" Even folded in on himself like he was, Po'Boy still flinched at the question. "Yeah, I know you have problems sleeping sometimes. You look like hell, did you sleep?"

Now it was Po'Boy's turn to be silent as he shook his head back and forth, the movement slow and cautious. He shifted, putting a knee to the floor, rising a little at what he must have thought was a challenge. Wrench sighed, with the way they were both dancing around the inevitable, they weren't getting any closer to what he needed, so he decided to just barge through.

"Po'Boy—" He got no farther before Po'Boy interrupted him.

"You call me Lewis." No smile, no anger, just a flat statement of what he wanted.

"No, I don't. Not always." Wrench shook his head.

"You call me Lewis *here*." His stare unblinking, Po'Boy waited.

"Yeah, well, not anymore." *There*, Wrench thought, *that should tell him where I am*. Po'Boy's head tipped to the side the slightest amount. Interrogatory without putting a single question to words. "Don't try and do your voodoo shit on me, man. Won't work. I've got nothing else to say. We all knew it was a short-term thing, just cutting the term shorter than expected."

Po'Boy's head tipped a tiny bit farther, and Wrench snorted. *Give what I get*. He stayed silent, matching Po'Boy's posture. A minute passed by, then another before Po'Boy spoke again. "Crissy's hurtin'.

You mean for that to happen?" Clamping his lips together, Wrench shook his head. The pain had been clear on her face this evening, he knew how devastated she must be by now. "She can't sleep."

"She call you? She okay?" *Dammit*, he thought, *shut the fuck up*.

"Naw, man, she ain't okay." Po'Boy's accent slipped back into his speech, something Wrench had noted he tried hard to curb when away from the club. "She's sorry as fuck about what happened."

Puzzled, Wrench asked, "What does she think she had to do with it?" Everything, every single thing had been his fault. Not hers. "What'd she say?"

"You wanna talk to her? Give her a call." Po'Boy angled his chin to the table in front of the couch, and Wrench turned his head, looking to see his phone lying there. "Unless all you got to say is what you cut her with earlier."

"I didn't cut her. She didn't do anything." *It was all me. Might as well say it as think it*. "This is on me."

"What's on you, Ty?" Po'Boy shifted, lifting his knee so he was on his feet, still squatting, but poised for movement. "Tell me what happened, lemme help figure out how we can deal with this. It impacts more than just you. I can't fix what I don't know."

"Fuck you. My goddamned president knows I'm—" He couldn't say it. If he once uttered the words, they were out in the world, couldn't be taken back. "Fuck you."

"Ace knows what? Who talked to him? Did Pony come into your CH and cause shit? Mother*fucker*." In an instant, Po'Boy pushed to his feet, pacing in a short arc across the room and back, wound tight as if he'd been fighting for hours. He turned to glare at Wrench. "I'll fuckin' kill him. I will. I'll kill him, Ty. He ain't gonna cause you any shit. No shit at all. Ain't happenin'. And you don't have to give up Crissy. I know you like her. More than. I can be gone city as far as you're concerned, but don't cut her loose. She...fuck, man, I think she loves you." Po'Boy snapped his fingers, then pointed to Wrench's phone. "Call her. Right now, give her a call. I'll head out. You get her over here and sort your shit with her. She ain't sleepin', cain't sleep, man. Her talking to Pony is eatin' her up. She didn't really say shit though, that's the kicker. I ain't sure what tipped Ace off the deep end because Pony'd only be thinkin' we were sharing her, like I done before." Wrench stared at him, not understanding half of what he said. "Pony gonna pay for anything he did, brother. I'll deal with IMC, no worries on that side of the pipe. Fuck him up, man. Don't give a shit we're patched, I'll fuck him up." Po'Boy shook his head. "Why are you fuckin' sitting there, man? Call Crissy, set that right at least. I'll clean up the rest and get you clear of anything."

Wrench flattened his palms on the arms of the chair, using them to lever himself to his feet. He took a step towards his phone, then turned and asked, "What's Pony got to do with anything?"

"He came over and talked to Crissy, looking for your ass. She offered up some info she didn't mean to. Don't hold it against her, man. Pony's an asshole when he wants to be. Probably shook her up." Muscles in Po'Boy's arm bulged as his hand clenched into a tight fist. "I'll fuck him up man, you tell her she don't have to worry about him again."

"Pony talked to Crissy? So? He wasn't at the CoBos' house tonight." Wrench squinted, trying to make sense of what Po'Boy was saying. "That don't matter."

Po'Boy stilled, footsteps coming to a halt and he stared at Wrench. "Then what the fuck do you think Ace knows?"

"He heard me talking. Had to have." Wrench pulled his foot back and kicked the table, sending the traitorous phone flying. "Fucking Truman got under my skin. My fault. Everything, it's all my fault."

"Slow down," Po'Boy got closer, putting a hand on Wrench's arm. He shook off the hold, but turned to face Po'Boy, putting himself right into

Po'Boy's face. So close he felt the breaths of air it took for the man to say, "Tell me, Ty. Tell me what Truman has to do with anything. Did you cross the bridge and go to Orleans? Were you at the suite today? At the bar?" Wrench nodded. "And Truman, who you know is an asshole, said something and got you worked up?" Grimacing, because when stated like that it sounded like school yard shenanigans, he nodded again. "Ty," now Po'Boy's voice was cajoling, pulling the story out of him against his will. "What'd Truman say?"

"Said you had a max limit with someone. Said six weeks was pretty much the top end for you." Lewis' head jerked backwards and he blinked, shaking his head, clearly confused. "I already know you fucked him." That caused Lewis' eyes to narrow, anger flashing dangerously in their depths. Ty didn't care; he pushed closer, arching his back so they were chest-to-chest. "We've been with Crissy for more than six weeks. I figured maybe it's per person. Maybe that's how it's gone longer. But then Greg spoke up—"

Lewis interrupted him, his tone deadly. "Greg? Fucking Greg got in on the show? Jesus, Ty, did you think about asking me anything? Fuck, man. Truman and Greg have been together since I dumped Greg. And yeah, I dumped his ass because he was so fucking one dimensional it wasn't funny. He didn't see me, didn't know me. Wasn't someone I could sit around and have a beer with, just to shoot the shit. He was someone I fucked. Period. He started pussyin' up, tryin' for something he couldn't ever be. All I ever wanted was someone I could be me with. Fuck." Lewis shoved closer, the tip of his nose brushing Ty's. "You're cutting me off, cutting Crissy to the bone because of something you didn't even give me a chance to respond to? *Jesus.*" He tilted his head, studying Ty's face. "I thought I'd found...doesn't matter what I thought, does it? You already decided for all of us. And what in fuck does Ace have to do with anything."

"Greg knew your name." Ty watched as Lewis' pupils expanded, and knew it for fear. "My phone, the call with Ace didn't disconnect. He heard everything. Called me for church. I went and it was just business, but I know he heard. He heard. You know how it is in the club. They might like to shock the citizens, but in a lotta ways they are worse than the holy rollers. Hell, I'm still struggling, and I've been the one here, with you."

Lewis stepped backwards, taking his heat with him and Ty immediately noted its loss. Noted and missed it. *Want it back*. Face twisted with anger, Lewis clipped, "Except you aren't with me. Because you talked to two old hens. Two busybodies who got their pussy hurt, so they fed you a fuckin' line. And—" He took another step back, one Ty matched with a stride forwards, trying to stay close enough to touch. "—you ate it up. Hook, line, and sinker. Chowed down on that bullshit. No fuckin' idea what you were tearing down when you took your hands to the wall, you still tore it all to shit. This? This shit"—he gestured between them, then swung his arm to include Crissy next door—"so fuckin' fragile. Newborn with wobbly legs, wandering close to the edge of a cliff. One stumble and it's all gone. And that happened. You fuckin' stumbled, didn't you?" His hand came up and he placed a palm in the middle of Ty's chest and pushed. "You fuckin' stumbled and took it all down. I've never had—" He shoved again, and Ty gripped his wrist, pulling them closer together. "—anything I wanted to keep like I wanted you and Crissy. Lies and speculation, and you trashed the whole thing."

Lewis pulled in a hard breath through his nose, blowing it out in a steady stream, staring into Ty's eyes. *Maybe I fucked up*. The look of loss on his face speared Ty's chest, pain blooming in its wake, and he did the only thing he could think of. *I for sure hurt him*. He hadn't thought things through. Been reacting instead of thinking, and now the idea of losing what they had ripped through him. Leaning forwards, he lifted a hand to cup the edge of Lewis' jaw, tilting his head the same slightest amount as earlier, but this wasn't a question, it was an answer. *I'm sorry*. He dusted Lewis' lips with kisses, soft and gentle, tracing the contours of his mouth with the tip of his tongue. *So sorry*. A muscle in Lewis' jaw jumped under Ty's hand, and he raised his other, curling his fingers into the waistband of Lewis' jeans, holding him in place while he tried to deepen the kiss.

Lewis resisted, mouth closed, and when Ty opened his eyes to look at him, he found Lewis staring at him. Pulling back for a moment, he trailed a finger along Lewis' strong cheekbone, then angled his head to cover Lewis' mouth again, nibbling and licking, fingers threading through the man's hair, cupping the back of his skull to pull him close. The pounding in his head intensified. *Let me in*. With a groan Lewis kissed him back, arms wrapping around Ty's shoulders, holding on. *Holding me*.

His dick thudded in his pants, blood pounding through his erection, and he ground his hips into Lewis', incapable of being this close, being this intimate, and not touching his cock in some way. A breath later, Lewis had taken control of the kiss, like Ty expected, and he carefully eased the intensity off, keeping Ty from coming in his pants right there.

I'll never have this chance again. The words threaded through Ty's mind, and he latched onto them. *My chance to do for him. He's always been the one caring for us*. Ty broke the kiss and buried his face against Lewis' shoulder, finding words escaped him. *Just do anything, idiot*. He nuzzled Lewis' neck and felt him stiffen. Something told him Lewis was seconds away from leaving, from shoving Ty off him and walking out the door.

Desperate now, Ty dropped a hand to Lewis' crotch, fingers molding the fabric of his jeans around his rigid cock, gripping and stroking, finger and thumb circling as much as he could. Again, and again, he slipped his hand back and forth. Releasing his hold, he shoved his hand down, firmly caressing Lewis' balls, knowing he'd won a reprieve when Lewis widened his stance with a groan.

Ty shoved his other hand between them, working at the buckle of Lewis' belt, drawing the tang out of the way and unfastening his jeans, the sound of the zipper loud in the suddenly quiet room. Sliding his hand inside, he circled the base of Lewis' cock, exploring the sensation of something so familiar, but incredibly different. Palm around the shaft, he eased Lewis free from the confinement of fabric, a smear of wetness along the inside of his wrist witness to how aroused Lewis was.

"Jesus, that thing gonna fit in my mouth?" Ty squeezed his eyes shut tight, shocked at the words which had come tumbling out, relaxing a tiny bit when Lewis chuckled and nodded, the movement trailing his hair across Ty's cheek.

"Yeah, it'll fit." Lewis hesitated, then tugged Ty closer, hips pumping, shoving his cock through Ty's loosely clasped fist. "If you're gonna give me head, that is. It'll fit. I ain't so big."

"You're pretty big." Ty turned his head so he could cut his eyes up to see Lewis' face. The man was smiling. *That's good, right?* He tightened his hand and stroked slowly, giving a tiny twist at the head, noting the difference no foreskin made. "Let's see."

He stepped backwards and crouched, then took a knee in front of Lewis, shifting until he was on the floor, heels of his boots digging painfully into his ass. Lewis' cock was right in front of him, so hard it curved upwards towards Lewis' belly, his sac obscured by the jeans. Ty shoved Lewis' pants down farther, halfway to his knees, wanting a clear field of vision. His sac hung heavy, lightly furred, and Ty wondered what that would feel like in his mouth. Curious, he leaned forwards and traced up the inside of Lewis' leg with his nose, the rough hair coarse on his cheek. A moment later heat hit his other cheek as he buried his face in Lewis' crotch, breathing deeply.

"*Fuck.*" The breathy curse came from above him, and he peered up, seeing Lewis' face angled down watching him. Arms straight at his sides, Lewis had fisted his hands and seemed to be working hard at staying still. Ty reached up until his fingers encountered one hand, gratified when Lewis immediately gripped his fingers, squeezing. Ty brought Lewis' hand to his head, smoothing the man's palm on his scalp, encouraging without words Lewis do what he would with anyone other than Ty. *Someone experienced*, he thought, shifting so his closed lips rested on the side of Lewis' sac. Opening his mouth, he sucked one ball into his mouth, finding the texture of the skin another thing that was known and yet intensely foreign.

"Jesus." Fingers clutched in Ty's hair, gripping tight but not pulling or directing, just holding. Holding on. *Holding me*. "Ty, you don't—" He rolled Lewis' ball with his tongue, then let it slip out, dipping lower so he could reach the other one, giving it the same attention and treatment. "Jesus, *fuck*." Lewis' fingers relaxed, threading through his hair, every movement cautious. "Baby, you don't hafta—" Ty released Lewis' sac with a last swipe of his tongue, then burrowed into his crotch again, the heat and scent he found there intoxicating. He turned his head and placed his mouth at the base of Lewis' shaft, licking and sucking. Frustrated with the naturally evasive movement of the cock, he raised a hand to grip it, holding it in place for his ministrations. Working up towards the head, he covered every inch of satin skin with his mouth, kissing and laving his tongue along Lewis' cock, no longer tentative, he was enjoying provoking the sounds pouring from Lewis' mouth. Praise and curses rained down, and he sought out the sensitive places, mapping them from every scarce reaction. Fingers tightening in his hair a silent compass needle pointing out the way.

When he reached the crown, Ty didn't hesitate to slide it between his lips, tightening them around the shaft as he flicked his tongue back and forth over the highly sensitive glans. "Jesus, Ty." A tang met his tongue that he recognized, having tasted himself on Crissy's mouth a few nights before. He noted a difference in flavor, Lewis' darker, more mysterious in many ways. He lifted one hand to Lewis' sac, balancing it in his palm, fingers rolling and tugging. "God bless, baby." Still flicking with his tongue, he gave an experimental suck, changing his grip on Lewis' cock, tightening his fingers and stroking up and down. Where he'd kissed and licked was slick, but not enough, so he slipped his hand up to where his mouth was working and slicked his fingers, making the return stroke smoother.

Lewis groaned, "Fuck. Ty."

He sucked and stroked, keeping the motions slow and firm, Lewis' cock fattening in his mouth, pulsing and delivering tiny drops of semen. Testing the boundaries of his comfort, he slid his lips up to the crown, sucking hard, and then back down the shaft until his lips met his fingers. Lewis tightened his grip on Ty's head, pulling him off and tipping his head backwards. He bent, swooping down to kiss Ty roughly, a hand on either side of his face, holding him still for Lewis to ravage his mouth, tongue tangling with Ty's in a sliding dance. Drawing back, he stared into Ty's face for a moment, eyes searching for something. "Baby," he whispered, and the single word was filled with so much emotion, fear and love, lust and longing, that Ty's chest contracted, his heart seizing. Ty lunged upwards, crashing his mouth into Lewis', kissing him hard. Lewis' moan rolled down his throat before he settled back on his heels again, cock once again poised at his lips.

With greater confidence, he wrapped his tongue around the head, sucking hard for a triplet of heartbeats before easing off, dipping the tip of his tongue into Lewis' slit, lapping up the spicy fluids steadily leaking there. He slipped a finger into his mouth alongside the cock, getting it wet and slippery, then he wedged his hand between Lewis' legs, tracing along his taint. Lewis groaned loudly, and his cock jumped in Ty's mouth, hardening more, swelling with anticipation. Ty touched the pucker, circling it with his knuckles as if he were going to knock for entrance. Finger to his mouth again, he slicked up his finger a second time, then sucked hard on Lewis' cock, one hand on the shaft with a pulsing grip. Other hand between Lewis' legs, he retraced his path from before, arriving at Lewis' hole just when he sucked hard on the head of Lewis' cock, teasing first his fingertip inside, then stroking deeper. One knuckle, then two, and he focused on the in-and-out motion, marveling at how like and yet unlike this was with a woman.

Angling his head, he looked up Lewis' body to see the man leaning against the wall, chin up and mouth open, silent but obviously enjoying what Ty was doing. Lewis had one palm flat against the surface beside his hip, the other tangled in his own hair, half covering his eyes. Ty swirled his tongue around the rim of the crown again and again, thrusting his finger deeper and wiggling it in tiny circles inside Lewis, watching as Lewis pulled his bottom lip into his mouth and bit down, staving off a cry. It was so silent in the condo, Ty imagined he could hear the clock in the kitchen. *No wonder he's being quiet now, probably afraid of freaking me out.*

Deliberately he made a slurping sound, then tightened his lips around Lewis' cock again, pulling it deeper into his mouth. Curling his tongue, working it along the length he could reach, Ty hummed. Softly at first, then with more volume, pulling the sound from deeper in his throat than Lewis could reach, letting the vibrations rumble up through his tongue and feeling the tremble in his lips, knowing it would be magnified for Lewis. His reward was a low groan, and he concentrated, sucking hard.

Pulling off with an audible pop, he gave another noisy slurp and lick along the length of Lewis' cock, then tipped his head to look up, seeing those intense eyes focused on him. He hesitated, then whispered, "Touch me, talk to me, don't make me feel like a freak, Lewis. I don't know what the fuck I'm doing. Can you cut me a break, man?" He smiled tentatively, and Lewis' lips quirked at the corners. With quiet passion, he repeated, "Touch me. *Please.*"

Heat engulfed his cheek as Lewis cupped his face with a palm, fingertips tracing along his cheekbone. Lewis knuckled his lips, pulling Ty's bottom one first to one side, then the other, seeming mesmerized with the movement, with how Ty parted them for Lewis to slip his thumb inside, with seeing Ty's tongue appear to wrap around the tip. "Jesus, Ty. You're so fucking hot. Watching you is…mmmm. So fucking hot, seeing my dick disappear into your mouth." Lewis tightened around Ty's finger, which was still moving with slow thrusts. "You're learning all my secrets, everything I dreamed you'd do." Lewis' other hand threaded through Ty's hair, fingers tightening. "Gimme your fingers, baby. Lemme lube 'em up again. I want you to give me two." He pulled his thumb from Ty's mouth, using the tip to lever Ty's mouth open wider. "Now, open wide, and suck me off."

Wet heat surrounded his fingers, then tight heat as he dropped his hand down to slip two digits inside. Lewis slowly thrust his hips forwards, and his cock slid over Ty's tongue, hand gripping tightly around the shaft, controlling the depth of penetration that way. Keeping his lips looser, he let Lewis fuck his mouth, matching the rhythm with his movements.

"Suck me, baby." Obeying the demand, he found the right combination of pressure and suction. "So fucking hot like this. Goddamned eager to please. Not just anybody. Me. You're pleasing me, and you love it." A groan and he wanted more of those. "I love it." Ty modified his stroke inside Lewis, adding a twist of the wrist when his fingers were buried deep, Lewis' moan shuddered through his cock and into Ty's mouth. He added an answering hum. "Jesus, yes. Fuck me like that. Wish it was your dick. Watched you with our Crissy, know you can work that monster. Worked her over good, Jesus, watching you was fucking torture. I knew. Knew you wanted. Know you want this. You and me both, Ty. You'd fuck me so good, baby."

Ty's cock jumped at those words, his heart rate spiking. *Yes, I want that, too.*

"You want that?" Lewis was like a mind reader, knowing every thought flashing through Ty's head. "You do. I know you do. Been thinking about it for weeks, something we never got a chance to carry through. Wanna fuck me here, against the wall? Wanna hold me in place and pound my ass? I can take a pounding, baby. You want it, you got it." Ty sucked harder, tongue dancing along the length in his mouth. Fingers working, he spread them inside Lewis, stretching him. "Hot as fuck, you handling me like this. You know what I want, every fucking time, baby. Every time, it's always you. So hot. You and Crissy." As he said their partner's name, Lewis' cock gave a pulse and heat hit Ty's tongue. "Fuck," Lewis hissed, "just the thought of her and you is enough to make me come. You suck me like that, you're gonna get a mouthful too soon. I wanna come when you're in my ass. Wanna come when you're pounding me. Deeper and deeper, fucking me hard. Get off, baby. Pull off." Ty ignored the stinging from his scalp, sucking Lewis harder, pulling him further into his mouth. "Jesus, Ty. No, baby."

He sucked hard, swallowing around Lewis, then pulled off with another pop. "You want it?"

"Jesus, yes. You wanna do that to me? Wanna fuck me?"

He stared at Lewis for a moment, then eased his fingers out and stood smoothly so they were chest to chest, face-to-face. "Yeah." It took him a minute, but he found his voice. "Yeah, Lewis. I want it." Lewis' eyes closed, and it looked like he was breathing a prayer. Then he turned around, chest and cheek to the wall. Pants already down to midthigh, his ass was right there, and Ty skimmed a palm across one curved cheek, digging his fingers in and rubbing, stroking, gripping and pulling. "What do I need to do, I don't want to..." His voice threatened to break and he let it trail off for a moment, taking his time before he continued. "I don't want to fuck it up."

Immediately Lewis gave him what he asked for, the answers coming readily. Practiced, maybe. "I like a little raunch. If you don't talk, I will. What you were doing before, finger-fucking me, that's all the prep I need. Don't go in completely dry—" Lewis twisted, looking over his shoulder at Ty. "—so if you need me on my knees first, just tell me." It was all so quickly negotiated, black and white. Settled.

"I have a packet of lube." Ty fumbled at his wallet, pulling out the small square. He'd gotten it a couple of weeks ago, an admission to himself of what he wanted, been wanting since the first time. He nearly dropped everything when Lewis reached out and plucked a condom from the folds, too. With a weighty look, he handed it to Ty, who stared at it, and then at Lewis, not understanding. *No, we're done with those.* Lewis held his gaze, and Ty watched as something passed behind Lewis' eyes he should have understood. Should have, but didn't. There was still arousal on Lewis' features, but it was tempered by an expression of certainty.

Ducking his head, Ty yanked at his belt, unfastening his pants with shaking fingers, shoving them down enough to get his cock and balls out, feeling the pressure of the fabric underneath as he smoothed the condom on, then liberally applied the lube. He leaned in and pressed a kiss to Lewis' spine, rolling his forehead there for a second. *What am I doing?* They were going a hundred miles an hour all of a sudden and he wasn't sure how to slow it down. "You want it here, like this?" *Maybe Lewis would prefer the bed, or the couch—*

His thoughts were cut off by Lewis' voice. "Yeah, here. Like this. With you." Lewis arched his back, pressing his ass backwards, and Ty groaned at the sudden pressure. "Fuck me, man." Lewis arched again, pushing back insistently. "You want it. I want it. Take it."

Ty heard Greg's voice in his head, *"Po'Boy doesn't do relationships. It's just sex to him."* His erection had already been flagging, the change in mood in the room breaking across him like a wave. Realizing this was what Greg had meant, that Po'Boy didn't need anything other than the act, killed the rest of his arousal.

"Hey?" Wrench was already stripping off the condom when he glanced up to see Po'Boy studying him. "You done, man?"

"Yeah. I'm done." He shoved his junk back into his pants, twisting to put his back to Po'Boy while he zipped up. By the time he'd turned around, Po'Boy had done the same. They were just two guys standing around. Could have been any two guys. Not two men who had shared an intimate act only moments ago. If he ignored the throbbing of his lips and ache in his jaw, he could forget the whole thing happened.

"What happened?" Po'Boy tilted his head that tiny amount he always did, just enough to indicate he was waiting for a response. "Just now, what was that?"

"What it was, Po'Boy—" He swallowed, feeling it in his gut when Po'Boy flinched. "—was me coming to my senses. You and me, we've worked for everything we have. Worked fucking hard. Today things nearly came toppling down around us. I think this—" He waved one hand, indicating the space between them. "—had already reached its natural conclusion." A muscle popped in Po'Boy's jaw, but he didn't say anything. "Crissy is a woman with a mind. If she decides she wants one of us, that's on her. She isn't something for us to argue over."

"You sayin' she ain't worth the fight?" Po'Boy spat out the question, squaring his shoulders in a way Wrench couldn't misunderstand. "Because I'll tell you you're a fucking idiot. She's worth fighting for. Fuck, she's worth fighting over. But you don't want her because she's somehow tainted from bein' with two men who were lovin' on her? Don't you fuckin' sweat it, man. I got her. I'll be whatever she needs me to be and you—" Po'Boy leaned closer, his expression fierce. "—can get fucked. I don't get what you're doin', but you were set on this from before me walking in here. I thought you were salvageable, this"—he gestured between them, much as Wrench had—"was salvageable, but I was wrong. You're a fuckin' idiot, and I got no time for such. Enjoy your goddamned life."

Po'Boy turned and without another word, swept through the door, slamming it so hard behind him the wall shuddered, the picture Wrench had of himself standing next to Bagger swaying dangerously close to falling off the nail that held it suspended. Wrench watched, fascinated as it wobbled wildly, then settled down, finally stilling, the frame out of whack, awry.

He whirled, facing the rest of the condo.

Empty.

"Fuck!"

***

Po'Boy

He stared at the phone as if it were a viper, turning in his grasp to lunge and pump poison deep under his skin. *Lotta things under my skin*, he thought. *Lotta poison inside.*

Flipping to recent calls, he assured himself he hadn't been caught in a nightmare. The phone had rung, and words had been said.

"Boy," greasy and rasping in the same breath, the voice from every nightmare slithered into his ear. *"I know your secret. You'll want to listen to me."*

He'd listened. Hadn't agreed to a damn thing, but he hadn't disagreed, either.

Chapter Fifteen
Po'Boy

"No, man. I gotta go." Po'Boy turned to face the door, not wanting to see the pain he knew would be on his brother's face. They'd been together forever, it seemed, but this would be something that would tear them apart. Abhorrent in the biker world, even if open mouthed kisses between brothers were used to shock citizens. "I can't…George,"—*here starts the separation*, he thought, *time to open up that first crack in our friendship, our brotherhood*—"this ain't something you can help me with."

Low and intense, Twisted's voice came at him from behind, pounding against and shaking his resolve to leave before he got kicked to the curb like a puppy who'd piddled on the carpet. "Don't go, brother."

"Man, I cain't stay." *Truth spoken*, he thought. It wouldn't be something he could ever put to words, but the torture of seeing Twisted with Penny ripped at him every day. Not the knowing she was what his friend needed. But that she could give the man everything he'd ever wanted. Family and a place to be himself, not whatever the club or world wanted from him or wanted him to be. But a place for him to just be. No, it was the knowing he'd found his own need answered with Ty and Crissy, but unlike Twisted, couldn't keep hold of his. *Everything slips*

249

through my goddamned fingers. "Glad as fuck you found what you did with Penny. She's your better half, no bout adoubt it. But I need...something different." That was dancing around facts he didn't want to have to put to words, while still not lying to Twisted. Their seventh-grade promise to each other still holding true. "I don't want to drag you down while I'm looking for that for me."

"Ain't dragging me down to let me help you find what you need, brother. I'm pretty sure I got an idea what it is." Closer, Twisted moved near enough Po'Boy could feel the heat against his back. Not as close as Ty had stood, though. The only man who'd ever known both sides of Po'Boy, and accepted both. *Gone with the tides*. Pain pierced him, then arms wrapped around him, pulling him back against the hardness that was his best friend's chest and he felt Twisted's muscles tighten, holding him in place. "Don't fuckin' quit on me, brother. You cain't go."

With a jerk and a lurching shove, Po'Boy pulled away. "I cain't stay. God*dammit*, don't do that shit. You don't know what I need. You don't know. Cain't know." Turning, he faced Twisted and shouted, anger rolling through his chest, making his throat tight, so his shout came out more of a whisper, "You cain't, George."

"You think I don't already know? Huh? You think this is news to me, brother?" Twisted made an impatient gesture with one hand, knifing the edge of his palm through the air. "Cut the shit, man. I know. I've always known. Love you how you are. Shit don't matter to me, not a fuckin' bit, and you fuckin' know it."

Po'Boy stood there, terror freezing him in place. He could swear his heart actually stuttered in his chest, the weight of panic so heavy the fist-sized muscle couldn't keep up, couldn't maintain the pace. *Is he saying what it sounds like?* Those recently received threats hung heavy in his mind, an outlined map of his destruction, perhaps already set into play. No words. Po'Boy couldn't find anything his mouth would agree to say, so he stood there silent. Mute in the face of what felt like a possible peril.

Twisted wasn't so afflicted, and he kept talking, sweeping the rug out from under Po'Boy in a way which meant they could never go back to before. "You're fuckin' gay. Have been. Shit like that don't change just because you want it to, brother." *He still called me brother.* "Life here ain't like it was when Jimbo was in charge. Fuck, man, life in the club ain't like it was five fuckin' years ago. Five years ago, woulda been a problem. Today?" Shaking his head, Twisted took a step towards him, stopping when Po'Boy retreated a step. "I've always known, brother. Since the first day in the fuckin' play yard back in Mandeville. Fuck, man, you think we'd be this close for this long and me not cotton on to the fact you like dick?"

Silent as a stone, Po'Boy locked his knees, horror making them weak. *Twisted knows, he's always known, and he stayed friends. Stayed by my side. Wanted me for the club.* His thoughts turned to the last big rally and meeting in the area, an even dozen clubs coming together to pay tribute to their dominant club: Incoherent. *Woulda weakened our position, folks knew about me.* Grover had well known the value of the cards he held and leveraged those to protect his son's surprise involvement in cartel business.

"Boy." The slippery voice had crept across the distance separating them, Po'Boy's arm in Grover's neck, holding him to the wall. "You do not want to do this. All you gotta do is stand down. Back off, and convince your friends to do the same." This meet hadn't been anything Po'Boy wanted, but the looming threat of that viper had sucked him in, bringing him here today.

Grover didn't seem worried, and Po'Boy realized his skin was powder dry. He ain't scared. Why? *Time to dig a bit. "The fuck you think's gonna happen here, old man? You ain't got no leverage. That boy of yours picked the wrong folks to back." He chuckled. "Shoulda stayed with the American bet, that's always best." He leaned harder, enjoying the sounds of Grover beginning to struggle for breath. "You ain't got a leg to stand on, man."*

"Got two of 'em, in fact." Face turning red, Grover managed to get the words out without wheezing. *"You and your boy, Georgie."*

Po'Boy tipped his head to one side, watching Grover's eyes. They never looked away, never flickered in nervousness, just stared at him. He's got something. Waiting, Po'Boy was finally rewarded with words which turned out not to be so rewarding, instead spinning his world on end. "Known Georgie for longer than you have, boy. Me and him, we was fuck buddies back when he didn't hardly have pubes. Your ass?" Grover made a dismissive sound as he stepped sideways, slipping out of Po'Boy's suddenly lax grip. "Paled in comparison. Now imagine how that man would feel if he was outed, and then found out it was your dear old daddy who did it? Tore down everything his granddad handed him, everything he's worked for."

Shaking his head, Grover straightened his collar, making a harsh tisking sound. "You think a man like him would be willing to forgive and forget? You've already lost everything, boy. You just didn't know it until now. Back down, and take your group with you. Leave my son his playground." Po'Boy stared, still disbelieving. "Me and you, we can keep a secret. You've proven that all these years. What's one more among family?"

With that final dig, Grover turned and walked through the door, leaving it swinging in his wake.

Resolved, Po'Boy shook his head, deciding to skirt the knowledge Twisted held, keeping every secret silent inside, he tried sidestepping the moment when he had to speak the words aloud. "I gotta go." Tipping his chin down, he broke the stare. "You love the club, you'll let me."

"Why now?" This might be the hardest question to answer, unless he was willing to be honest with Twisted. *First time for anything*, he thought with a snort, *withholding truth is nearly the same as lying.*

Twisted continued, "Brother, after everything we've been through, you gotta give me something. Don't do this."

"I..." He swallowed. *Fuck this is hard*. "I met someone." And he had, two someones who fit so well with him it still seemed unreal. *Gone and gone*, he thought, wishing with everything inside him that things were different. They weren't though, Ty and Crissy a shattered dream, but Twisted didn't need to know he wouldn't be running to the arms of a lover. Seeing Ty and knowing here was yet another man who wasn't willing to out himself, another man he couldn't have the kind of open and honest relationship he wanted, needed. *I need more than I've had, and Twisted needs what he's got. Means it's time to just go.*

"Who?" Of course Twisted would want to know. Was probably running IMC members and prospects through his head now, looking for another gay boy. "Someone you met recent like?" A shake of his head threw the idea away. Twisted persisted. "A member? Or someone you met from Orleans?" Another shake wasn't a lie, because the man he'd been dreaming about wasn't IMC, but wasn't from the Quarter, either. "Gonna make me play twenty questions? Fuck you, just fuckin' tell me, brother. I ain't givin' up on you. No way is that happenin', so just fuckin' tell me."

"That'll be something I won't miss, fucktard. You always pushin' like you know best. It's someone I've known a while, and before you ask the question I see on your goddamned face, yes, you know them. But I ain't gonna give them up, George."

"Fuckin' call me by my fuckin' name, Po'Boy." Growled, this seemed involuntarily ripped from his friend. "Stop your fuckin' shit."

"Twisted," he gave that, at least. "Brother." Gave that up, too. "Don't make this harder than it has to be."

"Fuck you," came the immediate response. "It doesn't have to be, brother. I piss you off and you actually fuckin' talk to me, you'll find you don't have to do this. I take you like you are, brother. No more, no less.

Exactly how I've always taken you. Club'll do the same, the ones who know you. Maybe there's others like me who know but were afraid to say anything. Afraid I'd push a scene just like this one. So I've been waiting. Maybe they're waiting, too." Po'Boy scoffed at the idea, and Twisted shook his head. "No, brother. Could be. Like me. See, I've been waiting on you to say something for a long time, until I realized how fuckin' deep you had that shit buried. Dug yourself a hole to China, stuffed your wants down that hole and then covered 'em up. Love you, brother. Not like that, not my way, but I am not going to judge you for what you need." He took a step towards Po'Boy, then another, until he was close enough to reach out and grip his bicep. "What I'm not willing to do is let you bail on us...on me, without a fuckin' fight. You're worth more than that, man. Worth a fuckuva lot, brother."

"Man, you keep me, you'll lose members. Incoherent would be at risk and I won't be the fucktard who puts your pappy's work on a dark path." Twisted's grip tightened to the point of pain, but he didn't say anything, letting Po'Boy speak his piece. "You need me gone, brother."

"Bullshit." Twisted shook his head. "I got intel you don't got, brother. I need you here, beside me, while we sort out this cartel shit. It's tied up in people we both know." He paused a moment, then spoke the name Po'Boy had been dreading for decades. "Grover's played his last card, brother. He's routing you with info I do not give one fuck about. Info I'll gladly speak to, because I know Jimbo already did, the night he took me outta Nondall's whorehouse. Ain't an OG in the club don't know what they saved me from. Him being your stepdaddy, I can only imagine. But—" Twisted leaned forwards at the waist, gaze intent on Po'Boy's face. "—he done fucked up. His spawn ain't worth the spit on my tongue, and I got an idea how to lay him out for the vultures. We'll sort it all, sort your shit, and we'll all be happy clams."

He repeated his words from before, "You need me gone, Twisted. I can't help with this."

"Fuck you. If I got a say—and we both know I have more than just a say—then you'll stay." Twisted's face cleared, worry leaching away and warmth infusing his features. He evidently had found an argument he believed in. "I ain't kidding about Grover's kid, Jeff. We gotta plan, brother. Plus, you're gonna hafta stay. Who's gonna keep my shit in line, if not you? 'Got your six.' Ain't that what you always tell me? Who's gonna have my six, you bail and run? You gotta stay."

"Club to the core. Ain't that what *we* always say?" Po'Boy turned the argument around, drew back, and aimed true. Saw the strike when his words hit home. "Twisted. Brother. I'm club to the core, and to save the club, it's gotta go down bad."

"Oh, no. Hell no. Fuck you sideways, ain't doin' that." Twisted's head came up, and he stared at Po'Boy, a wounded look on his face. "You find another home already?"

Having another patch lined up would have been a kill shot, and one he hadn't considered, but he dismissed it out of hand. "No. Never. But, you will cut me. You will. Listen to me, brother. Listen for a fucking minute and put aside what you want. It's the club, man. You need to cut me, and if I'm going to have a life that doesn't impact you and the club, you gotta do it in a way folks believe. I won't be going to another club. Fuck no, why would I do that when I have everything I've ever fuckin' wanted right here. But so it's believable, we gotta have a rift. A falling out."

Their gazes locked, and neither man spoke for a long minute. Twisted breathed in a shuddering sigh, one that voiced so much without a word passing his lips. When he did speak, it was something Po'Boy had to be, but still chilled his bones. "Out bad."

***

Wrench

"Naw, ain't got no issue with your boy, just wanna ask him a couple of things." Ace stared at Wrench from across the wide table, speaking to the cell phone laid on the surface in front of all the officers gathered today for church. Twisted had called, and Ace put him on speaker right away. As they had over the past two weeks, Ace's every action made Wrench nervous, had him overanalyzing things like putting a call on speaker. *Would he have done it like that before? Was this a chance to see if Twisted was going to out me?* Maybe that was what he was hoping for, since letting it happen in a meeting like this would mean it wasn't Ace who pulled the trigger.

Wrench swallowed hard and angled his head down, staring at the table, sweat breaking out across his shoulders as he listened with every fiber of his being.

Ace cleared his throat. "You wanna come here? This IMC asking for a meet?" That would be out of the norm, for sure. CoBos were allies of IMC, and formal meetings usually meant trouble they needed to tackle together. It wouldn't be trouble if Twisted was just calling Ace because Wrench wouldn't pick up Penny's calls for the past few days.

"Naw, Ace. Ain't nothing like that." Then, exhibiting either he expected the speakerphone or the call quality had indicated what Ace had done, Twisted addressed Wrench directly. "Wrench, just give me a goddamned call." An edge of threat entered his voice. "I got some fuckin' questions for you."

Breaking his silence, Wrench responded, "Yeah, I'll do that thing, when I got a minute."

"Fuckin' make a minute, brother." The word eased the sour in his stomach, a little.

Ace shook his head and shrugged, and Wrench grinned at him, surprised when Ace returned the expression. Wrench answered Twisted, "From boy to brother in under two minutes, I can probably make that call." Ace reached out and tapped the screen, disconnecting the call.

"What crawled up IMCs' ass these days?" Peanut, the CoBos VP since Bagger's death, leaned backwards in his chair. "I'd've thought Twisted would be pulling back, making fewer moves since he's got an old lady now. Especially since it's our Penny. I'm thinkin' he should have more of a care with her."

Ace snorted. "You seriously thinking our Penny would want him to change a thing? Jesus, Peanut, you know how she is. Been like that all her life." He cut a glance across to Wrench. "You think it's club, or just between the three of you?"

Fuck, does he think I'm with Twisted and Penny like I was Lewi—Po'Boy and Crissy? Nothing on Ace's face gave Wrench a clue, so he responded carefully. "Penny called a couple of times, and I was busy, sent her to voice mail. Wouldn't surprise me if she tried to enlist her man's help in making a connection." He curled his lip, letting a little of his known attitude towards Twisted show. Every man knew he'd gotten past his original dislike of the man, but it worked for laughs. "What would surprise me is if her old man extended that assistance." He snorted, shaking his head. "Jesus, make a purse out of it already." On cue, every man seated at the table laughed, leaning back, and the atmosphere in the room lightened.

Ace nodded at him, then looked around at the faces surrounding them. "Back to business, yeah? Sources say there's a big shipment headed our way. Diego's got a truck sittin' in a boat container, and word is that mother is full up with product for the far north. It hits the port down in Orleans, they got only a couple of route choices, and I expect they'll travel this direction, heading up through our territory. Wrench—" Ace tipped his head, directing a serious look Wrench's way, holding his gaze until Wrench nodded in response. "—need you to do your thing, brother. Activate what you need, talk to whoever has a fuckin' clue, but find the truck. They didn't ask permission to route this way, and we aren't about to fuckin' give it to 'em anyway. We find it, we torch it."

"Burn that mother," Peanut agreed with a nod.

Wrench glanced at the men surrounding him, seeing only trust and respect on their faces, then he looked at Ace. Pride shown on the man's expression and the feeling it generated was so unexpected it took Wrench aback. *I worked for a long time to earn it.* He shoved his chair back. "I'll start the net. See what I can scoop up." Standing, he leaned forwards, palm on the center of the club's emblem carved into the table. This was the closest CoBos had to an oath, and every man in the room had used the same gesture to underscore an important event, so they all knew what it meant. "I'm a Caddo Hobo, and I'll work my fingers to the bone for this club."

Ace stood, hands on his hips. He eyed Wrench narrowly, then nodded, seemingly satisfied. "I know you will, brother." Glancing around, Ace grinned broadly as he said, "Start the net, then call Penny. Save Twisted from our girl."

Shaking his head, Wrench headed out of the room to find privacy in order to make his calls. An hour later, he flicked a finger at a prospect to get him a fresh beer before dialing Penny, nodding his thanks when the bottle was set near his elbow on the bar.

"Finally, he calls." She didn't even bother saying hello, just opened with that, tone filled with sarcasm. "You know how hard I've been trying to get you on the phone, asshole?"

"You think comin' at me like that is going to earn you any points, Penny?" He lifted his beer and sipped, then grinned around the mouth of the bottle as he said, "How you doin', doll?"

"I'd be better if my best friend would call me back when I need to talk to him." Real hurt threaded through her voice, and he looked down, staring at the scarred wooden surface of the bar. "You too big and bad now for me?"

"No, honey. Just...got shit going on." He sipped his beer again, this swallow going down harder with his throat so tight. "Not an intentional slight, and you know it. If you'd needed me, you'd have texted when you didn't connect on the phone." He scoffed, the sound echoing in the silence she left between them. "Didn't have to sic your ole man on me. Fuck, that musta been a hard call for him to make."

"No." Her tone was flat, bland almost. Forced to be nothing of note, it shouted everything she said was noteworthy. "If he did make a call like that, it wouldn't be hard. Because he loves me."

Well, okay then. She wasn't pulling back from her anger, so he decided to let it go. "What'd you need, Penny?"

"I *need*," the emphasis was clear, "to know what the *fuck* is wrong with Po'Boy?"

That was the last question he expected from her, and his unguarded reaction probably revealed entirely too much. "What? Is he okay? What the fuck do you mean?"

"You tell me." Her response was so cryptic he wasn't sure how to respond. After a moment, she continued, "Po'Boy is Twisted's brother. Their connection is more than the club, deeper than a prospect's spewed 'ride or die' and you know that. Like you and me, how we go back before everything. What we have now tied it all together, history and present. Po'Boy and Twisted have that." She paused, and he waited. "*Had* that."

"Penny, what are you talking about?" Wrench leaned forwards, elbows to the table, phone to one ear, head cradled in his other hand.

"He's gone. Gave some bullshit excuse nobody believed and rolled out." Noise in the background of the clubhouse made Wrench look up, and he saw Dismal bringing in a large box, fingers wrapped around either end. Penny said, "Ty, there's talk I don't like. I'm in the truck for another two days, and can't get to him. I don't know what happened. But I know something did. Twisted is tore up and I can't get it out of him." She sounded frustrated, and he winced, knowing how it had to dig at her, not being able to find a way to help her ole man. "Jesus, I've fielded three calls about you, too, honey. People are worried about you."

"Nothing's wrong, honey." Wrench told the lie with a straight face, keeping his attention on Dismal's progress through the room. There were dark spots on his jeans, like he'd spilled gas on himself while fueling up. "And Po'Boy's always retreated to Orleans when he needed to, nothing different there."

"Why doesn't anyone know about your girl, then? If you and Po'Boy were in a...whatever you want to label it with that woman, why hasn't anyone mentioned meeting her?" Penny was tenacious when she thought she had an in, and Wrench knew he needed to shut her down for good. "Why?"

"Because it's none of their goddamned business. Who I fuck, or don't fuck, isn't anyone's business. As long as it doesn't hurt CoBos, then it's no skin off anyone's nose." Wrench lowered his voice. "And it isn't any of your business, either, Penny. I'm sorry if that hurts, but it's not. Hasn't been for a long time. If Twisted wanted a report on Po'Boy, he could have asked me. But I'm betting he doesn't know the exact why of this call, does he? I won't be sharing with him unless you push me. Leave it alone, honey."

"Ty, honey." Her words were filled with pain. "You were so happy. What happened?"

"Life." Throat tight, the sound of his voice was a harsh whisper. "The life. You know how it is."

"Can't you talk to him?"

"Nope." If he had to keep talking to her, he was going to strangle. Die right here, sitting at a table not twenty feet from men who would do anything for him. Anything, but accept who he loved. Wrench forced out another syllable. "Bye."

***

Crissy

Driving into the parking lot of the complex, Crissy scanned the spaces for any of Ty's vehicles and sighed when they were all conspicuously absent. If she didn't know better, she'd think he'd moved out entirely. Occasional sounds from within his condo put the lie to that. One morning she'd seen Sam sauntering to a car, and after living through that little walk of pain, Crissy had tried very hard not to listen too closely at night, glad her bedroom was on the opposite side of the building from Ty's.

He had moved on, that much was clear. Lewis had, too, a little slower, because he at least called or texted a few times in the beginning. Now, four weeks past B-Day—what she'd termed the breakup in her head—not so much. It had been eight days since she'd talked to him, and her last text had gone unanswered.

Well and truly done.

She parked and then sat in her car for a moment, trying to summon up the energy to climb out of the car and go inside. *At least I'm better now*, she thought, trying to convince herself. Desperately trying to not remember back to the first days when her emotions would rocket out of control at the least provocation. Thank goodness her boss was understanding, even if she knew he'd made the assumption her volatility was lingering grief over her sister's death.

Bag in hand, she made it up the walk and through her front door. Shoes to one side of the entryway, she dropped her purse and computer on the other, padding barefooted into the kitchen. She moved forward with her plans for another night of a frozen dinner eaten standing at the counter, no desire for anything more elaborate.

Later, she lay on her side in bed, e-reader in hand, finding herself skimming the same paragraph for the third time. She sighed and sat up, leaning against the headboard and picked up her phone.

I miss you.

So many unanswered thoughts in this text string. *I might as well be tossing scraps of paper into a fire*. She locked the phone but left it cradled in her hand, and not a minute later was unlocking it and returning to the text app.

I'm so glad you found love. Glad Bob wouldn't take no for an answer.

This had been one of Rhoda's favorite stories about her husband. How in the beginning she'd gotten cold feet and backed away, but he hadn't accepted it. He'd pushed against every wall she'd thrown up. Argued every reason she came up with about why they wouldn't work. She was a southern girl, through and through, and the idea of living in the frozen north had not appealed. But Bob returned to the well again and again, every time getting a little deeper with Rhoda, taking his first victory and turning it into a second, and a third. Over and over until finally Rhoda stood in the front of a church in Minnesota, pledging her life to his.

Missy's growing so fast. Maybe I should plan a trip up to see them.

When she moved back to Louisiana, visiting Bob and Missy often was something she'd intended to do. Staring down at the phone's screen, she mentally calculated how long it had been since she came to town. *Too long.* Shifting against the pillows, she glanced at the time and groaned. *At least it's the weekend, so I don't have to get up early.* The bed sprawled out too large beside her. Too large and empty. Her thoughts turned to the last time she'd seen Lewis lying beside her. It was the night everything went to hell, and she remembered every word spoken, every breath he'd taken.

Their shouting pulled her to the front of the condo and she was watching out the window when Lewis exited Ty's side of the building, not glancing back. With suddenly airless lungs, Crissy had watched in disbelief when he turned and disappeared into the shadows towards the end of the parking lot, then had seen his profile in sharp relief against the interior light of his truck when the door opened. Lewis climbed in and sat for a moment, head bowed over his hands clutching the steering wheel. Then he straightened and stepped back out of the truck, walking arrow-straight to her door.

She opened it as he reached the threshold and moved backwards, inviting him inside without a word. He'd crowded her against the wall, closing the door with a push of his heel as he wrapped strong arms around her, seeking solace as much as giving comfort. Face pressed to the side of her neck, he'd offered only two words. "I'm sorry."

She'd expected as much. Ty had been firm when he spoke to her earlier, and for all of Lewis' promises, she knew his attempt for the longshot it had proven to be. What she hadn't expected was the sudden piercing knowledge she was losing them both. Not until Lewis nearly left without speaking to her, not until his voice hit the air filled with a sadness that coated her soul. Not until his hold on her felt like a desperate goodbye.

Eyes closed, she leaned into his strength, pulling her dignity and resolve close, steadying her voice so when she spoke the pain was buried. "I know." Without pausing, she twisted free of his grip and stood on her own feet. Reaching out one hand, she waited, then when he didn't move, asked for one last boon from this man she'd come to love. "Stay tonight. Give me that."

She'd memorized these eyes, so expressive they seemed to show his every emotion, held this face and watched as he'd shattered inside her, kissed these lips even as filthy words of passion poured from that mouth. The moment the words hit the air she saw a multitude of expressions cross his features and took a chance, rolling up onto her toes, reaching to place her fingers across his lips, trying to lock inside the denial she knew was coming. "Please." Tracing the edges of his mouth with her fingertips, mesmerized by the feel of his skin under her touch, focusing only on the feeling, excluding any thoughts of him leaving. A sharp nod pressed his cheek into her hand, and she smiled.

Threading her fingers through his, she tugged and stopped, stymied when he didn't move, then shook her head in amusement as he leaned back to lock the door. She noted he didn't put the chain on, and wondered if he remembered Ty had a key. Then he was the one leading them towards her bedroom, fingers to the light switches along their way, leaving the space in darkness and shadows, his actions telling her she'd have him this night, at least.

He set her fingers to his belt, and she understood what he wanted. Building memories to last them past tonight. Focusing on her task, she took her time, not rushing, not wanting it to end but with the driving tension of knowing the reward would be sweet. A sweet frozen moment she would be able to pull out time and again, a comfort for them both. He was shirtless when she leaned in and scraped her teeth across one nipple, causing the first sound to burst from his throat, a full-fledged groan followed by a growling, "Woman."

That had given her pause, and she stopped her assault of his skin to arch back so she could see his face. Eyes closed, chin tilted upwards, he stood like one of the poses of Da Vinci's Vitruvian Man, arms lifted to the *side, feet spread slightly. Hair wild around his face from her fingers, he was living perfection. She didn't see the scars from a hard life, didn't see the marks left by his passage through the world. She saw only Lewis, her love. "Crissy," she told him, the single word a plea, and he opened his eyes and nodded, staring at her and brought his hands to her shoulders, holding her in place as he stepped backwards a stride.*

He undressed her slowly, kissing her mouth often, lips working side to side. He covered her skin with caresses from mouth and fingers, gracing every inch with his touch. She shivered, feeling gooseflesh crawling on her arms and he chased it away with the heat of his palms, stroking down until he gripped her hands, lifting them and matching each fingertip with his own, pressing so they were palm to palm, then he threaded his fingers through, locking his grip and backed towards the bed, taking her with him.

Once under the covers, they kissed, him on his side next to her, leaning over as she lifted her head and shoulders from the mattress, eager for the connection. "Crissy, my sweet Crissy." He murmured against her lips, "Gonna love on my Crissy."

And he had.

Every stroke of his hands on her skin etched into her memories. Every brush of his lips blazing a trail to her heart. She was ready for him long before he settled into place above her, hips cradled between her legs, rigid erection pressing against her core. Elbows locked, he stayed like that for a long moment, staring down at her, his gaze across her features almost a physical touch. "My Crissy," he said when he moved, hips arching back to bring his cock into alignment. "Mine."

She pulled in a hard breath as he entered her, filling her. Hands on his shoulders, she looked up at him, seeing his lashes clumping together, much as hers were. "Love me, Lewis."

His arms bent, and he gave her his weight with a groan, one hand sliding to the back of her neck, cradling her head to his shoulder as his other hand went behind her, holding tight. "I do."

Those were the last words he spoke. Not the last sounds, because he gave her groans and grunts, humming into her ear when she clenched tight around him, thrusting hard and deep to bring her over the edge, grinding the base of his cock into her clit as a final push. Then he lifted again and stared down at her as he plunged in and out, eyes covering every inch of her he could see in the shadows of her bedroom. When he came the expression on his face was fierce, mouth twisting, but he kept his eyes open and on her face, only collapsing on her at the end.

It had taken a long time for her to fall asleep, cradled in Lewis' arms. Much later, she woke in the darkness to his hands moving over her, cupping her sex before dipping a finger inside and then bringing it up to circle her clit. He played with her like that for a long time, bringing her to a climax twice before shoving the covers aside and making space for himself between her legs, tongue laving over her clit and thrusting inside. His fingers teasing as he pushed her until she orgasmed again, this one softly intense, driven to lingering shudders by his persistent attention. She groaned and buried her fingers in his hair, tugging his face away when he kept after her, the sensation from his tongue and lips, his fingers and scruff too much. Not enough.

Finally, he crawled up beside her and sprawled on his back, arm flung wide in an invitation she accepted, nestling against his side while he wrapped his arm around her shoulder. Covers tugged to her chin, she went back to sleep only waking in the morning to find him gone.

Smoothing the covers on that side of the bed, she leaned over and pressed a kiss to the empty pillow. "I miss you." Lifting her head, she stared at the wall standing between her and where Ty probably lay sleeping. She tried to keep the tremor from her voice when she whispered, "I miss you, too."

Resting back against the headboard, she picked up her e-reader, settling in for another sleepless night.

***

Po'Boy

He opened his eyes, blinking blearily at the moonshine coming through the window, and watched as the wind tossed treetops threw themselves in front of the sun's balance, unsuccessful at blocking out the weak light. *Fucking dreams*. Pinching with finger and thumb, Po'Boy applied pressure to the bridge of his nose, willing the stinging back.

He wasn't certain what woke him. Once the nightmares started in earnest, it could take a lot to pull Po'Boy out of their grip. The terror haunting his dreams had set itself in a tight spiral since things had ended with Crissy and Ty, circling closer and closer with every sweat-soaked wakening. Stomach pitching like he'd spent the day on a shrimp boat on the open Gulf, he'd wake unsure of where he was.

More than once he'd cried out for his mother, afraid the hand clutching the covers so tightly was his stepdaddy's. Not that she'd been around to help him when that part of his journey started. As if invited in by the thought, he saw a larger than life image of her dead face, blood crusting the inside edges of her nostrils, crimson bubbles passing out through her parted lips, each breaking skim of red spattering more of the substance on her cheeks and chin.

Shaking his head, he pushed to a half-sitting position, elbows to the sagging mattress behind him, head tipped forwards so his chin rested on his chest. Exhausted from the nights of interrupted sleep, he dozed in that position, head bobbing just enough to keep him on the cusp of being awake. *Fuck, I'm tired.*

The dreams hadn't been like this for a long time. In fact, he couldn't remember when they'd been so bad. Sleeping with Crissy and Ty had been a Godsend, because when he was with them, either nestled in the middle of his partners or being the biggest spoon to their cuddled sleeping arrangements, his dreams were sweet. Now, it was like the shades flew up when he went to sleep, memories coming at him double-time to make up the deficit.

Pounding at the door startled him, yanking his head upright and sending a hand to the nightstand where he noticed the tremors eased once the familiar weight hit his palm. On his feet now, he stepped into his jeans and strolled towards the rolling sounds still pummeling his front door. Easing to one side, he studied what he could of the figure in front of the door, gut rolling when he recognized the face of the man waiting for him to answer the demanding call.

Hand to the doorknob, he pulled it open abruptly, gun leveled at the man who had been so many things in his life: stepfather, nightmare, and now nemesis. Archibald Jefferson Grover.

Chapter Sixteen

Wrench

Staring across the table at Ace, Wrench ruthlessly controlled his breathing, praying the man didn't see how the pulse pounded in his throat, each beat of his heart taking up all available space, choking him. "The fuck you say?" As much as he didn't want to hear the story, he had to, because the ripples of gossip rolling through the biker community were brutal, filled with fear and pain. "Are you fucking kidding me?"

"Naw, man. Heard it from Wildman. He was Po'Boy's prospect, doubt he'd be spreading rumors like that if they weren't true." Ace scrubbed a palm across his chin, raspy whiskers making a sandpaper sound. "Jesus. Can you imagine being inside a whirlwind like that? *Shit.*" The last word was drawn out, extra vowels inserted as Ace shook his head.

Lips pressed tightly together, Wrench tipped his chin up, angling his gaze towards the ceiling. *What the fuck is the man playing at?* Po'Boy loved IMC, like Wrench loved the CoBos. That was one of the many things the two men had in common, a belief in the ideals and value found in the life. *If he really is…*his mind shied from the phrase, and Wrench tried again to wrap his head around what Ace had told him. "Tell me again." He kept his gaze turned upwards, focusing on a spot near the angle of the wall. The shadow there could resemble a spider, in some light looking real enough to cause more than one brother to throw things in attempts to dislodge what was seen as an unwelcome visitor. One party in particular had seen a blitzed-out Peanut climbing on a chair with shoe in hand, ready to show the shadow who was boss.

"Twisted met with him one morning. Shouting, but not enough anyone thought much of it, those two always got on like a house afire. Moonshine and Mason jars, you know? A call went out for officers. None of them are talking, but word is Twisted called him to the floor." Ace laughed, the jagged sound without humor. "Those two been ride or die since I can remember, man. This is hard to swallow. And you"— Wrench's gut soured, waiting for whatever Ace said next—"you're close with both, outside the club. What's your take on this?"

"Twisted actually took his colors?" He eyed the end of the curtain rod which cast the shadow, noting the cap was delicate and ornate, and looked nothing like a spider.

"Yeah, cut him right there as he stood. Left his vest hole-punched and naked. Wildman snapped a pic as Po'Boy walked out of the house." Ace's shadow danced up the wall as he lifted his arms overhead, the darkness clearly identifiable as a man, but from the shadow alone you wouldn't have a clue who. "Pic's making the rounds, brother. You ain't seen it yet, you will."

"Twisted called him to the floor and cut him? Only officers present, and no general message out to members yet?" Things weren't adding up. If a club cut a man, people were told, informed so they didn't fuck up and stay in touch. A cut member was shunned from the moment the blade hit the threads. They lost everything they'd worked for: club, brothers...the brotherhood.

"Yeah, not how I'd do it, either. I know what you're thinking, but if they were just sending him in quiet like, they wouldn't have cut him." A pause, the shadow of the man shifting and changing shape as Ace moved. "We've done that with you, had you go in naked to places. But you held your patches. We'd never have cut you for a run."

"Spider's back." Wrench lifted an arm and pointed to the shadow, noting idly how his hands trembled. "You look at the ceiling, you'll see it." He shifted his angle, pointing at the end of the curtain rod instead. "You look there, you know the spider's not real. But that's not what catches your eye at first. Your brain sees the thing that makes you the most nervous, draws your attention to the perceived threat, so you can deal." Straightening in his seat, he glared at Ace, seeing the same hope he had burning in his belly. "Ain't no way Po'Boy's out bad. No way in fucking hell."

Ace blinked slowly and stared back at him. A pained expression crossed his face, and he seemed to square his shoulders slightly. "You and me, we never talked about what I heard on the phone." Quick as a thought, Wrench was on his feet and headed towards the door, his body taking over with a response he'd never had before: flight. "Do not touch that fucking door." The barked order stopped him in his tracks, and he glanced over his shoulder to the man sitting at the table. Regret and anger were what greeted him, neither of which made sense if he was about to out Wrench. "Not my choice of topics either, bastard. But you're about to make another mistake."

Turning to face him even though every instinct told him to get out, Wrench waited, two words still dancing around his head, a shrieking alarm so loud it was hard to hear Ace. *Out bad.* Ace pulled his attention again, saying, "You done fucked up with Po'Boy. Don't let your shit get in the way of your good sense, son."

Faced with what he'd been fearing and dreading since that day in New Orleans, fighting to stay still as ordered, Wrench was unsure what the man was trying to imply and shrugged his confusion.

"Jesus. You ditched the motherfucker because you were afraid of what might happen. You've been a miserable bastard since. Climbing up everyone's ass when you didn't need to. Ty"—this wasn't Ace talking, this was Tommy Canton, his father's life-long friend—"you thought so little of us you didn't give us a chance to prove you wrong. Not my choice of partners for you, son, but if he matters, then you need to get your thumb out of it and dig deep to get back to where you want to be. He's out bad, that's all we know. You think it's a diversion, then let's work on that. We can call Twisted, use club relations as a reason, keep Po'Boy's secrets as best we can while we try to sort things out from where we stand." Pushing to his feet, Ace leaned towards Wrench, a palm out. "Don't run from the spider because your brain's tricking you into thinkin' that's what I am. Come on, son. *Let me help*."

***

Twisted

Thumb pressed to the underside of his brow, pressure applied against a pain that couldn't be eased, Twisted sat and stared at the tree line without realizing time had passed, only noticing when Penny walked outside. Glancing up, he saw worry and fear fight for dominance on her features, angling his chin down and looking at the boards between his boots before either could win. On the one hand, he was glad to his bones she was home. On the other hand, he knew it'd be far more difficult to avoid giving her answers when she was in his face.

The slant of the shadows had changed, edges becoming less defined, and he estimated he'd been home a couple of hours, not making it past the chair on the front porch. Bone tired and locked into the events of the past two days, he couldn't free his mind from the mire of thoughts and emotions, running the gamut from fiercely angry to hopeless. He realized Penny had come no closer, and didn't blame her, admitting as much with a warning, "Not fit company, darlin'." He took a chance at why she'd come out to where he sat. "Go ahead and eat. I'll be inside in a bit."

Silence, then the soft, sure padding of bare feet coming towards him. She climbed into his lap, wedging her way between his arms, folding herself against his chest. With a sigh, he wrapped her up, squeezing tight. *She always knows what I need*. He swallowed hard, then muttered, "Gonna be a while before I'm good, Penny. I cain't change direction on a dime."

"Did I ask you to?" She burrowed her face into his neck, pressing close.

They sat like that for an hour, then two, and Twisted only stirred when the annoying buzz of mosquitos became incessant. "Gonna get eat up you stay out here, darlin'. Skeeters are out in force tonight."

"I get eat up, you'll get eat up. We'll scratch each other's itch." He chuckled, and she snorted, then giggled as she lifted her head. "Not what I meant, but that's funny as hell."

"That it is." Tipping his chin towards his neck, he stared into her eyes, weighing his options. As the daughter of one club and queen of another, she knew about the life, knew there were many things he couldn't talk about with her. Still the pain clamping tight around his chest demanded some kind of release, and he knew if he could only share it with her, there would be some give in those iron bands holding him captive.

He'd constructed and discarded a thousand plans over the course of the past two days. Looking for anything which would put an end to what he prayed would remain farce and give Po'Boy the chance to come home. *Me and Chip, his only contacts*. A program too quickly put into place meant Po'Boy was hung so far out there to dry it'd take a miracle to get back with skin intact. Just the idea of him working without a net like this left Twisted with a sick feeling, like he was crawling out of his skin.

There was a fluttering touch along his bicep and then a sting followed by a growing burn. He jostled Penny when he reached across to slap the mosquito, leaving a smear of red behind. *Ain't bleedin' for your ass, motherfucker*. He paused, finally finding the words he needed to say. "You know me and Po'Boy been ride or die for a while. He's been my brother long as I can remember." Not a question, still he waited until she nodded, the softness of her skin sliding across his chest. "I don't say this lightly, Penny. The man can do no wrong in my eyes." He paused again, and she made a noise he took to be agreement. His heart swelled, because he knew Penny felt the same way, had a bond with Po'Boy that was nearly as strong. "No wrong. Nothing he could do would give me pause. So you can do what you will with the knowledge."

He stood abruptly, cradling her to his chest for a moment before he let her slowly slide down his torso. "Need to fog or light a candle, skeeters are gettin' bad." Without another word he walked away, leaving a stunned, speechless Penny behind him. *Do with that what you will, darlin'.*

The look on Po'Boy's face when Twisted had called him to the floor had been bad enough. The bogus charges they'd cooked up with Chip's help had run across Twisted's tongue and lips like acid. Collaborating with the enemy, but without specifying the individual, left everything up to the imagination. Knowing he'd been part of the club running cartel assets to the ground in Ponchatoula had made several officers cock their heads, but with Po'Boy not refuting anything, only two spoke out against the deed. Catfish and Ragman, both hard men to fool, and Twisted could only hope their act had been believable. The rest damned him by his own silence.

Knife held between numb fingers, Twisted had set to sawing the patches off the man's vest as he stood there, fists in hard balls at the end of each arm. There was no way to reassure him; any word spoken would expose the lie. Po'Boy didn't speak, teeth clamped so tightly it was a wonder they didn't shatter like glass in his mouth. He had to stand and take it, circumstances muted him as effectively as severing the muscle of his tongue.

Twisted could only imagine how Po'Boy felt to see the weathered patches in the hands of an officer, wonder at how light the vest must have seemed without the weight of the club on it. One thing he didn't have to wonder about was what Po'Boy had in his heart, because the agony was plain on his features. "'Bout fuckin' killed me to do it, brother."

Twisted looked around, realizing he'd stalked the entire way through the house, and was now standing on the back porch, where the skeeters were arguably worse than around the front, stinging bites blooming on his arms and neck as the bloodsucking insects honed in on vulnerable flesh. "*Fuck,*" he shouted, drawing his foot back and sending a table sailing over the rail with a hard kick.

* * *

Penny

She stared at Twisted's back as he stalked away from her and into the depths of the house. Incoherent's patch seemed to mock her from the center of his black vest, and images of the picture forwarded to her phone flashed through her mind. Po'Boy's back as he walked through the clubhouse door, the unfaded dark shapes of the rockers and patch glaring in the sunshine telling a story she didn't know how to read. *Do with that what you will.*

The expression on Twisted's face tore at her; she'd never seen him look as devastated. What struck her more than anything was the lack of anger in him. Oh, he was mad as a wet hen all right, but at himself. She could recognize self-loathing from a mile away, and her Twisted was eat up with it. What he wasn't was angry at Po'Boy. He wasn't angry or betrayed, wasn't disappointed. Fear, he had that by the bushelful, and when you stacked all of everything up beside the other, it was telling.

Ty will know what's going on, and he won't shy from telling me. She yanked her phone out and tapped a button, listening to the call ring beyond what she'd expect. Frowning, she was about to hang up when someone answered. "Fucking finally," she barked, then was shocked into silence when an unfamiliar voice responded.

"The fuck you want?" No nuance of recognition there. Penny double-checked the screen, making certain she had indeed called Ty. "Bitch, you got five seconds and I hang up." The attitude had to be club, no other answer, but who?

"No, wait." She stumbled for a moment, moving into club mode to say, "I'm looking for Wrench."

"Ain't we all, sweetheart?" That was a cryptic response, and she puzzled on it for a moment, then heard voices in the background she knew. *He's at the clubhouse.*

"Is that Ace? Let me talk to him." Laughter in her ear told her she'd forgotten herself, because there was no place in a club where a woman could demand something like that and have it handed over. "It's Penny, and I need to talk to Wrench, but if not him then Uncle Ace, please."

"Penny Dane?" Cautious respect crept into his tone, and she smiled tightly, humming her affirmation into the handset. Away from the speaker the voice called, "Ace, I got Penny. You said you were trying to catch her. She's on his phone, man."

Noise in the background and then Ace was on the line, barking his own questions at her. Hard and fast, he didn't give her a chance to respond individually. "Fuck, Penny. You okay? Where is he? Where'd Wrench haul his ass to? Twisted giving you anything, doll? Are you okay?"

Finally he paused for a breath, and she asked, "Why wouldn't I be okay?" Address that one first because it made the least sense. Given Ty's phone was at the clubhouse but he wasn't, it wasn't a far leap to know he'd left it intentionally when he rolled out to whatever destination he had in mind. Obviously something the club wouldn't approve of, but it wouldn't take a wizard to guess that one. He'd gone after Po'Boy, and given what she knew of their relationship, Ty was trying to protect the man from fallout if he could.

"You're okay." A statement this time, but he didn't bother to answer her inquiry, so she put it aside, listening carefully to what Ace said, and didn't say. "Wrench talk to you lately?"

"Why's his phone at the clubhouse and him not?" Countering with her own question, she left it hanging, again not surprised when he sidestepped it.

"He hasn't called you." Certainty in his tone, Ace was about to shut her down entirely, so she pulled out the tiny morsel Wildman had dropped when he sent the picture of Po'Boy around.

"He mixed in with the cartel business Po'Boy's trying to sort?" Put the lie to the out bad rumors, but this was Ace, and he'd been stonewalling supervisors and subordinates since before she was born. If anyone could hold the info close, it was him.

"Shit." *Bingo.* "You need to order something else from the menu, doll. If that's what you're thinking, then you're probably not feeling well. Which means anything we…" He paused a beat, selecting his words with care and she had a moment to wonder who was within earshot on his end. "…might deliver would need to be handled with care."

"You send me whatever you need. Let me help." She shook her head, knowing what he would say. *I had to try.*

"Take care, Penny. You know we love ya, honey." His voice roughened, growing thick, and he told her, "Do anything you need, and you know that's true." A brief pause then a click and the connection went dead.

Shit. Wrench was in the wind, and no one knew where he was. The text had indicated Po'Boy had worked a deal with the Columbians to transport a truck coming off a container, but she knew he'd never do that. None of IMC were hurting for money, and money would be the only reason for a member to pull that kind of betraying bullshit. So Po'Boy was floating around somewhere, and now Wrench had ghosted, too.

No way Po'Boy made a deal with the cartel. That was the story which had accompanied the picture, asking her if she'd known it was coming. Wildman had sent it and the text, and then called her, raging at how something like this could happen to a brother like Po'Boy. That was the emotion she would expect from Twisted, and that was what she'd been missing. *The man can do no wrong.* Not past tense, Twisted had been talking about right now, today.

Do with that what you will.

An angry roar echoed off the trees and around the house, shaking the air around her. Followed by a bang, then another, then a series of pounding crashes, each of which made the earth under the house tremble.

"I'll tell you what I'll do." She dug into her pocket for her phone a second time, lifting it as she dialed, "I'll do what I shoulda done yesterday, soon as I heard about this bullshit." The call rang twice, then connected, a voice she recognized sounding strong through the line. *Nothing but bullshit.*

"Hey, Penny. How are you, doll?"

Bullshit, she reminded herself. "I tell you what, Retro, I've been better. There's some kinda bullshit bug running around Louisiana, and we need to sort it out before your kiddos come visit."

"Tell me what you need."

***

Crissy

Driving into the city, Crissy glanced over when her phone rang. Seeing an unfamiliar number, she rolled her eyes and muttered, "No, I didn't win a cruise." Telemarketing calls were one of her least favorite things. She sighed. She didn't have many favorite things these days, but robo dialers were on the least fav list. A moment later the phone rang again, with what looked to be the same number. Fumbling for a moment with the controls on the steering wheel, she finally hit the right button to connect, just as the caller hung up. Smirking, she watched the traffic in front of her, knowing it was always congested at this time.

Her phone rang again, and without looking at the phone, she tapped the controls. A moment only then a rich, warm man's voice filtered through the car's speakers. "Is this Crissy? Crissy Emmerson?"

"If I say yes are you going to try to sell me something?" Signaling a left turn, she slowed and negotiated the entrance into the firm's parking lot. The client for this presentation was a law office, and she made a face as she drove past row after row of expensive cars parked in their lot.

Easy laughter, sounding warm even over the phone as he asked, "If I say yes are you gonna hang up on my ass?" Crissy came alert suddenly knowing this wasn't a sales call.

"Who is this?" She found a parking spot and angled her car into it, slamming it into Park and killing the engine. "Who are you?"

"My name's Retro," he said enigmatically, and she was puzzled for a moment before realizing it must be a club name like Wrench and Po'Boy. Before she could respond, he tried to reassure her, "We got friends in common, honey."

"What's happened?" Her heart leaped into her throat, threatening to cut off her air, and she wheezed a bit as she asked, "Are they okay?"

Silence for a beat then this Retro fella spoke again, all the warmth having fled his voice. "Wanna tell me what you think you know to jump to that kinda response?"

"Are they okay?" She repeated her question, fighting the sudden burning in her nose, fear settling deep into her chest. "Please."

Not as warm as it had been, still his voice had lost some of the starch this time around. "Imma goin' out on a limb here, and guessin' you're askin' after Wrench and Po'Boy. And that's just who I called to ask you about. But you comin' unglued on me ain't gonna help either of us figure out anything, honey. Suck it up, and pull your ass together." Softer, gentler, he told her, "Far as I know ain't nothin' happened to those boys, just no one can lay eyes on 'em. I hoped you'd either be with 'em, or seen 'em." He took a breath, and she found herself breathing with him, feeling steadier by the time he asked, "You better now, honey?"

She didn't bother responding to that, because with his call, with his questions, there was a sense of urgency weighing her down, as if the very air in the car had gotten heavier, oppressively so. Instead, she dove to the center of what she feared. "I live next door to Ty…Wrench, whatever. He hasn't been home for a while. A handful of days. Even after he broke things off with me and…" She pulled up short, remembering the fight she'd heard through the walls. "With me," she corrected, then continued, "he was home more than he was gone. I haven't talked to Po'Boy in days, but he's all the way over in Mandeville, and neither of them keeps a normal schedule."

"Wrench ain't been home? Are you sure?"

Shaking her head, she answered him, "Yeah, I'm sure."

"You been in his place while he's gone?"

Leaning back in the seat, she shook her head again, uncaring he couldn't see her. "No, I'd never…not even when we…it's his."

"We got a couple of alarms about the system disengaging and then engaging, like someone came in for something and then left not long after. Maybe fifteen minutes inside. Got any idea who that might be?"

Crissy started to shake her head again and then paused, thinking. Over the past weeks, she'd occasionally seen one person other than Ty heading into and out of his condo. One who he hated, if she could believe what he'd said. *He said a lot of things, but he's still gone.* Wrinkling her nose, she questioned, "Is it the same alarm sequence? I know I can set a special one for guests." She'd done that, passing them out on heart-shaped pieces of paper to both Ty and Lewis, receiving Ty's in return, delivered with the sweetest kiss which seemed to hold every kind of promise. She put the memory out of her head and twisting the key, started the car and sat, waiting.

Silence for a moment, then he cursed. "Fuck, how'd I miss that? Yeah, it's different from his master code. Who is it, honey?"

"I got this." Throwing the car into Reverse, she backed out of the parking spot, barely getting straightened out before spinning her wheels, leaving black strips of rubber. "I got this." She hung up on the shouting man she didn't know, aiming her car for the exit and back to Slidell. "Fucking Sam Rotain."

Chapter Seventeen
Po'Boy

Po'Boy waited in silence, or as much silence as he could manage. It was hard and becoming more difficult by the second as the pressure on his hand increased. Twisting his neck, he looked, even as he told himself not to, and saw the balloon-like swelling of his fingers, skin stretched taut. Purple with pooling blood, he didn't know how much more strain his flesh could take without bursting. For a moment he reconsidered the silent thing, because while screaming wouldn't help, it couldn't hurt.

The trap was simple, and elegant. Noose around his ankle, tight and secure, positioned where he couldn't reach. It had been laid in a hallway, rag rug tossed over it to conceal the presence of the rope. All it took was him creeping through the darkness looking for Deuces, and a step in the wrong place. Snap, the trap tripped, and he'd been dragged down the hallway like a rabbit lure at hound races.

The one on his hand was harder to explain, but he remembered reaching out for something, anything to slow his terrifying rush up the hallway. Pulled to a jolting stop, his shoulder joint stretched to near breaking, anchored to a point somewhere along the path. Once the shock wore off, he'd looked up to see a thin wire wrapped around his hand and wrist. But the motor pulling on his leg hadn't stalled. *Oh, no.*

That bitch is quality machinery. Fuck. Hadn't stopped and was actively pulling, whining as it worked overtime to continue its job. The wire around his wrist was small, thin, and looked disturbingly like a cheese slicer against his skin.

Images from text books ran through his mind, of men suspended from ropes, tied to four horses, one for each appendage. Drawn and quartered, but in his case he figured it was halved. The sound of the motor changed, nearly stalling, and he hoped this meant the clutch was giving out. *Fucking finally.* Then another sound rattled through the hallway, and he twisted his head to look towards the front of the building. Standing in the opening was a man. He wasn't moving, was just standing there quietly. From the tilt of his head, Po'Boy knew he was looking down at him. Not moving, not jumping to help, not saying anything.

Not friend, then. *Can't hurt to ask.* It did hurt like a motherfucker just to lay there, so asking was where he'd head.

"Little help?" Rough and hoarse from holding quiet for so long, Po'Boy watched as the man's head swung back and forth, slowly. "Oh, come on, man. You can't be fuckin' serious."

"As a heart attack," the man told him, stepping forwards and into the light shining through a window in a room opening onto the hallway. Slender, with long red hair pulled low on his neck into a simple queue, the man looked like anyone you might pass on the street. Nondescript, dressed in clothes which wouldn't pull someone's gaze twice. He was everybody, and nobody. "You're in quite the pickle, Po'Boy."

Well, fuck. If he knows who I am, then I'm screwed. The motor whined and stuttered, then caught, and at the resulting yank, Po'Boy felt the cable around his hand break the skin, finally.

Chapter Eighteen

Crissy

Standing at the door, she dithered for a moment, unsure, then lifted a hand and knocked briskly. Ty's truck was in the lot, but his bike wasn't, so Crissy figured she had a fifty-fifty chance of him being home. If he was, then she'd call Retro back and let him know.

That was a man who didn't give up easily. When she refused to answer any of his dozen calls while she drove like a bat out of hell back to Slidell, he'd left two very detailed voice mails. One about what bad things could happen to a nice girl like her if she stepped into the wrong person's path, and one about all the ways she could contact him "when you fuck up, because you're gonna fuck up, woman."

Thirty seconds with no response to her knocking had her stepping to the side where the keyless pad was hidden behind a panel. Thirty more seconds and she was inside, soundlessly closing the door behind her, reaching to the side to enter the code a second time, disarming the alarm. She swept the living area with her gaze, marking the disarray so unlike Ty's normal housekeeping. He might not be a neat freak, but he seemed to appreciate tidy.

This room was far from orderly. There were beer cans on the floor next to the furniture, mostly empty bottles of liquor on the end tables, and open takeout containers on the coffee table in front of the sofa. His boots were missing from their normal place near the door, but the thing that chilled her bones was the sight of his club vest hanging off the back of a dining room chair. If his truck had been the vehicle missing from the lot, she wouldn't have thought anything about the vest being here, but given he was evidently out on the bike, him not wearing the symbol of his association with such a powerful group made her decidedly uneasy.

The silence in the condo was oppressive, the air stale, scents of rotting food teasing at her nostrils. Thinking hard, she put it at about a week since she'd seen his bike, but it didn't mean he hadn't been back in between. Still.

When her phone rang, she startled, thumb moving to decline the call, flipping the button to silence the device without looking to see who had called.

Walking through Ty's home was eerie, and she found herself tiptoeing to keep her footsteps as silent as possible. Everywhere she looked there seemed to be another jarring detail. A glass with beer foam residue sporting a bright red lipstick stain on the rim. A small pile of ammunition, with several bullets arranged in a circle, butt down to the table. Dirty pans in the sink, burnt and unidentifiable food caked in the bottoms. A disassembled gun on a towel on the kitchen table.

She got to Ty's room and hesitated, one hand resting on the doorknob. It was the only closed door inside the condo, and the smell of decaying and spoiled food hung heavy in the air, churning her stomach. With a shallow breath, she gripped hard, turning the knob and easing the door open.

Not certain what she was seeing, for a moment she stood stock still, staring with mouth open at the disaster that greeted her. While the rest of the condo could be politely termed untidy, this room was destroyed. Pillows and mattress were slashed and ruined, feathers and foam everywhere. The mattress was half-off the frame, angled against the far wall as if it had been tossed there. The dresser drawers all stood open, hanging wildly akimbo, the clothing tossed here and there. Shirts were shredded, holes and rips in each one she could see.

The closet door hung open and the hangers were in tangles, empty and shoved together so they looked like knots of metal. Debris littered the floor, and Crissy couldn't catalogue every item, but it looked as if everything in the room had been touched and demolished. Everywhere she looked, she found more ruin. The thing her eyes kept returning to was on the wall over the bed, and while she couldn't tell what it was, it filled her with a slippery unease.

She took a step, then another, finally coming close enough to see it was a picture pinned against the surface with a knife. The huge blade bisected the image, and it took a moment before she realized it was of her, Ty, and Lewis. Not one she'd ever seen, this was taken at Plaisirs Caches in New Orleans, with the three of them at the bar. She was leaning into Lewis' side, and Ty had draped himself over their shoulders. Smiling at a private joke; there was no mistaking the intimacy between the three of them.

Focused on the picture, when her phone vibrated in her hand she dismissed the call, not bothering to try and recognize the number. A moment later it vibrated again, and she looked to see a text on the screen. The words chilled her, causing Crissy to look around, ensuring she was indeed alone. **You're in the house**. It seemed too much like the script of a bad horror movie, so it was nearly a relief when the next text identified the caller. **Retro callin u again now**.

The phone rang and she accepted it, putting it to her ear. Before she could speak, the man's voice barked at her. "You stupid or somethin'? You went to Wrench's place, and you're inside. Tell me what you see." A clear demand in a tone which said the person on the other end of the line was accustomed to being obeyed. Crissy didn't hesitate, providing a quick rundown of what she'd seen.

"Condo itself is messy, and if you know Ty, you'll know it's not his way, so I'm guessing he's not been the one here the past week or so. But the bedroom—" She hesitated, swallowing hard as she eyed the picture fixed to the surface of the wall with a knife she assumed was used to create most of the chaos in the room. "—it's different. This looks personal. It's…everything is destroyed. It looks like an angry genie blew up anything belonging to Ty." She paused. "That's to say…everything."

"Anything stick out, honey?"

"Yeah, sorta. There's a picture of—" Wrinkling her nose, she tried to decide how to approach this bit of information. "—us. But we didn't know anyone was taking it. Anyway, it's nailed to the wall." She hesitated again, then said, "Well, not nailed. There's a knife…a big one."

"Where were the two of you when it was taken?"

Shit. He'd made an assumption, and she had to set him straight, not knowing what it might all mean, but setting him straight might be the ruination of one of the men she loved. *I love them*, she told herself, the feeling in her chest bridging any additional fear. *If they're in trouble, I don't care what might happen, as long as I can keep anything physically bad at bay.*

"It's not just me and Ty in the picture." She cast about for a moment, trying to remember his question, then finished with, "Plaisirs Caches in New Orleans. It's a bar."

"I know the place," he assured her, and then made an intuitive leap which shouldn't have been a surprise, given the clues he'd already pieced together. "It's the three of you, right? You and Wrench and Po'Boy?" Then he made another leap, one that made her wince for her two men. "It's a picture of the three of you out together, like on a date."

Focused as she was on the contents of the room, at the words coming from the phone pressed tight to her ear, a touch on her shoulder had her shrieking and jumping away. She swung around to find a man standing behind her, someone she'd only seen once before. She barely had time to scream before his fist was swinging towards her face. An instant later pain burst in her jaw like she'd been hit with a brick, and she staggered backwards, tripping and falling over the shredded clothing on the floor. Lying on her back, she stared up at him, blinking in a futile effort to keep the blackness from sweeping over her. Through all this, the phone stayed in her hand, but with the ringing in her ears she couldn't tell if Retro was still talking.

***

Twisted

Listening carefully, Twisted tried to make sense out of what Retro was telling him. After a minute, everything clicked, and his blood ran cold. *Fucking shit, the ruse worked.* Too well, it seemed, if Po'Boy and Wrench's woman was caught up in it all. Now he just had to sort out who'd cottoned onto what was going on, and hope like fuck the woman was okay when he found her. The fact he would find her wasn't a given, but he couldn't allow any other thoughts to even enter his head. He knew she needed to be unharmed, or Po'Boy would give him an assbeating like none other.

"Are there eyes in the place, or on the lot?" He broke in, interrupting Retro's rant about the two men going off the grid. "You're talkin' Wrench's place, right? Don't he own the complex? You talk to Ace, see if he got any insight?"

Silence, then Retro spoke carefully. "I have not called Ace. While Wrench can be an asshole, I like that asshole, didn't wanna cause problems when I wasn't sure there was even shit to share. I like your asshole, too, but I got the feeling I wasn't causin' Po'Boy any issues because you—" The sound of a sigh came through the line. "—know more than most how life can bend around ya." A pause, and Twisted waited, knowing Retro was working through things in his head. "You know where they are."

Not a question, but he answered, knowing honesty would help find the gal faster. "Nope, I got no fuckin' clue where. But I can give some insight on the why."

"And the woman? What is she to Wrench?" Twisted held his silence, waiting, and as he expected, Retro put it all together from whatever clues he had. "What is she to Po'Boy? I know from the limited digging I've been doing the three of them have been seen around New Orleans, where Po'Boy's got his place. And I know she is not just Wrench's next-door neighbor, but something more. Those two boys, they've been the talk of the party more than once, leaving like they do and heading out together. Assumption is they were doin' the woman. No harm, no foul. But her reacting the way she did, I'm getting there's more to this. You wanna lay it out for me before we go farther?"

"Don't you think we need to be working out how to find out who took her?" A soft gasp behind him and Twisted turned to see Penny standing there, hand covering her mouth. "Hey, baby. I'll be off the phone in a minute." That was a clear indication he needed privacy, and given she didn't usually buck his demands, the fact she took a step towards him was a surprise. "Penny—" he started, and she cut him off.

"Is it Crissy? Is she in trouble?"

"Shit, is that Penny?" Retro's voice held a thread of amusement mixed with regret. Probably because he knew how she could be.

Before Twisted could answer either of them, Penny got his full attention. "I called Ace. Tell Retro after I got off the phone with him, I called Ace. He already knows, too. So if something's up with Crissy, we need to know."

"Wanna tell me why you think there'd be somethin' up with this Crissy chick?"

Shoulders back, Penny stood and stared at him. "Wrench came to me early on, wanted to talk about what was going on with him and Po'Boy and this Crissy. If she's in trouble—" She held her hand out, palm up and he watched it tremble as she said, "baby, we gotta wade in."

"Baby doll, I'm not sure Po'Boy—"

She cut him off again, and he thought he heard Retro snort laughter on the other end of the call. "Po'Boy isn't here, Twisted. He's not here, and neither is Wrench. I don't know why, but I suspect you have something to do with some of that." She held up a hand, palm facing him. "I know you can't tell me everything. But if she's in trouble and they aren't here, then we have to wade in."

"She's got a point, man."

"Sure, now you wanna chime in with your two cents' worth? Now you bought me my old lady's wrath if I don't do some kind of shit to make right whatever fucked up play you had going with this chick went sideways?" Twisted tipped his head down, looking at the toes of Penny's boots. She was dressed for riding. *Shit*. She'd expected something. Maybe not this call, but she'd expected a call. *Fuckin' lucky I was still here*. "You got a point, and you cover that motherfucker with your hat. Jesus."

"Crissy was in Wrench's place, said it was trashed like someone's been squattin' there. But she said his bedroom is trashed, as in *trashed*, and she said there was a picture of the three of them pinned to the wall with a knife. About then she encountered someone who evidently came into the condo behind her. I'm guessing she didn't arm the alarm because we got nothing on the entry logs. Sounded like she took a hit or two, man." Twisted's neck angled, and he looked away from Penny, not wanting her to see the look he knew would be on his face at the knowledge. "Chatter, a lot of noise, then a voice."

"Who?" Po'Boy's face came to mind, him talking about Crissy and how she'd bridged the gap between him and Wrench in a way that made them all better. *She took a hit or two.* Twisted remembered coming out of hell to see Penny next to a dead man, her hands bloody, her face bruised. *She took a hit or two.* "We'll kill the motherfucker."

"You know Thorne? Sam Rotain's old man?" Nothing more or less than he expected, and Twisted held his peace, trying to not react. He made a noise and Retro seemed to understand he couldn't speak. "Pretty sure it was Thorne."

***

Crissy

There was no slow rise to consciousness. One moment she was entirely unaware, and the next Crissy was fully immersed in noise and pain. When she opened her eyes, she saw the noise was coming from a radio alarm clock. Blinking 12:00, it seemed to be stuck in "get the fuck out of bed" mode, shrieking again and again at a high volume. The pain started in her head and radiated down through her jaw and into her back, and had her squeezing her eyes closed. She tried to move and woke more pain, one side of her ribs aching sharply.

When she woke, she also recalled, not just what she'd seen in Ty's condo, but what had happened to her. She remembered where she'd seen her attacker before and wasn't surprised his was the first face she saw now. "Thorne." That came out as a bare murmur, since it hurt to talk, because talking meant moving her jaw, and just tensing to force out the single word had the pain levels jacking up to unbearable. He hadn't yet realized she was conscious. Across the room, he stood in front of a window in what she believed must be a motel. *It's sure not the condo.*

With the distance she would have to cover, there was no way she could take him by surprise as he had her. On that thought, remembering the fist that had barreled toward her face, she thought, *fuck it* and decided to take care of one of the problems at hand. The unceasing racket from the alarm. Lifting her arm gingerly, she tested the bounds of the pain, finding it bearable. *Thank God*, she thought, pressing the button on top of the clock. At the sudden silence, Thorne jerked around to look at her, and Crissy found herself staring in surprise at what she saw, because he didn't look like a criminal, which of course he was, because he'd knocked her out and kidnapped her. Instead the expression on his face was nearly grieving, eyes swollen and red, and she wondered at the source of his anguish.

"Where is she?" His mouth was hard, lips thinning as he asked an incomprehensible question. Trying to hold her jaw still, Crissy shook her head. *She who?* "Where is she?" Thundering the words, he took two fast steps in her direction, and she saw his hand curling into a hard fist. "Where." Another step. "Is she?"

Thorne loomed over her and Crissy pushed at the mattress with her heels, trying to gain a little room. Wincing at the pain, she clenched her teeth together delicately, then hissed, "Who?"

"Fucking Sam. Sam." He pounded the mattress between her knees, and she pushed harder, sliding her back up the headboard, slipping sideways against the pillows. "Fucking Sam, where is she?"

"I don't know." He jerked a fist towards her face, and she flinched back, her chin knocking the point of her shoulder painfully. Tears stung her eyes and she held her breath until the agony subsided. "I was looking for Wrench." Instinctively she used Ty's club name, trying to map her way through a minefield she couldn't even see.

"Fucking Wrench." He twisted away, back towards the windows, and she saw the butt of a gun sticking out of the waistband of his pants. "She liked his goddamned dick. Had a way of making sure a man knew he weren't the first." His words so bizarre she could only stare at the back of his head for a moment. "Figured Wrench would come back, know where she is."

"You were in his condo." Speaking came easier this time, and she pushed away from the headboard, angling her hips towards the edge of the bed.

"Figured he'd be back, or she would." He turned, staring at her, his reddened eyes eerie in the light filtering through the thick curtains. "But you showed. So then I thought you'd know where he was, way he was all up in your business all the fuckin' time. Where is he? You gotta know, right? He's your old man, right? You're his old lady?" He shook out one fist, and she saw the knuckles were bruised. "You gotta let Ace know I didn't mean to hurt you, right? Gonna let Wrench know? He gonna be pissed, and I'll take my beating, but I had to get you out of there before she came back."

She shook her head, not a negative response, just not understanding. *Is he insane?*

Thorne's lip curled and he angled his chin to the side, staring at her out of the corner of one wide eye. "Aww naw, you gotta tell 'em. You gonna tell 'em, right? Gonna let 'em know? I didn't mean to hurt you." He lifted a hand beseechingly, taking a step closer. "It's just a little blood, mostly. Just a tap, you just gotta get cleaned up. I just tapped you. It's only a little blood, honey." He semirepeated himself, and she flinched when he came towards her and pointed at her face, the gesture bringing him too close for comfort. The skin under her nose pulled and prickled, and Crissy lifted a hand to find dried blood coating her skin. "You wanna clean up?" Thorne offered again, gesturing towards the bathroom.

The way he switched back and forth between angry and overly nice made her gut clench. Working off that feeling, she tested her legs, finding them only a little wobbly. "Yeah. If I could." Unwilling to turn her back on him, she moved towards the bathroom blindly, feeling every backwards step before trusting her weight to it. Slowly but surely she made her way through the doorway, hand on the knob as she stared at him. *Will he really let me just walk in there?* "Thanks." Before she could push the door closed, he had crossed the room, placing a big hand flat on the door.

"Leave it open." She nodded, disappointed. That emotion forgotten when she turned to face the mirror, gasping. Eyes mapping her face, she took in the damage she'd only felt so far. Black and blue bruising on her jaw and cheek claimed a space on her face she could barely cover with a single hand, and her chin and neck were hidden behind a dried layer of blood. The effect was as ghoulish as any Halloween makeup she'd seen and she could only stare for a moment. "You all right in there?" His voice came from outside, not near, so he'd probably moved back to the windows. In response she turned on the water, dropping a clean washcloth into the sink's basin, waiting for the stream to warm.

Cleaning up took longer than she'd expected, terror still thrumming through her made working around the tender areas a more difficult task than it seemed. She heard the rumble of his voice several times, caught a glimpse of his form pacing in and out of the mirror's reflection, crossing in front of the windshields and roofs of vehicles she could see through the window. Staring at her image, she recognized the fear in her eyes as she struggled to make sense out of the few things he'd said.

As far as she could tell, there were only two things that didn't quite ring true. The first was though she'd seen Sam around the condo, Thorne claimed to be the one camping out, which didn't make sense. The second was even if he'd been the one to knock her out and bring her here, he was flat scared of both Wrench and whoever this Ace was. The fear in his face had echoed what she'd seen in her own features, and he hadn't been acting. Since he seemed to think she was Wrench's significant other, she could work that to her favor.

She rinsed out the washcloth, frowning at the reddened stains that remained. Swallowing hard, she lifted her eyes to her reflection again, consciously lowering her shoulders as she pulled in a steadying breath. Thorne's voice sounded again, and she turned towards the door, walking out of the tiny room which was no haven, and into what felt like the lion's den.

***

Wrench

Shoving hard with his boots against the pavement, Wrench backed the bike into his space with an economy of movement that spoke to familiarity. Heeling down the kickstand was second nature as was thumbing the kill switch on the bike. A moment later he stood to one side, key in hand, and had turned to walk towards his condo. As he had for weeks now, he focused on the car he'd already looked for, parked in front of Crissy's place. He remembered the first time he'd seen her, one corner of his mouth curling up as he murmured, "Butternut."

"Wrench." Key to the door, he heard his name shouted from across the parking lot and pushed the door open as he turned and watched Pony trotting his way. "Jesus, man. Answer your fuckin' phone once in a while." Wrench pushed a hand into his pocket, coming out empty when he remembered leaving it at the clubhouse. *Shit.* Pony asked, "Where the fuck you been, man?"

"Out." Not a sanctioned run, he'd been looking for Po'Boy, and wasn't about to talk about that with an IMC member, no matter they were friends. Pony reached past him, holding the door open as Wrench turned to walk inside, stumbling over Wrench's boots when he stopped in his tracks. "What the hell?"

"Jesus, you're a slob now?" Pony knew him better than that, and from the corner of his eye Wrench saw him pull a pistol out of his vest. Wrench matched the movement, the familiar weight comforting. "Tell a brother when you pull shit like this." He pulled the door closed, the security of a locked entryway less comforting than it could have been.

"Yeah, don't you know I'm messy?" Easy banter covered the sound of their advancing footsteps, and would hopefully soothe whoever had done this, if they were still here. Wrench turned to the side and saw his alarm blinking green. It hadn't been armed. "You want pizza?" He covered the kitchen, saw it empty, saw Pony doing the same to the main living area. "I could order some."

Moving up the hallway, he left the bathroom for Pony, checking the first bedroom, losing sight of his friend for a moment while he opened and checked the closet. Pony laughed softly, and said, "Pizza sounds good, man. I'm starved." The shower curtain rattled.

Back in the hallway, he glanced back at Pony, tipping his head towards the master bedroom. One room left to check, and he felt Pony's presence at his back as he pushed the already ajar door open. Chaos greeted him, and he tried to look past it to ensure the room was empty. By the time he turned from the closet, Pony was stepping out of the bathroom, and both men lowered their weapons to their sides. "Empty, brother," Pony said, then whistled low. "Who in the *fuck* did you piss off? I need to know so I can avoid that shit."

"Hell if I know." Gaze flicking from one thing to the next, he surveyed the damage. "Jesus, whoever it was did not go gentle." He bent, using the finger of one hand to flip items over, tossing them to one side. "All my shit, man."

"What's that?" At the question, he straightened to see Pony pointing behind him and turned towards the bed, freezing in place. "Vicar's," he pushed out between clenched teeth. "Fuckin' Vicars?" Stepping towards the machete, he stared at the picture of Po'Boy pinned to the wall. The background was familiar. Po'Boy in Plaisirs Caches, and he remembered that night, suddenly fighting against going hard. With a grunt, he leaned closer, angling to see around the blade, all thoughts of sexy times pushed out of his head when he saw the rest of the image. Crissy in the curve of Po'Boy's arm, Wrench pulling back after kissing a stunned Po'Boy, leaning over his two lovers in a way that screamed intimacy. It was an image he would have framed if he knew it existed, would have brought out time and again to look at, as he did the ones on his phone.

Not able to pull his eyes from the picture, he reached up and wiggled the blade, capturing the photo between his fingers as it fluttered free.

"Got a fuck of a lotta red here, brother." Pony's words pulled him around, and he made his way around the bed, stopping short at the drying pool of blood on the floor. Not a spray or splatter like from a gunshot, it was an impressive amount soaking the carpet. He took another step and felt something hard under his boot, pulling back and kicking a ruined shirt to one side to see a familiar rectangle shape under the next layer of clothing. Toeing things aside, he leaned over and picked up the phone, using his thumb to activate the screen.

Fear froze him, because he was staring at another image, this of himself and Po'Boy, both of them grinning up at the camera. Taken so long ago it nearly seemed a lifetime, this showed what had been the beginning of things for the three of them. "Crissy," he muttered, "it's her phone." Scanning the floor, he took in the amount of blood again, then looked at the blade he'd tossed to the floor beside the upended bed. It didn't have any staining on it that he could see, but there could be a dozen reasons for that. With the clothes tossed everywhere, it would have been easy to wipe it clean before leaving it in the wall. The screen darkened as the phone went back to sleep, and he thumbed it again, focusing this time on the missed texts and calls. With shock, he recognized the Alabama number and shook his head. Lifting his eyes to stare at Pony, he asked him, "What in fuck would Retro be doing calling Crissy?"

Chapter Nineteen

Po'Boy

He groaned, the noise sounding thin to his ears, and opened his eyes. Blinking to clear his vision, Po'Boy strained to see, looking for any clue to tell him where he was. Light from across the room hit a mirror on the wall at a known angle, and he sighed, relaxing minutely. *The suite*. He swallowed and sighed. *Fuck of a dream*. Not his normal nightmare, but the idea of Grover dispatching him to trip traps in an unknown house was weird enough to classify as a nightmare.

Then he tried to move.

Pain blasted through every muscle, yanking away the comforting thoughts of being safe in a familiar place. He strained against the bonds that held him still, arching to see above his head, catching a metallic glint at his wrists. His feet were similarly secured, and his balls tried to crawl up into his belly when he realized he was naked on the bed, legs spread wide, exposing his privates to the chilly air.

Shivering, he pulled at first one leg then the other, finding no give in whatever shackled him. Fucking hell. He scanned the room. Not seeing anything or anyone to tell him what was going on, there were no clues as to how he'd gotten from that house to here.

Over the next few hours, he kept testing the bindings on his legs, working the handcuffs back and forth on the headboard with no success. The wound on his wrist reopened, making his skin slippery, but the cuffs were too tight for him to have any hope of slipping through. Each movement was hard, agonizing and coming at a cost of pain-filled nausea.

Thoughts of the redhead filled his head, and he concentrated on what the man had said before he'd lost consciousness.

"You made some serious enemies. Did you know there are two separate contracts out for you?" Facing away from Po'Boy, the man stood framed in the windows, ignoring the groans Po'Boy couldn't contain. *"Though each is decent enough on their own, together they were enough to get my attention."* He rolled a shoulder, a motion Po'Boy recognized as settling the strap of a holster. He's got at least one, *he thought.*

Standing still, the man presented an attitude of patient waiting, which echoed his movements and words from earlier. He put Po'Boy in mind of a hunter, willing to be silent and still for hours waiting on an elusive moment in time when fates aligned, gifting them with a perfect shot. Is he hunting me? *"So I did some looking, poking around where I normally wouldn't, and I found some very interesting things about you."* He paused, glancing over his shoulder to where Po'Boy lay. *"Ralph Lewis."* Another pause, then he finished with a word which had never been part of Po'Boy's name, *"Grover."*

Turning back to the window, the man shook his head. "You're an interesting fella. Looking at you, a body would never know you had money, that you came from money. But I'm betting it's not something you knew, either."

"You got the wrong guy," Po'Boy gritted out, listening to the motor chatter for a moment before it resumed its grinding whine. *Jesus, give*

up the fuckin' ghost already. *"I ain't got nothin' a body would want. I'm just a poor boy."*

The man chuckled, the sound low and intense. *"That's rich. You're funny."* Snorting, the guy glanced at him again, his gaze locking with Po'Boy's. *"You come from money. Your momma never told you, did she?"* Po'Boy stared at him. *"Yeah, she left you in ignorance. Probably hoping with ignorance comes bliss."*

The pulling cables shivered, stuttering again, then the sound increased in pitch until it was shrieking, a metallic clatter signaling the end of life for the motor. There was still tension on the lines, but it was a relief to know he might not lose his hand after all. *"I done told you, I ain't got anything of note."* He kept his speech to the patter of the bayous. *"I ain't nobody. Don't know what nonsense you're spewing, but you're barkin' up the wrong tree with me."*

"Your momma was Shirley Lewis, of the Baton Rouge Lewis family. Your great granddaddy was into lumber and land. He bought up a bunch of land, all kinds of land in all kinds of places. Up in Mississippi, over in Texas. Wound up with land that happened to sit on a gas field. Your granddaddy knew his business and held onto the rights with a tight fist. One of the reasons he weren't happy with your momma getting knocked up like she did. He had a man all hand-picked out for her, and she bucked him every step of the way." He realized the man had adopted a near copy of his speech patterns and grimaced, knowing playing the fool wouldn't work here. The guy snorted. *"Yeah, your granddaddy weren't happy. But he kept track of her, and when she had a boychild, he kept track of you."*

"So what, he probably had a dozen kids and they've had a dozen kids, so now you think they're all out to kill me for my part of his estate?" Bending his knee, he pulled his leg up, finding some slack, reaching up to try and loosen the cable from around his hand.

He stopped, stunned by what the man said next.

"Nope, Ralph Lewis Grover, you're the only child of an only child of an only child. It's all yours. Or your heir's." Turning, the man put his hands on his hips, fists balled and elbows to the side. "You even know you got an heir?"

"Fuck are you talking about now?"

"Well, one of the lists I saw showed you as Ralph Lewis, which is what I expected. But the other"—shaking his head, the man stepped closer—"had you down as Grover's kid. So I did some digging. Did you know he adopted you? Made you his kid, first thing when he married your momma."

Po'Boy's head snapped back, and he stared up at the man, stunned.

"Yeah, I didn't think so. Now, cast your mind into what pathways that leads you." Stepping back, the man leaned his shoulders against the wall. "I got some time. I can wait."

"I don't have to think. Fuckin' Jeff." Man had stepped in the deep end of the pool. First cartel, then putting out a contract on Po'Boy. Nothing that's going to help extend his life expectancy.

"Got it in one. Must say, color me impressed. Shouldn't be surprised, though, everything I read on you said you were smart. So imagine my surprise when I heard you'd been stupid."

Po'Boy was nearly lost inside his head, trying to sort out the idea he might be worth enough to put a hit out on. Nearly, but not quite. Beyond Jeff, there were two questions in his head. "Who dropped the other paper? And what do you mean, I've been stupid?" He could think of a dozen MC rivals who might want him dead. "What's the payoff? How much are you gonna make on me?" That would narrow it down, and since he wasn't dead yet, there was every chance he could get out of his one. Fingers under the cable, he wiggled it back and forth, finally slipping his hand free, losing more skin and flesh in the process but counting it progress nonetheless. He sat up, loosening the noose around his ankle, feeling the rush of blood painfully in his foot, pins and needles making him hiss. "Jeff and who?"

"You fucked a girl." He studied his hands, curling one palm up, fingers curved.

"That's it? All you're givin' me? No more than that? Man, I've fucked a lot of gals." He rubbed his hand, avoiding the painful wound on his wrist. "That's not as big a clue as you might think."

"Well—" Casually dipping into one pocket, the man pulled out a blade, flipping it open with a relaxed motion, applying the tip to each fingernail in turn. "You fucked a girl, then you fucked her sister. Then, you fucked that girl's cousin." Eyes angled up, he stared at Po'Boy, wanting to watch as whatever bomb he dropped detonated. "And that cousin? He wasn't happy when you were done with him. He's got family money, too. He rolled up an offer and threw it in the waters, knowing he'd sweetened the bait with enough to get a bite." The guy shrugged. "I knew about the other offer, so I bit."

Sounds outside heralded the arrival of other parties, something Po'Boy could do without, not seeing where it could be a winning situation for him, given this guy's offhand attitude. The door at the front of the house opened, and Po'Boy twisted on his ass, rolling to his knees and then his feet as he turned to face this new threat. "You gettin' paid to deliver breathing?"

"I already got paid. No more work is needed on my part."

Po'Boy glanced at him. "What?"

"You got friends, as well as enemies, Po'Boy." With a single word cementing his knowledge the man had thoroughly looked into him, Po'Boy tried to split his attention between the known and unknown. "Tell Retro I left you alive, yeah?" Strolling to a door, the man opened it and, leaving it standing wide behind him, walked through.

"Lewis," a familiar voice purred his name, and he turned to face Sam Rotain. She was holding a pistol steady in one hand, as casually comfortable with the weapon as someone raised around them would be.

"Lewis," an also familiar voice gritted out his name, and he stared over Sam's shoulder at the man following her into the building. "Fancy meeting you here."

"Greg?" He barely got the stunned question out when Sam raised her arm, locking her elbow as she squeezed the trigger. Po'Boy threw himself to the floor, yanking his weapon out and firing at her. His wrist couldn't hold against the recoil, and he shouted in pain, fighting to try and line up the barrel again. Greg rushed towards him, gun in hand, the grip coming down in a rush that pulled darkness with it.

Being in the suite now meant Greg hadn't been a hallucination. Being tied up as he was, meant Sam hadn't been one, either. At the moment, he couldn't decide which was worse. From Grover's rental house in the country to his suite in Orleans, he'd gone from the frying pan into the fire.

The sound of a key in the lock alerted him, and he was staring at the door through slitted eyes when it opened, admitting Sam, followed by Greg. Ignoring him stretched out on the bed, they carried bags of what looked and smelled like takeout from Plaisirs Caches to the small kitchen area. "I don't see what you like about Truman. He's kind of a douche." Sam set her bag down and turned to face Greg.

He shrugged, turning his back on Po'Boy as he placed his bag on the countertop. "He's a power top, and I like dick."

"Jesus, don't remind me. The idea of you takin' it up the ass makes me sick." Sam faked a shiver, grinning broadly.

"Fucked you up the ass, you seemed to like it." Greg reached out, trailing his fingers down Sam's arm. "We get the asshole behind me hard, we can figure out something we'll both like." He leaned forwards, pressing his lips to hers, pulling back a moment later to finish, "Guarantee."

Sam looked at Po'Boy over Greg's shoulder, the grin fading. "Still not sure why he's not dead. I thought you said you'd paid someone to kill him."

And there it was. Proof of the redheaded man's information falling out of Sam's mouth like it was a food order at a diner. Po'Boy stared as Greg turned to look at him.

"Yeah, I'm still not sure about that, either. But," he twisted to face Sam, "this could be fun."

Jesus fuck.

***

Crissy

Easing the car to a stop in the underground parking space, Crissy glanced at the man seated beside her as she turned off the lights. In the illumination of the garage, she watched as Thorne picked at the skin of his knuckles, not looking up, seemingly lost in thought. She glanced around, reaching for a moment to the console before remembering the car he'd had her drive had the gearshift on the steering column.

"We're here," she said unnecessarily, not wanting to startle him. They'd ridden the whole way from Slidell in silence, broken only by his repeated checking of the magazine on his gun. The metallic slide and snap sounded again, and she stared at his hands moving so familiarly on the weapon.

You grew up around guns, she reminded herself again. *Got your first deer at nine-years-old*. Fascinated at how his fingers danced through the motions, she shook her head slightly. *Yeah, but I've never seen a gun held by a madman*. Jury was still out on his mental state, and his twitching made her wonder if he was a tweaker, coming down off an unstable high. That would account for his rambling monologue in the motel.

The tiny house he'd taken her to after they left the motel had been in his family for generations. Thorne had described the convoluted family tree that brought it to his ownership, but she'd only tried to follow for a few minutes before realizing he was lost in a sea of memories which had nothing to do with what was going on today. She reached and retrieved the pistol from underneath her leg. The arsenal he'd unveiled behind a plain, wooden door had been the reason for their visit. Gathered and stashed there, he promised her the gun in her hand had never been used for more than target practice.

When she'd lifted an eyebrow in confusion, he explained it meant if used in "self-defense," and he'd used the air quotes when saying the words, it would be a clean burner to drop "at the scene," another phrase deemed deserving of those curved motions of his fingers.

Then he'd showed her a map on his phone with a green dot and a pulsing red one.

The green dot was his phone's location, where they were in the middle of nowhere outside Slidell, surrounded on all sides by thin strips of blue, the waters of the many bayous they'd driven past and around on their way to the shack. The red dot was Sam's phone.

When Crissy enlarged the map, bringing the street and nearby business names into focus, she'd been shocked and then saddened to see the address was that of Lewis' condo. In that moment she was nearly undone, struggling to hold her tears back, remembering again Retro's voice on the phone talking about the three of them together. Then she remembered the confrontation on Ty's sidewalk, where he'd casually talked about having sex with Sam. Fear drove her thoughts, and she struggled to hold back tears. It didn't take them long to replace me. *Thorne saw her near to losing it and tried to console her, missing the* mark with his, "She don't mean nothin' to him. Wrench never glommed onto her like he did you. She was just wet and willing."

"They're at Po'Boy's place in New Orleans," she finally choked out, and he eyed the phone with distrust, as if it could grow fists and strike at any moment.

"Don't change nuthin'," he muttered, thrusting the phone and an extra magazine of rounds her direction. "Bitch got him. Think about his place. She trashed it. He knew about that place of Po'Boy's, so could she."

Swallowing hard, she bit down on the inside of her cheek. "Retro said folks hadn't seen either of them, but he didn't have any indication anything bad had happened." She'd meant to remind herself, but said it aloud, only realizing it as Thorne stiffened and turned woodenly to stare at her.

"You fuckin' know Retro?" He shook his head. "You best buds with Twisted and his Shiny Penny, too?"

"What?" She shoved the magazine into the back pocket of her jeans, and reached up, cradling her jaw for a moment, the clenching of her teeth setting up a fierce throbbing.

"Nothin'. Got what we want, now let's go. Follow the bouncing ball." Walking out, he headed towards the car and she paused on the tiny front porch, pulling the door shut behind her.

"Don't you want to lock it?"

At her question, he laughed, and she saw the man who might have attracted Sam, the expression lifting fifteen years off his face. "Gel, we deep in the bayous. Ain't nonesuch gonna bother thangs here. Hell, half the parish is kinfolk. They need, they'll use, then return. It's our way."

"You got a key?" Thorne's voice startled her out of her head, and Crissy nodded. It was on a carved wooden keyring Lewis had left on her nightstand the last time he slept at her house. A peace offering, maybe. An invitation, possibly. She hadn't asked, and he hadn't given an explanation, and then they'd simply stopped talking. She'd kept it like a talisman, never intending to use it. "Let's go then. See what we find."

She was out of the car, pocketing the keys when he spoke again. "You got it in you to deal shit out to Sam if needed? If she's hurt your men? You got that in you?"

Crissy stared at him across the top of the old car, unrepaired rusty dents dotting the surface, the rancid smell of well-used fishing tackle drifting up from the inside. Used and abused, the car wasn't cared for. But it wasn't breathing, either. No matter what, Sam was a person, and Crissy didn't know if she could hurt her. As she stared at him, thoughts of Ty's recitation of Sam's instability, and how Sam had threatened her fluttered against her resolve. She recalled the way Lewis' face had blanched at the mention of the sister's name, Sabrina. Then she remembered the condition of the condo, how Ty's bedroom had been destroyed, and thought about the deranged attitude it spoke to. The woman could have hurt either of them, badly. The knife, impaling the image of the three of them. *What if she's already...* "If I have to, yeah."

As she spoke, Crissy felt a stillness settle into her soul. Whatever this was she was feeling, doggedness or determination, it must have shown on her face, because Thorne told her, "Yeah. I get that now. Let's go see what we see."

Holding the loaded pistol tight against her leg, she led Thorne up the stairs, pausing for breath as they reached Lewis' floor. Laughter drifted down the stairwell at one point, and she had looked up, glimpsing two masked women in evening gowns leaning over and staring at them. *How surreal.*

Checking the hallway through the small square of glass, she tugged the fire door open, murmuring, "This is it."

"Slow and easy, gel," Thorne urged as she slid the key into the lock. His quiet encouragement helped steady her, and with a deep breath, she turned the knob and slowly pushed the door open, glad when the lights inside were bright, helping disguise their entrance. Slapping sounds from inside the room had her gut clenching, and she slipped around the edge of the door not sure she wanted to see what was happening, but like driving past a wreck on the interstate, unable to look away.

Three bodies. Lewis was splayed near the center of the bed, head tipped to one side, naked and exhausted. On the other side of him there was a man on his knees behind a woman, powering into her, the sound a result of each impact of his thighs on hers. Sam. Her head pillowed on Lewis' belly, one hand in view, and it took Crissy a moment to realize she cradled a knife in that hand, positioned perilously close to Lewis' side. A moment later and she recognized the red stripes covering his thighs and belly were cuts, shallow but still bleeding. Another moment and she knew the way his head lolled with each movement of the mattress meant he wasn't asleep, he was unconscious. *What if he's...* She refused to let her mind follow that thought into the darkness.

Sam's head came up and she stared at Crissy, mouth open and working soundlessly. Then the man groaned, fleshy ass quivering and flexing as he shoved hard once, then a second time. He hadn't stilled when Sam pulled away, yelling, "Thorne," as the man shouted, "Jesus, Sam!" He twisted to face the door, hard cock bobbing side to side, glistening wetly in the bright lights. "Who the fuck are you?"

Thorne pushed past Crissy, gun lifted to shoulder height and Crissy winced when he casually backhanded the man with the barrel. The blow knocked him off the bed where he slithered into a heap on the floor, silent, dick already going soft against his thigh. Sam was shoving backwards on the mattress, knife in hand, eyes only for Thorne. Lips closed tightly, she glanced down at Lewis, then over at Crissy and back to Thorne, a grim smile flattening her mouth into an ugly line.

Before Crissy could react, Sam had thrown herself prone beside Lewis, lifting the knife to his throat.

"Stop, Thorne." Sam's shout wheezed, as if she'd been running for miles. "I'll kill him. They'll look to you, you know they will. Club don't care about bitches. You'll never get your diamond. I'll kill him."

Thorne stopped at the end of the bed, looming over the two figures on the mattress. "You fucking bitch. You'd jack with me just to do it, wouldn't you? Jesus, what the fuck did I ever think you did for me?" He gestured with the gun in his hand, continuing his tirade, while Crissy moved towards Lewis, eyeing the ropes anchoring him to the legs of the bed. Beyond Sam, she saw his hands were cuffed together, the metal chain running around a spindle in the headboard.

"I'll kill him."

"No, you won't." Crissy didn't know where the words came from, but she didn't try to stem them as she fell to her knees at Lewis' feet, fingers working at the knots, breaking fingernails off to the quick in her haste. Breaths coming fast, she said, "If you were going to, you wouldn't have brought him here. You'd not be trying to impress on him how you're so hot you can be fucked on the bed beside him. You're just along for the ride." She finished loosening one rope and shoved Thorne to the side so she could reach the other one.

Her brain raced, trying to find a way to keep both Thorne and Sam busy while she got Lewis free. "Guy on the floor is the one you're after, Thorne. He's the one who was fucking Sam. He's the one who wants your woman. Po'Boy would have bailed if they hadn't tied him down."

She finished with the second rope, wincing as another nail tore free. "You sure Sam's worth the trouble?" There was a groan from behind Thorne, and he turned away. Crissy kept her eyes on Sam, still trying to goad her away from Lewis. Taking a chance on something Thorne had mentioned, Crissy said, "I see a sad little girl trying to pretend she's as good as her sister. Trying, and—sorry to say, honey," that was directed at Sam, "—you're failing. Never gonna be half the woman your sister is."

Sam's face twisted in rage and she hurled herself down the mattress, knife in hand. Crissy fell to her back, hitting Sam's belly with both feet and clumsily lofting her overhead to crash down next to the dresser. Back on her feet, she faced the taller and bigger woman, knowing only that Lewis was still handcuffed to the bed. He hadn't moved, and his feet were chilled in a way that scared her. *What if he's...* her brain again shied away from the thought.

She shouted, "Get Po'Boy loose. He'll help you deal with that guy, Thorne." She shook her hands out to the sides, telling him the same thing she'd told Retro so many hours ago. "I got this."

Chapter Twenty

Po'Boy

He pulled himself up from blackness, clawing his way towards the voice he'd heard. *Crissy*. Crissy was here. She'd said his name, his club name, showing him she knew all of him. Then she'd uttered the most bizarre and yet reassuring statement. "I got this." In that instant, he believed her. It didn't matter what got thrown her way, she'd have his back. He remembered a moment in time months ago, on a run when he'd overheard a pair of men talking about Twisted's Penny, one of them saying, "God, I'd give a fuck of a lot to have someone like that at my back," and his thought at the time had been, "Wouldn't we all?"

"My dream woman," he garbled, tugging at the restraints still holding his wrists in place over his head, realizing a moment later his legs were free. Pushing with his feet, he folded up next to the headboard and stood, balancing awkwardly on the shifting mattress as he surveyed the room from a half bent over position. The first thing he saw was the duo on the floor next to the bed, where Thorne was methodically beating a man's head in with the butt of his gun, hammering hard over and over. "Jesus."

He scanned the room as he strained, pulling on the top railing of the headboard to dislodge it from the rungs holding the thing together.

Crissy circled Sam in the open space between the bed and bathroom, and before he could do more than open his mouth they were grappling, the blade in Sam's hand flashing in the lights. He bent his legs and heaved powerfully, hearing wood crack and break, cursing himself for buying quality furniture, then the rail finally pulled free and he let it slip out of the encircling cuffs, stepping off the bed and to the floor, nearly falling when his ankle tried to give way. He glanced over at Thorne. Exhausted by his efforts, the man had settled to one side of the body on the floor. With the blood and bruising, he had to look twice, but Po'Boy eventually realized it was Greg lying there.

No time to consider it now, he heard a feminine shout, and heart in his throat turned to see Crissy leap backwards, her hand lifting to cover a growing red stain on her shirt. Without thinking, Po'Boy sprang at Sam as she lunged forwards, bringing his arms over her head, gripping her face and skull with his hands and twisting fast, the sickening feel of bones popping in his grasp overshadowed by the clench in his chest at the extensive bruising on Crissy's face. *She's hurt.* He dropped the now still Sam to the floor, then stepped over her to get to Crissy, meeting her in the middle and cupping her face in his palms. "Baby doll," he whispered, staring at her. She looked up at him, her eyes tracking across his face. "What the fuck happened?"

"You weren't…you were…I thought you were dead." Crissy gasped for air, and he pushed away, kneeling so he could look at her side. A shallow slice across her ribs meant it was panic taking her breath. He rose and curled himself around her as best he could. Backing away from where Sam's lifeless body lay, he positioned them near the wall so she couldn't see Thorne and his grisly companion.

They'd stood like that only moments before Crissy pushed back. Po'Boy lifted his arms and released her, and she began cataloging the slices Sam had laid in his skin. Each touch of the blade had been a threat of greater damage, as Sam had asked the same question again and again. "Where's Sabrina?"

Crissy finally satisfied herself, folding into him again. That was all it took, even in a room with two bodies, exhausted, sickened by what Sam and Greg had tried to do to him, their coarse jokes bringing back memories of his stepfather, all it took was the feel of Crissy for him to start getting hard. Tipping his head down, lips to her ear, he told her, "Missed you, honey."

Naked as he was, she couldn't have missed how his cock was aimed her direction, and she laughed, a bare tinge of hysteria bleeding through as she said, "I feel ya," both meanings of the words making him laugh, too.

"Lemme get free and then I gotta make a call." He looked down, seeing her face tipped up. He watched as she bit her bottom lip, letting it slide slowly out from between her teeth, knowing it was her tell that she was thinking hard about something. *It's gonna sink in eventually.* He'd killed a woman in front of her. Forget it was to keep her from getting hurt worse than she did, forget the things Sam had done to him. *I'll be a monster now.* Taking one final look at her, he dipped his face close and brushed his lips across hers, side to side, pressing firmly, kissing her. "Proud of you, honey."

She pulled back and her gaze focused on him for a long moment. "I thought you were dead. I wanted to..." Her eyes narrowed and she hesitated a moment. "...to kill her." Po'Boy rested his cuffed arms on her shoulders, wrapping his fingers in her long hair and tugging her head backwards as he swooped in for another kiss. "I did." Her lip curled, lifting in a silent snarl and he felt her heart pounding. "I do." Pushing against his chest, she shoved back and he lifted his hands, letting her slip away. "Jesus." The look in her eyes was wild, whites showing all around the iris and she stumbled as she backed away. "God, I fucking want to kill her." Without another word, Crissy whirled and seemed to see Sam's crumpled body for the first time. Freezing in place, her hair slid across her shoulders as she angled her head down and to the side. Thorne rose to his feet and Po'Boy looked at him, seeing Crissy's head come up, too.

"She goners?" Thorne toed Greg's leg, pushing it an inch or two and then letting it settle back into place. "This one, too." He looked around the suite for a moment, then back at Po'Boy. "How you wanna handle this?"

Crissy moved, reaching into her pocket and pulling out a phone. Po'Boy lunged but was too slow and she'd dialed before he could reach her. Expecting to hear her give out the address to the 911 operator, he was shocked into stillness when instead she greeted someone he never imagined. "Retro, you said to call you if I needed anything. Well—" She looked around the room and then back at Po'Boy as she finished. "—I kinda need something."

***

Wrench

"Brother," Wrench greeted Retro tersely, glaring out the front window of the condo. He heard Pony rustling through things behind him, recognized the flapping of plastic as he shook out another garbage bag. "Whatcha got for me?"

In the minutes since getting home, Wrench had texted Retro for details of his contact with Crissy, getting a brief message back to hold on. He had also reached out to Twisted, catching only wind as he rolled over to voice mail. In fact, every contact he'd attempted had been a bust, and he was beginning to wonder if there was more going on than he expected. Pony told him not to be paranoid, because if there was shit going down, they would both have received a call out.

So the phone in his hand ringing was a relief, and he wanted to cut directly to the chase, no time for niceties. "Tell me you got something."

"I got a lot, brother." Retro didn't delay but what he had to say was so far from reassuring, Wrench found himself having to fight to hold onto his stillness. "You were in the wind, Po'Boy was in the wind, kinda expected to find the two of you together, but that's a no-go, obvo. Your gal, Crissy, she's smart as fuck. I talked to her to see if she knew who'd been going in and out of your place. She did, and damn, the woman's a force when she's tweaked, brother. Does not bode well for you." Wrench made a noise and Retro got the hint, putting them back on track of whatever he knew. "I didn't have it installed in time, but need you to know I'm aware you're in your place because I can see you. Wave at the kitchen, we got a camera in there." Wrench whirled and stared into the kitchen, seeing a small, black oval attached to the wall above his cabinets, not something he'd installed, and not something which was present the last time he'd been home.

"What the fuck?" He gaped. "Who the fuck did that? Why?"

"Yeah, it was clear someone was heading in and out of your place, so Twisted and Ace wanted to see if we could find out for certain who it was. Whoever it was would avoid the guy we parked in the lot, so they were clearly not wanting to be seen, which meant we all wanted to see them even more." Retro paused. "I can get you the footage, but from what I've heard this afternoon, it's a moot point."

"Jesus. Where's Crissy? That's what I fucking texted, man. I got some kind of bullshit here, and it looks like she's tied up in it. We got red, too, brother, and that's got me on edge." He could hear the anger building in his voice and tried to tone it back. "You got a point, then make it fast."

"Crissy was there, and was taken."

Those six words stole the breath from his body, and his chest heaved, futilely trying to suck in more. Retro was silent through this and Wrench glared at the camera, knowing the man could see his reaction. "Shoulda led with that, *brother*," he finally gritted out between clenched teeth. "Tell me what I got to go on, because from the looks of things, if taken from here, she's in a bad way."

"She's good. Swear, Ty." The compassion in Retro's voice nearly broke him, and he closed his eyes, twisting his neck and angling his chin down and away from the camera. "Swear, brother. I was moving heaven and earth to find her, coming up absolutely dry. Then about forty minutes ago, she called me for a fucking clean-up crew."

"Where is she?"

"Orleans. She's in New Orleans." Wrench was already striding towards the door. "She's at Po'Boy's place down there…y'all's place. I got a crew on the way."

"I'll be there in twenty." Wrench slung a leg over his bike, Pony's presence barely registering.

"It's thirty-five miles, brother."

"I'll be there in twenty," he repeated, then disconnected and shoved the phone into his pocket, the roar of bikes next to him pulling his attention. He looked over and saw not only Pony, but all the other CoBos and IMC members in the complex had mounted up, ready to ride. With a nod to Pony, he started his bike, the back wheel spinning for a moment then catching, propelling him out of the lot.

Fifteen minutes later he led the string of bikes into the underground parking, angling his into the first open parking he saw. Kickstand down, he had stalked through the doors before the columns had fully even entered the space. Moving up the stairs two treads at a time, he rounded the landing to see the door at the top propped open. Wrench hadn't paid much attention to the vehicles in the garage, but given the number of vests he saw milling in the hallway outside Po'Boy's suite, there must have been a half a dozen bikes he hadn't noticed. Giving Twisted a chin lift, he pushed past the man and into the room, sweeping the area, gaze locking on where Po'Boy stood with his back to the door, IMC vest in place on his shoulders, arms wrapped around Crissy, her hair the only thing visible.

Across the room in a handful of steps, Wrench didn't pause, didn't give any headspace to who might be there, who might be watching, or who might give him shit for what he was about to do. He found he didn't give that first fuck, because after the past weeks, after agonizing over a decision he'd known was wrong only minutes after making it, he needed to have his partners in his arms, needed to have his hands on them. Pressing tight to Po'Boy's side, he wrapped his arms around both of them, and when Po'Boy lifted his head, Wrench captured his mouth in a hot, wet, and very deep kiss, with tongue, in front of God and everyone.

When he tore his lips off Po'Boy's, he heard the familiar low, rolling chuckle which made his dick get hard every time, Po'Boy muttering, "Damn, baby."

A hand cupped his jaw, and he looked down to see Crissy's eyes were lifted to meet his. A deep bruise had spread to cover most of her jaw on one side, purple and black warring for space under her skin. Even with that she lifted to her toes and kissed him hard, sweeping his lips with her tongue, diving inside when he opened for her, battling back as he took control of the kiss, finally breaking it with a series of soft lip brushes, finishing with his forehead resting against hers, both of them panting for breath.

Chapter Twenty-One
Po'Boy

Penny shook her finger in Po'Boy's face and he clicked his teeth at her like a snapping turtle, threatening to sever one at the joint if she left it too close. She stood beside him at a folding table, both their hands nearly covered to the wrist in a mixture of flour and cornmeal. Across the way he watched as Crissy bumped Wrench with her hip, scolding him quietly for sneaking one of the small hushpuppies she'd just taken out of the fryer. Half the members of their two clubs had been out running trotlines last night, hauling in enough channel and blue catfish to feed the more than one hundred people expected at the fish fry today.

Not a celebration, that wasn't their way. No, this was just another party.

At least to the outside world.

Po'Boy looked around, noting who was in attendance, and who was not. *Ain't no easy roads.* He and Wrench both knew there'd be bullshit to deal with, in and out of their clubs. *Clubs*, he thought with a wince, was area number one where there was a known discontent because of them being what they were to the other. He knew eventually one of them would have to make a leap unless something more radical happened upstream in the Caddo Hobos and Incoherent. It wouldn't do to have a house divided, not when it came to club business, and them being high-level officers made that a long sight more challenging.

Not today, though. Today was about brotherhood and friendships, with Twisted hosting members from at least a half a dozen clubs who crossed alliance lines. Still, the missing faces were noted.

It had been three weeks since Wrench claimed him and Crissy in a way no one present could mistake. Po'Boy had heard the story a dozen times, and it had grown in the telling, as was the way of things. How Wrench had torn out of his condo like the devil was nipping at his heels. About the hundred-mile-an-hour ride across the causeway, Wrench's bike weaving in and out of traffic, uncaring of protocol, willing to leave everyone behind if it got him to the suite a half a second earlier. Of the walk of fame, Wrench reportedly shoving Retro's cleaners out of the way to get to him and Crissy. Wildman had summed up the kiss in a handful of words that made Po'Boy roar with laughter. "Coulda made me gay, man kissed me like that."

I'm a lucky bastard.

A bump at his shoulder pulled his gaze down and to the side where he saw Penny grinning broadly up at him. "Fish ain't gonna bread itself." She reached out, grabbing a handful of raw fillets and dropped them into his bowl of the flour and meal mixture.

He smiled, enjoying how easy that expression was to call up these days, and bumped back. "Better watch out, Twisted gonna breed you any day." She flushed, the rosy coloring flooding her cheeks and quickly looked down. "Oh, fuck me. He already did." Remembering their earlier conversation, he dropped his voice and asked, "You okay with that?" Red curls falling around her face, she mumbled something, and he jostled her again. "Yousa, don't fuckin' try and bullshit a bullshitter, it don't never work, doll. Tell me true, you okay with that?"

319

"I didn't know what to think at first, was…shocked." Head down, she focused on where they were working the squares and rectangles of the sweet meat through the seasoned breading, gaze following his hands when he reached out for more fish. "Took me a week straight to pull up the courage to tell him."

Deftly flipping the pieces onto the growing pile of fish ready for the fryer, he asked, "What'd he say?"

"Wasn't what he said that convinced me." Angling her head up, she looked at him from the corners of her eyes, looking a little coy and pleased with herself. "Apparently, my Mr. Bell likes the idea of me being pregnant." Her meaning clear, Po'Boy couldn't contain himself, he threw his head back and roared laughter, Penny trying to shush him, her attempts entirely unsuccessful.

"What's going on over there?" Wrench's question made Po'Boy look back at where he stood next to Crissy, and he smiled.

"Nothin'. Just Penny Dane being the funny-as-fuck gal she is." Wrench's eyes narrowed as they flicked between Po'Boy and Penny. "Serious. Yousa's fulla the funny. Hell, Wrench, you been her friend for life, anyone should know, should be you." Now Crissy was squinting at him, and he found the paired expressions hilarious, throwing his head back again. "Fuck, I'm a lucky bastard," he muttered through the laughter, not surprised when he heard Penny respond, "Yeah, you are."

A couple of hours later, Twisted cornered him, beer in each fist, handing one over when Po'Boy reached for it. He felt the vibe coming from his oldest friend, and instinctively scanned the people standing nearby. Wildman and Chip were close, but not so they'd overhear anything. Wrench and Crissy stood nearer the bonfire. Po'Boy approved of their position, Crissy leaning back against Wrench's chest, her hands wrapped around his wrists, his arms crossing her and holding tight. Looking back to Twisted, he lifted the beer in thanks, saying only, "Sup?"

"Jeff's been handled."

Those three words brought a wave of anger to Po'Boy. Anger he'd had to share about Grover, and in sharing, find out details of how Twisted already knew the man. Their experiences similar, and yet not, the freedom the man had in his own house severely truncated in the whorehouse where Twisted had grown up. Still, knowing his stepfather had targeted a much too young George had pissed Po'Boy off like none other. Retro had provided some info, and with Wrench and Twisted at his back, Po'Boy had paid the assclown a visit that ended in red. *Best percussive therapy I ever had*, he thought, not caring what that made him.

"What's that mean for me?"

"Hopefully means all the papers been cleared and you got no more house arrest on your radar."

"Thank God." He'd been stir crazy after the first week. When his leg and shoulder healed enough he felt like getting out and into the wind, he'd been told to stay close, stay in as much as he could stand, because the hitman hadn't been joking; there was significant incentive for someone to take him out. "Not that I wanted to get lead poisoning, but fuck, it's been shitty."

"Yeah, sure it's been *hard*, holing up in a house with lotsa flat surfaces and a woman who looks at you like Crissy does." Twisted snorted, the humor audible in his tone when he finished with, "And a man who ain't scared of tying your ass down."

"Oh, baby. It was just the once, and you can bet I liked it." Po'Boy grinned and Twisted returned the expression. "Least after that, Retro came and got his fuckin' camera."

"Jesus." Twisted's shoulders shook with his laughter. "You are one fucked up bastard."

"I'm a *lucky* bastard. That's what I've been tellin' myself, at least."

"You're that, too." They stood in silence for a moment, the party swirling around them, people moving from group to group to share stories and cement friendships a little tighter.

Brotherhood. A precious thing.

"Fuck." Po'Boy swallowed hard, forcing the stinging in his nose back. "I nearly gave all this up."

"No fucking way, brother. I wouldn't let ya go. Not ever. You my ride or die, man. Need you." Twisted's hand wrapped around his arm, pulling him close. "That shit we started, though? We're gonna have to see it through. Just finding a different way, because ain't no way anyone'd believe you gone out bad after all the shit over the past couple of weeks. Still, gotta see it through."

He pulled in a deep breath, letting those words settle inside him. When Twisted showed at the suite, he'd had Po'Boy's cut with him, patches already sewn back into place by his own hands. He hadn't waited a moment before settling it onto Po'Boy's shoulders.

"So, if I ain't out bad, does that mean I'm in good?"

"Fuck yeah, brother." Twisted stared at him a moment, eyes glittering in the firelight before he turned to look at the flames. "Fuck yeah."

***

Retro

Retro shook his head, wanting to put this conversation behind them. "Not a big deal, brother."

Po'Boy angled his chin, squinting against the light from the fire. He looked a mix of skeptic and pissed, which was better than just being pissed, Retro supposed. "You had my woman's back. That's a big fucking deal to me."

Wrench spoke for the first time, shoving his hands deep into the front pockets of his jeans. It looked like it took all his will not to lean into Po'Boy and Retro wondered if he realized how much his body language telegraphed. "All through the shit, you had Crissy's back. Po'Boy's right, we owe you."

"Then call it a marker owed, yeah?" Retro tipped his head to the side, sweeping the hair off his shoulder and out of his face. Normally tamed in a braid or tail, he'd left it free today for some reason, his mane now an annoyance from being in the wind on the ride over. He glanced over his shoulder, seeing Mudd standing nearby. Close enough to support, but far enough to give the illusion of privacy for their conversation. "We got a system, and this was a good test of it."

"System?" Wrench was squinting his eyes now. "Y'all dumped everything, right?"

"Well, yeah. Eventually." Retro grinned, then reached up to push another hank of hair out of his face. "Fuck." Gripping it behind his head, he stood casually as if he posed like this every day. *Jesus, I'm such a poser.* With a sigh, he gave them what they needed to be at peace. "We do a four-day vat bath in DMF and water. Then whatever we're treating goes under a rack of grow lights " He winked. "—not that we use them to grow anything, ya know." Po'Boy lifted his thumb and finger to his lips, miming puffing and they both laughed. "Twelve hours later, they are DNA-free and ready to be packaged. No worries about anything coming back your direction, the deliveries were multitude, and widespread. Hard to make a cohesive package after that."

Po'Boy blew out a hard breath, then rolled his shoulders, shedding tension with every movement. "Marker owed," he agreed, holding his hand out to Retro. He accepted the grip, clasping Po'Boy's wrist and let the man pull him into a one-armed clinch. In his ear, Retro heard Po'Boy mutter softly, "Marker for life, brother. You got a need, you make a call, I'll be happy to answer. Anytime. As my Crissy says, I got this."

Straightening, Retro stared into his friend's face, seeing an ease there he envied. "Are you? Happy? Are you as happy as you look?" He didn't know where the question came from, it just blurted past his lips and he shook his head quickly. "Don't gotta answer that one. It's writ large on your face."

"Yeah, I'm fuckin' happy." Po'Boy responded anyway, then reached out and rested one palm on Wrench's shoulder, thumb digging into the muscle over the collarbone. "Really fuckin' happy."

Head dipping, Wrench laughed quietly, willingly stepping closer when Po'Boy pulled. "I'm happy too, if anyone's interested."

Retro watched as the two men leaned close, seeing the natural way these two fit together. *Meant to be*, he thought, then looked across the broad lot again, his gaze arrowing towards his old lady. Without looking away, he asked, "You seen Twisted? Need to ask him about my kids."

"Oh, yeah," Wrench said, "Penny told me you were fostering them here. That happening soon? It'll be good for your gal to learn the world from different points of view. You're smart to do this, man."

"Yeah, real fuckin' smart," he muttered, then shook his head. "It's been busy, but soon as I can make it work, I'll be parkin' two of 'em here for a bit. I got…" He trailed off, deciding what to say, and after everything he'd shared with these men, he opted for honest, betting on their loyalty. "I got shit in my house, brothers. Shit I gotta clear."

Po'Boy responded immediately, validating the warmth spreading through Retro's belly, his bet parlayed into a win. "Anything you need, brother. I mean that. Anything you need."

***

Crissy

Curled in an armchair, Crissy thumbed the screen of her phone, navigating to the text app. Used less and less frequently, she saw the last entry in the string was more than a month old. She flipped to her messages with Bob, smiling at the last picture of Missy he'd sent only a couple of days ago. Her texts to Lewis and Ty were daily, sometimes hourly, if her men were in a mood to tease. Texting Rhoda was no longer her go-to coping mechanism, and she wondered if maybe the one-sided conversation had served its purpose.

I want you to know I will always love you.

Leaning her head back, she blinked fast, dispersing the threatening tears.

Remember when I said you'd tell me to go for it? Crissy smiled, her thumb gliding from letter to letter. **I went for it in a big way.**

In the weeks since the events in New Orleans, her men had taken every opportunity to remind each other how good this was between them. They'd also introduced her to all the people who held important places in their lives. Each encounter nerve wracking, since Crissy knew her behavior with the two men would be the topic of conversation long after they'd left to go home. Still, Lewis and Ty made it bearable, because they were just so damn comfortable with each other, and her, and her with either or both of them.

No jealousy, that had been a topic Lewis had introduced, in his delightfully blunt way. She rolled her eyes, remembering.

"We want to keep this all hunky dory sunshine, then we're gonna need one ground rule." He was lying next to Ty, facing Crissy across Ty's chest. Ty's fingers stroked through her hair, smoothing and arranging it, careful of any tangles he encountered.

Almost idly, Ty asked, "One rule? You? Only one? I find that hard to believe." She smiled at Lewis' offended expression, rolling her cheek against Ty's shoulder, pressing her lips to his chest.

"Fuck, yeah. One rule. Like the one ring thing, this will rule everything we do from here on out." Lewis mimicked her actions, but instead of a kiss he bared his teeth, nipping and pinching Ty's skin.

"Ouch, fucker." Ty's hand on her head stilled and his other gripped Lewis' hair, tipping his head back. "No biting."

"Watch out, Crissy. The no-fun police are in bed with us." Lewis reached across, threading his fingers through hers and brought their joined hands down to Ty's crotch, cupping her fingers around his thickening cock. "I think you should get ready to distract him, soon as I tell him what not to do."

"Go ahead, tell me the rule." Ty's voice hitched in the middle, in time to Lewis' encouraging stroke. "Tell me the rule, then I'm gonna use whatever I like to shut your mouth."

"Gonna give me a mouthful, baby?" Lewis was comfortable uttering endearments towards both of them, and she knew Ty liked hearing it, because his breath hitched again. "Okay, one rule. Doesn't matter what we do with each other, as long as it stays with the three of us. You fuck our Crissy and I'm not here, I'll wanna hear about it, but that's all. No jealousy, and if you feel the green monster raising its head, say something and we'll address whatever's needed. When you and me get it on—"

He stopped talking when Crissy lifted her head and stared down at him. "I wanna watch." Ty's belly jumped as he laughed and Lewis smiled. "I'm serious. Y'all are hot as anything every time you put hands on each other. Y'all get it on? I wanna watch." She twisted her neck, angling to look up at Ty. "At least the first time."

Ty's cheeks were red, but he gamely nodded.

I'm so lucky, Rhoda. I wish you could have met them.

Crissy smiled, because in a way, meeting Ty and Lewis had been instigated by Rhoda. If she hadn't set everything up, Crissy would probably have followed Bob and Missy to Minnesota and her whole life would be different.

Thank you. My big sissy, always looking out for me.

Her thumb moved across the screen again and she slid the window with the conversation down, prompting the phone to ask for confirmation before completing the command. "Love you," she whispered, tapping the Archive button.

***

Po'Boy

Po'Boy looked around, shaking his head in amusement and grinning. He called, "What kinda party we havin', baby?" On the dresser was a set of lingerie, sheer brassiere displayed at an angle on top of tiny panties. On top of those were a cock ring and a vibrating dildo. *Oh yeah, my woman's in a mood.*

Soft footsteps from the bathroom and he tipped his head to see Crissy sauntering out, frilly satin fabric barely covering her tits and cunt. "You like?" This was a coy question, but it trembled along the edge of being nervous, and he knew Crissy putting herself out there like this wouldn't happen again if he got his response wrong.

In the months they'd been together, he'd learned a lot about their Crissy. Learned a lot about Wrench, and since the event—something Crissy always designated with air quotes—they were seldom apart, but when they were, it wasn't something anyone worried about. They all knew they'd come back together at the end of the day. As they had since the beginning, if the spirit moved them—and it moved them a lot—the makeup of the lovers didn't matter. Him and Ty—because they were still their most real when they were in bed—or him and Crissy, Crissy and Ty, or the three of them, it didn't matter who was doing the loving, because jealousy didn't have a place in their home.

Without looking around for Ty, without looking around at the very comfortable home he'd bought for them in Ponchatoula, a town midway between Mandeville—where Incoherent's mother house was—and Baton Rouge—where the Caddo Hobo's house was—without doing anything except focusing on their Crissy, he answered her honestly.

"Oh, yeah. I definitely like, baby." He prowled towards her. "You look good enough to eat, and darlin', I got a hell of a hunger. Worked one up soon as I walked through the door and saw your shoes lined up against the wall." He nearly chuckled at the sweet confusion on her guileless face. "I like everything I see, honey. From the first time I met you, sittin' your sweet ass on a stool next to a complete stranger and letting him strike up a conversation. The laughter that poured from your lips was heady, and I'm still drunk on you from that day."

He didn't stop moving when he reached her, wrapping his arms around her and turning them so he could back her towards the bed. "I liked what I saw the next mornin', too. Hair all over the fuckin' place, and so fucking pretty it took my heart a minute to decide it could keep beatin'. Then you let me in there, wrapped me up in your arms and cooed in my ear, your voice just as sweet as the ass I had in my hands."

"Lewis," she murmured, chin up, bright eyes locked on his face.

"So fucking much in like with what I saw." He paused, dipping his mouth to brush against hers. "I kept you for hours upon hours, unwilling to let go." Pulling back, he saw her eyes had gone watery, and he cupped a cheek in his palm, brushing his thumb softly against her parted lips. "Then I got to see you with our Ty, and I liked that a lot, too." He raised his voice an octave, ignoring her rolling eyes when he cooed, "Lewty. Oh, Lewty." Her curved lips put the lie to her feigned annoyance. "Like that, too. Best thing, though? See you lovin' on him, see you takin' his cock right where mine had found a home, watching as you made room in your heart for both of us." Pulling in a hard breath, he stared down at her, stopping them at the edge of the mattress. "I most definitely like."

"I like, too," Ty's voice came from the doorway, and Lewis let Crissy twist in his arms as he looked that direction, eyeing the obvious bulge in their partner's crotch. "Oh, yeah. I like." He moved, and Lewis got to watch him stalk towards them, then felt the heat of Ty's body as he wrapped himself around them. "I look at you and I see the sweet klutz who clocked me in the dick—"

Crissy tipped her head back with a groan. "Am I ever going to hear the last of that?"

Ty dipped his head close, and Lewis heard him whisper, "Nope. Get used to it, butternut. That's the only time in my life I want to remember being bagged. You..." Ty's voice trailed off as he traced his nose along her cheek and pressed his lips to hers. Lewis' cock got impossibly hard as her mouth parted under Ty's, their tongues tangling gently together. "You were the cutest thing I've ever seen, trying to explain what you nutted me with. Then you pulled out those damn batteries."

Lewis bent and placed his mouth on Ty's neck, working the muscle there with lips and teeth, feeling Ty's groan as much as hearing it. "She got some toys over on the dresser. Good thing she's got an economy pack of the damn things, yeah?"

Crissy buried her face in his chest, and Ty lifted his head, staring into Lewis' eyes as he leaned in for a kiss. "Fuck, yeah. We're gonna par-tay!"

THANK YOU FOR READING *TREADING THE TRAITOR'S PATH: OUT BAD*!

In this story, Penny's culinary skills are on display again, and while she might be cooking individual dishes at the time, her intention is to have enough leftovers to provide a basis for a good jambalaya. Here's her recipe, which actually is mine.

Cheatin' Quick Jambalaya

What you need to find in your fridge:

- Two pounds cooked ham, chicken, or a mix of the two, chunked
- One pound fried sausage, boudin preferred, chunked
- Creole spices like Tony Chachere's, Zatarian's, or King Creole
- Small amount flour
- One cup chicken broth
- Green onions
- Sweet onions
- Bell peppers
- Celery
- Two cups cooked rice, dirty or white
- 10-12 ounces whole corn, canned or frozen, drained
- Oil or grease, enough to coat a large skillet

Want to make your own creole spices? Easy 'nuff:

- Combine a quarter teaspoon each of onion powder and garlic powder. Add a dash or more of oregano, basil, thyme, black pepper, white pepper, cayenne pepper, and paprika. Salt to taste.

Preparation

- Heat the skillet until a drop of water dances in the oil.
- Veggies get cut up and tossed in with the meat. Don't overcook, remember the meat is pre-cooked, so you're just heating that stuff up. Veggies should be softened, but not cooked through.

- Dust contents of skillet with flour and seasoning, and stir to coat evenly. Add broth and bring to a boil for a minute, stirring to keep from sticking. Add rice and corn in small amounts, stirring. Takes a few minutes, but once everything is good and hot, you're ready to serve your cheatin' quick jambalaya.

Enjoy!

PO'BOY'S PLAYLIST

Po'Boy's music is an eclectic mix, much like the character is. Po'Boy's playlist: bit.ly/ntnt-outbad-playlist

ABOUT THE AUTHOR

Raised in the south, MariaLisa learned about the magic of books at an early age. Every summer, she would spend hours in the local library, devouring books of every genre. Self-described as a book-a-holic, she says "I've always loved to read, but then I discovered writing, and found I adored that, too. For reading...if nothing else is available, I've been known to read the back of the cereal box."

Also by MariaLisa deMora

Alace Sweets

A dark thriller, this book is not a light read. Filled with edge-of-your-seat suspense, this intense story commands the reader's attention as it drives towards the explosive ending. Alace Sweets is a vigilante serial killer, with everything that implies and is sure to trip all your triggers. Be ready.

At seventeen, Alace Sweets turned a corner in her life, taking the wrong shortcut home from school.

Resisting the harsh knowledge her attackers will never be made to pay for their actions, Alace takes a stand. Justice must be served, and if fate's scales are out of balance, she's determined to set things right as best she can.

When the laws of men fail, the rules of Alace prevail.

5-Star Reviews for Alace Sweets

"deMora has a superb story-line and exceptional character development. All of her characters have such depth that will intrigue the reader..."
~Turning Another Page

"Hot, sweet, dark thriller."
~Beth D

"It will keep you on the edge of your seat and give you chills."
~Escape Reality Book Blog

"Disturbing, haunting, sickly; yet hot, sexy and heart racing!"
~Amanda L

"From the first page [deMora] pulls you into the world she has created and you do not even try to escape..."
~Little Shop of Readers Blog

"A must read for all those dark, gritty romance fans out there."
~Sweet & Spicy Reads

"You will find yourself so drawn into the story that the outside world is blocked out and your locking the doors and turning on all the lights."
~Danena F

"Don't judge me for bonding with a vigilante serial killer, she's more than what she does."
~iScream Books

"Thrilling...chilling...full of suspense, nail biting edge of your seat excitement."
~Tracey H

"Every time MariaLisa deMora picks up her pen (or opens her computer), she creates characters you want to believe in."
~Gail S

"Intriguing dark storyline, beautiful love story and nail-biting conclusion, what more could a reader ask for?"
~Manda M

"This book takes you a dark and twisted ride that is gripping..."
~Renee Entress' Blog

"This book is dark and gritty and I literally had to take a day off from reading it because it's that intense."
~My Girlfriend's Couch

"This is my favourite book so far from this author ... I recommend this book if you enjoy dark romantic thrillers."
~Cheekypee Reads and Reviews

"There's not enough stars to give this book and 5 just doesn't really do it justice!"
~DeLane C

"I couldn't put this book down from page one! Tried to stop & go to bed but couldn't sleep thinking about Alace and got up & finished the book."
~Debbie M

"MariaLisa DeMora, wordsmith that she is, made this a story of the enlightenment of a woman and finding love in a life where she has had none."
~Kat W

"Whatever deep dark trench [deMora] pulled a character like Alace from should be revisited again and often."
~Confessions of a Serial Reader

ADDITIONAL SERIES AND BOOKS

Please note that books in a series frequently feature characters from additional books within that series. If series books are read out of order, readers will twig to spoilers for the other books, so going back to read the skipped titles won't have the same angsty reveals.

Rebel Wayfarers MC series:

Mica, #1
A Sweet & Merry Christmas, short story #1.5
Slate, #2
Bear, #3
Jase, #4
Gunny, #5
Mason, #6
Hoss, #7
Harddrive Holidays, short story #7.5
Duck, #8
Biker Chick Campout, short story #8.5
Watcher, #9
A Kiss to Keep You, novella #9.25
Gun Totin' Annie, short story #9.5
Secret Santa, short story #9.75
Bones, #10
Gunny's Pups, novella #10.25
Never Settle, short story #10.5
Not Even A Mouse, short story #10.75
Fury, #11
Christmas Doings, #11.25
Gypsy's Lady, #11.5
Cassie, #12
Road Runner's Ride, novella #12.5

Occupy Yourself band series:

Born Into Trouble, #1
Grace In Motion, #2 (TBD)
What They Say, #3 (TBD)

Neither This, Nor That series:

This Is the Route Of Twisted Pain, #1
Treading the Traitor's Path: Out Bad, #2
Trapped by Fate on Reckless Roads, #3 (TBD)

Other Books:

With My Whole Heart
Alace Sweets
Hard Focus

More information available at mldemora.com.

www.ingramcontent.com/pod-product-compliance
Lightning Source LLC
Chambersburg PA
CBHW050034030726
47506CB00001B/265